Emily Forbes is an award-winning author of Medical Romance for Mills & Boon. She has written over thirty-five books and has twice been a finalist in the Australian Romantic Book of the Year Award, which she won in 2013 for her novel *Sydney Harbour Hospital: Bella's Wishlist*. You can get in touch with Emily at emily@forbesau.com, or visit her website at emily-forbesauthor.com.

Sue MacKay lives with her husband in New Zealand's beautiful Marlborough Sounds, with the water on her doorstep and the birds and the trees at her back door. It is the perfect setting to indulge her passions of entertaining friends by cooking them sumptuous meals, drinking fabulous wine, going for hill walks or kayaking around the bay—and, of course, writing stories.

Also by Emily Forbes

The Perfect Mother for His Son
Marriage Reunion in the ER
Rescued by the Australian GP

A Sydney Central Reunion miniseries

Ali and the Rebel Doc

Also by Sue MacKay

Brought Together by a Pup
Fake Fiancée to Forever?
Resisting the Pregnant Paediatrician
Marriage Reunion with the Island Doc

Discover more at millsandboon.co.uk.

PREGNANCY SURPRISE IN BYRON BAY

EMILY FORBES

PARAMEDIC'S FLING TO FOREVER

SUE MacKAY

MILLS & BOON

First published in Great Britain 2024
by Mills & Boon, an imprint of HarperCollins*Publishers* Ltd,
1 London Bridge Street, London, SE1 9GF

www.harpercollins.co.uk

HarperCollins*Publishers* Macken House, 39/40 Mayor Street Upper,
Dublin 1, D01 C9W8, Ireland

ISBN: 978-0-263-32166-1

07/24

PREGNANCY SURPRISE IN BYRON BAY

EMILY FORBES

MILLS & BOON

For Ned and Finn

In the time it has taken me to write 40 books
you have grown from babies to young adults.

I am so proud of you both. You are amazing men;
kind, intelligent, handsome, polite and funny.

You would both make fabulous heroes and I hope
you each get your own happily-ever-after one day.

All my love,

Mum

CHAPTER ONE

MOLLY PRESCOTT CHECKED the time as she stepped out of the surf at Clarkes Beach and picked up her towel. She cursed softly to herself. She'd need to hurry if she was going to make the meeting on time.

Who was she kidding? She was definitely going to be late, she thought as she dried her face and wiped her arms with her towel. The clinic manager, Paula, had organised a quick breakfast meeting to introduce everyone to the new locum doctor who was coming up from Sydney to provide cover in the Byron Bay clinic for a few weeks. But there would be enough staff for him or her to be introduced to until Molly arrived. She wasn't the most senior doctor on staff, she'd only been there for six months, and maybe no one would even notice if she was late. Or maybe they had come to expect it. Timekeeping was one thing she had difficulty with. She was always trying to squeeze too much into her day and time was constantly getting away from her as a result. It was a perpetual struggle. She hadn't won the battle yet but she hoped that one day she'd miraculously develop a time-management gene.

Punctuality had been one thing, along with resilience and independence, that she'd hoped might improve with her move to Byron Bay. Here in the northern New South Wales coastal town she had only a short commute to work—nothing like the fifty-minute trip she'd made twice a day back in Sydney—but instead of improving, she'd just filled that extra time with another activity—her daily swim.

She quickly towelled her blonde hair before throwing a T-shirt over her swimsuit and jogging up the beach. She still had to get home to the apartment she rented with Gemma, one of her colleagues, shower and then make the quarter of an hour walk from Lighthouse Road into town. She would have liked to have taken a detour past The Top Shop to grab some breakfast but she didn't have the extra ten minutes that would take.

She really should have cut her swim short today but it was her favourite way to start the day, she needed it for her mental health and it was an important part of the process of finding herself. Swimming gave her time to reflect on what she wanted out of life. After wasting years of her life with her ex-boyfriend, finally saying goodbye to Daniel was supposed to be a turning point in her life. Her plan had been to move to Byron Bay and to make time and space to work on herself. She no longer wanted to worry about pleasing others. She no longer wanted to seek attention. From her father. From her ex. From anyone.

She shook her head. She didn't want thoughts of Daniel encroaching on her mind. She was putting her past behind her, moving on from a bad relationship. Moving in general, she reminded herself as she checked her watch again, hoping her tardiness would be forgiven. Her consulting list didn't start until ten o'clock on Wednesdays so no one should expect her to be there at quarter to eight.

Molly's shoulder-length hair was still damp when she arrived at the clinic and she knew the humidity of the summer air would make it kink but she certainly couldn't have spared the time to blow-dry it. She sneaked into the staffroom a few minutes before eight, quite pleased with her effort, and relieved to hear Tom Reynolds, the senior doctor whose leave necessitated locum cover, still going around the room introducing the staff to the new locum.

She could smell coffee and she headed for the machine to grab a cup, along with a muffin, sending a silent thank you to Paula for organising food. She added milk to her coffee and took a bite of her muffin just as she heard Tom say, 'And, last but not least, is Dr Prescott.'

The room was full and many of the staff were standing, as there weren't enough chairs for everyone. Molly could hear Tom but, being only five feet four inches tall, she couldn't see to the front of the room. But Tom had obviously seen her tardy arrival.

She quickly tried to swallow the muffin and school her expression to casual nonchalance in an attempt to convey that she'd been at the back of the room all along as opposed to sneaking in thirty seconds before.

'Molly, this is Dr Williams.'

All she could see was the top of what she assumed was a man's head, although it could have been a tall woman. She waited for her colleagues to part, not expecting them to reveal a familiar face.

'Theo?'

She hadn't seen him for four years, but he looked just

the same. Tall, close to six feet, with broad shoulders that belied his otherwise slim physique. His thick black hair, cut short at the sides, was swept away from his forehead above dark eyes that widened a little, the only indication that he was as surprised as she was.

'Hello, Molly. It's been a while.' He nodded slightly but only managed a half-smile. He didn't look all that thrilled to see her and she couldn't blame him.

Four years had passed but all of a sudden it felt like yesterday. And not in a good way.

She felt the long-forgotten heat of embarrassment, could feel the blush creeping up her neck and into her face, and knew her cheeks were now stained pink.

She tried to school her features to mirror his. Trying on a mask of pleasant surprise rather than abject embarrassment as she wished the floor would open up and swallow her.

She dropped her gaze, focusing on her coffee, as Tom continued speaking. She let her colleagues close the space and shield her from view as the colour faded in her cheeks.

'While I have you all here, I had a call from the organisers of Schoolies Festival. They need a few more volunteers for the weekend so if any of you can spare a few hours they'd love to hear from you. I think any clinical staff would be qualified to help, but, for any admin staff who are interested, as long as you have a police clearance and your first-aid accreditation, you can sign up too. Paula has the contact details.'

Her mind drifted as Tom continued speaking about the imminent influx of teenagers who would be descending

EMILY FORBES   11

on Byron Bay for the next ten days to celebrate the end
of their school lives.

She threw her unfinished muffin into the rubbish, her
appetite deserting her as the memories flooded in. She
hadn't seen Theo since their university graduation ceremony and she hadn't spoken to him since they both
attended the same party to celebrate the end of their
final exams prior to graduation. The last words they'd
exchanged had come just after she'd unceremoniously
kissed him.

Mortified about her behaviour and still feeling the
sting of rejection, she had avoided him at graduation as
she'd tried to pretend nothing had happened. She'd been
immensely relieved when he'd appeared reluctant to seek
her out too.

But the feeling of embarrassment returned now as she
remembered her foolishness. She knew she'd behaved
badly. Drunk and emotional, she'd acted impulsively and
then tried to pretend nothing had happened. Theo had
treated her with kindness and compassion and she'd re-
paid his kindness with the assumption that he'd welcome
her impulsive kiss, even though she'd been in a relationship. Albeit an emotionally complicated one.

He had kissed her back—she hadn't drunk so much
that she'd forgotten that—but when he'd asked if she
would take Daniel back if he had cheated on her she
hadn't replied. She'd known she would. She'd done it
every time. And Theo had known it too. He'd stood up
and walked away.

She didn't want to be twenty-five again. She hadn't
always made good choices four years ago but she had

matured; life had a way of forcing you to grow up. She was rebuilding herself and she didn't really want to see someone who knew the old Molly, who knew the mistakes she'd made in the past, on a daily basis. Someone who she felt had judged her and found her lacking.

After four years she was still embarrassed and ashamed of her behaviour. Of the kiss. She'd acted carelessly and then realised she didn't want to be the girl who cheated on her boyfriend. She didn't want to be the cliché. Her boyfriend had cheated on her—often—but she didn't want to play tit for tat. She wanted to be the bigger person and kissing Theo had been a mistake. She shouldn't have put him in that position.

She could feel herself being watched and she lifted her eyes to see Gemma grinning at her from the other side of the room. Gemma raised her eyebrows, darted her eyes in Theo's direction and mouthed one word. *Wow.*

Molly glared at her and Gemma started to cross the room as Tom wrapped up the meeting and the rest of the staff began to disperse.

Molly had been vacillating over whether or not she should approach Theo. If she did, how should she behave? What should she say? Four years was a long time. Especially considering what had happened between them. So, at least Gemma's arrival meant she didn't have to make that decision. She could talk to Gemma instead. That would give her time to compose herself and work out how to manage this unexpected turn of events.

'Oh. My. God. Talk about tall, hot and handsome,' Gemma said as she reached Molly's side.

Molly glanced around, hoping Theo wasn't within

earshot, and was relieved to find he'd actually left the room. She really didn't want to have this conversation with Gemma in the middle of the staffroom but it looked as though that was what she was getting.

'Where have you been hiding him?' Gemma asked.

'Theo?' Molly feigned indifference, knowing she felt anything but. 'I haven't been hiding him anywhere. I haven't seen him for years.'

Gemma was watching her closely. 'He's not a skeleton in your closet?'

Molly shook her head and turned away to gather the left-over breakfast items. Wrapping the platters of muffins and fruit and putting them into the fridge for later gave her an excuse to avoid Gemma's gaze as she tried to stop the blush from returning to her cheeks.

'So, you don't know if he's single?' Gemma continued.

Molly felt a twitch of jealousy. *Theo was hers.* But that was ridiculous. *She* was ridiculous. Gemma was quite entitled to fancy Theo.

'I have no idea, but I thought you were taking a break from dating?' she replied as she closed the fridge and started stacking empty coffee cups into the dishwasher.

Gemma had recently been dating a pilot but it turned out he had a girl in several cities and she was currently single. 'It only takes one man to change my mind. But tell me if he's off limits.'

'Why would he be off limits to you?' Molly asked as she closed the dishwasher and switched it on.

'Several reasons. If you fancied him, for one. After all, you saw him first. Or if he's an ex of yours then I'm not going there.'

'I told you, he's not an ex. There's no history between us,' she said. She knew she was massaging the truth very slightly but she wasn't about to share all the embarrassing details. 'We studied together, that's all.'

'You've never mentioned him.'

'Why would I?'

'Because he's gorgeous and he works for Pacific Coast Clinics.'

'I didn't know he did.' She'd only been employed at the clinic for six months. She knew there were several associated clinics throughout New South Wales, and she knew the locum was coming from one of them, but she hadn't bothered to look at the staff list across all the different locations. There'd really been no need. 'You'll have to work fast—he's only here for six weeks,' Molly said, trying to sound light and breezy. It sounded like no time but Molly feared it might feel like an eternity.

'No.' Gemma shook her head. 'Looking like he does, I bet he's not single and I'm not going to get burned again.'

Molly didn't try and persuade her friend otherwise. Besides, she could be right, Theo could be spoken for already.

Molly wiped the bench, dried her hands and she and Gemma headed for their consulting rooms. She planned to use the extra time before her list started to follow up some of her patients, check their results and organise referrals. But her mind kept drifting.

She and Theo had studied medicine at university together but they hadn't been close friends. They'd moved in different circles. He'd spent a lot of his time in the library, she'd spent a lot of time in the university bar with Daniel, when they'd been 'on' again.

When their circles had overlapped she'd got the impression that Theo had judged her choices. She knew they'd been questionable but, at the time, her choices had made sense. At least in the world she knew.

She remembered Theo had a way of quietly watching people, taking stock, and once, in just a few moments, he had accurately summed up her and her relationship with Daniel, which had frustrated her. She hadn't wanted to hear his opinion. She'd wanted to be seen as strong and confident, not weak or scared, and she definitely hadn't wanted to admit that he'd been right.

There were so many things in her past she'd rather not think about. The present was about making better decisions. She was using her time in Byron Bay to find herself. To work on herself. She'd grown up, the middle of three sisters, always feeling as though her father would have preferred to have sons. She was constantly trying to prove that girls could do anything boys did, trying to be the perfect daughter. Then the perfect girlfriend. She'd been desperate for attention, desperate for affection.

She realised now that had been a big factor in her relationship with Daniel. Her father had ignored her mother, herself and her sisters and Molly had been flattered by Daniel's interest in her. He was intelligent, good-looking and popular and she'd been so desperate for attention she'd overlooked the negatives—his lies, his unfaithfulness, his unkindness. Her younger self had been happy just to have someone take notice of her and she knew she'd been conditioned to believe that everyone cheated—her father had certainly been guilty of the same offence on several occasions—and so the young Molly hadn't stopped to think about whether Daniel's attention was positive or negative. She hadn't cared. But not any more. She knew now that she didn't need someone else's validation—especially not when it was thinly-disguised emotional abuse. Now, away from her family and single for the first time in years, she was just trying to be the best version of herself. Whatever that was.

Here in Byron, she wasn't a sister, a daughter, a girl-friend. She was just Molly. A doctor. A friend.

But seeing Theo reminded her of the old Molly, the one she was trying to leave behind. She didn't want to be reminded of that girl.

She'd need to avoid Theo. And seeing as he was only in Byron Bay temporarily, it shouldn't be too hard.

Theo Chin Williams tried to concentrate as Tom Reynolds showed him around the clinic. He schooled his expression to make it look as if he was listening but he wasn't sure he would retain any of the information. His mind was too busy going back over old times. Back to Molly. He'd been stunned to see her at the clinic today. He hadn't seen her profile on the Pacific Coast Clinics website and he knew he would have noticed it, which meant it wasn't there. She must be new to the practice.

Four years was a long time but Molly hadn't changed. At least, not in appearance. She looked exactly the same—petite, blonde, shiny. Theo had always seen an aura of lightness and joy about her. With the exception of one memorable occasion, she'd always presented as

a happy person. She'd been popular at university. She'd
been fun and people had been drawn to her. He knew he
had been. But they had mostly moved in different circles and Molly had barely noticed him. Except for that
one night.

He remembered their last encounter. Their only intimate encounter in the seven years they'd been acquainted.
Molly had cried on his shoulder, confided in him, kissed
him and they hadn't spoken since.

He had admired her from afar for many years before
that fateful night. He'd put her on a pedestal and hadn't
been able to resist kissing her back when she'd abruptly
and unexpectedly kissed him, but he'd been convinced
she would never choose him over Daniel and so he'd
walked away, wishing he were brave enough to stay.

At the end of the staff meeting he'd wondered if he
should approach her, but what would he say after four
years? They weren't friends, they were acquaintances at
best. And then Tom had steered him out of the staffroom
to embark on a tour of the clinic, taking the opportunity
away from him.

Which brought his mind neatly back to the matter at
hand. Back to the reason he was in Byron Bay—to work.
He was here for the next six weeks in a locum capacity
but he'd also been tasked with some problem-solving.
The Byron clinic was the newest addition to the Pacific
Coast portfolio, a group of medical centres owned by his
parents and managed by his mother, and she had flagged
some issues, which Theo had been entrusted with sorting out. Between treating patients and going over the
clinic's books and operating procedures he had enough

on his plate. He didn't need to add Molly Prescott to his list. His mother was a perfectionist who expected nothing less than one hundred per cent effort at all times. He knew he was expected to return to Sydney with answers, and possibly solutions, to the issues she'd raised. He had plenty to focus on and his mother would not be pleased if he let himself get distracted. She wasn't interested in excuses, only in results.

Molly was a blast from the past but one that didn't need revisiting. He didn't need the distraction. Reminiscing wasn't a priority for him and he got the impression it wasn't high on her agenda either.

He forced himself to concentrate on the guided tour he was being given. He knew Tom's leave started today and he knew he would be expected to step up to the plate and take on a patient load immediately. He needed to focus. He hadn't seen Molly for four years. He could put her out of his mind for another few hours, at least while he was at work. He was older and wiser now, no longer infatuated. They had both moved on.

He could ignore the fact that she still glowed, still made the air around her shimmer. He could ignore the fact that his heart rate had escalated when their colleagues had parted to reveal her standing there and he could ignore the fact that his hands had perspired and his mouth had gone dry.

He could ignore her.

Molly scrolled through patients' test results on her computer screen but couldn't find the headspace to pick up the phone to pass any results on. She was being extremely unproductive. She was unsettled and she hated to admit it but Theo's arrival was responsible. She really thought she'd been making progress since she'd moved to Byron Bay. She was growing in confidence, no longer having to wonder what life with Daniel would have in store for her, whether she would be in or out of favour, whether she'd be fighting for attention or battling for his affection. She was on the path to independence and she didn't want Theo's arrival to pull her backwards. But she was stronger now, she wasn't the same girl any more, and she would show Theo that. Or just avoid him and allow him to see that for himself.

She nodded to herself, encouraged that she'd found a solution. She earmarked a couple of patients for the receptionists to call with non-urgent results and decided she'd go and grab another coffee before her consulting list started. Perhaps that would kick her brain into gear. Into the present and off the past.

On her way to the kitchen, she passed Paula's office. The practice manager had a large internal window looking out to the reception area. Molly glanced through the window and saw Theo leaning over Paula's desk, deep in conversation and pointing at a computer screen. What on earth could they be discussing? She paused briefly as her curiosity got the better of her, before realising she didn't want to be caught peering in at the unexpected tableau. It was none of her business and if it had been anyone but Theo she wouldn't have given it a second thought. Why did she find him so interesting?

Not wanting to go down that rabbit hole, she continued on to the kitchen but couldn't resist glancing through the window as she returned with her coffee. Theo was still there.

Molly kept walking and just as she reached the reception desk the front door to the clinic burst open and a very distressed middle-aged woman barrelled in, holding the door for her male partner. The man was overweight and sweating, not unusual in the humid air of Byron Bay, but Molly could see he was having difficulty breathing.

The woman plonked him on a seat and rushed to the desk, ignoring the other patients waiting to be attended to. 'Please, we need to see a doctor. My husband isn't well.'

'Are you a patient of the clinic?' the receptionist asked as Molly hurried around the desk and into the waiting room.

The woman shook her head. 'No. We're here on holiday. My husband has been complaining of indigestion, over-indulging I think, but it's got so bad this morning he's finding it hard to breathe.'

The clinic was not technically an emergency clinic but because they were right in the centre of town they got a lot of walk-ins. Despite the sign on the door giving the hospital's details, if the clinic was open people just turned up. The hospital had recently undergone extensive upgrades but, being a ten-minute drive out of town, it wasn't nearly as convenient. Especially for the tourists.

Molly sat down next to the man. 'My name is Molly, I'm one of the doctors.' He turned towards her but she could see he was having difficulty taking her words in. He was rubbing his sternum but it seemed to be an unconscious movement. 'Why don't you come with me and we'll get you looked at?' she continued.

She was concerned he was displaying symptoms of a cardiac episode. She could call for an ambulance but she knew from experience that dealing with any emergency was better done behind closed doors and out of the reception area. She wanted to get him somewhere with some privacy. He'd walked into the clinic, she just hoped he'd be able to walk into her consulting room. She didn't fancy her chances of breaking his fall if he toppled over.

'I'll take him, if you can get some details,' Molly told the receptionist.

The man stood, unsteadily, and Molly instinctively gave him her arm for support. 'What is your name?'

'Warwick,' he replied breathlessly.

Molly took him into the examination room where they had an ECG machine, just in case she needed it. She pressed on the footplate under the treatment bed, lowering it so Warwick could sit down. She lifted the back support and helped him to lift his feet.

'Can you describe to me what you're experiencing?'

'I'm having trouble breathing. It feels like someone is squeezing my lungs.'

'Does it hurt?'

Warwick nodded.

'Is this the first time you've had this pain?'

'It's the first time it's been this bad,' he said, not without some difficulty.

'Are you seeing a doctor for any chronic health conditions? Do you have any allergies? Any heart issues? Angina? Diabetes? Anxiety?'

Warwick shook his head.

'Are you taking any medications?' Molly asked as

she wrapped a blood-pressure cuff around his arm and pressed the button to inflate it.

'Tablets for high cholesterol.'

Did he not think that was a condition worth mentioning? she thought as she looked at the reading on the monitor. She was surprised to find his blood pressure was within normal limits but noted his heart rate was rapid.

'I'd like to take a closer look at your heart. Have you ever had an ECG done before?'

Warwick shook his head again.

'I need to stick some electrodes onto your chest. Can you undo your shirt for me?' Molly asked as she turned her back to prepare the ECG machine.

'I don't…' Warwick's sentence faded away behind her. She spun around.

Warwick's eyes were closed. Was he breathing?

Molly looked for a rise and fall in his chest.

Nothing.

'Warwick?' She shook his shoulder before grabbing his wrist and feeling for a pulse.

Nothing.

She dropped the back of the bed, lying him flat.

She suspected he was in cardiac arrest.

She needed help.

She darted out of the room, snatching the defibrillator kit from the box on the wall outside Paula's office, and yelling instructions to Crystal at the reception desk as she flew past. 'Call an ambulance. Code blue.'

Through the window of Paula's office she could see Theo sitting by the desk.

She needed help and there was no time to go looking

for it. She scanned the corridor, hoping someone else might materialise but, of course, no one did.

It would have to be Theo.

She stuck her head through the door. There was no time to worry about the past. She'd have to shelve her plans to avoid Theo.

She needed help.

She needed Theo.

'Theo!' She all but shouted his name, barely waiting for him to look up before she was already turning back to her exam room. 'I need you. Patient in cardiac arrest.'

CHAPTER TWO

THEO LIFTED HIS head as he heard Molly call his name. She'd already turned on her heel and was heading along the passageway by the time he moved. As he stepped into the corridor, he was immediately enveloped by the scent of oranges hanging in the air and he was transported straight back to the night Molly had kissed him. Her hair had smelt of oranges then too. It was the scent of her shampoo. Now was not the time to be distracted, though. He hurried after her, catching up to her as she ducked into a clinic room. Her words trailed behind her. 'Middle-aged male, sudden cardiac arrest. No reported prior history.'

Theo nodded and said, 'I'll start compressions.' This wasn't how he'd imagined their first conversation would go but there was no time to waste. There was no time for the past.

Molly was avoiding eye contact, which piqued Theo's curiosity. Four years ago, they hadn't been friends, but they hadn't been enemies either—at least he hadn't thought so. But a cardiac event was a stressful situation. He couldn't expect her to spend time making him feel welcome.

Pushing his curiosity aside, he ripped open the buttons on the patient's shirt, exposing his chest and belly as Molly quickly opened the defibrillator kit and pulled out the pieces she needed. He leaned over the patient and placed his hands on his sternum, beginning chest compressions as Molly worked behind him.

Theo counted out loud and tried to ignore Molly as she moved around him. But it was difficult. She was hard to ignore. Each movement she made disturbed the orange-scented, perfumed air; he could feel where she was even when he couldn't see her. She squeezed behind him, putting her hands on his hips, obviously trying to keep him in position, trying not to disturb his rhythm, but her touch nearly made him lose track of his count.

'Fifteen.'

Molly's arm brushed his as she reached across to press the sticky pad onto Warwick's chest and a spark of awareness surged through him.

'Twenty.' His voice was husky. He cleared his throat and focused hard. Now was not the time to be thinking about Molly Prescott as anything more than his colleague.

He continued compressions as Molly placed the second pad onto the patient, this time without any further contact with Theo. She connected the pads to the machine and it began to issue instructions in its automated voice.

'Stop CPR, analysing rhythm.'

'Shock advised.'

Theo could hear the whine as the power built up in the defibrillator unit.

'Stand clear.'

'Clear.' Theo lifted his hands, holding them in the air, and repeated the machine's instructions. Molly stepped back from the bed and pressed the flashing red button. Theo stayed close. The patient was large and he was worried he could fall when the shock was delivered.

The patient lifted off the bed as the machine delivered a charge, trying to shock his heart out of fibrillation and restore its normal rhythm.

Theo and Molly waited but there was no change.

'Continue CPR.'

The machine continued its instructions.

'Are you okay to continue and I'll do the breaths?' Molly asked.

Theo nodded and resumed chest compressions. He knew the AED machine would expect two minutes of continued CPR before performing another analysis.

Molly opened the face-shield container and placed the shield over the patient's mouth and tipped his head back. Her left hand cupped his chin and Theo noticed her fingers were bare. She wasn't wearing a ring.

As Theo approached the count of thirty, Molly was preparing to give two breaths. Despite the fact they'd never worked together before their movements were smooth and coordinated. Theo reached thirty counts and paused and Molly bent her head and breathed into their patient. The transition from compressions to breaths was seamless.

Molly was standing opposite Theo now, keeping out of his way, and he watched the top of her head as she bent over the patient, her blonde hair falling over her face. She tossed her head to shift the hair from her eyes as she tilted her head to check for the accompanying rise of the patient's chest, making sure her breaths were reaching his lungs. Theo had to stop himself from reaching across and tucking Molly's hair behind her ear. He didn't think she'd appreciate the help but his fingers ached to touch her.

He returned his focus to his patient's chest as Molly finished her second breath, making sure he wasn't caught looking at her when she straightened up.

They continued administering three more rounds of CPR. Two more long minutes before the machine interrupted them again.

'Stop CPR, analysing rhythm.'

'Shock advised.'

'Stand clear.'

Another jolt. But still nothing.

Theo continued with a fifth round of compressions. His shoulders were starting to complain—the patient was large and Theo was using a lot of effort, but he couldn't quit.

'Analysing rhythm.'

The defibrillator deliberated a possible third shock.

'No shock advised.'

'Check pulse.'

Molly checked for a pulse. 'I've got something!'

Her eyes met his. She was grinning, her smile was wide, full of relief and achievement, and Theo felt something tug at his heart. He smiled back. A proper smile this time, not the uncertain half-smile he'd bestowed on her earlier in the staff kitchen.

He let his hands drop and breathed out as Molly cried, 'We've got him!'

Theo could hardly believe it as the patient's eyes opened, a look of confusion on his face.

'Hello, Warwick.' Molly turned her attention to their patient and Theo felt a chill as her smile was directed at someone else. 'You gave us quite a scare.'

Warwick. That was the patient's name, Theo thought as Molly picked up the phone and buzzed the reception desk, asking Crystal to send the paramedics in when they arrived.

'We're going to send you off to hospital now and get you sorted out,' Molly continued as the door opened and Paula ushered the paramedics in, followed by a woman who Theo assumed was Warwick's wife. She made a bee-line for their patient but Molly, who had her eyes trained on the woman, inclined her head slightly in Theo's direction. He understood her gesture—he needed to keep the wife out of the way while Molly did the patient handover. He steered the woman to a chair in the corner.

'Is he okay?' she asked. 'What happened? Why is the ambulance here?'

Theo didn't have much information but he had enough to pass on to the wife and hopefully ease her concerns.

'He's all right now but he needs to go to hospital.'

'For indigestion?' The woman was frowning.

'He went into cardiac arrest,' Theo explained gently. 'Your husband's heart stopped. We had to resuscitate him. He needs to go to hospital and he'll need further tests done.'

'He had a heart attack?'

'Cardiac arrest,' Theo repeated. 'It's a bit different from a heart attack.' Technically they were two different things but he didn't have time to go into that detail and he doubted if she'd remember much of what he told her anyway. 'Warwick will be seen by a cardiologist. They'll be able to give you more information.'

In his peripheral vision Theo could see the paramedics slipping an oxygen mask over Warwick's face as Molly took a final blood-pressure reading and removed the sticky pads from his chest. Warwick was transferred to the paramedics' stretcher as Molly removed the cuff.

'Can I go to the hospital with him?' Warwick's wife asked.

'Of course.'

Molly and Theo remained behind as the paramedics wheeled the stretcher out, followed by Warwick's wife.

Theo went to the sink in the corner and filled two disposable cups with water. He handed one to Molly as she sat on the edge of the bed and let out a large sigh of relief.

'Thank you,' she said as she took the cup from him.

'Are you okay?' he asked.

She nodded. 'You?'

He smiled. 'Yep. Can't say I was expecting that on my first day though. Is Warwick a patient of yours?'

Molly shook her head. 'I've never seen him before. They're tourists, here on holiday.'

Theo frowned. 'But there's a hospital in Byron Bay. Why did they come here?'

Molly sipped her water. 'It happens a lot. We're in the centre of town. We're a lot more convenient.'

'But you're not an emergency clinic.'

'I know. But they thought it was indigestion.'

Theo wondered how often this occurred and what impact it had on the practice. On the staff. GPs weren't emergency physicians and the clinic certainly wasn't equipped like a hospital ED. Warwick had been lucky today.

'Warwick was lucky you knew what you were doing,' Theo said.

'I was lucky you were here too. Sorry, to throw you in the deep end. That's the first real emergency I've had to deal with in the six months I've been here.'

Six months—that was one question answered.

'What brought you to Byron Bay?'

She shrugged. 'I needed a change of scenery.'

He wanted to ask about Daniel. He wanted to know if he was there too, if Molly was still with him, but there was no subtle way to phrase that question so he let it lie. Her bare ring finger was no clue. Lots of doctors didn't wear rings for practical reasons. It was easier to keep your hands clean if you didn't wear jewellery.

Molly finished her water, stood up and began to tidy the room. She threw out the used sticky pads and packed the defibrillator away after checking that there were more pads in the kit. 'Would you mind putting this back for me?' she asked as she held out the kit, back to avoiding eye contact. 'It goes on the wall outside Paula's office.'

Theo took the kit and left the room, unasked questions still swirling in his brain. But he'd been dismissed. Sent away by Molly. No longer needed.

He returned the kit before heading to the consulting room that had been allocated to him. He ran the cold water in the basin and rinsed his hands to cool them down. He stared into the mirror as he let the water run into the sink, looking at his reflection and wondering if Molly had seen the changes he saw in himself.

He knew he had grown as a person over the past four years but would anyone else notice? Would Molly? Did it matter?

Theo had grown up caught between two cultures, on the outside looking in at kids like Molly and her friends, kids who were comfortable in their skin, who knew where they belonged. He'd never felt completely at ease. He'd often felt he was drifting lonelily between his Asian heritage and his Aussie upbringing. Fitting in nowhere.

His mother was Taiwanese. She'd moved to Australia as a teenager and had met his Australian father at medical school. But although his parents came from different backgrounds their goals were almost identical. Their level of contentment was directly proportional to their level of success—they aspired to successful careers and to raising successful children. But there was some irony there, Theo knew, given that his maternal grandparents had emigrated from Taiwan to look after his sister and him while their parents established their careers and then grew their businesses, having little to do with raising their own children.

Theo was bilingual. Speaking Mandarin with his grandparents, he'd worked hard to cultivate an Australian accent so that he'd fitted in at school, but he'd known there were more differences between him and his classmates than just an accent. He and his sister were officially Chin Williamses, but Theo had refused to use Chin on his paperwork, preferring to stick with the more Anglicised Williams. Even that hadn't seemed to help. He hadn't eaten the same lunches, he hadn't played sport, his parents and grandparents had never attended assembly or the Christmas concerts and had only occasionally made it to a music recital. He'd given up wishing for attention beyond what he'd garnered by his results. If anything, he knew that was partly what had motivated him to do well at school—it was the only time he'd got any recognition. Any positive attention.

A stint working overseas after graduation had taught him a lot about himself and the world. He had returned knowing the importance of his skills and the importance of human relationships and as he'd settled into his career as a doctor he'd found an identity that had started to fit him. It didn't matter what grades he'd got at school or university once he had his degree. It didn't matter if he played sport, had gone to parties or out on dates. All that mattered was whether he could help his patients. And he had no difficulty with that.

Seeing Molly had thrown him momentarily. He had never expected to run into her here. He'd had no idea she worked for Pacific Coast Clinics. The company was owned by Theo's parents but managed by his mother, a general practitioner, while his father concentrated on his career as a plastic surgeon. They had added the Byron Bay clinic to their stable eighteen months ago but Theo had never given the practice on the upper New South Wales coast much consideration. His time was consumed by his job in Sydney and by his parents' expectations. He was always expected to work harder and longer than the other employees, to prove his value, his skills and his suitability as heir apparent.

He knew he was expected to take over the clinics one day, and he wanted that. But he also knew it wouldn't be handed to him on a plate. He was expected to work for it, and work hard. His parents could just as easily look for an outside investor or one of the other staff members to take over as they could hand him the reins. But they wouldn't be happy. Failure was not an option for a Chin Williams.

When other children had been playing sport and joining teams he'd been doing extra homework or attending tutoring. Not that he'd found schoolwork difficult, but his parents had wanted him and his sister to excel in everything. To be the best. When he was a teenager and schoolmates had been going to parties he'd been at home doing practice exams. His only hobby was playing the guitar and that had developed from the piano lessons he'd been made to take as a child. As a teenager he'd taught himself the guitar and he had entertained fantasies of playing in a band until that dream had been squashed by the demands of university.

His parents and his maternal grandparents had told him, repeatedly, 'You'll never get anywhere without hard work,' and he had to admit, they had a point. He was good at his job and was working hard to establish himself, working harder than the next doctor, trying not only to meet his parents' expectations but to prove to everyone else that he wasn't getting by on his connections.

Personal relationships were another story. He'd had one serious relationship since finishing university, but she had wanted more of his time than he'd had to give. He was only twenty-nine. He figured there was still plenty of time for relationships in his future.

Now, thinking about relationships led him back to

thinking about Molly. He was curious to know what her life had looked like for the past four years. But curiosity was dangerous. It was distracting. Besides, did it really matter? He'd be gone in six weeks and Molly would be firmly back in his past. He needed to stop thinking about her and remember why he was here.

His mother had put her faith in him, her trust, and Theo knew that wasn't easy to come by. He had a job to do in Byron Bay—two jobs: one as a doctor and the other to evaluate the clinic. Its profits had been falling and he had six weeks to figure out why. Normally his mother would have looked into this herself. She'd told him as much. She'd looked over the books but she wanted to see how the clinic functioned in person, but an upcoming overseas conference where she was a keynote speaker had made that impossible so she'd sent Theo in her place. Killing two birds with one stone. He would fill the locum position and get her some answers. Failure was not an option.

Finding out he'd be working with Molly Prescott was a surprise but he wouldn't let it be a complication. They had worked well together today but they weren't friends. They had never been friends and there was no reason to think things would be any different now.

Yes, he'd had a major crush on Molly at university. Yes, he had admired her from a distance. She always seemed so sure of herself and her place in the world and he'd been a little envious of her confidence back then. She was pretty and positive and popular, but there had been one night when he'd found out that she was vulnerable just like anyone else.

He could only remember seeing her let her guard down that once, and it had stayed with him. Not just because of her vulnerability, but because of what else had happened.

He knew the kiss Molly had bestowed on him had been spontaneous, he knew he'd just happened to be the man in front of her when she'd needed comfort, but that hadn't stopped him from kissing her back. And he couldn't pretend the kiss hadn't been incredible. And for a fleeting moment he'd imagined it could be something more than what it was. But just because he wished it didn't make it true.

She'd chosen to kiss him that night, but he knew she wouldn't choose him again permanently. She'd made that much clear. And so he'd walked away.

It had hurt at the time. He had always had Molly on a pedestal, wanting her to notice him, and for a brief moment in time she had.

None of that mattered now. The past was the past. Four years later they were equals. Colleagues. What Molly thought of him now shouldn't matter. He didn't usually care what people thought of him. He was used to existing in his own world. He expected to be judged on his achievements, not for who he was. Molly had been the exception; he had wanted her to see him. For her to see Theo. For some inexplicable reason Molly Prescott had been the only exception in his world.

But as much as he'd like Molly to see the new, confident Theo, she couldn't be an exception again. He wasn't going down that path. He wasn't going to bring up the past. They weren't friends. They were temporary colleagues.

He'd do his job and be gone in six weeks, putting Molly

Prescott behind him for the second time. He'd be in and out of Byron Bay before she even had time to notice.

Molly sat down as Theo left her room. She wondered if he'd noticed that she'd almost pushed him out of the door, but she needed a moment to catch her breath alone. All thoughts of tidying up were forgotten as she sat and gathered herself together. She closed her eyes and took a deep breath. Her hands were shaking and she clenched her fists to control the tremor. She knew it wasn't just Warwick's medical episode that had got the adrenalin racing around her body. It was Theo.

All it had taken was a look, one smile, the briefest contact, and she was catapulted right back to the night of their kiss. Everything she'd tried to ignore, how he'd listened, how he'd smelt as he'd held her while she'd cried, how he'd made her feel when he'd given her his attention and how he'd tasted when she'd kissed him, all came rushing back. She liked to pretend she'd forgotten but she knew that was a lie. And now he was here she knew she'd been kidding herself if she'd thought she could pretend it was all in the past.

Molly stared into space as she thought about that night.

She'd had a few drinks, everyone had, but she'd mostly been exhausted and emotional after their final exams. And when she'd seen Daniel in a suspicious embrace with another girl she'd completely lost her temper. It wasn't the first time she'd caught him cheating on her, and she'd been furious. She'd confronted him and they'd gone into the garden and had a massive argument. He'd denied any wrongdoing, she'd been positive he was lying, and he'd left her alone and gone back to the party.

Theo had found her sobbing and he'd sat with her while she'd blubbered all over him. She hadn't been so drunk that she didn't remember every little detail of their encounter. She'd talked and cried and he'd listened. And then they'd talked to each other. For hours, it had felt like. Molly couldn't remember anyone talking to her for that long. Couldn't recall anyone taking what she said seriously. She was so used to being the life of the party. Being fun. Hiding her insecurities behind a smile and a laugh. But Theo had been interested in what she had to say. And gradually she'd started to feel better. She remembered leaning on his shoulder and then she'd looked up and he'd been watching her with his dark eyes and she'd known he was really seeing her. And then she'd kissed him.

She hadn't asked, she'd just done it, and he'd kissed her back.

She remembered everything. From what they'd talked about to the kiss. Especially the kiss. It had been amazing. Incredible. As if he'd known her for ever, as if he were another half of her. They'd been so in tune, as if they'd kissed a thousand times before, in a thousand different lifetimes. There had been no awkward clashing of teeth or noses. No hesitation.

She'd never been kissed like that.

And then he'd walked away.

And in the months that had followed she'd wondered if she should have grabbed his hand as he'd walked away. If she should have made a different choice. But she'd made the same mistake she'd always made and had forgiven Daniel. And had let Theo go.

She'd been insecure, meticulously curating an image of a girl content with her life, and she'd always been so careful not to let her guard down. Theo had seen her at a weak moment. He had seen and heard too much. She'd never told anyone what happened and she had never spoken to Theo again. She'd moved on with her life, moved on with Daniel and pretended that night had never existed.

She was a different person now. She was finding her independence and didn't need reminders of the past. The spontaneous late-night kiss they'd shared would have to stay consigned to history. And history shouldn't be repeated. Some things needed to be let go. Several years and many reincarnations of her relationship with Daniel had come and gone before she'd finally learned the value of leaving things behind and divesting herself of bad mistakes. It was a lesson she'd do well to remember.

CHAPTER THREE

AFTER THE RATHER dramatic start, the rest of Theo's first day went smoothly. A couple of billing enquiries had come up that he'd discussed with Paula, leaving him feeling as if he was already making headway with his mother's task. He saw a few patients of Tom's, easing himself into the locum role, before heading to the pub for something to eat.

He sat at the bar nursing a pre-dinner beer. He'd have to find time to get to the supermarket tomorrow. He couldn't eat out every night and he didn't want to eat out alone.

'Hey, Theo.' He was jolted out of his musings by the sound of his name. Matt, one of the physios from the clinic, was standing beside him. He nodded in the direction of Theo's drink as he ordered a beer for himself. 'Can I get you another one?'

'Sure, thanks.'

'I heard you had an eventful first day.'

Theo laughed. 'Yeah. Luckily it turned out okay, but I'm hoping it's not always like that.'

'It's usually pretty chilled here in Byron. This place is all about a good work-life balance.'

'Work-life balance.' Theo laughed. 'I'm not sure what that means.'

'Well, let's hope you have time to find out while you're here. Six weeks, right?'

Theo nodded.

'Have you been to Byron before?'

'Never. Born and bred in Sydney but never been here.'

'You went through med school in Sydney with Molly?'

'Yes. Did she tell you that?' Theo was surprised. He'd got the impression Molly hadn't shared their history.

Matt shook his head as he paid for their beers. 'Gemma did.'

That still meant Molly had told someone. 'I didn't know Molly was in Byron Bay.' He hadn't seen Molly since their graduation ceremony. When it was obvious she and Daniel had patched up their differences. She'd avoided him. He'd left her alone.

He'd felt both disappointed and vindicated when he'd seen them together at graduation. He'd guessed correctly that she would take Daniel back after the party and he hadn't wanted to get caught in the middle of their on-again-off-again romance. He didn't need the headache. As much as he'd been attracted to Molly, and he could admit that he was, he didn't want to be a pawn in her game, cast aside when she went back to Daniel, as she'd done several times throughout university. Being rejected was a form of failure in Theo's eyes and failure was unacceptable, therefore, the sensible thing to do was to reduce his exposure to that risk by removing himself from the situation.

But now he thought again about her bare finger, the

lack of a ring, engagement or wedding, and wondered if she was still with Daniel or if she'd come to her senses over the past four years. He hoped for her sake that she had.

'I managed to convince her to make the move up here after she broke up with Daniel,' Matt said.

Theo bit back a smile. Hearing that Molly had broken up with Daniel was good news, but he wondered if it would be like all the other times she'd broken up with him. Was it going to be short-lived or was this it? 'They were still together?' He knew he was fishing for information but he was curious to know what had happened and he took some small measure of satisfaction in hearing Molly and Daniel were no longer a couple.

'Yeah, they were. It's been almost a year since they broke up this time so I'm hoping she's finally done with him. He's not a mate of yours, is he?' Matt added, as if suddenly realising he might be stepping on toes. 'He would have been at university with you too.'

Theo nodded. 'He was in our year but we weren't mates.' Theo and Daniel couldn't have been more different. Theo's parents had worked hard, built a successful business, but they had started with nothing. Theo didn't know Daniel well, but Daniel had clearly been born with a silver spoon in his mouth. He had the arrogance and general disdain of others less fortunate. He had a strong sense of self-importance, an expectation that people would listen to him—not because he had good ideas but because he had grown up having people tell him that he was special. He wasn't Theo's type of person. Theo had never been told he was special. He'd been brought up to work hard, to let his achievements speak for him, but that meant he didn't dare to fail because if he wasn't achieving, then who was he?

He did wonder, though, what it was that had finally made Molly see the light and break up with Daniel. Or had he broken up with her? At university it had always been something that Daniel did that had triggered their breakups. But Molly had taken him back time and time again.

But he wasn't going to ask Matt those questions. It really wasn't any of his business. Molly wasn't his friend; she was just a part of his past. That was where she needed to stay.

Fortunately, Matt had moved on from the topic of Molly. 'What's your trivia knowledge like?' he asked. 'We've got a regular team together for the weekly pub quiz if you'd like to join us. We're down a player—it's usually Tom.'

Theo hesitated. He wasn't sure how Molly would feel if he joined the group. He'd got the impression she wasn't that thrilled to see him.

'No pressure, we're not playing for sheep stations,' Matt said when Theo didn't reply straight away. 'And in the interests of full disclosure, we don't expect to win. We order pizzas and have a few drinks, that's it.'

Theo was assuming Molly would be there. She might not. He made a decision. 'As long as you don't expect me to answer any sports questions,' he replied.

'That's my area of expertise.'

A contest where there were no expectations on him to excel? To be the best? To win? That was a novelty for

Theo and one that had some appeal. Perhaps it was time to embrace that work-life balance Matt spoke of. 'Okay, then, sounds good.' He picked up his fresh beer and followed Matt to a table at the back of the pub. It wasn't as if he had anything better to do.

He went round the table, introducing himself to some unfamiliar faces, and as he sat down he saw Molly and Gemma arrive. Her double take when she saw him at the table didn't go unnoticed by him. She looked at the seats around the table. She and Gemma were last to arrive. There was one spare seat on the bench beside Theo and another at the other end of the table. He could tell Molly intended to sit at the far end but Gemma got there first, leaving Molly to sit with him.

Her hip bumped against his as she sat down and immediately she shifted away from him. Could she not bear to be close to him? He moved aside slightly, trying to give her more space. He didn't want her to feel crowded. She looked a little skittish, as though if he said or did the wrong thing she'd get up and leave. Flee. She gave him a smile, but it wasn't her usual full-blown, all-encompassing smile that he remembered. He could see the tension in her shoulders, in her eyes.

She chatted to Matt's partner, Levi, who was a school-teacher, and then took charge of the answer sheet. Theo suspected that was so she could avoid having to talk to him. That was okay. He didn't need her attention. He wasn't twenty-five any more. He was comfortable in his own skin now, successful, mature. He didn't need to be in awe of Molly any more. Didn't need to be seen by Molly.

* * *

Molly knew she'd given Theo short shrift when she'd sat down. She would have preferred to sit somewhere else. She was still on edge.

Working so closely with Theo had reawakened her memory of the kiss. It had been unexpected and amazing. The way it made her feel had surprised her back then, but she'd attributed that to her heightened emotional state and the alcohol. But that didn't explain why she'd had a similar reaction today when Theo had smiled at her and when her arm had brushed against his. He triggered feelings that startled her. Feelings that were out of her control. She didn't like that. She wanted to maintain control.

She was afraid to look at him. Afraid he'd see what she was feeling in her eyes. It really wasn't appropriate and she'd needed time to gather herself together, worried that if she sat beside him he'd know what she was thinking.

So when she'd been forced to take the spot next to him, she took it upon herself to be the scribe for the group. It gave her an excuse to avoid eye contact but just because she wasn't looking at Theo didn't mean she wasn't aware of his every movement, his every breath. He reached for his drink and his arm brushed hers and the pen skittered over the paper as her skin burned in response to his touch. She tried to focus on the others in the group as the questions began.

Levi had politics and Australian history covered, Gemma was a geography nerd and Matt was all over the sports questions. She was normally good at the trivia questions but her focus was terrible and answers she could normally give without even thinking about eluded her, putting them in the bottom third of the results with two rounds to go.

Theo had contributed a few correct answers in the early rounds but everything changed in the music round. He answered every question correctly, even arguing his case successfully with Levi about the original name of a band and insisting Molly use his answer. They scored full marks and closed the gap on the top two teams. He looked so pleased with his efforts that Molly couldn't ignore him any longer. Not when every other member of the team was so excited to be in with a shot of winning.

'Wow. That was impressive,' she said as Matt took the answer sheet up to the scorer's table. 'How do you know so much about music?' The questions had been varied, it wasn't as if they were all focused on one genre, but Theo had been flawless.

'Music was a big part of my family. My mother believes studying a musical instrument helps to develop the brain so my sister and I had no choice but to learn something. I started with the piano but eventually taught myself the guitar and I have always loved listening to all sorts of music. I really wanted to be in a band but my sister is a classical violinist with the symphony orchestra so, as one of only two children, I was expected to follow in my parents' path and study medicine.'

'You didn't want to be a doctor?'

'I wanted to do both. I spent a lot of time at live gigs, soaking up that atmosphere, until it became impossible with the time commitments and hours needed to devote to study. But it's still my way of relaxing.'

'Do you still play the guitar?' Molly asked, realising she knew nothing about him really.

He nodded.

Molly couldn't play an instrument. She could never sit still for long enough to learn. She played netball, a lot of netball. That was much more her speed.

He had musician's hands, slender fingers, fine bones. But Molly supposed they were good doctor's hands too. Gentle. Tender. She lifted her eyes to his face. He had a shadow of a beard on his chin and jaw, slightly darker where a moustache would grow, and his eyes were almost black in the dim light of the pub.

'Molly, are you ready for the last round?'

Matt's question interrupted Molly's thoughts and she jumped and dragged her gaze away from Theo. She reached for a fresh sheet of paper to record the answers but Theo reached for it at the same time and his fingers landed on hers. A burst of heat shot up her left arm and Molly dropped the paper in a fluster. She tucked her hand under the table, opening and closing her fist until the tingling subsided and normal feeling returned and she was able to rest that hand on the answer sheet to stabilise it as she wrote. Her heart was racing and she could feel a frown of concentration creasing her brow as she struggled to keep focused and keep up with the answers her team was peppering her with. Theo's knee bumped against her thigh as he reached for his drink, disrupting her focus even further, and at the end of the round she got up quickly, needing to put some distance between her and Theo lest she make another silly mistake.

* * *

It was impossible to avoid Theo completely though as
the next morning, as she was rushing into the clinic, late
as usual, he was waiting for her in her consulting room.

He handed her a coffee and a paper bag.

Molly took the coffee and peered inside the bag to find
it contained a doughnut. 'What's this for?'

'An apology.'

Molly frowned. 'Apology?'

'I get the impression you would prefer me not to be here.'

'Here?'

'In Byron Bay. Working at the clinic. Coming to the
quiz night. Anywhere really.'

Theo's dark eyes were flat as he watched her closely.
His eyes lacked their usual shine and made her feel uncomfortable. Had she made him feel unwelcome? That
hadn't been her intention.

'Can we call a truce?' he asked, taking her silence for
affirmation of his thoughts. 'I don't know why you don't
want me here but I'm hoping we can get on as colleagues.
I promise I'm not going to bite you. Or kiss you again.'

'You remembered.' Of course he did. But she wasn't
sure how she felt about him putting that information out
there between them. She was part mortified, part pleased.
She didn't want to be forgettable but she would have preferred the incident to be wiped from memory. His memory. She was no longer the insecure girl who was looking
for attention and seeking validation and she worried that
Theo might still see her as such. Despite her having resolved to overcome the damage that Daniel had done,

that her parents had done, she feared her insecurities hadn't been erased completely, and having her past and present collide could destabilise her carefully laid plan of reinvention.

'That kiss was a lot of things but forgettable wasn't one of them,' Theo said, and Molly could feel herself blushing as he continued. 'I promise I'm not here to cause drama. I don't want to make things difficult for you.'

His dark eyes were gleaming again, his gaze gentle, unchallenging, and Molly knew he wasn't looking for an argument, he was offering her a way out. Telling her he had moved past their last encounter so she could put it behind her too.

'I'm only here for forty days. Do you think you can put up with me for that long?'

She nodded, rather unconvincingly she felt, but she couldn't ignore his question altogether. It wasn't a case of putting up with him. It was a case of maintaining her composure. She knew she'd crossed a line the night she'd kissed him but it had been so nice to have someone ask her if she was okay, to have someone listen to her. She hadn't expected the kiss to tip her world sideways. And for one crazy minute she'd been tempted to take a chance and see what would happen if she chose Theo. But for so long she had been hiding behind a mask. One that Daniel hadn't even cared enough to see behind. She'd been the loudest in the room, the funniest, the brightest and she was terrified that if her mask slipped Theo might not like what he found behind it.

But she still wasn't sure she'd be able to handle being colleagues without being awkward. She got the feeling

Theo could read her innermost thoughts. That he could see into her heart and soul, and she didn't want him to read her thoughts now. She didn't want him to know she'd never forgotten him or the kiss either. Those days were long gone.

Theo was the last one in the clinic on Friday night. He had spoken to his mother and run through the issues he'd already identified within the clinic and then returned to the spreadsheets when the call ended, but the figures were swimming in circles.

He kept thinking about Molly and wondering why it was that they found themselves together in this town. Was it fate, as his mother and grandparents would attest to, or was it simply a coincidence, as his father would say? And, either way, did it mean anything?

His logical side told him it didn't, but he still couldn't concentrate. Work could wait for another day, he decided as he shut down his computer.

But now the weekend stretched ahead of him. He had no plans. He never did—he was normally working.

He wondered what Molly was doing. But if she had plans she hadn't included him, not that he expected her to, and nor had he asked her what she was up to.

He had to admit he still felt a pull of attraction, chemistry, a buzz when he was around her. She still bewitched him, that hadn't changed. But he wasn't going to make a move. He was only here for another month or so and it was almost as if they'd agreed to ignore one another for that time. Despite their truce, they'd barely said a word to each other for the past two days.

He switched off the lights and locked the clinic behind him. He walked through town, heading for the beach and home. Town was busy and loud but he assumed it was par for the course on a Friday night before remembering that the Schoolies Festival started this weekend. Hadn't Tom said the festival organisers were looking for volunteers? Perhaps he should look into that. It might fill up his time. He couldn't spend all weekend looking at spreadsheets.

Work-life balance. That was what he needed. He wasn't sure if spending his weekend volunteering in the first-aid tent counted as finding work-life balance but he didn't really know any other way to live. He'd been brought up to work hard, study hard, commit one hundred per cent to his endeavours and reach his goals. He understood the work bit but what about the life bit?

Time off was rare and he usually spent it in the gym—not because he loved it but because he knew the benefits—and to relax he turned to his music.

He unlocked his front door, picked up his guitar from the lounge, grabbed a beer from the fridge and headed out to the deck that overlooked the beach. He finished his beer and then played some chords as he looked over the ocean. He let his mind empty as the notes floated around him, accompanied by the intermittent blink of the lighthouse to his right and the stars overhead.

Molly pulled on a pair of jeans and the green T-shirt she'd been given to wear as her uniform for tonight. She and Gemma had done their regular Saturday morning walk up to the lighthouse followed by a swim, but had forgone their usual time on the beach as the sand was already being overrun by the school leavers who had arrived in town for the Schoolies Festival, which officially started today. Molly had spent the afternoon cleaning and doing the grocery shopping before she headed to the foreshore, where she would volunteer her time in the first-aid tent for the first night of the festival.

Having volunteered last year, she thought she was prepared for anything but what she wasn't ready for was seeing Theo, also wearing the green volunteers' T-shirt, walking into the tent in front of her.

'Theo! What are you doing here?'

'Volunteering.'

Molly frowned. 'Why?' Their little contact this past week had meant she was beginning to think she could navigate working with him, treating him as just a doctor she had been to university with, as a nine-to-five weekday colleague, but she hadn't counted on spending Saturday night with him as well.

'Tom said they were short of volunteers and I figured I didn't have anything better to do this weekend.'

Molly immediately felt guilty. Hadn't anyone from the clinic offered to show him around? What had happened to small-town hospitality? 'You didn't check out the beaches or the town?'

'I thought I'd avoid the beaches until after the festival— I'm not sure I wanted to share it with a thousand school leavers. I did take a drive up into the Hinterland but that still left me with a Saturday night to fill.'

Perhaps she should have sent him off with Matt. That would have meant she could avoid the situation she now found herself in, namely spending the next few hours together, she thought as they were greeted by Steph, one of the volunteer coordinators.

Steph introduced Theo and Molly to the other volunteers—Justin and Priya, both first aiders—before showing them around the large tent, which was actually several marquees joined together to create different spaces. The front section of the tent was set up as a dispensary where first aiders could hand out water, sunburn cream, painkillers and lollies to the festival-goers. A cluster of beanbags had been arranged in one corner of the tent to give kids a break-out space if they needed a chance to chill, and a couple of smaller tents at the back had been furnished with beds where treatment for minor injuries or ailments could be administered away from the crowds.

'It's fantastic to have you both here tonight,' Steph said as they returned to the front of the tent. 'We are grateful to have as many volunteers as we can get but always happy to have some with more medical experience. We've got some nurses and paramedics helping throughout the week too. Your expertise won't always be needed but occasionally we can have more serious injuries and, because the hospital is a ten-minute drive out of town, it's not easy for the kids to present to emergency, and we don't really want them turning up there as the first option for every little mishap. The first-aid tent helps to triage the load.'

'If we do need to send someone to hospital, how do we manage that?' Theo asked.

'We can call an ambulance in an emergency or, if it's not critical, someone from the Red Frogs brigade can take them.'

'The Red what?'

'Red Frogs are another volunteer group,' Steph explained. 'They're affiliated with a church group so they're separate from the first-aid crew, not all of them have first-aid skills, and they provide general support, emotional support, advice and information. For a lot of these kids this week will be the first time they've been away from home without some sort of adult supervision. Some of them get in over their heads and need support, others can find the whole experience a bit overwhelming. The Red Frogs act kind of like a big brother. Or sister. Support without judgement. They will drift in and out of our tent over the course of the night but they're around all week for the students. The kids can download an app that lets them contact Red Frogs for assistance or company, and they've been known to offer everything from pancake cook-ups, room visits and cleans to emotional support, walking kids home and handing out lolly frogs,' she said as she pointed to a huge bowl filled with red frog-shaped lollies that sat on one of the counters. 'Theo, why don't you take a few minutes to familiarise yourself with the treatment spaces before it gets busy? Molly can show you the ropes.'

'You've done this before?' Theo asked as Steph left them to it.

Molly nodded and headed for the treatment area, knowing it was easier to talk to Theo if she wasn't looking at him at the same time. That way she could avoid the fluttery feeling she got every time she looked into his eyes. 'I volunteered last year,' she said. 'I came up for a holiday and one week of my trip just happened to coincide with the Schoolies Festival. Matt and Levi volunteer with the Red Frogs and Matt talked me into helping out. I really enjoyed it.'

That wasn't the whole truth. Matt had invited her for a holiday when she'd broken up with Daniel and, to keep her occupied while he was at work, Matt had suggested she lend a hand during the festival. She had enjoyed it and it had kept her mind busy, given her an excuse to avoid Daniel's phone calls and given her a chance to experience life in Byron. 'I felt like I really got to know some of the locals and it was a big part of helping me to make the decision to relocate here permanently.'

'What presentations were you dealing with?' Theo asked.

'Sunburn and dehydration during the day, drug- and alcohol-affected kids later on, plus the odd broken bone and a concussion or two, but be prepared for anything,' she said. 'The first night was pretty hectic last year. The kids tend to party hard over the first weekend and then calm down as the week progresses and the excitement wears off. Once the exhaustion and hangovers kick in, they can't continue on at the same pace.'

The end of Molly's sentence was drowned out by loud cheering and yelling coming from the beach. The first-aid tent had been erected on the grassy plateau overlooking the beach, between the surf club and the pub on the corner, and the noise from the sand competed with the sound of music from the hotel. Drawn by the commotion, Theo and Molly wandered back to the front of the tent.

Sunset was approaching and the Norfolk pines cast long shadows on the lawn where several teenagers sat, feasting on takeaway. Main Beach stretched out in front of them, full of school leavers. The foreshore was an alcohol-free zone. Those who were old enough could drink at the pub, but, judging by the volume of noise and some of the rowdy behaviour, it looked as though plenty of those on the beach had made their way there from the bar. Behind them the pub was also busy, music blared from the speakers and Molly knew there would be a live band later in the night.

Her attention was drawn back to the beach where the sounds of cheering were being accompanied by rhythmic clapping. From their slightly elevated vantage point she could see a large group of kids on the sand forming a circle around four others. The circle gave the tableau the effect of a bullring. Within the circle were two boys, each with a girl sitting on top of his shoulders.

'What are they doing?' Theo asked.

The two girls each held what appeared to be long sticks but Molly knew they were actually beer cans that had been taped together.

'Playing beer-can jousting,' she said.

As the crowd cheered and clapped the two boys ran towards each other, the girls bouncing on their shoulders. The girls had the beer-can sticks thrust out in front of them, aiming at their opposition number. Molly heard Theo's sharp intake of breath as the stick of one girl glanced off the other girl's shoulder, causing her to overbalance. She tumbled into the sand as the crowd clapped and whistled. Molly held her breath until the girl got to her feet and bowed to the crowd as the other girl held her arms aloft in a victory pose.

The boys retreated to opposite sides of the circle and

a new girl took the place of the one who had fallen. She waited for someone to hand her the jousting stick before the boys ran at each other again.

'Shouldn't we stop them? Someone is going to get hurt.'

Molly was watching through half-closed eyes, as if that were going to make the activity safer, but as the words left Theo's mouth she saw one girl rear backwards as the jousting stick hit her in the face. As she fell, she took all the other combatants down with her and suddenly there was a pile of bodies in the centre of the circle. The crowd, which seconds before had been loud and boisterous, fell silent.

CHAPTER FOUR

WITHOUT DISCUSSION MOLLY and Theo sprinted to the beach.

Theo pushed his way through to the middle of the crowd and Molly followed closely behind him, letting him clear a path for her. All four kids were kneeling in the sand as Theo and Molly squatted beside them. The boys appeared to have got out of the contest unscathed but the same could not be said for the girls. One had a nasty gash above her eye, which was bleeding profusely, and the other girl was clutching her mouth as blood streamed down her chin.

'Let me see.' Molly didn't bother introducing herself. Her green T-shirt identified her as a first aider and her tone implied authority. The girl took her hand away from her mouth and Molly could see a gap where a front tooth should be.

Molly looked up and saw Justin, one of the other volunteers. 'We're looking for a lost tooth,' she said, assuming the girl had started the day with both her front teeth. Looking for the tooth would be like trying to find a needle in a haystack, but it would keep everyone busy while she and Theo sorted out the injured girls.

She helped her patient to her feet while looking around

for Theo. He was still squatting in the sand next to his patient. He'd ripped off his T-shirt and had it pressed against her head wound, stemming the blood. His skin was smooth and golden and his shoulder muscles flexed as he reached for the girl's elbow to help her stand. With difficulty Molly dragged her gaze away from Theo's bare back and naked chest. It was a struggle. It was a reflex re-action to let her eyes roam over his body, but she couldn't afford to get distracted.

'If you find the tooth, give it to Justin. Try not to touch the root of the tooth.' Molly issued instructions to the crowd. 'Justin, I'll send someone down with a container. If by some miracle it is found, bring it up to the tent as quickly as you can.'

She and Theo helped the girls up to the first-aid tent while dozens of kids dropped to their hands and knees and began sifting through the sand.

Molly and Theo sat the girls on adjacent treatment beds, not bothering to pull across the curtains that sepa-rated them. She pulled on a pair of surgical gloves and opened a container of saline, pouring some into a small specimen jar and handing it to Priya, the other volun-teer. 'Take this down to Justin,' she said. 'If they find the tooth, get Justin to put it in there and bring it back to me.'

Priya raised her eyebrows. 'You think they'll find it?'

Molly shrugged. 'Stranger things have happened.' She had no way of knowing if they'd have any luck but they had to try.

She poured some saline into a cup and handed it to her patient. 'Rinse your mouth and spit into here,' she said as she held a stainless-steel bowl out for her. She handed the bowl to Steph, who was hovering nearby, to empty. 'Is there an after-hours dentist on standby this week?' she asked Steph.

Steph nodded as she rinsed the bowl.

'Can you give them a call and see if they'll meet us at the surgery?' Molly asked as she tore open a packet of gauze and held it to the girl's gum to soak up the blood and stem the bleeding. All the blood was coming from the gum. Her lip was intact so she wouldn't require stitches. Hopefully the tooth would be found but, either way, she needed a dental review.

Molly glanced over to Theo as Steph left the area and Priya returned, without the missing tooth. Theo put her to work helping him cut sutures as he stitched the girl's head wound. He was still shirtless, Steph would need to find him a new top, but Molly secretly hoped she wasn't in too much of a hurry. She admired Theo's physique while she admired his handiwork. His stitches were small and neat and Molly doubted anyone would be able to tell that a plastic surgeon hadn't done the job. He was applying a dressing over the stitches when Justin appeared, triumphantly holding the jar of saline, complete with the missing tooth.

'You found it!'

Justin nodded and handed the jar over to Molly. She opened the lid, put the jar on the bed and changed her gloves. She opened a fresh packet of gauze before removing the blood-soaked wadding from her patient's mouth. She carefully removed the tooth from the jar and pushed it back into the socket.

'Bite down gently on the gauze,' she told her patient

as she placed the fresh wad under the repositioned tooth. 'It'll hold the tooth in place until we get you to the dentist.' Molly turned to Justin. 'Can we get one of the Red Frogs to do the transfer to the dental surgery?'

Justin nodded and he and Priya took Molly's patient, leaving Molly alone with Theo and the second girl. He was doing a concussion test before he checked on any allergies and gave her some tablets for pain relief. Once he was finished and had given her the all-clear, Molly grabbed another Red Frog to take the girl back to her accommodation to rest. Priya, Steph and Justin all drifted back to the front of the tent and suddenly it was just the two of them again.

Molly pulled off her gloves and threw them in the bin before sanitising her hands. Theo did the same and then picked up the spare T-shirt Steph had left for him and pulled it over his head. Molly tried not to be disappointed. Wasn't this exactly what she'd been trying to avoid? Letting herself get too close to Theo, letting him get too close to her. And this definitely counted as too close.

'What a stupid game that is,' Theo said as he tugged the T-shirt down over his stomach. 'They're lucky someone didn't lose an eye.'

Molly smiled. Theo was so incensed. She knew it wasn't funny but it was hard not to find his reaction a little amusing. 'Anyone one would think you were seventy-nine, not twenty-nine,' she said. 'Didn't you ever do anything stupid when you were younger?'

'No, never,' Theo replied, but he was grinning and Molly wasn't sure if he was pulling her leg or not.

'Did you go to Schoolies Week?' she asked.

Theo shook his head. 'My parents took my sister and me overseas when I finished school. I think it was their way of making sure I didn't get into any trouble. My parents both had high expectations. My sister and I didn't get a lot of freedom. It wasn't until I went to university that I really had a chance to test the waters and you'd think spending time at music gigs I'd push a few boundaries, but I was always conscious of my grades. I couldn't afford to let things slip. Failure wasn't an option in our house so I never really went wild. You?'

'Did I go wild or did I go to Schoolies?'

'Both.'

'I did go to Schoolies. And lived to tell the tale, obviously.'

'Did you have fun?'

'Definitely.' She smiled. 'It was the first time I'd been away with my friends without any parents. We had an absolute blast. But if it makes you feel any better, the police will crack down on the kids a bit later in the night. Apparently on the first night they like to take a couple of kids off to the police station on some trumped-up charges, urinating in public, underage drinking, that sort of thing, which serves to scare the majority of the kids into behaving a little better. There will still be some who want to push the boundaries but most of them don't want to get sent home or spend the night in a cell. They've paid a lot of money to spend a week here—forking out for accommodation, entertainment, meals, drinks—and they don't want to miss out on the fun, so things will calm down.'

As if to back up her point the next couple of hours were relatively quiet. Molly had to extract a nasty splinter from a boy's hand and Theo sent another to hospital for an X-ray on a suspected broken toe, and then it was mostly handing out bottles of water and vomit bags before sending kids home under the supervision of the Red Frogs.

'I'm starving,' Theo said when their shift ended at midnight. 'Is there anywhere we can grab a feed this late?'

'The pub will be open,' Molly told him. 'And they provide volunteers with a free cheeseburger and fries, or a tofu burger if that's your preference. It is Byron Bay, after all.'

'Sounds good. Would you like to join me?'

'Sure.' She justified the extra time with Theo by telling herself she was hungry so it made sense to grab some food. And it would ease her guilty conscience that no one had thought to play host and had left Theo to his own devices on his first weekend. But really, she had enjoyed his company tonight.

'That was an interesting night,' Theo said as they waited for their burgers. 'I must say I didn't expect to find myself tending to exuberant teenagers in a tent on the beach at midnight as part of my time here.'

'No, it's a bit left of centre, isn't it?' Molly laughed. 'It suits Byron Bay though.'

'I didn't expect to find you here either. I always imagined you married to Daniel and living in Sydney.'

His comment surprised her. His assumptions were probably reasonable enough, but she was surprised to hear he'd thought about her at all. 'And yet, here I am,' she said, 'neither of those things.'

'Here you are,' he agreed. He was looking at her intently and Molly could feel her heart beating in her chest as she stood in the spotlight of Theo's attention. His dark eyes held her in their thrall as she held her breath, waiting for some sort of personal declaration she felt was coming.

'Order for Molly!'

She jumped, startled out of her reverie by the everyday sound of her name being called, and the moment was lost. Theo glanced over his shoulder and their connection was broken as he went to collect their burgers.

'Do you want to eat here?' he asked as he handed her order to her.

Molly shook her head. The pub was still busy and noisy, filled with school leavers intent on celebrating into the wee hours of the morning, and she needed some peace and quiet, some time to sort out the thoughts in her head. 'I've had enough of exuberant teenagers tonight,' she said, copying Theo's earlier description. 'I'll have mine to go.'

'Are you walking home?'

'I should be but I drove into town. I was running late.' She smiled and Theo laughed.

'Again.'

'Again,' she said. 'I parked at the clinic.'

'I'll walk with you to your car.'

Molly was about to say she'd be fine, it was only a short walk, but she realised she wasn't quite ready to say goodnight to Theo. She didn't want to admit that seeing him half undressed might have had something to do with that. But regardless of his state of dress they'd worked well together tonight and she was feeling much more comfortable with him.

'Okay, thanks.' She ate a couple of fries as they walked and then picked up the previous thread of conversation.

'Why did you assume I'd be married to Daniel?' she asked. She was intrigued to know if he'd spent a lot of time thinking about her, but of course she couldn't ask him that.

'You seemed so serious about him, so convinced he was the right man for you. I thought you might have married him. But I was pleased to find out you haven't.'

'You never liked him,' Molly stated. She knew that. Theo had made that clear.

'I didn't dislike him. I didn't like him for you. I thought you could do better.'

Molly smiled. She wasn't offended by Theo's view. She agreed with him now. 'You were right,' she said. 'But I needed to figure that out for myself. It turns out I'm not a very fast learner when it comes relationships, but I had no intention of getting married.'

'To Daniel?'

'To anyone.'

'Really? Not ever?'

'Marriage seems like a strange commitment to make. To be bound to someone until the end of time. I think it just opens you up to heartache and I haven't seen anything yet to make me change my mind. I'm focusing on myself and on my career. Taking some time out for self-reflection.'

'And what are you discovering? I assume you're not about to swap life as a doctor to move to the hinterland and grow herbs?'

'Only medicinal ones,' she teased.

'A worthy pastime, I agree,' he said with a smile that made his eyes gleam and her heart skip a beat, 'but that seems a waste of a medical degree. Or is medicine not a calling for you?'

Molly looked at Theo as she wondered how much she should admit. 'To be honest, becoming a doctor wasn't my idea. The careers advisor at school suggested it as an option. She thought I'd get the grades and I thought if I got into med school it might make my dad notice me. I am the middle of three girls and I always thought Dad was disappointed that he didn't have any sons. He never had a lot of time for us—he was the headmaster at a boys' school and he spent a lot of time at work—and I thought if I became a doctor I might suddenly become worthy of his attention. The school he taught at was very academic and there was the expectation that almost all of the students would go on to university and to study prestigious courses. Law. Medicine. Engineering. Politics. Medicine was something I could imagine doing.' She shrugged.

'Did it work?'

'Nope.' She threw her empty fries container into a council bin and unwrapped her cheeseburger. 'Turns out it wasn't our gender that was the issue. My father wasn't a faithful husband. I had always assumed he would spend more time with us if we were boys. I never considered that he was not at home because he was cheating on my mother. When I was fifteen, I saw my father with another woman. He told me my mother knew. It turned out she did know and she chose to stay with him anyway. For a long time I believed that was normal behaviour in a marriage and I decided that if that was the case, then I didn't want to get married. Marriage should be about commitment, trust, fidelity and love. I didn't see it being about any of those things.

'And then I met Daniel and he was the same, but I thought I could be the one to get him to change. To commit. I don't know why I didn't look for a faithful partner instead.' She paused, unsure how to continue, not sure if Theo would judge her but needing him to understand who she had been back then. 'Dad was a serial philanderer. He had plenty of opportunity. He is handsome, charming— the mothers of his students couldn't get enough, apparently. What I couldn't understand was why my mother didn't kick him out. So, I asked her that question. She said she didn't know how to survive on her own, or as a single mother, and she was scared of what her future would look like if she left.'

Theo was looking at her and she knew what he was thinking. 'I know. I was doing the same thing with Daniel, taking him back every time he apologised and promised to be better. I'd take him back hoping this time he meant it but knowing it wouldn't last. I was repeating my mother's mistakes but at least I hadn't married him. I knew I could take care of myself financially. That was another big reason why medicine appealed to me—it was a high-income-earning job that would give me financial independence. If I was never getting married, I needed to earn my own money. I never wanted to be dependent on someone else for my financial security. Luckily for me it turned out that I love being a doctor.'

Unlike for her mother, it wasn't financial security that had influenced her decisions and kept her in a relationship with Daniel. Molly had spent most of her life wanting to be seen and she'd been afraid that if she wasn't Daniel's girlfriend any more, if she wasn't part of the cool crowd, then she'd suddenly become invisible again. That fear had been real enough to keep her going back, long after it was good for her.

She kept her eyes focused on the footpath. She hadn't expected to talk about Daniel, hadn't expected to share her thoughts with Theo, but he was a good listener and she felt safe with him. They'd worked well together tonight, and she'd been comfortable in his company while they were busy and, somehow, that feeling continued as they walked side by side in the dark, making it easy to confide in him.

'I kept telling myself I could leave whenever I wanted, but I never did. Not permanently. I'd break up with him and then take him back. Time after time after time. I'd invested so much time and effort into that relationship that it made it hard to throw it away, but I'm done now. I've been here nearly six months and I'm surviving. Better than that, I'm happy here. Away from my family. Away from Daniel. It was the best decision I ever made.'

'What made your mind up?'

'After the last time he cheated on me I realised I was exactly like my mother, just without a wedding ring. Normally the pattern would be he'd cheat on me briefly, give up the other girl and convince me to give him another chance. I suppose I'd always let him get away with his behaviour, I'd condoned it in a way. Once I became aware of the situation with my parents and had seen how my father treated my mother, and how she put up with it, I think I came to believe that it was just the way men were. The way relationships were. The way my relationship was.

'But the last time was different. He wanted me back but wanted to keep seeing the other girl as well. I had just enough self-esteem to reject that sordid offer. I had a career, my own income, no dependants. I didn't need Daniel, but it wasn't until I finally realised that I didn't want him, or the life that he was subjecting me to, any more that I did something about changing things.' She smiled. 'It's ironic really—you told me the same things years ago. But I wasn't ready to hear it then. Matt helped.'

'Have you and Matt been friends for a long time?'

'No, we met playing social netball before he moved up here, but it think it was a case of the planets aligning. He was back in Sydney for a mutual friend's engagement party when Daniel and I were on a break. Another one. Matt convinced me to come up here for a holiday and I loved it. But when I got back to Sydney I realised I needed to make the change and I left for the last time.'

'That was brave.'

Molly shook her head. 'Not really. It was well overdue but I was glad to make Daniel someone else's problem.'

'Is he still with her?'

'I don't know. I try not to think about him if I can help it.'

'Ah.'

Molly frowned. 'What?'

'Is that why you weren't happy to see me? Because I reminded you of Daniel?'

How was it possible that Theo had more insight into Molly than she'd had into herself? 'You didn't remind me of Daniel, but you did remind me of a time in my past I'm not proud of. You reminded me of the person I was then—insecure, dependent, like my mother—all the things I swore I wasn't going to be. I wanted to believe that I was growing as a person, that this move to Byron Bay was the start of a new life, a new me, and your arrival brought back some of my insecurities.

'Until I realised that I couldn't put that onto you. I'm responsible for myself and I know I'm not that person any more. I've made some tough decisions and I've made some good ones and some bad ones, but I'm starting to think the good are outweighing the bad now. Moving here has been a good one. I love the job, my colleagues and the town.'

'I'm pleased. You seem happy.'

'I am. And I've got a chance to figure out who I am now. Who I want to be and who I want to be with. I haven't been on my own since I was seventeen. This is my time to work on myself.'

'Do you think this is a permanent move for you?'

'I'm not sure. But I think it could be.'

'You like it here? You're not missing the rat race of Sydney?'

'Not at all. I love it here. The job is great, the people are lovely. It's fun. What about you? Is Byron Bay casting its spell over you yet? I would have thought the rock star part of you would like the vibe of Byron.'

'You know what, I kind of do. It's a lot more relaxed here, isn't it? I feel like even the drama of tonight will be forgotten by tomorrow. People seem to live in the moment.'

'That's a good way of putting it. I'm not sure that it's

sustainable for a lot of people to live like that but it's appealing for a little while. Something to be said for being able to stop and smell the metaphorical roses.'

'Even the clinic seems a little less frenetic. Often I feel like I'd get more job satisfaction if I could spend more time with my patients but there never seem to be enough hours in the day. But the past few days have been a revelation. I've enjoyed having more time and longer consults.'

'I think that's one nice thing about regional medicine. We get the chance to know our patients a bit better,' Molly said as they reached the car park.

The walk had taken a lot longer than it needed to and Molly realised they'd both been dawdling, so caught up in their conversation there hadn't seemed any need to hurry. Perhaps the slow pace of Byron Bay was to blame or perhaps they had been happy to spend more time in each other's company.

'This is me,' she said as she pushed the button to unlock her car. Theo reached for the door and opened it for her. She stepped into the opening and then spun around to face him. 'Thanks for keeping me company and thanks for listening.' Listening was still one of his strong suits.

'Any time.'

Molly leant her back on the car, reluctant to get in, reluctant to say goodnight. 'Can I give you a lift home?' she offered.

'Which way are you headed?'

'Up the hill.' She gestured to her right. 'Towards the lighthouse.'

Theo shook his head. 'I'm the other way. It's only a short walk.'

He was standing close, on the same side of the door as her. He had one arm resting along the top of the door, keeping it open. If Molly stood up straight, if she leant forwards and moved away from the car, she'd almost be touching him. She closed her hand into a fist and forced herself to keep it by her side, resisting the sudden and ridiculous desire to reach for him.

She maintained her position, frozen in place, too scared to move, knowing if she straightened up as she'd have to do to climb into the car it would bring her closer to him. She was scared of what she might do then.

Theo hadn't moved. He was watching her with his dark eyes and, worried that he might read her thoughts, she dropped her gaze.

But that was a mistake.

Now she was looking at his mouth.

He had an amazing mouth. His lips were full and soft and just begged to be kissed. But that hadn't ended well last time and she didn't want to repeat the same mistake, no matter how tempting. She shouldn't have kissed him four years ago and she shouldn't kiss him again. Not now. She was avoiding relationships, taking time to work on herself, but when Theo was standing in front of her it made her wonder if complete abstinence was a step too far.

But kissing Theo wouldn't serve any purpose other than to satisfy an urge and she'd learnt her lesson. It hadn't been fair of her to kiss him spontaneously four years ago and she wasn't about to do it again. Next time they kissed it would be consensual. Next time she would ask first.

Molly shook her head—what was she thinking? Next time! She was getting carried away in the moment. She needed to ignore the frisson of awareness and the shiver in her belly that she got whenever Theo smiled at her or whenever his hand touched hers or whenever he took off his shirt. It shouldn't be impossible. Even though it felt as if it might be.

Once again Molly tried to keep her distance from Theo over the next few days. The pull of attraction she'd felt had frightened her. She didn't want to get involved. She didn't want to be in a relationship. Relationships complicated life, made her part of something else, someone else, and what she really needed was time alone, time to be by herself, time to figure herself out. She'd been asked out a few times since moving to Byron Bay, but it was easy to turn down those invitations when there'd been no chemistry. But it was becoming hard to ignore the spark of awareness she felt whenever she saw Theo.

The connection she felt was strong, the pull powerful. It shouldn't have surprised her, she'd felt it before, four years ago but that was exactly why she needed to keep her distance. Her brain and her body were at odds with each other. One pushing. One pulling. One resisting. One capitulating. She was worried she'd do something stupid if she spent too much time with Theo.

It was easy enough to avoid him in the mornings because she was always dashing in the door at the last minute, and she cut down on her caffeine intake to avoid bumping into him in the staff kitchen. Thankfully there was no quiz night at the pub this week because of the

Schoolies Festival, so by Thursday she thought she might make it through the whole week without seeing him. Until she found herself face to face with him at the hydrotherapy pool.

Thank God he wasn't actually in the pool, but standing beside it, fully clothed, talking to Matt. But still, her stomach flipped and her hands became clammy. If she hadn't been taking a patient through in preparation for their first hydrotherapy session she would have turned on her tail and fled.

She needed to get a grip. She was being ridiculous. She tried reminding herself why she meant to keep her distance from him but when he saw her approaching and smiled at her she couldn't remember a single reason.

She sent her patient to the change rooms and, telling herself it was just the humidity of the indoor pool making her hands clammy, she forced herself to keep walking, one step at a time, towards Matt. And Theo.

Matt was explaining the benefits of hydrotherapy to Theo. 'I'd really like to get into the pool more often, but I just don't have the time between patients,' Matt said. 'We need more staff in order to run more regular sessions.'

'Is the pool used for anything else?' Theo asked as Molly waited for her patient.

'Like what?'

'Kids' swimming lessons? Aquarobics?'

Molly frowned and wondered why Theo was asking all these questions.

'No,' Matt replied.

'So it is underutilised.'

Matt nodded as Molly waved her patient over.

'Matt, this is Susan Ford. She's got her first hydro session today.'

Matt took Susan off and Molly walked out of the pool area with Theo. 'What's with all the questions?' she asked.

'I was just curious to see how it all works.'

She didn't understand why it mattered. He was only a locum. 'You don't have hydrotherapy in the Sydney clinic?'

'No. We don't have any allied health facilities. This clinic has a different operating structure. I'm just trying to see what works and what doesn't.'

That still didn't explain his interest, but it wasn't really any of her business. Perhaps he was thinking about offering hydrotherapy back at his clinic in Sydney. If he wanted to get to know the intricacies of the clinic, that was his choice. She just needed to worry about getting through one more day until it was the weekend, when she could relax and not have to worry about bumping into him.

Molly grabbed a handful of red lolly frogs from a bowl in the first-aid tent and sat on the edge of a treatment bed, swinging her legs as she popped a lolly into her mouth.

'I thought they were meant for the kids,' Theo teased her.

Molly's heart leapt at his voice and she almost choked on the lolly.

Her hope that he wouldn't also be volunteering on the last official night of the Schoolies Festival was well and truly quashed. There seemed to be no way of avoiding him completely. He was constantly popping up in her vicinity, so much so that she wasn't really all that surprised to see him tonight.

'I don't think they'll miss a few,' she replied. 'This is what keeps me coming back.'

'Not my company?'

'I didn't know you were going to be here.'

'I had a good time last weekend and figured I could lend a hand again. The gig came highly recommended,' he said with a smile.

He had a really lovely smile, Molly thought, not for the first time. She'd miss seeing his smile once he returned to Sydney. She'd miss the way it made her feel. But every time he smiled at her she felt her resistance to spending time with him crumbling just a little bit more until one day she feared she wouldn't have any resolve left. And where would that leave her? Throwing caution to the wind and kissing him again?

She shook her head. She couldn't do that. Perhaps she was experiencing a simple case of sexual frustration? Perhaps she needed to rethink her relationship ban— maybe she needed to go on a date and try casual sex. That might get thoughts of Theo out of her head and let her start a clean slate.

The only problem was she'd never had a one-night stand or casual sex and she didn't know if she could. But that might be her best option, she thought as she put another lolly frog in her mouth and looked for something to do to keep her hands busy and her mind engaged on something other than Theo.

* * *

The first few hours of their shift were fairly routine. They handed out plenty of water and treated a boy who'd got into a fight and broken a bone in his hand, but they hadn't been called upon much at all.

The kids were down at the beach where a DJ was playing and the rest of the volunteers were milling around the edges of the rave, handing out bottles of water and keeping an eye on things. Molly and Theo were alone in the tent, waiting for anything more serious that might need their expertise.

Though she'd been on edge initially, she'd gradually relaxed into things. Even though she sometimes felt as if Theo could read her mind, she knew that wasn't really the case. He didn't know that she'd wanted to kiss him again. He didn't know that she'd been deliberately avoiding him because of it.

She was finding him easy company. His company wasn't the issue. He wasn't the issue.

She was.

She was still worried she'd give into temptation and kiss him again.

Should she apologise for deliberately staying out of his way this week after revealing so much?

Maybe she should do that right now, she thought. They were alone. There might not be a better time.

She swallowed the red frog, ready to apologise, when two girls burst into the tent supporting a third girl between them.

CHAPTER FIVE

'OUR FRIEND ISN'T feeling well.'

Molly and Theo hurried over to the girls and ushered them to the back of the marquee. The girl in the middle was unsteady on her feet and Molly doubted she'd be able to stand without the support of her friends. Her eyes were unfocused, her pupils dilated.

'What's her name?' Molly asked.

'Tayla. Tayla Adams.'

'Let's get you up onto the bed,' Molly said as they guided Tayla through the tent to the treatment area at the back. Molly drew the curtain around them to afford some privacy as Theo helped Tayla up onto the examination plinth, physically lifting her when it became apparent that she had neither the coordination nor the comprehension to follow instructions.

'Has she been drinking?' Molly asked. She'd learned over the years never to assume the cause of a patient's symptoms. While she knew it was a fair assumption, there could be other causes, other factors at play.

But Tayla's friends were nodding. 'Vodka shots.'

'How many?'

The two girls looked at each other. 'Maybe ten.'

Molly wasn't certain they were telling the truth. Perhaps they didn't know the answer.

'In how long?'

'Since nine o'clock.'

It was now midnight.

Whatever the number of drinks Tayla had consumed it was obvious she'd drunk more than she could handle. Molly couldn't believe the girl was still standing, let alone conscious.

Molly could see Theo checking Tayla's wrist as she spoke to the friends. She knew he was looking for a medical bracelet or tattoo to indicate an underlying condition. Like her, he wasn't assuming that alcohol alone was responsible for the state Tayla was in. For all they knew she could have diabetes, epilepsy or be on medication that reacted with her alcohol consumption.

'Does Tayla have any allergies or any health problems? Is she diabetic? Epileptic?'

'No.'

'Does she take any prescription medication?'

'No.'

Molly hoped the girls' answers were correct. She looked at their patient, wondering if she should be asking her these questions. But one glance told her that Tayla was not going to be able to help her. Her eyes were glassy. She was conscious, but only just.

'Has she vomited?'

The girls shook their heads. 'She said that her hands and feet were tingling and that she couldn't breathe properly.'

'Has she taken any drugs?'

The girls hesitated. They were looking at each other, avoiding eye contact with Molly.

'It's okay,' Molly told them. 'You need to be honest. We need all the information you can give us in order to help her.'

'She had two caps of MDMA.'

'Temperature forty point two degrees.' Theo had a blood-pressure cuff wrapped around Tayla's arm and was holding a thermometer in her ear. 'Heart rate one hundred and ten.'

Molly knew that ecstasy, the common name for tablets of MDMA, could lead to hyperthermia, especially if Tayla had been dancing, which was highly likely given that most of the festival attendees had been gathered on the beach with the DJ.

'We all had lots of water. Not just the vodka,' the girls added.

Unfortunately that wasn't always the right thing to do. If Tayla's body couldn't process the water it could cause fluid to build up around her brain, which could cause headaches, dizziness, nausea, and even seizures.

'Molly.' Theo's voice held a note of warning. Molly turned around and saw that Tayla's eyes had rolled back in her head. Her mouth was open and Molly could see her tongue had swollen and she was having difficulty breathing.

'Girls, you need to wait outside.' Molly addressed Tayla's friends, who were now crying. She did not have time to deal with them as well. She drew back the curtain and ushered them out, relieved to see that Steph, the volunteer coordinator, was back in the tent. 'Steph, we need an ambulance. Accidental overdose, alcohol and ecstasy. Teenage girl, no significant medical history.'

Steph nodded in reply before Molly retreated back into the cubicle, pulling the curtain closed to block Tayla from her friends' view. She was just in time. Tayla was having a seizure, most likely related to her hyperthermia. There wasn't anything Molly and Theo could do except keep her safe. Theo was on one side of the bed and Molly quickly stood opposite him, both of them in place to ensure Tayla didn't fall off the bed.

The seizure didn't last long, maybe thirty seconds, but it felt a lot longer. Molly helped Theo to roll Tayla into the recovery position before checking her vital signs again. Her heart rate was still high and her temperature was still elevated. The risk of another seizure was not out of the question.

'Can you grab some wet towels?' Theo asked Molly. He was wedged in behind the treatment plinth and Molly was able to get out more easily. 'We need to try to bring her temperature down.'

'Do you think we should give her a saline drip?' Molly asked when she returned with the damp towels.

Theo shook his head and took a couple of towels from her. Together they draped them over Tayla. 'No. If the seizure was due to cerebral oedema extra fluids could make it worse.' There was no way of knowing whether Tayla's convulsion was related to her temperature or fluid retention around her brain. They were simply making educated guesses and trying to minimise further harm. 'She needs to get to the hospital.'

'I'll check on the ambulance ETA,' Molly said as they

finished laying towels over Tayla. She returned moments later with the paramedics in tow.

Theo did a patient handover as Molly began disconnecting Tayla from the equipment. They reached for the blood-pressure cuff at the same time, Molly's hand coming down a fraction after Theo's, her fingers resting over his. She jerked her hand away but not before she felt the warmth of his skin flow through to her.

Her hand tingled. 'Sorry.'

'Don't be,' Theo replied as he glanced up at her. 'It's fine.' Molly's heart skittered in her chest as her pulse skyrocketed but Theo's eyes told her she had no need to be nervous around him.

She turned away to gather herself together. She was conscious that they weren't alone and disappointed and relieved at the same time. She was a mess of contradictions.

When she wasn't with Theo her resolve was strong. She resolved to be pleasant, friendly but not familiar, but when she was with him, one smile, one accidental touch sent her pulse racing and she forgot that she was going to keep her distance. All she wanted was more of him.

The paramedics had rolled Tayla onto a transfer board as Theo gathered the towels. Together they slid Tayla from the bed to the stretcher and Molly followed the paramedics as they wheeled Tayla out, giving herself another minute to catch her breath and restore her breathing to its normal pace.

She thought Theo might remain in the treatment area but she was aware that he was behind her. Right behind her. She couldn't see him but she could feel him.

'Is she okay?' Tayla's friends were waiting in the tent and Molly turned her attention to them, letting them distract her, even as she saw Theo move in line with her on the opposite side of the stretcher.

'She should be fine,' Molly told them. 'She's asleep now but she's very lucky to have friends like you.' Molly was talking to the girls but she glanced over at Theo as she spoke. He was watching her with a smile on his face and she knew they were both thinking of the night when he had taken care of her.

Molly smiled back. He had been a good friend to her that night. Something she wasn't sure she deserved. She really did owe him an apology.

'Where are they taking her?' The girls' question brought Molly back to the present.

'To the local hospital. She'll probably need her stomach pumped.'

'Couldn't you give her something to make her vomit?' they asked.

'That's not how we do things now. And Tayla needs to be monitored overnight. She needs to go to hospital. Do you have phone numbers for her parents? They need to be told about what's happened.'

'No.'

'I'll get it sorted,' Steph said as the paramedics opened the rear doors of the ambulance. 'If you girls would like to go to the hospital I'll get one of the Red Frogs to take you,' Steph offered, leaving Molly and Theo free to return to the treatment area.

Molly busied herself tidying up, packing up equipment

and throwing away discarded single-use items. The activity meant she could avoid looking at Theo.

'How will Steph find Tayla's parents?' Theo asked.

'The schools all have an emergency contact listed,' she said as she stripped the protective sheet off the treatment plinth. 'Steph can call the number for Tayla's school and they'll get in touch with her parents. It's a bit of a roundabout way to do it but it's better than nothing. Ideally if we had a contact number we could have spoken directly to the parents. Doing it this way means they'll have to call the hospital once they are notified and then chase down the information.'

'We can wait.'

Their shift should have finished an hour ago and Molly was beat. She threw the sheet into the rubbish bin and lifted her gaze to look at Theo. 'It might take them a while to get in contact with Tayla's parents. The hospital will deal with it. I don't know about you but I am exhausted.' She almost said *ready for bed*, but stopped herself at the last minute. She didn't want to complicate things. 'I'm going to head home,' she added right before she collapsed onto the treatment plinth. She lay back and stretched her legs out and let out a big sigh. 'As soon as I can make myself stand up again.'

'Are you hungry? Did you want to grab a cheeseburger from the pub?' he asked.

She shook her head. She was hungry but she didn't feel like negotiating the noise and bustle of the pub. She was exhausted but she knew the adrenalin pumping through her system would keep her awake for hours. Even so, the pub was more than she could handle at the moment. 'I'll make a cup of tea at home. I need peace and quiet. That was a bit hectic.'

Theo held out his hand, offering to help her up. 'Come on, then, I'll walk you to your car.'

She couldn't refuse his hand. That would look odd. She lifted her arm and put her hand in his. His fingers wrapped around hers. Strong, safe, familiar. He pulled her up as she swung her legs over the side of the bed.

'I didn't drive today,' she said as she stood up, dropping his hand. 'Would you believe I had time to walk?'

Theo smiled and Molly's heart skipped a beat. 'Wonders will never cease.'

'I wish I had driven now,' she admitted. 'I'm not sure I can be bothered walking up the hill.'

'I'll walk home with you, if you like.'

She shook her head. 'You don't need to. I'll be fine.'

'I'm happy to do it. I'd feel better if you let me and, besides, I can pick you up if you collapse with fatigue.' He was still smiling and Molly found she couldn't turn down his offer. She didn't want to. Despite her misgivings, he was easy company, and she was finding she enjoyed spending time with him. She knew it was only her own thoughts that were complicating the situation.

They said goodnight to Steph and left the next shift of volunteers to man the first-aid tent. The beach party was still in full swing and the music followed them up the hill towards Molly's house. She was grateful for the background noise—she was suddenly nervous and the music disguised the lull in conversation, covering their silence.

As they walked further from the centre of town the music and the light faded. Stars shone above them and up ahead the lighthouse stood bright and white and magnificent against the dark sky as it sent its beacon of warning light across the ocean.

'Have you done the lighthouse walk?' Molly asked, desperate to make conversation to fill the emptiness. She felt uncomfortable in the dark and quiet. The silence felt far too intimate. She was afraid she was making herself vulnerable to questions from Theo that she might not want to answer. He seemed to have a knack for getting her to talk about herself and she'd already divulged more to him than she had planned to.

'No, not yet.' Theo's voice was deep, blending into the blackness of the night, and Molly felt it reverberate in her chest.

'You have to make time to do it,' she told him, 'and you should really make sure to get up early to watch the sunrise from there. That's a non-negotiable when you're in Byron. It's a pretty special experience.' The lighthouse building itself was gorgeous but, because the lighthouse stood on the most eastern point of mainland Australia, the view across the Pacific Ocean was amazing. Theo couldn't leave Byron Bay without making that walk.

'Will you do it with me?'

She'd left herself open to that one. But the idea of watching the sunrise with him appealed to her. It was a magical experience and an iconic Byron Bay activity. She'd just ignore the fact that most people would also consider it a romantic experience. 'Sure,' she replied as they reached her apartment building. 'This is us.'

'Us?'

'Gemma and me,' she said as she entered the code and

opened the building's front door. 'I'm going to put the kettle on. Did you want a cup of tea?'

'We won't disturb Gemma?'

Molly shook her head as Theo followed her inside. She headed for the stairs that would take them up to her apartment. 'She's in Brisbane for her grandparents' sixtieth wedding anniversary.'

'That's an impressive achievement.'

'I can't believe people can be happily married for that long,' Molly said as she stepped into her apartment and headed for the kitchen to flick the kettle on.

'You don't think that's normal?'

'Not in my experience.' She'd only seen evidence to the contrary, which was why she was determined not to go down that path. 'Certainly not my parents'. Are yours happily married?'

Theo shrugged. 'Mostly, I think.'

'What's their secret?' she asked as she passed Theo the tea canister, letting him choose his flavour, before filling his mug with boiled water.

'I'd like to say love, but I actually don't know if that's the truth.'

'They don't love each other?'

'I don't know. I've never heard them say they do. I don't remember them telling my sister or me that they loved us either. I guess I've just assumed they do.'

Theo's comments weren't making Molly change her views on marriage. It really didn't have a lot to recommend it, in her opinion.

'So what makes you think they're happy?' she asked.

'They don't seem *unhappy*. They have a lot in common. And common goals. As long as they're achieving those goals, I think they're happy.'

'I think people get comfortable and settle for a situation that perhaps isn't ideal. I know I did,' she admitted. She'd learnt a lot from her relationship with Daniel and she was proud of herself for getting out of it. And she had no intention of putting herself in that position again.

Theo finished his tea and stood up.

'I'm just going to call the hospital and get an update on Tayla,' she said. 'Do you want to wait?'

He nodded but moved from the kitchen and crossed the living room to stand near the front door. Molly wasn't sure if he was giving her space to make the call—he could still hear her talking and she was going to tell him the outcome anyway—or if he was just preparing to leave. She didn't want him to leave. She watched him as she waited for her call to be picked up, afraid to take her eyes off him in case he vanished before she had a chance to say goodnight.

'This is Dr Prescott,' Molly said as her call was answered. 'I sent a patient to the ED via ambulance earlier tonight. I'm just calling for an update. Her name is Tayla Adams.'

Molly had visiting rights at the hospital and she knew the ED staff would be able to tell her the basics of Tayla's condition. That was all she needed to know.

'She's stable,' she told Theo when she finished the call. 'Full of remorse and regret, I suspect, but she's okay.'

'We've all done something we've regretted after a few too many drinks,' Theo replied.

'About that—'

'I'm not talking about you,' Theo said, cutting Molly off mid-sentence and making her wonder again how he knew what she was thinking.

Molly frowned. 'What did you think I was going to say?'

'You were thinking about the night you kissed me, weren't you?' Molly nodded and Theo continued. 'I was too but I was talking about me. About my regrets.'

'Yours?'

Theo nodded. 'I regret that I walked away. I've always wondered what would have happened if I'd been brave enough to stay.'

'Why didn't you?'

'I expected you to reject me. I didn't believe I deserved you but that didn't stop me wishing and hoping you might see me for who I was. Wishing I'd been braver. Wishing I'd kissed you a second time. I should have had the courage to find out. I was too scared of rejection, of failure, but what was the worst that could have happened? I'd get my heart broken. I was young. It could have been worth it. And I always wish I'd asked you why you kissed me.'

'You want to know why I kissed you?'

He nodded.

'Because you were gorgeous and kind and for the first time I felt like someone was listening to me and that was a powerful thing. Do you remember what you said to me?'

Theo shook his head. 'I wanted to tell you that you had terrible taste in men,' he said, 'but I don't think I did. I didn't think you would listen.'

'I wouldn't have listened,' she admitted with a small smile. 'I *should* have listened but I was determined to make Daniel love me, determined to make him faithful, so I put up with his behaviour and kept going back to him. I saw it as a challenge, something I needed to overcome. I tolerated his behaviour, his treatment of me, instead of walking away because that's what I'd seen my parents doing. Parents can have a lot to answer for. But you're right—you didn't tell me that. Do you remember talking about what we were going to do after graduation?'

'Yes.'

'You were going to work overseas. You told me I should go too. You told me I didn't need to go to work at the hospital in Sydney. I didn't tell you at the time but working overseas sounded exciting. It sounded like an adventure but I knew I wouldn't go. I wasn't brave enough either. I couldn't see myself as separate from Daniel. I made a choice. And then I wondered if you judged me for it. If you found me weak, unambitious, scared, and I was afraid I was all those things.'

'No.' He shook his head. 'I thought you were beautiful and kind and smart and funny and that you deserved so much better than Daniel.'

Molly felt tears well in her eyes as Theo's words washed over her.

'I'm sorry I behaved badly,' she said.

'It's okay. I'm just glad that you finally came to your senses. Even if it did take you a long time,' he said with a smile that took any judgement out of his words.

'I'd invested so much time and effort and energy into the idea of Daniel and me as a couple that it was hard to walk away. And I'm sorry for kissing you. I should have apologised then.' She finally gave the apology that had been haunting her. 'It was a mistake.'

'Was it?'

She shook her head. 'Not the kiss itself. I knew what I was doing. I wanted to kiss you. But it wasn't fair. I was in a relationship and I shouldn't have done it.'

'No. It wasn't fair. But I didn't handle it well,' Theo replied.

They were still standing in her doorway. He was close. If she reached out a hand she could rest it on his chest. It reminded her of this time one week ago. When they'd been standing by her car and she'd resisted the urge to touch him. One part of her knew she'd made the right decision. Another part of her regretted that she'd avoided temptation.

She wanted to touch him.

She wanted to kiss him.

She wanted to ask him to stay.

She wanted a lot of things. None of which she imagined she'd get.

The living room light wasn't on and Theo's dark eyes were hard to read in the dim light. What was he thinking? What did he want? What was he waiting for?

'But we're older and wiser now,' he said. 'And if you wanted to kiss me again it might be different.'

'Really?'

He nodded. Slowly. His gaze was fixed on her face. It was unwavering, steady and calm.

She was a bundle of nerves.

Her head waged a war with her desire. She was taking a break from dating. But she was curious to know what would happen, what a kiss might lead to. And one kiss did not mean they were dating. The chemistry was still there, she didn't think either of them would debate that. There was a spark every time they brushed past one another. With every glance they shared Molly felt as if the rest of the world ceased to exist. Theo could answer questions Molly hadn't even asked. He knew what she was thinking. They had a connection she'd never felt with anyone else.

It was only a kiss.

Her heart was racing. She could feel the blood pounding in her veins, could hear her heart beating.

Was this a bad idea?

She couldn't decide.

Her gaze dropped lower, moving from Theo's eyes to his lips. There was only one way to know for sure.

CHAPTER SIX

THEO WATCHED MOLLY'S thoughts as they played across her face. He knew the attraction he felt wasn't one-sided. Their connection was real. The chemistry, the buzz he felt when their hands brushed, the buzz he felt when he made her smile, he knew she felt the same.

It had been the same four years ago. They had come together as if they were made for each other. He remembered every detail of that night. He'd tried to forget but seeing her again had brought back every memory—both painful and miraculous.

He'd been foolish to think he could ignore her this time around. The attraction was impossible to ignore.

He had been drawn to Molly from the moment he saw her on their first day at university. He'd waited seven years for her to notice him. Seven years to touch her. Seven years was a long time and the kiss had only made things worse. The kiss they had shared had been amazing but he'd known it wouldn't lead to anything more. And that had been heartbreaking.

Molly and Daniel had had a turbulent relationship but Molly always went back to him and Theo hadn't for one moment thought their one kiss would change anything.

So he'd walked away. Never knowing if things might

have turned out differently if he'd stayed, if he'd taken a chance, if he'd kissed her again, if she'd realised that staying with Daniel would be a mistake.

Molly was still looking at him, her lips slightly parted. He could see the tip of her tongue. He watched as she licked her lips, watched as her gaze dropped to his mouth.

He knew she was thinking about kissing him. He just couldn't tell if she would.

He could remember how she had tasted four years ago. She'd tasted of raspberries—sweet, juicy and soft. He wanted to know if she still tasted the same.

He hadn't been brave enough to take a chance four years ago. He needed to be brave now. What was the worst that could happen? She could reject him again, but he'd survived that once before and something was telling him that this time would be different.

He didn't want to wait any longer. It had been four years and six days since he'd last kissed her. That was long enough.

'It's only a kiss,' he said before he dipped his head and claimed her mouth with his.

Molly closed her eyes and parted her lips and a little moan escaped from her throat as she offered herself to him.

Theo accepted her invitation and deepened the kiss, claiming her, exploring. Their first kiss had been tender. Their second was intense. This one was hungry and desperate and demanded a response. She clung to him and he held onto her. He wasn't going to let her go. He lost himself in the warmth of her kiss.

* * *

Theo's kiss was commanding, demanding. Gone was the reserved young man. He'd been replaced by a confident man who had seen her desire and could give her what she wanted.

Her heart raced in her chest and she could feel every beat as Theo's lips covered hers. She closed her eyes, succumbing to his touch. She opened her mouth and Theo caressed her tongue. She felt her nipples peak in response as he explored her mouth.

His hands wrapped around her back, the heat of them burning through her T-shirt. She melted against him as her body responded to his touch and a line of fire spread from her stomach to her groin. She deepened the kiss, wanting to lose herself in Theo.

She was aware of nothing else except the sensation of being fully alive. She wanted for nothing except Theo.

His touch was so familiar that it felt like she'd spent a lifetime in his arms. That made no sense but Molly felt as if she belonged there, in his embrace. She felt safe. She felt special. She felt seen.

But the kiss was over way too quickly. Between the hammering of her heart and the heat of Theo's kiss she was completely breathless. She needed to come up for air.

'I should go,' Theo said as they separated.

'You're going to run away again.'

'No. I'm not running. I'm not going anywhere. I'm giving you time to think about what you want. Giving you time to think about whether this is something you want to explore. What happens next is your decision.'

He kissed her again. Lightly this time, the gentlest

of touches, so soft she wondered if it was nothing more than her imagination, before he opened the door and said goodnight.

Molly closed the door and leant against it.

Her legs were weak, her knees shaky but her mind was crystal clear, focused, certain. She didn't need time to think. She knew exactly what she wanted. She wanted Theo.

She had wanted the next time to be a mutual decision, consensual. She didn't want to take liberties, didn't want to take advantage, but now she knew Theo wanted it too, wanted her, and she didn't want to give him time to change his mind.

She spun around and flung open the door, desperate to call him back, worried he might have already disappeared.

He was standing right where she'd left him. He hadn't moved.

'You stayed.'

'I stayed.'

'I know what I want,' she told him as she reached out her hand. When he didn't reach for it Molly panicked. Was he going to turn down her offer?

Bu the moment passed and he said, 'You're sure?'

She nodded. She wasn't sure if she would regret her decision but she was prepared to take the chance. At the moment she had two choices—to invite him in or to let him go—and the first option was far more appealing. 'If we find we've made a mistake we can pretend nothing happened,' she said with a smile. 'We know how to do that.'

'We do indeed,' Theo agreed as he took her hand and let her lead him back into her apartment.

Theo pushed the door shut and pulled her to him. He spun her around and she felt the door press against her back. She was grateful for the support as her legs turned to jelly as Theo pressed his lips to the soft spot under her jaw where her pulse throbbed to the beat of her desire.

His lips covered hers as his fingers slid under the fabric of her T-shirt, warm on her skin, setting her on fire. She pulled her shirt over her head, reluctantly breaking the kiss, desperate to feel his skin against hers. She tugged his shirt out of his jeans, pressing her hands into his back.

Theo snapped open the button on her jeans and pushed them to the floor.

'Which one is your room?' he asked.

'Down the hall on the left.'

He picked her up, as though she weighed nothing at all, and Molly wrapped her legs around his waist. She could feel his erection straining against his jeans and she knew he wanted her as urgently as she wanted him.

He kissed her as he carried her to her bedroom and she was astounded that he managed not to crash into any of the walls.

He laid her down on her bed and ran his hand up her thigh. She was wearing only her underwear; he still had far too many clothes on. She reached out to him and slid her hands under his T-shirt, feeling the heat coming off his skin as she dragged his shirt up his back before pulling it over his head.

He bent towards her, kissing the hollow at the base of her neck where her collarbone ended. She tipped her head back and his lips moved down to the swell of her breast. She felt herself arch towards him, silently crying out for his touch. His hand reached behind her and with a flick of his fingers he undid the clasp on her bra and her breasts spilled free. He pushed her back, gently laying her down beneath him before he dipped his head and covered her nipple with his mouth. She closed her eyes as bolts of desire shot from her breasts to her groin. As his tongue caressed her nipple she could feel the moisture gathering between her legs as her body prepared to welcome him.

She heard him snap open the button on his jeans and opened her eyes to watch him divest himself of the rest of his clothing. His erection sprang free as his clothes hit the floor. He knelt between her legs and she slid her hands behind his back and ran them down over his buttocks. They were round and hard under her palms.

Theo moved his attention to her other breast as she moved one hand between his legs, cupping his testicles before running her hand along the length of his shaft. She heard him moan as her fingers rolled across the tip, using the moisture she found there to decrease the friction and smooth her movements.

She arched her hips towards him and he responded, removing her knickers and sliding his fingers inside her. She gasped as he circled her most sensitive spot with his thumb. He was hard and hot under her palm; she was warm and wet to his touch.

She was ready now. She didn't want to wait. She couldn't wait.

She opened her legs and guided him into her, welcoming the full length of him.

He pushed against her and she lifted her hips to meet his thrust. They moved together, matching their rhythms as if they'd been doing this for ever. She had her hands at his hips, controlling the pace, gradually increasing the momentum. Theo's breaths were short and Molly didn't think she was breathing at all. All her energy was focused on making love to him. There was no room in her head for anything other than the sensation of his skin against hers, his skin inside hers.

Theo gathered her hands and held them above her head, stretching her out and exposing her breasts, and he bent his head to her nipple again as he continued his thrusts. She wrapped her legs around him, binding them together. The energy they created pierced through her, flowing from his mouth, through her breast and into her groin where it gathered in a peak of pleasure building with intensity until she thought she would explode.

'Now, Theo, do it now,' she begged.

His pace increased a fraction more and as she felt him start to shudder, she released her hold as well. Their timing was exquisite, controlled by the energy that flowed between them, and they cried out in unison, climaxing simultaneously.

Their bodies had been made for each other and their coupling had been everything Molly had expected and more. They had been unified by their lovemaking and it was an experience Molly would treasure for ever.

Molly had fallen asleep with Theo curled against her and she woke up in the same position. Theo's hand cupped her bare breast. His breath was warm on her shoulder. He was breathing deeply, still asleep, but Molly needed to use the bathroom. She lifted his hand from her breast and slid out of bed, moving slowly, trying not to wake him.

She went to the bathroom and then looked for her phone. She checked the time even though there was nothing she needed to do today. It had been late when they'd fallen asleep and it was late now, almost eleven in the morning. She plugged her phone in to charge in the kitchen—it had spent the night on the lounge room floor in the pocket of her jeans and was almost out of power—and flicked the kettle on before going back to the bedroom.

Theo was awake and Molly was suddenly overcome with a bout of nerves. What if he had regrets about last night?

He greeted her with a wide smile and she relaxed. 'Good morning,' she said.

'It's a very good morning,' Theo agreed as he reached for her and pulled her back into bed.

He ran his fingers up her thigh, cupping the curve of her bottom. Molly closed her eyes and arched her hips, pushing herself closer to him. He bent his head and kissed her. She opened her mouth, joining them together. Theo ran his hand over her hip and up across her stomach, his fingers grazing her breasts. He watched as her nipple peaked under his touch and she moaned softly and reached for him, but he wasn't done yet.

He flicked his tongue over one breast, sucking it into his mouth. He supported himself on one elbow while he used his other hand in tandem with his mouth, teasing her nipples until both were taut with desire. He slid his knee between her thighs, parting them as he straddled her. His right hand stayed cupped over her left breast as he moved his mouth lower to kiss her stomach.

He took his hand from her breast and ran it up the smooth skin of the inside of her thigh. She moaned and thrust her hips towards him as her knees dropped further apart.

'Patience, Molly. Relax and enjoy,' he said, and his voice was muffled against the soft skin of her hip bone.

Theo put his head between her thighs. He put his hands under her bottom and lifted her to his mouth, supporting her there as his tongue darted inside her. She knew she was slick and wet, and she moaned as he explored her inner sanctum with his tongue. She thrust her hips towards him again, urging him deeper.

He slid his fingers inside her as he sucked at her swollen sex. His fingers worked in tandem with his tongue, making her pant, making her beg for more.

'Theo, please. I want you inside me.'

But Theo wasn't ready to stop. Not yet. He had waited years for this. He wanted to taste her, to feel her orgasm. He knew she was close to climaxing and he wanted to bring her to orgasm like this. He knew this was a skill he possessed.

He ignored her request as he continued to work his magic with his tongue, licking and sucking the swollen bud of her desire. He continued until Molly had forgotten her request, until she had forgotten everything except her own satisfaction.

'Yes, yes… Oh, Theo, don't stop.'

He had no intention of stopping.

He heard her sharp little intake of breath and then she began to shudder.

'Yes. Oh, Theo.'

She buried her fingers in his hair and clamped her thighs around his shoulders as she came, shuddering and gasping before she collapsed, relaxed and spent.

'God, you're good at that,' she said, and he could hear the smile and contentment in her voice.

'Thank you.' He lay alongside her, his hand resting on her stomach as she cuddled into him.

He felt her hand on the shaft of his penis. 'Now it's your turn,' she said as she slid her hand up and down. 'And I want to feel you inside me. Please?'

'Seeing as you asked so nicely,' he replied as he gave himself up to Molly's rhythm.

She cupped his testes with one hand as the other encircled his shaft. Theo could feel it pulsing with a life of its own as Molly ran her hand up its length. She rolled her fingers over the end and coaxed the moisture from his body. Theo gasped and his body trembled.

She sat up and straddled his hips.

'Give me a second,' he said. He rolled onto his side, careful not to dislodge Molly, and found his jeans lying on the floor by the bed. He pulled his wallet from the pocket and retrieved a condom. He opened the packet and rolled it on in one smooth, fast movement.

Molly sat above him, naked and glorious, and Theo felt another rush of blood to his groin as she brought herself forward and raised herself up onto her knees before lowering herself onto him. Theo closed his eyes and sighed as she took his length inside her.

She lifted herself up again, and down, as Theo held onto her hips and started to time her thrusts, matching their rhythms together. Slow at first and then gradually faster. And faster.

'Yes. Yes.'

'Harder.'

'Oh, God, yes, that's it.'

He had no idea who was saying what, all he knew was he didn't want it to stop.

'Now. Yes. Keep going. Don't stop.'

Just when he thought he couldn't stand it any longer he felt Molly start to quiver and he let himself go too, breathing out as his orgasm joined hers in perfect harmony. She was insatiable but their timing couldn't have been better.

They lay together looking up at the ceiling, breathing heavily as they recovered before Molly sat up suddenly, the sheet falling to her waist as she turned to look at Theo, a horrified expression on her face. 'We didn't use any protection last night!'

It had been the last thing on his mind. And obviously on hers too. They'd been too focused on their needs and desires, ignoring all practicalities.

Theo could feel the colour drain from his face. He sat up. 'You're not on any contraception?' he asked. 'Not that I'm saying it's your responsibility.'

Molly shook her head. 'I stopped taking the pill when I moved here.'

Damn. He'd been so caught up in the moment last

night that he hadn't even made assumptions about contraception. He hadn't even stopped to think. 'I'm sorry.
We should have had that conversation. I've let you down.'

'We're both to blame,' Molly replied, sharing the responsibility. 'I certainly didn't stop to think.'

'What would you like to do?' he asked. 'Do you want
to take a morning-after pill?'

That was their best option. It wasn't perfect by any
means, but it was their only choice.

Molly nodded.

'I'll go and get one,' he offered. 'And I should get more
condoms too if we're going to keep doing this.'

'Are we going to keep doing this?' she asked.

'Why wouldn't we? I enjoyed it. And I hope you did
too. There's no reason that I can think of to stop.' He
picked up her hand and kissed her fingers, one by one.

'I'm supposed to be finding myself,' she said, 'not getting into another relationship.'

'I'm only here for four more weeks. I don't think a few
weeks would qualify as a relationship.'

'Plenty of people have relationships that last less than
that.'

'Well then, maybe it just depends on what we want
to call it? What about hot, steamy, no-strings, no-
commitment sex? Is that off limits too?'

Theo was smiling and despite the situation Molly
found him impossible to resist. 'I hadn't thought about
it, but you've made me realise that I miss sex.'

'I don't think you should deprive yourself, then. If it
will help you sleep better at night, why don't we call it a
holiday romance?'

'Neither of us are on holiday though,' she argued with a smile.

'Friends with benefits? A summer fling?' he proposed.

Molly shook her head. 'I can't think while I'm naked.'

'All right, then, you can get back to me on that. I'll go to the pharmacy now and when I come back I'll take you out for lunch.'

'You don't need to go to the pharmacy. Go to the clinic. There'll be morning-after pills in the dispensary cabinet. Do you have a key for that?'

'Yes. Do I need to sign it out?'

Molly shook her head. 'No. And there will be condoms in the nurses' room, just in case we get carried away again. They give them out at the safe sex talks they run.'

A wide grin lit up Theo's face. 'Maybe we should sign up for those.'

He kissed her before he got out of bed, affording Molly a very nice view of his bare backside as he retrieved his clothes. 'I'll go to the clinic, duck home for a shower and come back for you.'

Molly stretched her arms and legs out and felt several muscles complain. Despite her regular swims and her walks up to the lighthouse there were some muscles that obviously hadn't had a thorough workout for a while. Her sheets smelt of sex and she probably did too. But she didn't mind—the sex had been amazing and she was glad she'd given in to the temptation. It had been worth breaking her temporary vow of celibacy.

Theo had been worth it.

She finished stretching and, with a smile on her face, headed for the shower. But her smile faded as she remembered their lack of contraception. The morning-after pill worked by delaying ovulation by several days but her menstrual cycle was irregular and she had no idea where she was at. She crossed her fingers and hoped everything would be okay. Not every instance of unprotected sex resulted in a pregnancy, she reminded herself. It would be fine.

CHAPTER SEVEN

THEO STRETCHED HIS legs under the table and managed, with some difficulty, to keep a wide smile off his face. He felt good, last night and this morning with Molly had been spectacular, and he felt as if he'd won the lottery. He'd suspected he and Molly had a chemistry that was off the charts, not that he had much to compare it to, his relationship history being limited to one semi-serious one and a few short-lived, casual romances. He prided himself on being a considerate lover and knew how to please women, but he preferred it when there wasn't too much expected of him from an emotional viewpoint. He wasn't sure if he possessed those skills. That was a work in progress.

But Molly made him want to try. He imagined she would be worth it.

But he was only in Byron Bay for four more weeks. What could he achieve in that time? When he had returned from the clinic earlier this morning Molly had agreed to a summer romance, but Theo suspected that wouldn't be enough for him. Not after last night.

He breathed deeply, inhaling the orange fragrance of Molly's shampoo. He was relaxed, he wasn't thinking about work, his mind was still and quiet, which was a rarity for him. Molly's presence today was calming on his mind if not on his libido.

He wanted to celebrate but Molly didn't seem to share quite the same level of enthusiasm. He was enjoying his lunch but Molly's lack of appetite suggested she had something on her mind. The table next to them at the little café in Brunswick Heads was occupied by a family with two small children and her gaze kept flitting towards the slightly frazzled mother and the toddler in a high chair.

'Is everything okay?' he asked.

'God, I hope so,' Molly replied as her gaze flicked, yet again, to the table beside them before she turned back to face Theo, concern in her blue-grey eyes. 'I really don't want kids.'

That was a segue he hadn't expected and her comment surprised him. She sounded so adamant. 'Not at all?' he asked.

'I don't think so. Certainly not right now.'

'You and Daniel didn't talk about it?' He wasn't sure if it was wise to bring Daniel's name into the conversation, but Molly had dated him for years and Theo was curious to know how serious they had really been.

Molly shook her head. 'Never.'

Theo looked across to the family at the adjacent table. The toddler smiled in his direction and Theo smiled back and then pulled a funny face.

Molly watched him. 'Do you want kids?'

He nodded. None of his past relationships had ever progressed to the point where he could see a future, where he could imagine starting a family, but that hadn't meant he didn't want one. He was hopeful that, one day, he'd fall in love, get married and have children. In his heart, he believed he could love and be loved and he wanted, one day, to have a family of his own.

'Why?' she asked, and he tried to ignore the slightly incredulous tone in her question.

'I want to be able to love someone unconditionally.' In his mind that was a partner and children. It was a dream he'd had but never voiced. Until now. 'I think having kids could be tremendously fulfilling and rewarding if you have them for the right reasons.'

'I'm not so sure,' Molly disagreed. 'The way I see it, mothers in particular have to sacrifice their freedom and independence to raise a family and I'm only just getting mine back. I lost sight of my independence when I was with Daniel and I have no intention of giving it up again any time soon.'

Molly was rubbing the palm of her hand with her opposite thumb in a nervous gesture. Her frown was creased, her worry obvious.

'Well, if it makes you feel any better, the chances of getting pregnant from one episode of unprotected sex are slim, and even slimmer considering you've taken the morning-after pill,' Theo said, knowing what was on her mind and trying to calm her fears. He kept his voice low, conscious of the family at the next table, and tried to pretend that her thoughts didn't bother him.

She was being honest, and he had to acknowledge and appreciate that, but her opinion surprised him and raised the first question mark in his mind. He'd pictured himself with a wife and kids one day. He didn't have a specific timeframe; he knew that was a luxury of being a male. But it was something he wanted in his future, and hearing Molly's thoughts made him wonder if perhaps they weren't as compatible as he'd like to believe.

He reminded himself they had agreed only to a summer romance. Their compatibility past Christmas was irrelevant.

But, after last night, he wondered how hard it was going to be to say goodbye and relegate her to his past. Again.

Molly had chosen to take Theo to Brunswick Heads, fifteen minutes north of Byron Bay, for lunch. She told him it was to avoid the Schoolies Festival but, in the back of her mind, she thought it was a sensible choice. Going out in Byron, they were bound to run into someone she knew and she wasn't ready to explain why they were having lunch together.

The café she'd chosen was one of her favourites but being seated next to a young family had freaked her out a little, making her head ache with thoughts of 'what if?'. A post-lunch walk along the beach, hand in hand with Theo, the sound of the waves crashing on the sand and the feeling of the salt spray and sun on her face, had gradually calmed her mind until she felt confident that all would be well, and by the time they headed back to Byron she was feeling less panicked and more like her normal self.

She pointed out landmarks to Theo as she drove them back to town, slowing down as she approached an intersection on a narrow road as another car was headed towards them from the opposite direction. As she eased off the accelerator there was a flash of movement, a flash of red, to her right.

All of a sudden the flash of red became a person on an e-scooter. Molly saw him look to his left before careening straight onto the road. Straight into the path of the other car that was approaching from his right. The car had no time to swerve and only barely enough time to slam on its brakes. But even that wasn't enough to enable the driver to avoid the impact.

Molly hit the brakes instinctively and watched in horror as the scooter rider bounced off the other car's bonnet and was flung into the air before crashing onto the road in front of Molly's now stationary car. Thank God she'd stopped—if she hadn't she would have run straight over him.

Molly and Theo sprang from the car and rushed to the rider's side.

A second rider, a female, dropped her scooter on the footpath and ran into the middle of the road, screaming.

The driver of the car that had hit him raced over. 'Is he all right? He came from nowhere. I didn't have time to stop.'

'I know,' Molly said. The driver was obviously in shock and understandably concerned. 'We saw the whole thing. He looked the wrong way. He didn't see you.'

The rider's eyes were open, his expression suggested he was wondering what had happened, but at least he was conscious and breathing. He'd been wearing a helmet and that was still fastened under his chin. He was lucky. Most scooter riders Molly saw didn't bother with a helmet, even though the law required them to wear one. It might have just saved this man's life.

'Don't move,' Theo said as it looked as if the man might attempt to get up. 'We're doctors, let us check you over first.'

The man, who was of Asian appearance, frowned as he looked at Theo, but didn't reply. Did he have a concussion or did he not understand the question? Molly wondered.

He looked at the young girl who was squatting beside him and spoke to her in a foreign language that sounded to Molly like Mandarin.

To her surprise, Theo replied.

She'd had no idea he spoke a second language. It just reminded her of how little she knew about him.

She sat by as a spectator as Theo, the rider and the young woman had a conversation. The man was gesturing to his right arm and shoulder.

Theo was speaking now, his words accompanied by hand gestures. He opened and closed his fist before bending and straightening his elbow. The injured man copied Theo's movements, somewhat hesitantly, but he was able to complete the two actions.

Next, Theo demonstrated lifting his arm away from his body but the young man shook his head. He said a few words but Molly couldn't tell if he was refusing or unable to perform that movement.

He pointed to the tip of his shoulder where the collarbone and shoulder blade met.

'What's he saying?' Molly asked.

'It hurts to move his shoulder.'

Theo spoke to the young man again but without any

accompanying actions. The man nodded and Theo ran his hands gently over the man's clavicle and shoulder blade.

Molly watched. Theo's hands were gentle, his fingers long and slender. Just a few hours ago those same hands had been tangled in her hair, cupping her breasts, between her legs, bringing her to orgasm. She closed her eyes. What was the expression? Still waters run deep. She'd always thought of Theo as being reserved but she'd definitely seen a different side to him last night and this morning. He was passionate, considerate and was it any wonder she'd found herself agreeing to a summer fling? She wasn't about to deny herself a few weeks of pleasure.

Theo spoke and then translated for Molly. 'I think he's fractured his clavicle. Can you call for an ambulance? And then we need to get him off the road.'

Molly's phone was in her car. She went to fetch it, moving her car to the side of the road in the process, while Theo helped the man, whose name was Leung, to his feet. Theo brought him over to Molly's car and let him sit in it to wait for the ambulance.

Molly dialled 000, gave their location, and explained there had been a car versus e-scooter accident.

'They're sending an ambulance and a police car,' she said as she hung up. The police would breath-test the driver of the car involved as well as Leung. Molly suspected Theo would need to explain that process too. Theo was still talking to Leung but Molly could recognise only a few words—'Byron Bay', mostly.

Theo gave a patient handover when the paramedics arrived and Molly got more information then.

'We have a twenty-four-year-old male who was riding

an e-scooter when he collided with a car. He has injured his right shoulder, suspected fractured clavicle.'

The paramedics asked a question, which Theo relayed to Leung and then repeated the answer, in English, to the paramedics. 'Yes, he has travel insurance.'

Another question. Another translation. Another response, 'No allergies.'

'Will there be a translator at the hospital?' Theo asked as the paramedics prepared to put Leung onto a stretcher.

'If there's not then the hospital use a dial-in translator over the phone,' the paramedics explained.

The police arrived and Theo gave them a description of the events before they breath-tested the involved parties. The crisis over and their patient strapped securely to the stretcher, Theo and Molly were finally free to head off.

'I could use a beer,' Theo said. 'Shall we go to my place? It's only around the corner.'

They got back in her car and Molly followed his directions, driving through town and onto Childe Street where Theo's accommodation was one of a dozen or so houses. It was single storey, tucked in among the sand dunes. Theo led Molly past three bedrooms and a bathroom, a simple layout with pale wooden floors and white walls, but Molly's jaw dropped as she stepped from the passage into an open-plan kitchen living space. The back wall of the house was glass and over the top of a low hedge of native plants Molly could see the ocean. The water looked to be mere steps from the back door. Theo unlocked the large glass door and slid it back, connecting the house to a deck that led straight onto the sand. Molly could see a narrow path stretching between the salt bush giving direct access to Belongil Beach.

She was drawn to the deck and stood taking in the view. It was the same ocean that she could see from her house, but standing here it felt as if the sea were close enough to touch, as if she could reach out a hand and dip it in the water from the comfort of the house. It would be incredible to live somewhere like this. It felt a million miles away from the busyness of Main Beach.

'This is amazing. I had no idea these houses were here,' she said as Theo reappeared holding two beers he'd fetched from the fridge. He passed one to her and she took it and sat on the end of a sun lounger, facing the ocean.

'It's pretty incredible,' he said. 'I've come to love this spot in the past few weeks. Nothing beats sitting on the deck with a beer at the end of the day, watching the waves roll in. Well, almost nothing,' he added with a grin and Molly knew instinctively that he was referring to last night.

Theo took a seat behind her, straddling the sun lounger, and Molly leant on him, resting her back against his chest. 'How on earth did you find this place?'

Theo wrapped his arms around her and Molly relaxed into his embrace. 'A friend of my sister's owns it. She's overseas. She doesn't rent it out but she lets friends and family use it. I think she was pleased to have someone in it during the Schoolies Festival.'

She closed her eyes and listened to the waves breaking on the shore. She could hear the sea from her house if the windows were open, but here it sounded as if the water were lapping at her feet. The real world receded into the distance as she lost herself in the sounds of the sea, the tang of the salt air, the warmth of the sun on her face and the touch of Theo's hands on her skin.

Molly caught the yeasty smell of Theo's beer as he sipped his drink. She'd forgotten all about hers.

'I had no idea you spoke a second language,' Molly said. 'That you are fluent in Mandarin.'

'You know I'm mixed race, right?'

'Of course.'

'My dad is Australian; my mum is Taiwanese. She moved to Australia from Taiwan to finish her schooling, met my dad at university when they were both studying medicine and they married. I grew up speaking English and Mandarin. Mum's parents moved here when my sister and I were little to look after us, basically, while Mum and Dad worked. We grew up speaking Mandarin with them.'

'You said both your parents are doctors.'

'Dad is a plastic surgeon and Mum is a GP. Lian Chin.'

Molly frowned. 'Lian Chin. That's the same name as the doctor who owns Pacific Coast Clinics.' She sat up and spun around to face Theo.

Theo nodded. 'That's my mum.'

'You're the boss's son? Why didn't you say anything?'

'Why does it matter? It's not relevant. Is it?'

Molly hesitated. It felt very relevant. It felt as if he was hiding something. Why wouldn't he have told people? Told her? That was the real question. She frowned. 'Why didn't you tell me?'

'I just did.'

'I meant, why didn't you tell me earlier?'

'I don't want people to think I got where I am because I'm related to the boss.'

'Can you honestly tell me that's not why you're here?'

'The staff in Sydney were asked if anyone wanted to cover here for Tom's leave. Being so close to Christmas, no one did. I am here because no one else put their hand up so, as the boss's son, I had to fill the gap. But I didn't want to be judged by my name or by my relationship to Lian. My surname is officially Chin Williams but, because it isn't hyphenated, I usually just go by Williams. It was a habit I developed in high school, a strategy to help me fit in, to seem less Asian.'

Molly sensed there was more to this situation than Theo was telling her, but she let him continue rather than pushing for him to disclose more.

'All my life I've been judged on my achievements,' Theo continued. 'My results at school and university. My contribution. I've been expected to excel and been criticised if I fall short. I've never been praised for the person I am, only for what I've done. I don't want to be seen as the boss's son. I want people to see me. Theo. Can you understand that?'

Molly was nodding her head. 'I can. I wanted my father to see me and so I created a personality for myself—a persona—to try to make me stand out from the crowd. It became a protective mechanism. I became the person I wanted people to see. Now I'm just trying to be me. The best me I can be. So, yes, I know what it's like to feel invisible, to be judged or misjudged.'

Theo's phone buzzed with a text message.

'It's from Matt,' he said as he read it. 'Inviting me for a barbecue dinner tonight.' He sounded surprised.

'That's nice,' Molly said. It was, but she wasn't sure how she felt about it.

'You don't sound convinced. What's the catch?'

It was one thing agreeing to have a summer romance or to being friends with benefits, it was another thing spending time together in public. Did she want everyone to know what they were doing?

She knew she didn't. Just as she believed Theo's business was his, hers was hers. 'There's no catch,' she said. 'Matt and Levi host a regular Sunday night barbecue. Gemma and I usually go.'

'Are you going tonight?'

She nodded.

'Shall we go together?'

Theo didn't seem to have the same concerns as her. He seemed quite comfortable with the fact that they were sleeping together but that didn't make them a couple. They'd agreed to being friends with benefits. Did that mean that everyone else had to know what they were doing or could they keep it between themselves? How did she want to play this relationship in public? Because, no matter what they called it, and even if it was only going to be short-lived, it was a relationship of sorts. She had never had a one-night stand and anything more than that had to have some level of connection, didn't it?

What had she agreed to exactly?

'I need to go home and change. Can I meet you there?' she stalled to avoid answering his question directly. 'Their place is halfway between here and home.' She wanted to keep their dalliance between them. She didn't want to share it, she didn't want to talk about it, she didn't want to discuss it and she didn't want to hear everyone's opinions on the subject. She didn't want the others to know.

Theo nodded. He either didn't notice her hesitation or he chose to ignore it.

The night had started off well. Theo had noted that Molly had avoided arriving with him but that hadn't bothered him. This 'thing' between them was new and they hadn't discussed what, if anything, they were going to tell people. But when everyone was discussing their weekends and Molly completely wiped him from her recount, with the exception of their shift at the Schoolies Festival, he couldn't help but feel slighted. He didn't expect her to share every intimate detail with her friends, but did it matter if they knew Molly and he had gone out for lunch? Why was she pretending the day hadn't happened? Was he not good enough for her? Was he something, someone, she wanted to keep secret?

And could he be upset with her if she *was* keeping secrets?

He was keeping secrets too. He couldn't in complete honesty say that his presence in Byron Bay had nothing to do with being a Chin Williams. His mother had requested he go to Byron Bay on her behalf. He'd told a half-truth. He certainly hadn't told Molly the whole story.

He took his guitar out onto the deck when he got home and wasn't surprised to hear that the first few chords he played had a melancholy note.

Would he ever be good enough?

Would he ever be good enough for Molly?

The sad notes kept coming, his fingers seeming to find them of their own accord.

Was he prepared to be a closely guarded secret?

Was Molly worth the angst?

He was only in Byron for another month. Should he walk away now? Save himself from inevitable heart-break?

No. He'd walked away before and regretted it, he thought as the chords he played became stronger, more determined. Failure no longer had the same hold over him. He was willing to take a chance. Molly was worth a shot. He was still fascinated by her, intrigued by her, attracted to her, and he wouldn't walk away again.

'Theo?' The intercom on his clinic phone buzzed and he heard Paula's voice. 'Do you have time to see a walk-in patient? I have an eighteen-year-old male here who's complaining of abdominal pain.'

'Sure. I'll come and get him.' Theo was pleased to fill up his diary. Too much time on his hands meant too much time to sit and think about Molly. He was still try-ing to figure out what had been going through her mind last night, and getting nowhere, so more work was a wel-come distraction. He didn't even mind that this was ex-actly the sort of patient who should be presenting to the hospital ED or even the Schoolies Festival first-aid tent which was open for its last day rather than the medical clinic. As long as he was prepared to pay for a consult.

That thought reminded him again of Molly—their first shared patient, Warwick with the cardiac arrest. He hadn't been charged for his consult, but Theo needed to remember that not everything was about money. He'd become a doctor because he wanted to help people. He had worked overseas after finishing uni, in Third World countries—he definitely wasn't about the money—but he knew his mother wouldn't be happy about giving their expertise away for free. Not if patients could afford to pay for their services.

'Will?' He called for his patient.

A teenage boy stood up slowly from a chair in the corner of the waiting room, slightly unsteady on his feet. He had his right arm held across his stomach and as he stood he reached out with his left hand to stabilise himself on the wall.

'Are you okay?' Theo asked, even though it was obvious the answer was no.

'Just a bit dizzy.'

He was tall and lanky, his face pale. He was flanked by a couple of friends, one of whom put an arm around his waist and lent him support. Theo looked at the group. 'You're here for the Schoolies Festival?' They looked about the right age and all looked a little worse for wear, as if they'd had a late night and hadn't had enough coffee or fried food yet to cure their hangovers.

Will looked worse than the rest. Unable to stand up straight, his face pale and drawn, he was obviously in pain. It looked as if he was suffering from more than a simple hangover.

Theo let Will's mates help him into the examination room but ushered them out once Will was lying on the treatment bed. He seemed coherent and was able to understand Theo's conversation. He'd call the other boys back if he needed them.

'What seems to be the trouble, Will?' he asked after introducing himself.

'I've got some discomfort in my stomach, just here.' He was holding his hand over the left side of his abdomen, just below his ribs.

'Sharp or stabbing pain like a knife or tenderness like a bruise?' Theo asked.

'Like a bruise. But there's no bruise I can see.'

'You're dizzy as well?' Theo checked, recalling his comment from the waiting room.

Will nodded and then closed his eyes, the movement of his head obviously unsettling him. 'That could have something to do with my hangover.'

'When did you last have an alcoholic drink?'

'Last night probably about ten o'clock.' That was twelve hours ago. 'I wasn't feeling too good then. We'd been drinking since lunch and I started feeling a bit off.'

Theo wasn't surprised. But he needed a better explanation as to Will's symptoms. 'Off?'

'Dizzy. I thought I'd had too much to drink.'

'And when did you first notice the tenderness?'

'This morning.'

Theo clipped an oximeter to Will's finger and then took his blood pressure.

'I was wondering if I could have alcohol poisoning?' Will asked. 'Would that give me stomach pain?'

Theo assumed Will had consulted Dr Google and wondered if he should advise him against it. 'That would be likely to make you nauseous but unlikely to present as tenderness in a specific area unless you'd strained a stomach muscle through vomiting. Have you vomited? Had any difficulty breathing? Lost consciousness in the past twelve hours?'

'No.' Will shook his head.

His blood pressure was lower than normal and his heart rate was rapid.

'I need to have a look at your skin. Can you lift your T-shirt up for me?'

Will pulled his T-shirt up, exposing his abdomen. His skin was unblemished. It was lightly tanned but not enough to camouflage any bruising.

'I'm just going to feel your abdominal organs.'

Theo started on the right, gently palpating Will's liver before moving across to the left side. His appendix didn't appear to be giving him any discomfort and Theo reached across Will and lifted the left ribcage slightly with his left hand before pressing his right hand in and up under the ribs. 'Can you breathe in for me?'

The spleen moved down, allowing him to feel the inferior margin. That was a little concerning. The spleen wasn't normally palpable except in very thin adults. If they breathed in the spleen could pop out from under the ribcage.

There were a few red flags, the elevated heart rate, low blood pressure and abdominal tenderness, but they could just as easily indicate side effects of a few days of hard partying as Will celebrated the end of his schooldays.

'Have you had a knock or blow to your stomach in the past couple of days?'

'We were playing beer-can jousting yesterday and we

got knocked over and one of the girls fell and landed on me. Her knee went into my stomach. I didn't think anything of it until this morning. I looked for a bruise but I couldn't see anything.'

Theo had a sense that something else was at play.

'I'm just going to lie the bed flat,' he said as he stepped on the control pad to lower the back of the bed and prepared to do an additional test. 'I want you to lift both your legs into the air and tell me if you feel any discomfort with that movement.'

Will did as he was instructed and Theo saw him wince as he lifted his legs. Will grabbed at his left shoulder, reinforcing Theo's interim diagnosis.

'I think you might have damaged your spleen,' he told him. While Will's symptoms matched any number of things, that last test was quite specific and, combined with the other results, Theo was fairly certain he was looking at signs of a damaged spleen.

'I'd like to send you to the hospital for some tests.'

'What sort of tests?'

'A CT scan to check for damage to your spleen caused by blunt force trauma, for example, someone landing forcefully with their knee on your spleen, and an ultrasound to check for blood in the abdominal cavity. I just need to get an assessment organised.'

Theo wanted to send Will for a specialist opinion, but he had no idea whether it was something that the hospital could provide or if he needed to send his patient to a larger town with better access to specialist clinics. Gemma wasn't at work yet. He would need to ask Molly for advice.

'I have a teenage boy, a Schoolies participant, who has presented with abdominal tenderness and dizziness,' he told her when he found her in the staffroom. 'I'm concerned that he's damaged his spleen.'

'Are you sure? There are several things that present with similar symptoms.'

'I know, but there's one fairly specific test, which was positive,' he said before explaining the test.

Molly frowned. 'I've never heard of that test. How did you know about it?'

'When I was working in Cambodia and Indonesia there were lots of scooter accidents. It was fairly common to patients presenting with abdominal pain after getting handlebars in the abdomen. I was shown that test over there. We probably saw more than the average number of damaged spleens over there, caused by the blunt trauma of a handlebar into the spleen, and that test was pretty reliable. Unfortunately, there wasn't the same access we have here to scans, diagnostic tests or even blood tests. If we suspected spleen damage it was a case of monitoring and hoping that it was minor enough that it would resolve. Non-surgical intervention was our usual treatment option. Often our only treatment option. But what I wanted to know was whether I can send Will to hospital here for further tests. Can we make that referral?'

Molly nodded. 'There are general surgeons at the hospital. Make a phone call and advise that you're sending a patient for scans and review. Is he here with friends?'

'Yes.'

'If he's not critical then he can call an Uber and go with friends.'

'Okay. Thank you. Have you got another minute?' he asked, waylaying her as she was about to leave.

She waited.

'Is everything okay between us?'

'What do you mean?'

'Last night. I thought we'd have a good time together. I thought we'd agreed to a summer fling but then you brushed me off and brushed over our weekend. As if you were embarrassed. If you're having second thoughts, please just tell me. I'd rather you were honest with me.'

Molly shook her head. 'I'm not having second thoughts, I did have a good time, but the whole thing was a bit un-expected. I didn't know how to behave and it made me self-conscious. I didn't say anything because I didn't want people to think we were in a relationship. I don't want to be in a relationship.'

'We agreed to keep it casual,' Theo said. 'Don't worry about what other people think. All that matters is how we feel. If you're not having a good time, we call it quits, okay?'

Molly nodded.

'And don't feel you have to include me in everything you do,' he continued. 'We're not dating, we're just hav-ing fun. Let's just relax and enjoy the next few weeks and make some memories. If you need space, just tell me. Promise you will talk to me, that you'll tell me if there's a problem.'

'Okay.'

CHAPTER EIGHT

MOLLY'S ALARM BUZZED, rousing her from her sleep. She reached for her phone to hit snooze, disturbing Theo in the process.

He rolled over and pulled her into him, holding her close.

He kissed her shoulder. His lips were warm and soft. He trailed his hand from her hip down her thigh and up again, sliding his hand between her legs. Molly shifted her weight and opened her legs. She seemed to be constantly aroused when she was with Theo. A glance, a smile and especially a touch of his hand, even the lightest of touches, all had the power to trigger her libido. And there was no denying how compatible they were in bed. But outside the bedroom they had been getting on just as well. Molly enjoyed Theo's company. She used to feel he was judging the old Molly—although it turned out she was her harshest critic—but she got no sense of judgement any more. He was happy in her company, as she was in his.

And she had decided that there was no point pretending otherwise. They were seeing each other casually and she'd admitted as much to her friends. She and Theo had no expectations of each other of anything bigger, anything permanent, so there really was no need to hide their summer romance from anyone. She'd been slightly surprised to find her friends were all unanimously positive in their support of the romance, but Molly had stressed that it wasn't going to be anything serious—their affair would be over almost before it began. A line would be drawn through it when Theo returned to Sydney.

She wasn't thinking about how she would feel then—she still didn't like to examine her feelings too closely. She was still telling herself it was a summer fling, although she was worried she was in deeper than she'd planned to be.

Theo's fingers were working their magic and Molly forgot about the alarm she'd set until the snooze button went off. Reluctantly she covered Theo's hand with hers and stilled his movements.

'What's the matter?' he asked.

She rolled over and apologised with a kiss. 'Nothing. But if we want to see the sunrise we need to get up.'

'It's still dark,' Theo complained. 'I'd rather stay in bed with you. There will be another sunrise tomorrow.'

'It's forecast to rain tomorrow,' Molly said. 'You can't come to Byron and not see the sunrise from the lighthouse at least once. We can come back to bed after our walk.'

'Is that a promise?'

She nodded and kissed him again before throwing off the covers and pulling him out of bed. They did need to get going if they were going to make it up the track before sunrise.

* * *

Molly and Theo leant on the white wooden fence at the top of the hill. The lookout was almost deserted save for a couple of other early risers. The lighthouse stood tall behind them. It was a gorgeous building, but Molly and Theo were focused on the horizon to the east. The sky was getting lighter, a pale azure blue tinged with pink and orange as the golden orb of the sun began to glow on the edge of the ocean.

Theo moved to stand behind Molly and wrapped his arms around her waist, resting his chin on the top of her head and inhaling the orange perfume of her hair. They stood in silence, mesmerised by the colours of nature, waiting to be among the first people to see the sun rise in Australia on this day.

Seagulls and cormorants wheeled in the sky above their heads and the tang of the sea carried to them on the warm breeze. Theo breathed deeply, taking time to feel the moment, committing it to memory. He knew this experience would stay with him always, long after he'd returned to his life in Sydney.

'This is incredible,' he told Molly. 'Thank you for bringing me here.' He had been brought up to be busy, to be achieving, and found he was always thinking about something. He was comfortable here in Byron Bay. With Molly in his arms. He felt at home. He knew he had a job to do but he still had time and space to breathe. It was a rare state for him. 'It's not often I feel completely at peace,' he added.

'What are the things that bring you peace?' Molly asked.

He could count those things on one hand. 'Playing the

guitar—not performing, but playing on my own with no one to hear. It's cathartic and freeing. Watching the sunrise at the Temple of Borobudur in Indonesia—that was a very similar experience to today.' And being with Molly.

But he didn't include that last one, knowing it would be very likely to frighten her. They weren't at a point where they had serious conversations. He knew they might never be. That she might never want that.

The sun was well and truly above the horizon now. The rich pinks and oranges had faded, leaving just a cloudless blue sky and a new day.

'But every day is a new beginning. A chance to start again. What are your plans for your new future? Where do you see yourself in five years?' He tried to gently gauge her thoughts.

'Five years!' Molly exclaimed. 'I haven't really thought about it. Have you?'

'I might be running the clinics by then.'

'Is that what you want?'

'It's what's expected,' he replied. 'I've imagined other options plenty of times, but I've never seriously considered doing anything else. Maybe I should just stay here,' he said, and he was only half joking.

The sun was on Molly's face. She was glowing. Her hair was like spun gold and her eyes were the colour of the sky. She looked like an angel and he knew there was nowhere else he'd rather be.

He studied her closely, committing the vision to memory, knowing he would take that image with him when he left.

* * *

Molly couldn't believe another week had passed. The year was rapidly drawing to a close, Christmas was three weeks away and Theo was over halfway through his stint in Byron Bay. She had to admit that she was enjoying spending time with him. She'd relaxed, realised her friends were happy for her and no one was judging her. She was free to do as she pleased. Theo gave her the space she needed and was happy to see her on her terms. It had been a fun few weeks.

The weekends had passed by in a blur of sun, the sea, sand and sex—not always in that order—and the weekdays had been filled with work and the myriad social activities that were part of the fabric of daily life in Byron. The days were busy and so were the nights.

It was Friday again and Molly and Theo were the last ones at the office. Theo's consulting room door was open when Molly went to see if he was ready to leave. It was Gemma's birthday and they were meeting friends at the Railway Hotel for an open mic night. Theo was on the phone but motioned for Molly to come in.

'I've got a few ideas. I'll talk to you again once I've got more information,' Theo said as he ended the call, but not before Molly worked out he was on the phone to his mother and they were talking about the clinic.

'Is everything okay?' she asked.

Theo nodded and switched off his computer before standing up. 'Mum just had a few questions about the clinic.'

Molly looked expectantly at Theo, waiting for him to expand.

He pushed his chair under the desk and Molly waited. 'The clinic's profits are down and she wants my opinion on a couple of things,' he said.

'What sort of things?'

'She's looked at the books but while that gives her the bottom line it doesn't indicate the reason why the figures have dropped. She wants to know what I can tell her.'

'She wants you to spy on us?'

'No.' Theo frowned. 'Why would you think that?'

'Because you were talking about getting information.'

'Why do you always think the worst of me?'

'What do you mean?'

'You accused me of keeping my relationship with the boss, my mother, a secret, when really it just wasn't relevant.'

'But it is relevant now, isn't it?' Molly argued. 'You wouldn't be reporting back to her about profits if you weren't her son.'

'This has nothing to do with the fact we're related and now you're accusing me of being a spy.'

'All those questions you were asking Matt about the hydrotherapy sessions—you were looking for information for your mother, weren't you?' Those questions that had seemed so random now made sense.

'Yes, but I'm not spying on *you* or any of the staff. I'm looking at the figures, at the way the clinic operates.'

'Does anyone else know what you're doing?'

He nodded. 'Tom was aware and Paula has been helping me with the data. I've been looking at where we can make money or save money, if there's a service we should be offering or one that isn't viable. It's not so much a staffing issue as a practice management one. I haven't been hiding this, Molly. Why don't you trust me?'

Molly thought about Theo's question. He was right, she was always questioning his behaviour, looking for reasons to push him away. 'You know trust is an issue for me. People I've cared about have let me down. A lot.'

'Have I let you down in any way?'

Molly shook her head. 'Not yet.'

'Why do you assume I'm going to?'

'Because men I care about seem to,' she admitted. 'My father. Daniel. People lie to me, people cheat and I've been gullible before, believing things I know I shouldn't, and not trusting my instincts.'

'I'm not keeping secrets from you,' he said. 'This is simply an admin issue, part and parcel of running the business. If there's anything that affects you, I'll tell you,' he added as he wrapped an arm around her shoulders and dropped a kiss on her forehead. Her hurt feelings gave way to guilt. She'd made this about her. She expected to be let down, but he hadn't done anything to her. She knew he was under no obligation to tell her about what he was doing. She wouldn't have expected Tom to tell her anything in the same situation. Theo didn't owe her an explanation just because they were sleeping together. They weren't in a serious relationship. That was her choice. She couldn't have her cake and eat it too.

'I'm sorry—again,' she apologised.

He dropped a kiss on her lips before releasing her from his embrace. 'It's okay, just remember we're on the same side,' he said as he went to the cupboard in the corner of his consulting room and retrieved his guitar.

* * *

Theo forced himself to join in Gemma's birthday festivities and leave Molly's comments for another time. But he couldn't deny her comments had upset him. Why did it always seem to be two steps forwards and one back, or maybe even one forwards and two backwards with her? She was so afraid of letting him close. He understood that she was fearful and he agreed, trust needed to be earned, but it hurt when he knew he'd done nothing to make her think she couldn't trust him. It made it difficult to prove that he was trustworthy when she was inclined to make assumptions. Inclined to tar him with the same brush as her father and Daniel.

It shouldn't matter. Their relationship wasn't serious. But he didn't want Molly to confuse him with other men in her life.

He took his guitar out of its case and began to tune it. Strumming the strings calmed him down and he was able to take some comfort in the fact that Molly had admitted she cared about him. But how much was what he wanted to know.

'Are you going to sing, Theo?' Gemma asked.

'I'm not sure,' he replied. He didn't know if he was in the right mood to sing in front of people tonight.

'These sessions are popular so you should put your name down. You can always decline later,' Matt said. 'I reckon we'd all be keen to hear a new voice. The talent can be a bit hit and miss.'

Encouraged by their group, he signed up to sing, and when he returned to the table Gemma said, 'Molly told me you worked overseas. Can I pick your brains?'

'Sure. Did she tell you I worked with an aid organisation so we were clinic-based, not hospital-based? Is that what you're thinking of doing?'

Gemma nodded. 'I think I'd like that. Where did you go?'

'I spent two years in Cambodia and Indonesia.'

'You'd recommend it?'

Theo nodded. 'It was one of the most amazing experiences of my life.' He had loved the freedom of being away from the expectations of his parents. There were other expectations but they were manageable, he wasn't expected to be better than anyone else, he was only expected to be as good, and that had felt liberating. 'It was challenging a lot of the time, but knowing that we were actually making a difference was unbelievably rewarding. Everyone should be entitled to health care. It's a basic human right, not a privilege, and to be able to deliver that to people was incredible.'

'Why did you come back?'

'My parents expected me to go into their business.'

'What's that?'

'The clinic.'

'Pacific Coast?'

Theo nodded. 'Lian Chin is my mother,' he told them. 'My parents set up the clinic and my mother runs it.' He figured there was no point in keeping his relationship hidden. They'd find out eventually.

'That must make things hard for you at times,' Gemma said.

'It has its ups and downs,' he admitted.

He was aware of Molly watching him. She'd been quiet

since they got to the pub and he wished he knew what she was thinking. Did she still think that he was hiding something from her? Or did she think, after his conversation with his mother, that he thought medicine was all about the money? That wasn't his mindset. After working overseas he knew that money was much less important than helping people. But that didn't mean it wasn't important at all.

He strummed a few chords on his guitar and, using the cover of his music to keep the others from overhearing, he said to Molly, 'Everything okay?' He wasn't going to sit there and second-guess what she was thinking.

She smiled and nodded. Her smile reached her eyes and Theo relaxed. Perhaps she wasn't upset with him at all, he thought as he was called up to the stage.

He debated whether or not to sing a love song to Molly before thinking better of it. He didn't want to embarrass Molly or himself. She might have said everything was okay, but that didn't mean she was ready to listen to him sing her a love song in public. A Christmas song was another option. Christmas was fast approaching and the streets and businesses had their decorations on display, but the audience possibly wasn't the right demographic for Christmas carols. An Aussie rock classic might be a better choice.

The crowd loved his rendition and demanded a second song as he wrapped it up. Molly was smiling and clapping along with the rest of the crowd. He'd do it for her.

'If you recognise this one, sing the chorus with me,' he invited as he launched into 'I Still Call Australia Home'.

This song had a slow beginning and as he kept his

gaze on Molly and sang he reflected on how comfortable he felt in Byron Bay. He was reminded of the freedom he'd had when he'd worked overseas, where he was expected to do his job but no more or less than the other doctors working with him. Here was the same. Here he was just Theo. Not the boss's son, despite what Molly might think. Here he was just Theo, especially when he was with Molly. Then he forgot about anything else.

Molly was still smiling when he finished the next song and she welcomed him off stage with a kiss and, suddenly, all was right in his world again.

At midday on Monday Molly knocked on Theo's door and invited him to lunch in the staffroom.

'What's the occasion? Another birthday?' Theo asked.

Molly shook her head. 'No. I hope you don't mind but I asked everyone to spend some time thinking about what is working in the practice and what isn't. I thought they might have some suggestions or opinions that you haven't thought of and that you could add to your report.'

Molly was trying to make up for what she thought of as her unkindness, the accusations she'd made about Theo last Friday. He had tried to help her four years ago and she hadn't listened. He needed help now and it was her turn to listen. She wanted to help.

'You did? Why?'

Oh, God, had she got it wrong? He hadn't wanted her help at all.

'I thought it was my chance to help you. A way of saying sorry for all the times I've misjudged you.'

'Thank you.' Theo smiled and gave her a quick kiss

on her cheek and Molly breathed a sigh of relief that he wasn't annoyed with her for interfering. 'Let's go.'

Paula, Matt and Gemma were already seated around the table, buzzing with ideas. Molly knew Theo had already got data from Paula, and a few suggestions regarding administrative issues, but she also knew Paula was keen to be involved further.

'Okay, let's start with what's working well.' Molly got the ball rolling.

'Our consulting lists are consistently around ninety per cent booked. For both the physios and GPs.'

'Do you think we have enough staff. Is there need for more?' Theo asked.

'We've got room for more but I don't think the demand is there. Summer is a bit busier but winter is steady also,' Paula replied.

'I think we could get more use out of the pool if we had more staff,' Matt added. 'An extra physio might let us maximise its potential in terms of rehab, but alternatively we might be able to rent it out for swimming lessons or aquarobics, as we talked about, Theo. It's an expensive asset so it would be good to get more income from it.'

'Paula, you said we have room for more staff. If we don't need more GPs or treating physiotherapists, what are some options for the vacant consulting rooms? And why are they vacant?' Theo wanted to know.

'The consulting rooms that are available to be booked by visiting specialists aren't being used as often because the new hospital is finished and they're going there instead,' Paula said.

'Who else would be willing to take on a permanent

lease of some of this space?' Theo looked up from his note-taking to look around the group assembled at the table.

'I think allied health staff could be a good value add to the clinic. A podiatrist, a dietician, a psychologist. Someone like that might be interested in renting space on a permanent basis. Even a dentist is an option,' Molly said.

'Or we could open up those offices and make better use of the space,' Matt suggested.

'As what?'

'We could combine spaces to make a Pilates or yoga studio. I don't think that would be hard to do. The building has been added onto over the years and doesn't present as a new modern space and doesn't work as well as it could,' he answered.

Theo was taking notes. 'All good points, thank you. There's one final issue that I think is worth raising,' he said. 'Are we billing efficiently and adequately?' He directed his attention to Paula before turning his gaze to the others around the table. 'Paula has given me access to the books and I realise this query is only a small component, but every little bit saved or earned may make a difference.'

'What do you mean?' Paula asked.

'On my first day here, Molly and I treated a walk-in patient, the gentleman who went into cardiac arrest.' Theo waited for Paula's confirmation nod before continuing. 'The reception staff told me afterwards that he was only charged the government fee for that service. Not a regular consulting fee. Why was that?'

'It's what we've always done for emergency consults,' Paula explained.

'But we're not an emergency department.'

'They wouldn't have been charged if they'd turned up at the public hospital emergency department.'

'But we're not a public hospital either,' Theo replied. 'And private hospital emergency clinics charge hundreds of dollars to treat patients. We should too. We're not a public service. We should be charging full fees.'

'Emergency presentations can be quite stressful and it seems mercenary in those times to be talking about money,' Paula responded.

'I get that, believe me,' Theo replied. 'But if people are frequently using the clinic as their emergency department instead of going to the hospital, then if they have the means to pay for our service, they should be charged.'

'What about your comment last Friday? You said everyone should have access to health care as a basic right.' Molly felt she had to ask the question.

Theo nodded. 'That is my opinion and in Australia the government provides free or subsidised health care to people who need it. But Pacific Coast Clinics is a business—it needs to make a profit. We are not funded by the government and we should expect people to pay if they are able to and be prepared to have a conversation about finances if the need arises. If the reception staff don't feel comfortable doing that, is that something you could take on, Paula?'

Paula nodded as Theo wrapped up the meeting. 'Thank you, everyone, and thank you, Molly, for instigating the meeting. I should have asked you all for your opinions earlier but I'm used to operating on my own, but I appreciate your input.'

Molly tugged on her dress as she stepped out of the car. She'd bought a new outfit in celebration of the staff Christmas function, a sleeveless shirt dress that buttoned down the front, but it felt a little tighter today than she recalled it being when she'd purchased it. Perhaps she and Theo had been out for too many meals, she thought as she undid a couple of buttons at the bottom to give her room to bend her knees—the Christmas function was barefoot bowls and she needed to be able to squat to play. She'd just have to live with the button at her waist that was a bit snug.

'Who would like a glass of bubbly?' Matt greeted Molly, Theo and Gemma on arrival. He had an open bottle in one hand and several glasses in the other.

Molly took a glass and held it as Matt poured for her. She wasn't going back to Sydney for Christmas with her family this year, she had volunteered to work between Christmas and New Year so the other doctors could take holidays, so tonight was going to be one of her main celebrations, but as she brought the glass to her lips a wave of nausea washed over her. She felt light-headed. She wondered if it was something to do with her dress being a little tight at the waist or maybe she was just dehydrated. She was feeling a little hot.

She put the glass down on a nearby table and decided to start with a water. The water helped briefly. Until the finger food was passed around. Smoked salmon, chicken sandwiches, marinated prawns, all of it made her stomach turn.

Molly tried distracting herself by joining in an end of bowls, but all the bending made her dizzy. Eventually she gave up and went home, insisting that Theo stay and enjoy the evening, and just assuming she'd picked up a virus from somewhere.

She was lethargic and felt less than one hundred per cent for the next couple of days with bouts of lightheadedness but no vomiting and no temperature. She'd lost her appetite, with the exception of Vegemite toast, and reluctantly took Monday off work.

By Monday afternoon, she was feeling better, provided she wasn't looking at food and didn't stand up too quickly.

'Did you have a terribly busy day because of me?' she asked Gemma when she got home, feeling guilty because she knew her patients had either had their appointments cancelled or had been moved to Gemma's or Theo's lists.

'No, it was all fine,' Gemma replied. 'Theo says hi.'

She had told Theo to stay away but he'd phoned and messaged her during the day. There was no point in passing a virus around to more people. And in her mind a summer romance didn't include nursing care.

'I brought you something,' Gemma said as she handed Molly a bag.

Molly peered inside and her eyes widened when she saw the contents. 'What's this for?' she asked as she withdrew a box containing a pregnancy test kit.

'Just a precaution. You have to admit your symptoms fit this cause.'

'Don't be ridiculous,' Molly argued as she quickly calculated the time since she and Theo had had unprotected sex.

'When was your last period?' Gemma asked.

Molly couldn't recall. She remembered the lack of contraception two and a half weeks ago. The morning-after pill. Gemma didn't know about any of that. But was her period late? Maybe a few days late, although she couldn't be sure.

'There's no harm in doing a test,' Gemma said, and Molly gave in, knowing Gemma was unlikely to let the matter drop.

She felt the nausea return as she went to the bathroom and did the test. She left the little stick on the toilet seat, washed her hands and went back to the kitchen to put the kettle on. She needed to distract herself.

'Are you going to check it or am I?' Gemma asked as they finished the tea Molly made.

Molly wasn't sure she was game but said, 'I'll do it.' After all, it was her issue.

She returned to the bathroom. The stick was where she'd left it, looking innocent enough, until she got closer.

Two pink lines greeted her.

Molly picked up the stick before sitting down on the toilet lid. She closed her eyes and concentrated on breathing.

She heard the bathroom door open and looked up to find Gemma standing in the doorway, her eyes fixed on the stick that was still in Molly's hand.

'It's positive?' she said.

Molly nodded before promptly bursting into tears. Gemma stepped forward and wrapped her in a hug.

'Should I do another test? It might be wrong,' Molly said, her voice full of hope.

'A false negative maybe,' Gemma replied, 'but a false positive is unlikely.'

Molly knew Gemma was right. 'What am I going to do?' she asked.

'Nothing right now,' was Gemma's reply. 'I'm going to make you a piece of toast and another cup of tea. You'll eat and drink and take a breath. Take a minute.'

'This is not part of my plan.' Did she have a plan? She didn't really. Her plan had been to spend some time focusing on herself.

I should never have got involved with Theo, she thought, but she wasn't sure she really meant it.

She'd enjoyed spending time with him. Sleeping with him. Until now.

'What do I tell Theo?' she asked Gemma. 'We agreed on a summer romance, a "friends with benefits" type scenario. I don't think a baby counts as a benefit,' Molly said.

'Some people might think it does,' Gemma suggested.

Molly shook her head. 'No. We didn't plan on this. I didn't plan on this.' She'd told Theo as much.

'No kidding.' Gemma wrapped her arm around Molly and helped her to her feet. 'Come with me, I'll put the kettle on.'

Molly collapsed onto a stool at the kitchen bench. '*Do* I tell Theo?'

'Why wouldn't you?'

'Our relationship is hardly serious. And I don't want

to be tied to a man because of a mistake. I don't want to be tied to a man at all. The next relationship I'm in will be by choice, not circumstance.'

'In that case you only have one option because you can't, in all honesty, keep the baby and not tell Theo.'

'There is another option,' she said. 'Theo might not want anything to do with me or the baby.'

'But that would still mean telling him and taking that chance. Do you honestly think he wouldn't choose you and the baby?'

Molly didn't know what to think but she did know she couldn't terminate a pregnancy. She was filled with despair as she realised that a brief lapse of concentration was going to change her life. She hadn't planned on having children, but she knew she would struggle with a termination.

And that was the second time Gemma had used the word honest. Molly knew she was right. She had to be honest. She had to tell Theo.

It was only seventeen days ago that she'd told Theo she didn't want children. Could she do this? Could she raise a child? Could she do it alone?

Molly's hands were sweaty. She thought she might throw up but she knew tonight's nausea wasn't related to her pregnancy hormones, but to nerves. More than nerves. It was triggered by fear. She was going to tell Theo her news, their news, and she was terrified.

He might want nothing to do with her or the baby or he might want to be involved. Both options had pros and cons. Both options were equally terrifying. One would mean she would lose her independence. She would have to accommodate Theo in her plans and she'd be permanently tied to him through their child. They would be permanently connected and she did *not* want to be tied to a man out of obligation.

The other option would mean she would lose Theo. She was prepared to be a single mother but was that fair on a child?

Now that she was between a rock and a hard place she found that things were not so black and white. It was a lot more complicated in real life. Theory and practice were two very different things and she really had no idea how she wanted this to play out.

She'd have to put the ball in Theo's court and go from there.

She checked the time. She had ten minutes before Theo would arrive. She'd invited him for dinner. She had managed to avoid him at work—she knew she wouldn't be able to pretend everything was fine and the issue was not one she could discuss at work. Dinner was the best, the only, option and thankfully Gemma had agreed to make herself scarce for the evening and leave the apartment free for Molly and Theo.

Molly found a playlist on her phone and connected it to the speakers, using the music to settle her nerves. She lit the mosquito coils and placed one under the table and the other near the herb pots in the corner of the balcony. She finished setting the table and filled a jug with cold water. Bustling around kept her hands busy and her mind occupied.

Before leaving the house, Gemma had made a chicken

salad for Molly to serve for dinner. Molly couldn't face the thought of cooking and the idea of handling raw meat brought on another bout of nausea. If it wasn't for Gemma's help Molly would be serving toast with Vegemite—that was about all she could manage to prepare at present.

She switched on the fairy lights that were strung around the balcony and then turned on the Christmas tree lights. Gemma had decorated the house for Christmas, which was now only two weeks away.

Molly would have the apartment to herself over Christmas. Gemma was going to Brisbane but, as Molly had volunteered to work between Christmas and New Year, Matt and Levi had invited her to have Christmas dinner with them, and she was happy to have a reason not to go to Sydney. She would miss her sisters but she wasn't ready to leave Byron Bay yet. She had found some inner peace since moving here—although her peace had been shattered a little with the events of the past week—but that was another good reason to stay away from Sydney. She needed some time to work out how to announce the situation to her family. To work out how to tell them they would be grandparents and aunts.

She wasn't sure how that news would be received. She thought her sisters would be excited, she hoped her mother would be too, but there was no way of knowing. Her mother had learnt to guard her emotions a long time ago.

Molly wondered what Theo did for Christmas. He would be back in Sydney by then.

She wondered what his family would think of her news. Would he tell them?

Her musings were cut short by a knock on the door. Her heart skipped a beat when she opened it. Even though she knew it would be Theo the sight of him still took her breath away. He looked good.

He was wearing a pair of pale cotton shorts and a black T-shirt. His face was tanned and he looked healthy and strong and gorgeous. Molly knew he'd enjoyed his time in Byron and she was about to make sure it was time he'd never forget. One way or the other.

He kissed her and she closed her eyes and let herself imagine, just for a moment, a future where she could trust him not to break her heart. A future where they could be happy.

But any future they would have was now going to be complicated by her pregnancy. Things were never going to be the same. Never going to be simple.

As Theo released her she was overcome by a wave of light-headedness. 'There's beer in the fridge or water on the table. Help yourself to a drink. I'll be back in a minute,' she said as she fled to the bathroom.

She splashed her face with cold water and took two deep breaths before drying her face. She applied concealer to cover up the dark circles under her eyes and then rejoined Theo for a dinner that she couldn't face eating.

Gemma's chicken salad was delicious but Molly's appetite was non-existent. She picked at her dinner, moving food around her plate, while she tried to make conversation.

'Are you sure you're feeling better?' Theo asked. 'You're very quiet and you've barely touched your meal.'

'There's something I need to tell you,' Molly said

as she put her knife and fork together on her plate and pushed it aside. She could feel her dinner pressing against her oesophagus, threatening to make a reappearance. Theo was watching her closely, waiting. She almost felt sorry for him, he had no idea what was coming, but this was as much his fault as hers. He needed to hear what she had to say. 'I didn't have a virus. I assumed that I'd caught something but it turns out that wasn't the case.' She glanced away as she summoned up her courage before returning her gaze to Theo. 'I'm pregnant.'

Theo was silent. Molly waited, willing him to speak but at the same time dreading what he might say.

'Pregnant? Not sick?'

Molly shook her head. 'Obviously I'm one of those statistics you read about in the pamphlet that comes with the morning-after pill.' She must have ovulated before they had sex. 'Our timing wasn't great.'

'Pregnant. Wow.' A smile slowly spread across his face.

Molly frowned. 'You're not upset?'

'Upset? No. This is amazing,' he said as he stood and moved around the table, taking her hands in his and pulling her to her feet. 'We're having a baby.'

He wrapped her in a hug and kissed her and for a minute, Molly forgot that she was planning on doing this alone. This was not the reaction she'd anticipated and it felt good to share this moment with Theo. But that wasn't going to be her reality.

'How is this good news?' she asked.

'I've always wanted to be a father and I think, I hope, I'll be a good one. I've had plenty of lessons in how not

to raise a family,' he said, but he must have heard something in her voice because he stepped back, releasing her,
and looked into her eyes. 'You're not happy about this? I
know you said you didn't want children...'

She heard the note of hope in his voice and knew he
was counting on her changing her mind. 'I'm keeping it,'
she told him, giving him the news she knew he wanted,
'but we didn't plan on having a baby. We barely know
each other.'

'There are worse things that have happened. We're
not the first ones to find ourselves in this situation. We
can make it work.'

'Make what work?'

'Us.'

Molly shook her head and sat down. She needed a bit
of space, physically and mentally. 'There is no us, Theo.
We had no plans past the next two weeks.'

'We'll make plans.'

He made it sound so simple. But Molly knew it was far
from that. Unexpected tears welled in her eyes and she
blinked quickly, trying to stop them from spilling over.
'Neither of us signed up for parenthood.'

'That doesn't mean we can't do this.'

'Theo, we agreed to a summer romance. We didn't
agree to raising a baby.'

'What do you suggest we do, then?'

This was moving faster than Molly had anticipated.
She'd barely accepted the fact she was pregnant and she
hadn't expected to start making plans tonight. 'I don't
know. I'm still trying to work out how this happened.'
She felt sick.

'Shall I tell you what I'm thinking?'

Molly nodded. There could be no harm in hearing Theo's thoughts. Unless he wanted to take the baby and raise it on his own. Despite not having motherhood in her future plans a week ago, Molly knew now she couldn't give her child up.

'What if you came back to Sydney with me? What if we got married?'

CHAPTER NINE

'WHAT?'

He wanted to get married?

Molly shook her head.

That was a ridiculous idea.

Unexpected and ridiculous.

'I have no plans to move to Sydney and I don't want to get married.'

'Why not?' he asked.

'We agreed to a summer romance. We hadn't talked about anything after that and suddenly you're talking about spending the rest of our lives together.' Molly paused to take a breath, she could hear a slightly panicked note creeping into her voice and she needed to calm down. 'That makes no sense. I don't want to be trapped in a marriage because of a baby. And I don't think you do either.'

'Would you prefer I went back to Sydney and left you to it?' he asked. 'That's not going to happen. I barely saw my mother and father growing up. You know I was basically raised by my grandparents. I want to be present for my child. I want to be involved.'

'I'm not saying you can't be involved.'

'Maybe not, but you are saying you're happy to have

a summer romance but you don't want a relationship. You'll have my baby, but you don't want to marry me.'

'I don't want to marry anyone.'

'But I'm not just anyone,' he argued. 'I'm the father of your child. I don't want to be cut out of my child's life. If we're married that can't happen.'

'I'm not trying to cut you out.'

'But you want to make all the decisions.'

'Not all,' Molly replied, 'but I do want to be able to make some. Starting with whether or not to get married. I don't want to be told what to do, how to think, where to live.'

'I wasn't,' Theo objected.

'You just did! Literally three minutes after I told you the news you said, let's move to Sydney. Let's get married. As if I don't get a say.'

'Of course, you get a say, but would it be so awful to do this together?'

No, it wouldn't. In her heart she could see the future. But she couldn't risk it. The future wouldn't turn out as she hoped—she'd learnt that much. Happily ever after only existed in fairy tales.

Molly wiped away a tear. Theo had proposed out of honour. He hadn't proposed because he was in love with her. He hadn't proposed of his own accord. He'd proposed because of the circumstances, because he thought it was the *right* thing to do, and she couldn't accept. She would *not* end up like her mother—trapped in a marriage with a man who didn't love her.

'I don't want to lose my independence. My mother was hamstrung by her circumstances. She had no career and no money. I've worked hard to make sure I have financial independence. What I didn't always have was emotional independence. I was too busy seeking validation. Now I have both and I'm not prepared to give them up.'

'Commitment and dependence are not the same thing.'

Molly shook her head. Theo was wrong. 'I spent years being Daniel's girlfriend, Daniel's on-again-off-again girlfriend. The girl Daniel cheated on. Now I'm going to be someone's mother. I don't want to be someone's wife. I want to be me. Molly.'

'You will always be Molly. I'm not trying to change you. I'm trying to support you.'

But Molly was worried that support might end up feeling like control. She needed to breathe. She needed some space. 'We're not going to sort this out tonight.'

'I agree,' Theo said. 'We should sleep on it and talk tomorrow. But,' he said as he kissed her goodnight, 'I want you to remember this is good news and we will work it out.'

Molly collapsed on her bed after Theo left. She knew she should clean up but she was exhausted. Emotionally and physically.

Theo wanted to marry her.

For a brief mad moment she'd been tempted to say yes.

But he didn't love her. He just wanted to make sure he saw his child.

It was ludicrous to think that their story could end in marriage. In happily ever after.

She was having a baby; she was going to be a mother. She was going to co-parent with Theo. That was enough commitment for now.

Marriage was unnecessary.

And marriage without love was ridiculous.

'So, you'll let me know the date of your first ultrasound scan?' Theo confirmed as he signalled for their dinner bill. Just the thought of that first scan, of seeing his baby's heart beating on a screen for the first time, filled Theo with joy, a sense of anticipation and happiness more intense than anything he could have imagined.

'You'll come up from Sydney for it?' Molly asked and Theo nodded. 'How will you manage that?'

'I'll make it work. I'll take annual leave days. As long as you give me enough notice I can block out my diary.'

He was due to return to Sydney on Tuesday, in three days' time. His six-week stint was coming to an end and he still hadn't convinced Molly to move with him, but he had no intention of missing those milestones. He needed to show Molly he was serious about being involved and that started with the antenatal appointments. He hadn't figured out yet how he'd manage to attend antenatal classes—he assumed Molly would be going—but there was time for that. He knew there was a fine line to tread between being interested, being involved and Molly thinking he was trying to control her pregnancy. Her life.

He was so grateful that Molly had chosen to keep the baby and he was going to do everything in his power to support her, as well as make sure he was involved in the pregnancy and beyond. The huge responsibility of raising a child wasn't lost on him but it was a duty he would embrace. He would prefer to do it side by side with Molly, as partners, not co-parents, but that outcome was still a work in progress. Molly had taken it off the table but Theo wasn't giving up yet.

He'd invited Molly to dinner and they'd spent the night talking about logistics, which was important and necessary, but Theo knew there was also plenty being left unsaid. There was no discussion about how they felt. The conversation had been practical, not emotional.

Perhaps he should have cooked for her at home. In the privacy of his house maybe they would have been more honest with each other, more forthcoming about their feelings, their hopes and dreams. Perhaps he'd suggest that for tomorrow night.

He knew he was running out of time. He knew that once he moved to Sydney it would be harder to convince Molly that they should be together. He was worried it would be out of sight, out of mind. That was another reason he was determined to travel to Byron Bay for appointments. He wanted to remain in Molly's life.

Four days after hearing Molly's news he was still overcome with emotion, excitement and nervousness. It was exhilarating but terrifying all at the same time. He was determined to be a good father, a loving father, a hands-on father—all the things he'd missed out on— but working out how to make this happen was going to be a challenge.

He'd briefly considered staying in Byron Bay but he knew that ultimately he couldn't run the family business from there and that was what was expected of him, what he expected of himself. There were three clinics in Sydney—that was where he needed to be. It was frustrating but he'd figure out a solution eventually. He was not going to be an absent father. He could see a future with Molly. He just had to figure out how to convince her.

Trust was the key.

He needed time to show her that she could depend on him.

He hadn't suggested marriage again. He knew he'd got that wrong. She'd said she wouldn't marry him. He should take comfort from the fact she'd said she wouldn't marry anyone. But he wasn't just anyone. He was the father of her child.

'So, we agree, open lines of communication are important,' he said as he paid the bill. 'We will make this work. We both want to do what's best for our child. I'm sure all parents think they'll do things differently but I really want to get this right.'

'I do—' Molly's reply was interrupted by the sound of screeching tyres as a car rounded the corner outside the restaurant at speed. The noise level in the restaurant dropped as conversation among all the diners ceased when they heard a deafening crash and the unmistakeable sound of metal crunching and glass shattering.

There was a brief moment of absolute silence before a car horn blared and continued incessantly. Overlaying that came the sound of a second crash, duller than the first, followed by screaming.

Theo and Molly ran out to the street. A cloud of dust billowed in the air, choking the intersection.

Theo sprinted down the road, heading towards the screams and the dust, and Molly dashed after him. She rounded the corner and came to a stop, giving her brain a moment to process what she was seeing.

A car had careened up onto the footpath and was jammed between two concrete planter boxes, its nose against the wall of an old two-storey building that operated as a wine bar.

Molly knew the wine bar had an outdoor dining area on the street, under the veranda. The planter pots were supposed to act as a barrier, as protection for the outside tables, but somehow the car had flipped onto its side and slid in between the planter pots, taking out a veranda post in the process. The veranda had collapsed and she could see broken chairs and tables lying crushed under the weight of the veranda. She had to assume that, moments before, people had been sitting at those tables.

It was a confronting scene. Debris was strewn across the road as the dust began to settle and Molly's heart was in her throat at the thought of what carnage might be revealed. They needed to find out if there were people trapped under the building.

People were milling around—dazed and stunned—and Molly saw some crawling out from under the veranda. Bystanders helped them to their feet. Others had phones to their ears and Molly could hear them talking to emergency services. The police station wasn't far away and she expected they would be on the scene quickly.

She looked for Theo. They should start tending to the injured victims.

She found him clambering up onto one of the concrete planter pots to peer into the driver's car window. The window was cracked and he punched it, knocking it in, before reaching his hand inside.

Molly peered through the rear window of the car. She could see the driver slumped over the wheel. He was covered in white powder from the airbag, bleeding from the head. Theo was feeling for a pulse. She couldn't see a passenger on the other side of the car. That didn't mean there wasn't one, but the car was jammed tight between the planter pots and the building. There was no way of opening a door. No way of getting to anyone inside.

Theo climbed down from the car. 'He's alive but unconscious,' he said as they heard sirens in the distance.

'Could you see anyone else in the car?' Molly asked.

Theo shook his head as a young man emerged from the rubble at their feet. Theo grabbed him under his armpits and helped him stand. He was covered in blood and dust.

'You have to help me. My girlfriend is in there,' he said, pointing back under the building. 'She's trapped under the car.'

Molly saw Theo's quick glance in the direction of the car. 'Is she conscious? Breathing?' he asked.

Molly knew he was really asking if the girl was alive.

'I don't know.' Tears spilt from the man's eyes, making muddy streaks through the dirt on his face. 'Her leg is trapped; I can't get her out.'

'What's her name?' Theo asked as Molly put a hand on the man's arm, offering comfort through touch but feeling that was all too inadequate given the circumstances.

'Bree.'

Theo dropped to his knees and before Molly could

ask what he was doing he had crawled under the car and into the rubble.

Molly's eyes widened. What on earth was he doing?

The veranda posts creaked and groaned and dropped another couple of inches.

What was he thinking? He was putting himself in danger. For what? What did he think he would be able to do? He couldn't move the car.

Her heart was in her throat as she sent up a silent plea in the hope someone or something was listening.

God, please let him be okay. Get him out before he gets hurt. Before anything else goes wrong.

She rested her right hand on her stomach, subconsciously shielding her baby from harm. She knew it was a reflex action, instinctive, protective. She knew her baby was okay, but her baby's father was a different matter.

Staring at the black hole into which Theo had disappeared, she knew she'd made a mistake. She'd been an idiot. So fixated on maintaining her independence, her control, that she was risking everything.

She wanted Theo in her life. She *needed* him in her life. Not just for their child's sake. But for hers.

Molly was quite prepared to be a single mother. She had no issue with raising a child on her own or making independent decisions but, confronted with the reality of the danger Theo had put himself in, she realised her plan had a few flaws. She was quite prepared to raise a child as a single mother, but she wasn't prepared for her child not to have a father at all.

Now that Theo was in danger, she realised she didn't want to think of a world without him.

She didn't want to live without him. He made her happy. He made her a better person and she liked who she was when she was with him. Why was she refusing to accept that? Why was she resisting taking a chance on a serious relationship?

She admitted it would be difficult if he was in Sydney. *She'd* made this difficult. Not impossible, but not as easy as it could have been.

What if he was right? What if she could have commitment and independence? What if she could have a relationship with him without losing her identity? Without losing control?

It had to be worth a try.

She made a promise to herself. If, when, he came back to her they would have a conversation. They would make a new plan. She would tell him how she felt.

And if she lost him?

She shook her head to clear her thoughts. She couldn't think about that now. She needed something else to think about. Something other than Theo and the danger he'd put himself in. She turned to the young man who still stood beside her. She would let him distract her from her worries about Theo.

He was pale, his eyes were wide and he was starting to shake. He was in shock.

Molly turned to one of the bystanders. 'We need a blanket,' she said. 'Can you see if any of the restaurants have something we could borrow?'

The street was full of bars and restaurants and most had outdoor seating. Molly knew they would have blankets to ward off the chill on the odd cool night.

She turned back to the young man. 'What's your name?' she asked.

'Josh.'

'Josh, my name is Molly. I'm a doctor. I think you should sit down.' She guided him away from the crash site, not far away, just away from the damaged veranda. She didn't want to put him at risk if there was a further collapse. She got him to sit on the edge of the footpath with his feet in the gutter and wrapped the blanket around his shoulders when someone brought it to her.

'Are you hurt?' she asked as she sat beside him. He didn't appear to have sustained any major injuries. She could see a few abrasions and he had blood on his hands, but she wasn't sure whose blood it was.

He shook his head. 'But Bree—' His voice cracked and he couldn't finish his sentence.

'My friend who's gone to Bree, he's a doctor as well,' Molly told him, hoping that gave him some reassurance. She had to raise her voice as the emergency vehicles turned into the street with their sirens blaring. As the police cars, fire engines and ambulances pulled to a stop the sirens were switched off, but their flashing red and blue lights lent an eerie air to the scene.

Molly stood up to introduce herself as a policewoman approached.

'Do you need assistance?' the policewoman asked.

'No. Josh's injuries are minor, and the driver of the car was alive immediately after the accident, but my colleague—' Her voice caught as she thought about Theo. 'My colleague couldn't get to him so we don't know the extent of his injuries. We think he was alone in the car but we're not certain.'

'Where is your colleague?'

Molly pointed at the car. 'He's gone in there. There's a young woman, this man's girlfriend, trapped under the car. We don't know if there are any others.' She could see other people with bloodied heads, bloodied hands and torn and dirty clothes, but she didn't know if there were any others unaccounted for.

The policewoman nodded. 'Okay, thanks for the information.'

As she turned to leave, Molly stopped her. 'Can you take Josh to the paramedics? He's in shock and needs someone to keep an eye on him. I need to wait here.' Molly could have done it, but she wasn't leaving until she knew Theo was safe.

She paced up and down the edge of the road, her eyes glued to the crash site, willing Theo to reappear. Hadn't he heard the sirens? Didn't he know the cavalry had arrived? He could come out now, let the emergency services crew do their jobs.

Finally, he emerged.

'Theo, thank God.' Molly hurried to his side and threw her arms around him.

Over Theo's shoulder Molly saw a paramedic heading towards them. He'd obviously seen Theo emerge from the debris and assumed he was injured.

'I'm fine,' Theo said when the paramedic touched him on the arm. 'I wasn't caught up in the accident. I'm a doctor. There's a young woman trapped in the rubble and I went in to see if I could help her.'

'She's alive?'

Theo nodded. 'Barely.' He kept his voice low and Molly could see him looking around the crowd, searching for Josh.

'Her boyfriend is in one of the ambulances,' Molly told him.

Theo nodded again and gestured to a policeman and called him over. He didn't let go of Molly—was he supporting her or did he need reassurance as well? Molly tucked herself against his side, not willing to be separated from him.

'The car has pinned her against the wall of the building. She's trapped by her legs.' Theo addressed the paramedic. 'The car seems to have missed her abdomen and vital organs but I suspect she's losing blood from somewhere. Her pulse and respiration are elevated and she's drifting in and out of consciousness. It's going to be difficult and time-consuming to free her. She might not survive long enough to be freed and if she does then the process of releasing her could still prove fatal. Falling blood pressure is a major concern. I think we should have an air ambulance on standby. She's going to need to be transferred to a major hospital in Brisbane or Sydney.'

Theo turned to the policeman. 'And the veranda will have to be secured before we move the car.'

The policeman nodded. 'We've called in the engineers and the fire brigade will try to stabilise the structure while we wait. We need to clear the area now.'

'Come on, you need to get warmed up.' Theo was speaking to Molly now. She was still tucked against his side but she hadn't realised she was shaking. She hadn't realised she was cold.

Theo took her hand in his and led her away from the chaos and the trauma. There was nothing more they could do now. It was going to take some time to plan, prepare and complete the rescue and retrieval and emergency services were now in charge. 'Will you come back to my place?'

Molly nodded. She didn't want to be alone. She needed company. She needed to hold Theo, to feel that he was okay, unharmed and in one piece.

She held tight to Theo's hand. She thought it might be the only thing keeping her upright. Adrenalin continued to course through her system, making her legs shaky. Fear tainted her voice as she asked, 'What on earth did you think you were doing, going into that situation?'

Theo looked at her for a moment before he responded. 'There might have been something I could do. I had to try. All I could think of was what if that had been you trapped in there? Alone. Injured. What if I could make a difference? Imagine how terrifying it would be to be alone in a situation like that.'

Molly didn't have to imagine. She knew the level of fear. 'But it *was* you in there—I can imagine. What if you hadn't come out again?'

'But I did. I'm fine. Now we just have to hope that Bree will be too.'

'I need a shower,' Theo said as he unlocked his front door. He was still holding Molly's hand. He hadn't let go since they'd left the accident site, and she hadn't wanted him to. He stepped into the bathroom, taking her with him, and turned the taps on, running the shower.

Molly sat on the closed toilet lid as Theo fiddled with the taps, adjusting the temperature. She looked properly at him now and realised he was filthy. She hadn't noticed, she hadn't been paying attention to his clothes, she'd just been grateful that he was okay.

The bathroom was filling with steam, the fog reminiscent of the cloud of dust that had engulfed the crash site. Molly shivered as the memory tore back into her consciousness.

'I think you should have a shower too,' Theo said. 'It'll be the quickest way to warm you up.'

Molly could barely speak but she wasn't cold any more—she was numb. Frightened. Terrified. She still hadn't recovered from the idea that she could have lost him. She was well aware that he was leaving, which meant she was going to lose him in one form, but losing him to Sydney was better than losing him altogether.

Theo took her hand and helped her to her feet. As the mirror clouded with fog he began to gently remove her clothes. He unzipped her dress and Molly lifted her arms, letting him slide it over her head. The room was warm, thick with steam and moisture. He squatted down, running his hands down the length of her legs to undo the laces on her sneakers. She lifted one foot, then the other, as he slid her shoes from her feet.

His hands were on her hips now, warm against her skin. A tingle of awareness and anticipation surged through her as Theo slipped his fingers under the elastic of her underwear and pushed it from her hips. He stood up and moved behind her to undo the clasp on her bra. He wrapped his arms around her and his hands cupped her breasts. Her breasts were full and heavy, already changed by her pregnancy. His fingers ran over her nipple and it peaked immediately under his touch. Her breasts were far more sensitive than normal too. Another side-effect of her raging hormones.

Molly's knees trembled and Theo held her up with one arm around her waist. He half lifted her and helped her into the shower.

Molly pressed a hand into the tiled wall to support herself and let the hot water run over her as she watched Theo get undressed. His clothes were filthy and one leg on his cotton chinos was torn. In contrast his chest, when he removed his shirt, was smooth and tanned and clean. He kicked off his shoes and stepped out of his ripped trousers and underwear in one movement.

When he was naked Molly reached her hand out to him and pulled him under the water with her.

He cupped his hand at the back of her neck, sliding his fingers through her hair, and pulled her to him. He bent his head and covered her lips with his. His lips were soft and Molly sighed and leant into him as she opened her mouth. She parted her lips and let his tongue explore her mouth.

Her hands skimmed over his naked buttocks. They were tight and firm and warm under her fingers. She pulled him towards her, pressing her stomach against his erection. She wanted him closer. Needed him closer.

Her breasts, plump and ripe, flattened against his chest. She arched her back and her breasts sprang free.

Theo cradled one in the palm of his hand as he ran his thumb over her nipple. A throaty moan escaped from her lips as she tipped her head back and broke their kiss.

She reached down and wrapped her hand around his shaft. It throbbed under her touch, springing to life, infused with blood. She could feel every beat of his heart repeated under her fingers.

He ducked his head and took one breast in his mouth as Molly clung to him. His tongue flicked over her nipple, sending needles of desire shooting down to the junction between her thighs. It felt amazing but she wanted more. She was desperate for more.

She held onto his shoulders and arched her back as she thrust her hips towards him. His fingers slid inside her, rubbing the sensitive bud that nestled between her thighs. Her knees were shaking. She was incapable of thinking. She was far too busy feeling. Her body was a quivering mass of nerve endings, her senses heightened, touch, taste and smell being flooded with information courtesy of Theo's lips and fingers.

'I don't think I can stand any longer,' she panted. She was barely able to find the breath to speak. 'You'll have to hold me.'

He scooped her up in one easy motion and she spread her legs, eager to welcome him. She felt the tip of his erection nudge between her legs as she wrapped her thighs around his waist. She heard him sigh as he plunged into her.

She enveloped him as he thrust into her warmth.

God, that felt good.

She moaned as he pushed deeper.

'I'm not hurting you?'

'No.' The word was a sigh, one syllable on a breath of air.

She closed her eyes as she rode him, bucking her hips against his, her back arched. She was completely oblivious to everything except the feel of him inside her as she offered herself to him. His face was buried into her neck and she tipped her head back as he thrust into her, bringing them to their peak.

'Oh, God, Molly, that feels incredible.'

Hearing her name on his lips was her undoing. Her name had never sounded so sweet and she had never felt so desired. She gave herself up to him and as he exploded into her she joined him, quivering in his arms as she climaxed.

He kissed her forehead and her lips and held her close until she stopped shaking.

Molly was lying in Theo's arms. She was emotionally spent from the events of the evening and physically exhausted after their lovemaking, but she couldn't sleep. She lay in the dark and listened to Theo breathing. It was a sound she didn't think she would ever tire of.

She didn't want to lose him. How would she find her happily ever after once he was gone? Would their baby fill that void? She didn't think so. A baby and a partner were two very different things. She'd told Theo she was happy being single, that she was working on herself, that she didn't want a partner, but she knew now that she wanted Theo. She still didn't want to be married but that didn't rule out something more serious with Theo.

She thought she might be falling in love with him. That was unexpected but not as frightening as she might have once thought.

Should she tell him how she was feeling? No. She didn't want to be the one to take the risk. She'd told Daniel she loved him once. He hadn't said it back. She wasn't prepared to go through that pain again.

'Are you awake?' she asked.

'Yes.'

'Are you thinking about the accident? About Bree?'

'In a roundabout way. I'm thinking about our baby. About how life is short. What if something had happened to me today? I know you were worried. I should have thought about that before I rushed into trying to be a hero. If something had gone wrong I would have left you and the baby alone. I know you said you're happy to be a single mother but I don't want to be an absent father. I want to be around for our child. My father lived in the same house as me and I barely saw him. I can't stand the thought of being in Sydney if you and our child are here.'

Molly held her breath and hoped he wasn't going to ask her to move again. She didn't want to say goodbye to him, but she knew he would be gone in less than a week. And that was her doing. She had said she wouldn't move to Sydney. She'd told him she wanted to make her own decisions. But now she thought that perhaps they could have compromised, but she wasn't sure how or what she could have done. How were they going to make long-distance parenting work?

'What if I stayed here?' Theo said.

'Here?'

'Yes.'

Her heart had leapt with hope at his suggestion until reality swiftly kicked in. 'But you're supposed to be taking over your mother's business.'

'I might be able to do that from here.'

'Why would you do that?'

'Being around for my child is more important than living in Sydney. If you want to live in Byron Bay, that's where I'll be. I'm not prepared to walk away from my responsibility to my child.'

She had been terrified that she was going to lose him tonight when he'd disappeared under the building. She couldn't imagine her life without him in it. She'd be happy if he stayed but what would that mean for them?

'And what about us?' she asked. The baby was tying them together but what would have happened to them if she weren't pregnant? Was it a relationship that could have survived or would it have run its course with time?

'I'm not saying we have to be in a relationship, although I acknowledge we will have one of sorts because of our child, but what if we could have more than a summer romance?' he said. 'A proper relationship.'

'But not marriage?' Marriage was still a step too far. She wasn't prepared to give up her independence and that was how she viewed marriage. From her experience it wasn't a partnership. It involved compromise, she understood that, but from her experience one person always compromised more than the other. Theo hadn't said he loved her. If she let herself fall in love with him, she knew she would be the one to compromise. She would be the one with everything to lose.

'No,' he agreed. 'We can keep seeing each other but without pressure, without expectation. We need to find a way forward. Together. But we don't need to figure it all out tonight. We've got eight months to work out how we're going to navigate this. I just need to know if it's an idea you'd consider. If you'd be okay if I stayed?'

'Yes,' she said. 'I would.' She'd be more than okay with that. 'I think we should see what happens.'

'My mother is back in the country tomorrow after her conference. I'll call her tomorrow night and put my proposal to her.'

CHAPTER TEN

'I CAN'T BELIEVE you've done this.' Theo was on the phone to his mother. He'd called to discuss the possibility of him staying on in Byron Bay, he hadn't mentioned Molly or the pregnancy—that was a conversation best had face to face—but she had completely blindsided him with news of her own. And the news wasn't good. 'You didn't think to tell me?'

'No. It was my decision and it was too good an opportunity to pass up.'

'When are you going to tell the staff?' he asked.

'I thought you could do it tomorrow before you come back to Sydney. You won't be staying in Byron Bay now.'

'You want *me* to tell them?'

'Yes. Making tough calls is part and parcel of management. If you're going to take over the practice one day you need to be able to have these conversations. To take responsibility. Think of it as a learning experience.'

Theo wasn't sure he wanted the responsibility or the experience. In his opinion he was going to be the bearer of bad tidings without having any input into the decision. But he knew there wasn't much he could do. The decision had been made.

All his plans were unravelling.

* * *

Theo felt sick. His mother's news had cost him a night with Molly. He couldn't face her last night, not with this decision hanging over his head, and he'd made an excuse, told her a lie, and now he was hoping she didn't find out. He knew a lack of trust was a deal breaker for her.

He was the first person to arrive for the fortnightly Monday morning staff meeting. He wanted to make sure he had time to gather his thoughts and run through his announcement. No, not his announcement, his mother's.

He smiled at Molly when she arrived, only marginally late, but his smile felt forced. He then avoided looking at her, knowing he would have difficulty getting through the announcement if he caught her eye. He knew he would see disappointment in her expression.

'Most of you know that my mother, Lian Chin, is the owner of Pacific Coast Clinics. She has some news that she has asked me to pass on. It affects all of you. Some of you know that this clinic hasn't been performing as well as expected recently and Lian has decided that the Byron Bay clinic is no longer a required part of the business portfolio, and she has sold the property and is going to offer the practice as an ongoing concern to any potential purchasers.'

'What? We're losing our jobs?'

He could tell Gemma was incensed, but part of him was glad that it was Gemma who had spoken up. He wasn't game to meet Molly's gaze yet. 'The clinic will be offered as an ongoing concern, but the purchaser would have to find new premises. This site has been sold to developers.' He knew that financially the sale of the building made sense. It was a large landholding, on a corner site in the centre of town. But the decision did not sit well with him morally. 'We're hoping to find someone who wants to take the practice and the staff on.'

'And if you don't?'

'We've got three months before the site needs to be vacated. I'm hopeful that will give everyone time to find another job if we don't find a buyer for the clinic.' Theo's stomach felt as if it were lined with lead. He couldn't believe he was imparting this news and, by the look on the faces of everyone in the room, nether could they. 'I'm sorry, there's not much more I can tell you, but I'm happy to answer any questions that you might have, if I can.'

The room was silent. Nobody had anything to say. They were all stunned. Theo had been feeling included, feeling comfortable, as a member of staff, but that had all changed within the space of a few minutes, several sentences and one decision.

'I'll let you discuss this news among yourselves. You're welcome to ask me anything you need to throughout the day.' He thought the best course of action would be to leave the room and give them freedom to discuss the announcement without him present but as he headed for the door he saw Molly rise from her chair.

'Theo.' She had followed him from the room.

She closed the door behind her. 'What the hell was that all about?'

'I'm sorry, Molly.'

'You're sorry? We're going to lose our jobs and you're sorry! How long have you known about this?'

'I only found out last night. When I called Mum to discuss staying here.'

Molly laughed. 'Really. Did you ever actually intend to stay here?'

Theo frowned. 'Of course. We talked about it.'

'We talked about a lot of things. We talked about the practice and the issues it was facing. We gave you suggestions. Did you even discuss those with your mother or was this a done deal?'

'We discussed it, but she felt that selling the building made the most sense financially.'

'I thought you agreed medicine was about more than money.'

'I do. But this was her decision. I'm as upset by this as you are.'

'I don't think so. This doesn't affect you nearly as much. It's not your livelihood at stake. You have a job in Sydney.'

'What do you mean? I'm staying here.'

'Not on my account, you're not.'

'What does that mean?'

'You know how much this job means to me. This place. These people. I won't be manipulated into moving to Sydney. I can't believe you've done this to me.'

'I haven't done anything to you. And no one is asking you to move to Sydney. I was going to stay here. Why would I do that if I knew there was going to be no job? For either of us.'

'I don't think you should stay here. I think you should go back to Sydney. I think our relationship, for want of a better word, is done,' she said before she spun around and walked off, leaving him standing alone in the corridor.

The sun was shining on Sydney Harbour and it was a picture-perfect summer's day, but Theo was oblivious to his surroundings as he made his way across the city. His heart ached. He'd lost everything. Molly blamed him and he couldn't argue with her. In her eyes he'd taken everything from her and having him in her life was not enough of a consolation prize. He wasn't wanted.

He kept his head down as he walked through the clinic to his mother's office. He wasn't in the mood to make polite small talk with any of the staff. He was frustrated, heartbroken and angry. He knocked on Lian's door, his irritation manifesting in short sharp taps, loud and unapologetic. His mother owed him some more information.

'Why didn't you tell me you'd had an offer on the property before I went up to Byron?' he asked, barely able to manage a cordial greeting before launching into the root of his aggravation.

'Because I hadn't. The offer only came through once you were already there.'

'You still could have told me,' he argued. 'I thought you wanted me to look at options to make the clinic profitable and I thought we'd come up with some good ideas.'

'Many of those suggestions had merit,' Lian agreed, 'but some would have required quite a bit of capital investment. Once I got the offer to sell that made the most sense from a financial perspective as well as a time perspective. It was a lot of money tied up in the land. The site was worth far more as a development site. It didn't make financial sense to keep it.'

Try telling that to the staff, Theo felt like saying, though he knew that opinion wouldn't do him any favours.

'Can I ask why you bought the practice to begin with? Did it make financial sense at the time?' he asked.

'I wanted to expand, and I looked to invest in Byron Bay as it was a growth area, and I thought it might be a good option for retirement, but then I realised it's just a bit too far away to keep an eye on easily and your father and I decided we didn't actually want to retire, or even semi-retire, to Byron Bay. We like Sydney, our friends are here and it's convenient. It was a mistake to buy it.'

Theo's eyebrows shot up.

'What is it?' Lian asked when she saw his expression.

Theo shook his head. 'I've never heard you say you've made a mistake.'

'I've made a few,' Lian replied. 'But I hope I've learnt something from each one. If you can fix it or learn from it, it can be a positive. A mistake isn't a problem unless you repeat it.'

And that was when Theo realised that he'd made a mistake. And he'd made it twice.

Twice he'd walked away from Molly.

He'd let her down, unintentionally it had to be said, but that didn't change the fact that he hadn't supported her. He hadn't fought for her and he was ashamed of himself.

She'd pushed him away because he'd broken her trust and he couldn't blame her for that. He recognised that, for all her talk of independence, it was her fear of being let down that had led her to strive for that in the first instance. If she didn't depend on anyone she wouldn't be disappointed. His fears of rejection, of not being deemed good enough, had caused him to walk away, believing she didn't want him, only Molly had taken that to believe that he wasn't someone she could rely on. When what she really wanted was to be able to depend on someone. On him.

He should have fought harder for her.

He should have stayed.

His mother's words resonated with him. About mistakes but also about retirement. About finding somewhere to slow down. About Byron Bay.

That was where he should be. He'd found peace, acceptance and happiness there. With Molly. He could imagine growing old there. With Molly. And that was where he wanted to be, not in forty years' time but right now. With Molly.

The woman he loved.

He loved her.

He should never have left her.

Was it possible that together they could overcome their fears? That they could be stronger together?

Was it too late to win her back? Too late to tell her how he felt? Too late to make amends?

He had to try. He'd already lost everything. There was nothing more to lose.

He knew what he had to do.

'I have a proposal for you,' he said to his mother.

Molly stood beneath the lighthouse, a solitary figure, alone with her thoughts. She was up before sunrise, unable to sleep, but her eyes were closed now. She was leaning on the railing, facing east, listening to the waves crashing onto the rocks below her. The sound reminded her of Theo. Rolling waves were the soundtrack of their lovemaking.

She opened her eyes, looking for something to distract her, something to take her mind off Theo, but the ocean was empty and the horizon was only just beginning to glow.

It was Christmas Eve and he'd been gone for almost a week. Her heart ached. He'd broken it, smashed it, but she would have to find a way to deal with that, to deal with him, because even though he was gone, even though she had sent him away, there was no escape. He was the father of her unborn child and she knew that would connect them for ever.

Had she expected too much from him?

She hadn't expected to fall in love and that was when her expectations had changed. She'd said she wanted independence but then she'd changed her mind but hadn't told him. That was hardly his fault.

A life with Theo had, for a brief time, been what she wanted but depending on someone else frightened her, so much that she'd taken the first opportunity presented to her to push him away. By accusing him of letting her down, she'd sacrificed their relationship for her independence at the first hurdle.

Had she been too quick to judge? Should she have tried harder to work things through?

Had she made a mistake?

Maybe, but now she was stuck with the consequences

of her actions. Stuck with having to co-parent with Theo without being with him.

She'd acted hastily and she was as much to blame for the situation as he was. But that didn't lessen her heartache.

Would her heart ache so much if she weren't still in love with him? Unfortunately for her she couldn't turn love off like a tap. She had banished Theo but she couldn't banish her feelings and now she'd just have to find a way to manage. Given time, she might be able to do that.

She had thirty-five weeks until her due date. That might be enough time.

Or it might not.

With a little effort she pushed thoughts of Theo to one side. There were more pressing issues to deal with right now. She needed to get on with her life. The future she'd pictured briefly with Theo had changed completely. She needed to do something about finding a new job. She couldn't afford to wait. She was going to be a single mother; she needed to be settled into a job before she had the baby. She needed her new employer to find her invaluable. Her priority had to be her baby. Her heartache would ease and she'd eventually work out how to co-parent with Theo.

She turned south, looking away from the horizon towards the road leading to the lighthouse, imagining, over the sound of the waves and the seagulls, that someone was calling her name. She didn't expect to see anyone, she assumed it must be a trick of the wind, so she was surprised to see a familiar figure jogging up the path.

Her heart rate quickened as her body betrayed her.

Theo.

He slowed his pace as he approached her. Was he unsure of his reception? His dark eyes showed signs of fatigue—had he been sleeping poorly too? She curled her hand into a fist, forcing herself not to reach out to him, not to smooth the worry lines from his face. She wasn't the person to console him any more.

He stopped in front of her. Just out of reach. His eyes dark with apprehension.

'What are you doing here?' she asked.

'Looking for you.' His answer was matter-of-fact but his voice was soft and filled with longing and Molly's heart lifted with hope.

He was looking at her closely, his gaze intense, and she felt the familiar and not unpleasant sensation of her insides melting, turning to warm treacle. 'How are you?'

Molly almost laughed. His question was so brief, so minuscule compared to her feelings. She was devastated over what she'd lost, feeling sorry for herself and also annoyed that her first reaction to seeing Theo had been pleasure, but she didn't tell him that. 'I'm fine.' She could do brief.

'And the baby?'

His question brought a half-smile to her lips. 'The baby is the size of a sesame seed.' She was only five weeks pregnant. She knew the baby would be getting facial features now—eyes and a nose—it was developing into a tiny human, but it was still tiny.

'I know, but I've missed a week.' He shrugged. His tone wasn't accusatory, which was just as well. His banishment was his own fault. 'It's felt like a lifetime.'

She heard the heartache in his words but he had only himself to blame for that. Her heart was aching too. She didn't want to cover old ground so she repeated her question. 'What are you doing here?'

'I need to talk to you.'

'I'm not sure there's anything we need to discuss.' Her heart was bruised, her pride dented, her trust broken and the pain made her tone sharp.

'Please,' he begged her, 'can we sit down? Can you give me five minutes? It's important.'

The sun was only just starting to peek above the horizon. Molly had nowhere else to be and, she couldn't deny it, suddenly nowhere else she wanted to be. She nodded and let Theo lead her to a bench against the lighthouse wall. She sat and folded her arms across her stomach, keeping her distance, knowing if she let him touch her she'd be in danger of believing anything he said.

He reached for her but withdrew his hands as she crossed her arms. 'It may make no difference to what happens next, but it's important that you know this,' he said. 'I know you think I colluded with my mother, but I promise you she made all the decisions regarding the practice. I'm not trying to shift the blame to her. I'm telling you the truth. She didn't consult me about the sale. I knew nothing of it until twelve hours before I told all the staff.'

Hope died in Molly's heart. Had he come back just to rehash business matters? She admitted to herself she'd been wanting more, hoping for something personal. Hoping he'd missed her as much as she'd missed him. She sighed inwardly. He'd asked about the baby—was that the best she could expect? 'Why hadn't your mother told you about the sale earlier?'

'Apparently she only received that offer from the developers when she was overseas at the conference.'

'And you believe her?'

Theo nodded. 'I've seen the emails.'

'Why didn't you say anything to me as soon as you found out? Why didn't you give me some warning?'

'I didn't know how to tell you. I was afraid of what it might mean.'

'Did you even try to talk her out of it? We came up with lots of options—did you even discuss any of those with her? Did you try to fight for us?'

Theo nodded. 'I did but the reality was the offer to sell was too good to refuse. I agreed with her on that.'

Molly opened her mouth to interject.

'But I disagreed with her next move of giving up the practice entirely,' Theo continued, as if knowing what Molly was about to say. 'The town needs the clinic. She should have considered that and realised that not every health practitioner wants to run their own practice. She could have handled that better. This whole situation has taught me a few more things about my mother and myself. It was a unilateral decision and when I questioned her she told me it was hers to make. I know she intends for me to take over the business one day but the way this decision was made makes me question whether she will ever really let go. Whether the clinics will ever be mine to run as I choose. But I think I have found a solution.'

'Which is?' Molly's voice was flat. She was going through the motions, feigning polite interest, responding to Theo's words, when in reality she wanted to know if he'd really come back just to talk about work.

'I'm going to take over the Byron Bay clinic. I'll need to find another site but I'm going to keep it going. My way. Our way.'

'Our way?'

'I understand none of this might make any difference to how you feel about me, but I want to be here. I want to be where my child is. I don't want to be a part-time father. I'm not walking away again. I want to be here, with you. I want us to do this together.'

'Do what exactly?' Molly asked.

'Work together.'

'You want me to work in the clinic? Your new clinic?' What was wrong with men? Which part of independence didn't he get? Did he think that she would be grateful to have a job? She would, that much was true, but she wasn't going to work for him.

'I know how important your job is to you,' he said. 'How much you love the town. You want financial independence, job security and to be able to stay here. I think my solution gives us both what we're looking for.'

'But you'll still control my fate. My employment. I don't want to be controlled by anyone.'

Theo shook his head. 'I want you to work in the clinic if that's what you choose, but not as an employee. I want to make you a partner in the business. I want you to have the independence you need.'

'A partnership?'

Theo nodded.

'I can't afford to buy into a practice,' she told him. A

business partnership was appealing but she didn't even have money for a lawyer to draw up a contract, let alone money to start a business.

'It will be my gift to you.'

Molly frowned. 'A gift? You'd do that for me?' She tilted her head as she considered him. What did he want in exchange? she wondered.

'Yes. I want you to know you can trust me, but I thought a physical commitment would give you protection, a guarantee. No one will be able to take it away from you.'

Theo's eyes were dark and solemn, almost begging her to believe him. To trust him. Could she? She wanted to—desperately. 'Is that all you want?'

He shook his head. 'Not quite.'

She knew there would be more. There was always more.

'I want to raise our child together, not as two single parents but as a couple. I want to be in a relationship with you, if you'll have me. I made a mistake leaving here. I made a mistake leaving you. I don't want to give up on you, on us. I want to give you the world and I want to make a life with you. I want a family, people I can love without reservation. I love you, Molly.'

'You love me?' That wasn't the addition she was expecting. Once upon a time, just ten days ago, it was the extra piece she was hoping for but she'd let go of that dream. Now her heart leapt with hope.

'I love you.'

She heard the catch of emotion in his voice as he repeated his words. He loved her.

Could she possibly have everything she'd dared to dream of?

'I love you,' he repeated for the third time. He shook his head as if he couldn't believe it himself. 'I've never said that to anyone before.'

'Have you never been in love?' she asked.

'Once. With an amazing girl,' he said, and Molly steeled herself for what was coming next. 'She was bright and beautiful and she could light up a room. And I'm still in love with her. It's you, Molly. It's always been you.'

Molly's heart soared as she broke into a smile. She'd almost convinced herself that she didn't need anyone, that she didn't need him, but she knew that wasn't true. He loved her. And she loved him.

She had sacrificed their relationship for her independence only to realise that wasn't what she wanted after all. But now Theo was offering her everything. Independence along with a commitment and, best of all, his love, and she knew she wanted to make the same promise to Theo. She wanted to be his.

She reached for his hands as she said, 'I love you too. I didn't want to fall in love, but I can't resist you. I can't live without you. When you went into that collapsed building and I thought I might lose you that was the worst moment of my life. I realised I'd fallen in love with you, but then I thought you let me down and I convinced myself that I was better off without you in my life. I jumped to conclusions and I'm sorry. I'd been so afraid that you'd let me down that I made myself believe you had, just to prove myself right, just to make my expectations real, but I've been miserable. I've missed you. I've missed you so much.' She paused before finally uttering the words she needed to say. 'I love you too.'

Theo was beaming, his gorgeous grin stretching widely across his beautiful face. The morning sun fell on his face, turning his skin golden and making his dark eyes shine. He gathered her to him, wrapping his arms around her, and Molly lost herself in his embrace.

'What do you think?' he asked. 'Let's spend Christmas Day together and the next day and the next, and then we can celebrate a new year together and create a life for ourselves here where we can be happy. We'll have our work, our family, we'll have each other. Will you be my partner? In work and life?'

Molly sat back. She needed to clarify exactly what he was asking. 'Does your version of family look like a traditional one? I will be your partner, we will be a family, but I don't want to get married. Not yet. Maybe not ever. But that doesn't mean I don't love you. I want to be with you. I don't want anyone else, but marriage isn't for me. Can you live with that?'

'I won't deny that I would marry you in a heartbeat,' Theo replied, 'but, married or not, it won't affect how much I love you or our child. Married or not, I will still try to be the best partner, the best father, I can be. I'll be happy if I can wake up beside you every day. I want to spend the rest of my life with you. I love you and a wedding ring won't change that. I will love you just the same.'

The lighthouse towered above them, but Molly was oblivious to its beauty. All her focus was on the man in front of her. The love of her life. She was smiling now as she pulled Theo towards her.

'Then, yes, let's do this. Today, tomorrow and the next day. You and me together,' she said, before she kissed him with all her heart and soul. 'I love you.'

* * * * *

PARAMEDIC'S FLING
TO FOREVER

SUE MacKAY

MILLS & BOON

To Auntie Joc. Thank you for all the
wonderful memories. Love, Susan.

PROLOGUE

'HI. MIND IF I sit here?'

Leesa Bennett looked up at the guy standing in front of her with a beer in his hand and nodded. 'Sure.'

She was hardly going to say no when this was a communal party, in the park next to the apartment block where she lived. Though only for one more week before she was on the road heading north, home to Cairns. Back to her family and the world she'd missed ever since coming to Brisbane with her ex. If only she had known what awaited her here, she'd never have packed one bag, let alone all her belongings, to move south.

'Thanks.' The newcomer's voice was deep and husky, and a dark beard covered his lower face. A sexy combination, if ever she'd seen one.

Gasping, she swallowed a large mouthful of gin from her can and promptly coughed. Sexy? Definitely. But she didn't usually get in a twist about a hot-looking man. Didn't get in a twist at all these days, especially about men. One too many had made her life hell to be letting any others close.

'Easy.' A steady hand patted her back.

'Thanks.'

She sat up straighter and took a smaller sip. The guy

wasn't familiar to her, but then she didn't know everyone living in the block or attending the barbecue, which had been organised by the apartment tenants' committee. He hadn't been helping the other men cooking the steaks and sausages, but not all the men had. There wouldn't have been room.

'Did you have some food?' she asked.

'No.'

Not a great talker then. Suited her. She was feeling low and not in the mood for idle chatter, especially with a stranger. Even a sexy one.

There she went again. Sexy. Showed how long it was since she'd let her hair down and had some fun with a guy. Was it time to do so?

Now that she was finally leaving Brisbane it was dawning on her how she was closing a chapter of her life. A chapter that had been tough and full of hurt and that she was ready to leave behind. Still, she felt sad. The earlier dreams she'd had, of a wonderful marriage and a new life in an exciting city, had all turned into a nightmare.

She'd left her husband after accepting that he would never stop bullying her, even when she stood up to him. After being bullied at school, she knew there was only one way to go with Connor and that was to leave him. He'd get worse as time went on, not better. He'd tried to deny her a divorce, saying they had too much to lose and that he loved her to the end of the earth and back. So why demand she make the bed with hospital folds like his mother used to, and expect roast lamb for dinner every Tuesday, and make her wash the car on Saturday mornings even if she had to go to work? The list went on, but she'd put it behind her when she left him.

Only to end up working with another bully who thought he could tell all the female staff at the ambulance base what to do and when. Not the men. Oh, no, they were free to sit back and let the women clean the ambulances and re-stock everything. Not that any of them did, but that wasn't the point. That prat hadn't counted on her having already learned how to deal with someone like him. When he'd sacked her for standing up to him, she'd fought her dismissal with management and won, because they'd heard rumours about the man's attitude. After that she went on to stick up for the others he bullied and, in the end, he was the one to leave with his tail firmly between his legs.

Despite everything that had gone down over the last two years, in some ways she was sorry to be moving away. Brisbane was a great place to live, despite the feeling something was missing for her. She did have a great job lined up with the Flying Health Care service in Cairns, and spending more time with her family was high on her priority list, especially now her mother had been diagnosed with early-stage Parkinson's. Her grandmother's house was waiting for her, as Gran had moved into a retirement village and didn't want the house sold yet.

'You live in one of the apartments?' her companion asked.

'I do. A one-bedroom unit. It's great.' She watched some of the women dancing on the lawn to the music belting out from speakers hanging from trees. 'But I'm moving on in a few days, going back home to Cairns where my family are.'

'I've just moved up here.'

'So, you're not on holiday then?' She didn't really need

to know, but might as well keep the conversation ticking over and put her glum thoughts behind her.

He shook his head. 'No, I'm spending a couple of nights with a mate while I find somewhere permanent.' He drained his beer. 'I'm starting a new job in a couple of weeks.'

So, he could do talking when he chose. 'Doing what?'

'I'm a doctor. Going to work with the emergency service.'

'Right.' Small world. She decided not to mention she'd finished working in the same area one day ago. Her reputation went before her and, while most people thought she was great for helping her work mates face up to that prat, there were a few who thought she was nothing more than a troublemaker. 'Think I'll get another drink. Can I get you something?'

He stood up. 'I'll come with you.'

Not the answer she'd expected. He seemed reticent about talking too much, but he had sat with her so it could be he knew no one and wanted some company. She understood that. After all that had gone down over the last two years, she was cautious about who she talked to. People always took sides even when they didn't know the whole story.

That had been a major lesson she'd learned in all the turmoil. She used to be a slow learner, too willing to trust people even after being bullied at school. She hadn't recognised the signs when she married Connor. But she knew better now and was not going to hand over her heart so readily ever again, if at all.

'Grab some food while we're at it,' Leesa suggested.

'No, thanks.'

'Not into barbecues?'

Who wasn't? They were an Ozzie tradition.

His sigh hung between them. 'I had a big lunch.'

Okay, she'd shut up now. She might be feeling flat, but this was a party, and keeping quiet wasn't really her thing—not for long periods anyway. Digging into her chilly bin she grabbed another gin and popped the top.

'Who's your friend that lives here?' So she didn't know when to shut up after all. No surprise there.

At least he replied with a small smile, giving her a name she didn't recognise. 'Logan Brand. We met in med school.'

'I don't know if my apartment has been rented out yet, if you're interested. I'm on the tenth floor,' she added.

'I'll think about it.'

Taking a mouthful of her drink, she watched those who were dancing on the lawn and decided to join them. 'Into dancing by any chance?'

His eyes widened and he actually laughed. 'Yes, I am. Let's give it a whirl.' Without waiting for a reply, he took her arm and led her over to where people were shaking and wiggling, laughing uproariously about who knew what.

Leesa struggled to ignore the hot sensations his hand caused on her arm. Not only did he look sexy, he had a touch that sent her off balance. Blimey. So much for a quiet night. She was about to wiggle her ass in front of this guy. Best she went and sat down again.

Except they were already in the midst of the crowd and being jostled left and right. Her new friend's hand was now on her waist, making sure she didn't get nudged too far away from him. Moving in time to the music, she drank in the sight before her. Her companion might be quiet, but did he have the moves or what? Those firm hips swung all over the place, keeping a perfect rhythm to the music, while his feet were light on the ground and his upper body was a sight she couldn't ignore. She did try, but, hey, some things weren't meant to happen.

Settle, girl. You're leaving town in five days.

Yes, so why not have some no-strings fun with a sexy man?

Because she didn't usually hook up for one-night stands. That was why. Would it hurt to stretch the boundaries for once? Taking in the sight before her, it was hard to come up with an answer to that. Other than, 'Yes, go for it.'

'Why are you smiling so much?' he asked.

'Because I'm happy.' It was true. She really was. Gone was the sadness over this being the end of another phase of her life. Suddenly she felt there were opportunities out there she hadn't considered. Like letting go of her hang up over trusting a man not to demand her utmost attention all the time. She was probably overreacting because this man was hot, but did it matter? Tomorrow was another day. Tonight was to be enjoyed now. 'Nothing better than dancing.'

Nothing she was mentioning at any rate. He'd probably run away faster than a greyhound on the track. Even if he didn't, the last thing she wanted was him knowing what was going on in her mind, and other parts of her body.

He took her hand and whirled them around. 'Couldn't agree more.'

Thankfully he'd be thinking about the dancing and

would have no idea of the thoughts racing through her head. Fingers crossed.

Suddenly the music stopped mid-song. 'That's it, folks. It's midnight and as you know the council forbids music to be played in their parks after that.'

Leesa blinked. 'Where'd the time go?' She'd have sworn they had at least another hour to go. Went to show how much fun she'd been having dancing with Dr Sexy. What was his name? Did it matter? Dr Sexy suited him better than any other name she could come up with.

'Feel like another drink before you head upstairs?' he asked.

'Sounds good to me.' She had nothing important on in the morning so it didn't matter if she slept in.

'I'll get your chilly bin.' He sauntered across the grass, looking more at ease than when he'd first sat down beside her a couple of hours back.

Had she made him feel comfortable? Or had he just got over whatever had been keeping him quiet? Whatever. She liked him. She knew nothing about him, but that didn't matter. She was out of here on Wednesday and wouldn't be looking back, no matter what.

'Here you go.' He handed over a can and sat down beside her on the park bench, a beer in hand.

'Thanks.' She popped the can. 'Is your mate still here?'

'He and his girlfriend headed away to his apartment a little while go. I'm giving them some time alone.'

'You can come and checkout the apartment I'm in if you like.' *This late at night? Why not?*

He studied her intently. 'You sure? You don't know me.'

'You dance okay.' After dancing with him she really wanted to have some more fun.

A grin appeared. 'Then yes, I'll take a look at your place. I like the location and I know from my mate's apartment the place's kept in good shape.' So far, he was keeping to the script.

She could do that too. 'I've had no complaints in the time I've been here.'

'Which is how long?' He'd got a whole lot chattier. Must've liked her dance moves too.

When I left Connor.

'Over a year, give or take.' She stood up, suddenly restless. She wasn't into talking about her past. Plus, this man was attractive beyond reason, making it hard not to reach out and tuck herself into that amazing chest. Which would really have him thinking she was a fruit loop. Or a loose woman. Something she most definitely was not, but for some reason tonight she was ready to make the most of whatever this man had to offer. 'Let's go.'

'Give me your chilly bin.' He took it without waiting for an answer.

'Thank you.' Not that she'd have turned down his offer, even if the bin weighed less than a banana. It was nice being treated so well for a change. She had let her barriers down a little. Dr Sexy had been nothing but decent all evening. Throw in the growing need to have some me-time and he was getting more attractive by the minute.

In the crowded elevator Leesa found herself pressed firmly against his hard muscular body, liking every moment. His long body was a good fit. It wasn't often she felt comfortable with her height, but for once she did. Being taller than all the other girls at school had been another reason kids teased her. Apparently, girls were supposed to be slim and medium height. It had got better out in the adult world, but the sense of being different hadn't quite left her, especially when her ex had told her that she should be grateful he found her attractive.

As the lift became less packed at each floor Dr Sexy didn't move away, instead he stayed right beside her with his hand touching hers without actually holding it.

'Level ten,' intoned the metallic speaker.

They stepped out into the corridor. Without thinking she took her companion's hand, and didn't let go. His warmth felt so good she didn't care if this was a suggestive move. Which, come to think of it, it was. The realisation didn't change a thing. She couldn't remember ever feeling so relaxed but so fired up, her body melting on the inside for the first time in for ever. 'This way. My apartment's on the front of the building.'

He didn't drop her hand until they reached her door. Delving into her pocket for the key, she shivered. What was she doing? Showing this guy the apartment, or looking for that fun she wanted? Leesa's breathing stalled. He was watching her with the same need reflected in his deep blue eyes. Did she let him in? Or was this the opportunity to come to her senses and say goodnight?

'I can go if you'd prefer.'

His face was open and honest. The light beard covering his chin made her palms itch. Desire spiralled throughout her. Elbowing the door open she stepped inside. 'Come in.'

He followed her inside and closed the door quietly. Turning to face her, he said with a crooked smile that added to his sexiness, 'We haven't introduced ourselves. My name is Nick.'

Funny how they hadn't got around to mentioning names before. 'Leesa.' A lot of thumping was going on in her chest as she fell into those eyes. Beautiful. They stirred up her desire so it was now an eddy whirling from her mouth to her toes.

The chilly bin hit the floor with a soft thump as Nick reached for her, his hands on her shoulders pulling her close to that sensational body.

Slipping her arms around his neck she pressed into him, her breasts hard against his expansive chest, making her nipples tight as she lifted her mouth to his.

His sex was hard against her lower abdomen, telling her there was no doubt why he'd come up to her apartment. He wanted a first-hand view of the bedroom.

A view she was all too happy to share. But only when she'd had her fill of his kisses. He kissed like there was no tomorrow, devouring her while at the same time tender and teasing. She held him tighter, pushed closer and kissed him in return, giving way to the need taking over, going with him all the way until finally she had to have more.

Pulling back, she grabbed his hand. 'Come on.' Heading to her bedroom, she rued the fact she had to wait even seconds to get down and naked, but the condoms were in her bathroom cabinet in the ensuite. 'I need to get protection.'

'I've got some,' Nick told her.

'Cool.' A prepared man. She lifted her t-shirt over her head and dropped it on the floor. 'Then there's nothing to wait for.'

'You are in a hurry.'

She blinked. Did she sound too eager, when she rarely did something like this? 'Sorry.' Hello? Sounding like the girl who tried to placate people to keep them onside.

'Don't be.' Perfect answer. Nick touched her face so softly her eyes moistened. He really was special.

Better not let him get to her more than he already had. 'I'm not usually so fast to get this close to someone,' she whispered.

'Relax, Leesa. I'm not either. If you want to change your mind that's okay.'

'Hell no.' She was grinning like crazy. He really was awesome. She wasn't talking any more. His lips were soft as she kissed him. But not for long. Within moments he was returning her kiss with a depth that would've turned her on if she wasn't already wound up so tight—she was about to spring apart.

Somehow, they ended up naked on the bed, unable to keep their hands to themselves. Drinking in the sight of Nick's body she spread her fingers over his chest, his hips, his thighs and onto the throbbing erection teasing her, begging her to let him in.

All the while Nick's fingers were working magic on her heavy breasts, tormenting her with soft caresses, heating her already overheated skin, making her head spin. She wanted him. Now. But she didn't want him to stop touching her breasts.

Then his fingers walked lightly down her body to where her pulse was throbbing so hard the whole street could probably hear. He touched, ran his finger over her sex. Almost immediately she was coming. Her whole body quivered with the explosion of desire. 'Nick, now. Please,' she begged.

When he slid inside, tears spilt down the sides of her face. This was awesome. More than awesome. There was no word to explain the out-of-this-world sensations filling her from scalp to toes. Wrapping her legs around him she hung on for the ride, loving when he pushed into her, holding her breath when he pulled back. Then she rocked as she shattered.

Nick stood looking down at the woman who'd shared her bed and herself with him. Leesa. A lovely name to suit a lovely lady. She was special.

Sure, it had been one of those nights where a few drinks and sensational dancing had played a part in them getting together. But there'd been something more about her that attracted him. She was nothing like his usual one-night stands. She hadn't pushed him for any info, she'd taken what he'd said in reply to her questions and let him be. She was friendly without going over the top—until they fell into her bed and then there was no holding back.

He smiled widely. Then stopped. Unbelievable how a few hours with Leesa made him wonder if it was time to stop and question what he was doing with his life, why he was driven to keep moving on from job to job, city to city, every couple of years.

The fact his wife had waited until she'd had an abortion to tell him she'd been pregnant, and been having affairs for a while, had had him up and leaving and filing for divorce as soon as possible. But he'd always moved on from city to city, looking for something he wasn't sure he'd find.

'What about you, Leesa? When you love someone, is it with all you've got?' he asked silently. Because she had stirred him up, made him think about the impossible, even long for the life he'd always dreamed of again. Did that mean she could be the one to turn him around and help him settle down?

Of course, he knew the answer to that. Nothing was going to change because of an exceptional one-night stand. After his grandfather died, he'd spent most of his life alone, living with people in the welfare system who hadn't opened their hearts to him, who couldn't love him. Nothing about tonight changed that.

And yet his heart felt lighter and brought a flare of hope for something, someone, in his future. Something that hadn't happened since his marriage went west. The passion he'd known during the night could be a game changer if he was prepared to listen to his heart and not his head for once—as his mentor, Patrick Crombie, kept saying. The judge had saved his butt, and he'd always respect him for that, as well as the in-depth conversations they'd had over the years since.

But the night had been about Leesa. He would love more than one hot night with her. Might find more with her than only amazing sex. He shivered. What? Lower the barriers in place around his heart? Let Leesa in and risk being hurt yet again? Not likely.

But really, what was there to lose? She was heading away in a few days. They could have some fun and say goodbye at the end. Nothing unusual for him, but for once he wanted more.

Because of Leesa? Because he'd shared her bed once?

She'd been so refreshingly open, saying what she wanted without getting coy, he'd taken a second look at her. Different, for sure. But his nomadic lifestyle with few close friends hadn't made him out and out happy. If only it was as easy as stepping forward and holding out his hand to get the life he yearned for. But protecting himself had become ingrained as he'd grown up, first losing his parents, then his grandfather. He'd loved his wife, trusted her to reciprocate his love, and got that horribly wrong.

Leesa breathed heavily and rolled over onto her other side, that silky long hair spilling over the pillow.

Yes, his heart definitely felt eager for more. This wonderful woman had had his chest squeezing with something akin to love, had him thinking he might one day change his life around and find happiness. Another shiver as emotions flooded him. He wanted that so much it frightened the pants off him, despite believing he must be unlovable if his parents, grandfather and wife had left him for one reason or another.

Whatever steps he took it wouldn't be Leesa who followed him into whatever came next. She was heading away, while he'd just arrived in Brisbane.

Relief poured through him. He wouldn't be tempted to make a mistake and get hurt again. Then disappointment shoved aside the relief.

He more than liked Leesa. Way more. He had to get out of here before he gave into these warm feelings of longing—the hope of dropping this inability to settle down with someone and make love and happiness happen. He really wanted it all, and suddenly, all because he'd met this wonderful woman, he could see it just might be possible. Every thought came back to Leesa.

Time to go. Not only to reflect on what had happened in the space of a few passionate hours, and make sense of these new emotions, but to try and accept he was ready to make some changes in his life.

Moving quietly so as not to disturb her, he headed for the door, then paused. In the light thrown by the full moon coming through the window he saw a notepad and pen on

the kitchen bench. He couldn't help himself. He crossed
to the bench, picked up the pen and wrote.

Thank you for a wonderful night. N.

He didn't know if he was saying goodbye or setting
himself up for more enjoyment.

By six o'clock that night he had his answer. Pulling up
outside the apartment block he turned off the engine and
got out to stare up at level ten. Leesa had run around inside his head all damned day, even when he'd been looking
at available rental properties. Laughing, dancing, kissing
him, opening up to him. Smiling, sometimes not smiling,
just sitting beside him as they watched others dancing.

Oh, man, how she'd got to him. So much so that he
had to see her. He'd knock on her door on the pretext he
wanted to look around the apartment, properly this time,
as a possible option to rent. The location was ideal for
his upcoming job, and his mate was on hand, but that
had nothing to do with why he was heading up to her
floor and not stopping at level four where he was staying with Logan.

He and Leesa hadn't swapped phone numbers so he was
taking a punt she'd be at home. If she wasn't he'd come
back later, unless he'd managed to talk himself out of it.
Which he doubted was possible.

Leesa's face split into a warm smile when she opened
her door to his knock. 'Nick. I didn't expect to see you
again.'

Ignoring the thumping under his ribs, he asked, 'Is it
okay to take a look around the apartment to see if it suits
me?'

She stepped back for him to enter, her laughter tickling him on the inside. 'Let's be honest, you never really intended to inspect the place last night.'

He would've if that was all that had been on offer, but, 'You're right.' So did that mean he'd get it right this time?

'I just ordered pizza to be delivered. Want to join me? I can add to the order.'

Just like that he relaxed some more. 'Absolutely. Seafood would be great.'

'Take a look around while I deal with that.' She already had her phone to her ear. 'It won't take you more than a minute. It's kind of small in here.'

Except it did, because he paused in the doorway of her bedroom and stared at the bed where he'd had the time of his life with Leesa. He could picture her long, slight body pressed against his, under his, over his. Her tongue on his heated skin. Her fingers touching, rubbing, making him explode with desire.

'Nick? There a problem?' Leesa called from the lounge.

'Not at all.' Not anything he was mentioning. Stepping away, he turned and poked his head into the bathroom, where everything looked fine for his needs. At the end of the day apartments were apartments, and this one was in good condition and had everything he wanted. But there were still a couple more to look at tomorrow before he made a decision.

Or was he prevaricating? Because Leesa lived here? How that mattered didn't make sense since she'd soon be gone. Yes, but it would be where she'd lived, where they'd made love, where hot memories could tease him.

Once again, she interrupted his errant thoughts. 'Want a beer?'

He should leave while he still could. She was rattling his cage a bit too much. 'Love one.'

'What do you think?' she asked when they were sitting on the narrow deck watching the world go by below.

That I'd like another night in your bed.

He took a swig from his bottle, swallowed hard. 'About what?'

'The apartment, silly. Isn't that why you're here?'

Is it?

'It's fine. I've seen a few today and have agreed to look at more tomorrow, but really, it's a no-brainer. The location is ideal, my mate's handy, and I don't have any lawns to mow.'

Her eyes had widened. 'When I first met you last night, you didn't say as much in an hour.'

Yeah, well, you didn't know me then.

Still didn't, but he was working on it, because he couldn't walk away. They had a few days to enjoy if she was up to it, and hopefully by then he'd have worked this need out of his system. 'Like I said then, I didn't want to scare you off.'

'As if.' Her grin was wicked and winding him up fast.

'How long before those pizzas arrive?' Because eating was suddenly the last thing he wanted to do.

Her grin just got more wicked. 'Patience, man.'

'Are we on the same page?' He had to know or he'd blow a gasket.

'You mean, do I want to share my salami pizza?' Damn, her eyes were the sexiest he'd ever encountered.

'You got it in one.' The sound of a bell ringing cut through the air. 'Thank goodness,' he muttered. 'Unless you've invited the neighbours in.'

'No, just my mates from work,' she grinned. 'Relax, Nick. I'll go deal to with the delivery and then we can get down and sexy.'

He watched her walk inside, that sassy bottom making him hard just thinking about touching her. Twenty-four hours ago, he hadn't even met Leesa and now—now he wanted to fall into bed with her again and make love like there was no tomorrow. He wanted to leave his mark on her so she'd never forget him. He wanted to make more memories to hold close after she left town.

And yet he knew the old fear of being let down was lurking behind all the happy thoughts. There would be nothing to gain if he didn't take some chances, but that was a huge ask. Could he do it? Could he leave the past behind and get on with the future?

'I'd say by the look that just crossed your face we'd better eat first.' Leesa looked disappointed as she stood in front of him holding two pizzas.

On his feet in an instant, Nick took the boxes from her and placed them on the table. Then he leaned in and kissed her, lightly at first, then deeper and deeper until his head spun and Leesa was gripping him tight. He raised his head. 'Which do you want?'

She took his hand and raced to her bedroom. 'I've spent half the day thinking about this while not really expect-ing to see you again. I'm not going to waste any more time thinking.' She spun around in front of him, tearing her t-shirt over her head, exposing her lace-clad breasts.

He should've come up hours ago, to hell with looking at apartments. The best one in town was right here. 'Think-ing's highly overrated,' he groaned before his mouth found her nipple and she bucked against him.

* * *

Wednesday morning and Leesa was up at five thirty to see Nick out the door for the last time. She had a few last things to pack before the removal company arrived to box up the furniture and transfer it all to her gran's house in Cairns, and then she'd hit the road before the heat became unbearable. 'Thanks for some amazing nights,' she said before giving him one last kiss. A not-so-passionate kiss, since she was leaving town this morning and their fling was over.

They'd shared four incredible nights with little sleep and a lot of mind-blowing sex. How was she going to move on from that? *'Apart from the four days driving that lay ahead,'* she laughed to herself. There'd be plenty of time driving to consider her options about the future.

'Back at you,' Nick said as he returned her kiss. Stepping back, his arms dropped to his side. 'Thanks for everything, Leesa.'

'All the best with your new job.' She was filling in the air between them, wanting him to leave before she grabbed him tight and changed her mind about heading north. At the same time glad she could take in more of that honed body and beautiful face to brood over later.

'Drive safely,' he returned.

'Sure.'

'Good.'

Um… 'Bye, then.'

Nick spun away, took two steps, called over his shoulder, 'Bye, Leesa.' This time he kept walking all the way along the corridor to the lift.

Before he reached it, she was inside the apartment, closing the door and scrubbing her face with her fingers. The nights with Nick had opened her heart to really getting on with finding the life she wanted, once she got home to where her family and friends were. The new life might one day include a man she'd give her heart to and who'd love her to bits in return. Plus, children to love as well. A complete family. Yep, couldn't ask for more than that. If she was ready to try again.

At six thirty she slid into her car, buckled up and then flicked some music on—loud. Pulling out of the underground garage she glanced up at the apartment building one last time. 'See you, Nick. You're an amazing lover. I've had the most wonderful time with you.' Funny thing was they'd not talked about themselves at all. As though they both wanted to have fun without getting deep. Maybe that had been a mistake. And maybe it hadn't.

Indicating left, she turned onto the street and began the long haul home. All the way Nick stayed with her, reminding her there were decent men out there and that she only had to step up and be herself and she'd find one of them.

Sure you haven't already?

Unfortunately, the music couldn't get any louder to block out that annoying voice.

CHAPTER ONE

Fourteen months later

NICK TILTED HIS head and slid the shaver down his neck. Day one of another new job. How many jobs would he have held by the time retirement age came around? His hand pulled the razor down a second time, pausing as he stared at himself in the mirror.

He was tired of always moving on.

His eyes widened as the truth struck. He was? A truth he'd been denying since those wonderful nights in Leesa's bed. No, he hadn't forgotten her, no matter how hard he'd tried.

After rinsing the shaver, he made another clean line on his neck. Yes, he was ready to make some changes. The judge had been right there. It was time to settle in one place, and stay on in a job he enjoyed for more than a couple of years.

Since Patrick, as he now called the judge, had had a serious cancer scare a few months back, he'd become more persistent that Nick should stop wandering the country and follow his dreams of love and family. To see this strong man, who Nick had always thought the world of, looking so lethargic and ill had been such a shock. It'd woken Nick up in a hurry to the fact that no one knew what was around the corner, and that dreams should be followed, not avoided.

But did that include finding a woman he could love? Yeah, well, that requisite had been high on the list of reasons not to settle, because no one ever stayed with him for long, though there were no rules saying he had to fall in love to put down roots. Except he'd love to have a child and raise him or her, giving them all he could to make their life wonderful. Not like the life he'd had growing up in the welfare system after his grandfather died, but a life full of love and understanding, support and care.

The one man who'd understood him enough to give him a second chance, the reason why he was now a doctor and starting work today at Flying Health Care, had been Patrick. Judge Crombie could've sent him to an institution when he'd been caught stealing a car because he wanted to learn to drive, but had instead handed him some strong words of advice. 'Pull your head in, stop being an idiot and start behaving, or you are going to ruin your life for ever.'

Nick had always believed that Patrick had seen something in him that no one else had. If not for him who knew where he'd be now. Nick shook away the memory of being a hothead to get attention. No point looking back. His appalling behaviour had actually put him on the right path, something he'd be grateful for for ever, but that didn't make him ready to risk his heart by falling in love and believing he'd be loved in return. It didn't happen to him. His previous attempt had proven that, and he wasn't stupid enough to believe he'd get it right next time.

The fire alarm shrieked. And kept on shrieking.

'Great.' Nick dropped his shaver and hauled on his

shorts. Probably a false alarm, but he'd better play safe or someone would have to come looking for him. He tugged a t-shirt over his head, snatched his wallet and keys from the bench, ran to the door and swung it open.

The smell of smoke struck him. This was real. Supressing a shudder, he slammed the door shut and joined the crowd racing to the stairwell, including the neighbours he'd met briefly last night—two parents who were tightly gripping their children's hands.

'Can I take your daughter?' he asked his neighbour who had a wee girl clinging to her hand while her husband held the hands of two kids a bit older.

'You'd be a champ.' The woman shoved a child in his direction. 'Cally, this is Nick. Please hold Nick's hand tight and do what he says.'

No one stopped as hands were swapped. 'Cally, is it okay if I carry you?' Nick asked as lightly as he could. Walking down the stairs would be slow for the small girl, nor would it be safe in the panicked crowd.

'Yes.'

'Thanks, Nick,' Cameron looked over his shoulder as Nick swept the tiny five-year-old up and out of the way of people intent on getting down the stairs ASAP. 'Really appreciate it.'

Like anyone wouldn't do the same. 'No problem.' He concentrated on the stairs along with the pushing and shoving going on. It wasn't easy avoiding people. Each step seemed to take for ever, though the ground level was thankfully coming up fast.

Before he knew it, he was outside and handing his precious bundle over to her mother. 'There you go, little one.'

'I owe you a beer,' Cameron said as he looked around.

'What a nightmare. I thought it was a practice run, but that smoke's for real.'

'Move along. Everyone needs to congregate on the footpath on the opposite side of the road.' A policewoman was walking through the groups of shocked people. 'Out of the way so the firemen can get access. You all need to register your name and unit number with the two constables over the road. Do not go anywhere until you have.'

A small crowd had already gathered over there. Nick reached into his pocket. No phone. Damn it. He hadn't given it a thought when he'd grabbed his wallet and keys. How was he meant to inform his new boss, Joy, that he'd be late? Great. First day on the job. Not a good impression. According to Joy, he was meant to be going on a flight to Cook Town to pick up a young boy and bring him down here to the hospital for treatment. He needed to move. Fast.

He aimed for the front of the queue of tenants waiting to register their details. 'I'm sorry to push in, but I'm a doctor at Flying Health Care and need to get to work fast.' He might also be needed here of course. 'Unless I can help you out?'

One of the constables looked up. 'Got ID?'

Fair enough. In his wallet, he found his medical licence as well as the pass for the hangar he'd work from and handed them over. 'Here you go.'

'Thanks for the offer of help but the ambos are almost here.'

Nick realised sirens were approaching. 'That's good as I am supposed to be at work shortly. What is the time?' His watch was on his bedside table. When he was told he gasped. Where had the last thirty minutes gone? 'Right, I'll be on my way.'

'Hope your car's not in the apartment block basement.'

His heart sank. No phone. No car. Getting worse by the minute. 'I'll grab a taxi.'

'That ain't happening. The road's closed to all but emergency vehicles.'

Another officer stepped up. 'I'll take you to the airport.'

'Thanks, mate, but surely you're needed here?'

'They can do without me. So far it doesn't appear that anyone's injured, and plenty of other cops are waiting for the all-clear to go inside and check out the apartments to see what happened. It's important to get you where you're needed most. Come on.'

'Cheers, mate.' The guy seemed determined to give Nick a lift. Had someone close to him been saved by the Flying Health Care service?

'It's going to be noisy till we get past the traffic block,' the cop said as he flicked on the siren.

'Nothing I'm not used to on the ambulances.' Nick settled back for the crazy ride. 'You had much to do with Flying Health Care?' Might as well find out more while dealing with the frustration of the traffic jam.

'They flew our daughter to Brisbane Hospital when we were holidaying south of Townsville. She'd drowned and been resuscitated by the life guards but wasn't really responding to them. Scary time, I can tell you. Those guys are heroes.'

'Yes, they are.' Staring out at the backed-up traffic where kids crossed the road to a school, he wondered what lay ahead for him. That sense of finally wanting to stop and put down roots had returned.

Why now? Why here in Cairns? His apartment was like all the others he'd rented over the years since qualifying. A tidy place to cook a meal and put his head down after a long shift at work. He'd met people he enjoyed socialising with in every place he'd lived and worked. There'd been no pressure to get on and make the most of what he had. Yet less than a week in Cairns and the apartment already felt impersonal, despite the furnishings he took everywhere.

The town interested him. There were lots of beaches to enjoy, rural townships to visit, plenty of walking tracks. Nothing unusual except that, for the first time, he was considering staying around for longer than normal.

Leesa had something to do with that. Though he wasn't sure that was such a good idea. After all, this time the images of her smiles, laughter and sexy body were most likely overrated. She'd turn out to be a disappointment if he bumped into her again.

He laughed to himself. Give that time. A few weeks on the job and he'd probably be changing his mind. Except work was the one thing that always kept him grounded. Along with making him proud. He'd done well training to become an emergency doctor. He still relished every moment on the job as much as he had the very first time he'd stepped into an emergency department as a house surgeon.

'You're new on the block?' the cop asked. 'Haven't seen you around.'

'Moved up last week from Brisbane where I was on the ambulances.'

'You'll find it's not quite as busy up here. Though we do have our share of problems too. Like any town I guess.'

'There are high tourist numbers here and up the coast, aren't there?'

'Yes, but they cause less trouble than the locals. Mostly anyway.'

A road sign indicated the airport was ahead. Nick heaved a sigh of relief. 'That didn't take long.'

'Helps having the right bells and whistles.'

Now to face the day. Hopefully no one would be too disgruntled with him. More than half an hour late wasn't good, but it could've been a lot worse.

'Morning everyone. I'm Dr Nicolas Springer. Joy told me to come on out and get on board. She's tied up with someone from the hospital at the moment.'

You've got to be kidding me.

At the sound of that gravelly voice Leesa's head spun around. She grabbed the door frame of the pilot's cabin to stay upright as she came face to face with their new colleague. Dr Sexy himself.

What were the odds? It had been over a year since he'd left her bed for the final time after lots of the most amazing sex she'd ever known, and still her gut tightened when he spoke. Wonderful. Now what? She had to work alongside that voice. Unless she gagged him every time they shared a shift. 'Hello, Nick.'

His eyes widened. 'Leesa? I knew you'd moved up here and figured we'd probably bump into each other somewhere on the job, but I didn't realise you worked for this lot.'

She could feel her face redden as memories of his hands on her body swamped her. Not appropriate. They were colleagues now. Yeah, so how to stop this reaction? Carry a bottle of cold water all the time?

'Would that have made any difference?' she snapped in an attempt to get back on track. It wasn't as though she'd been hankering for more time with him. No way. Those nights had been so wonderful it was unlikely they could be repeated. Besides, she still didn't do trusting men when it came to her heart. Though she was moving closer to thinking it was time to try again and to hell with the past. And, if she were honest, she had to admit that her passionate fling with Nick had gone a long way to letting her guard down.

'To me accepting the job?' He shook his head. 'Not at all.' He glanced past her and saw the pilot looking back at him, and repeated, 'Hi, I'm Nick.'

'Darren, your pilot today.'

Leesa stepped back as the men shook hands.

The last thing she wanted was to feel Nick's touch. She'd turn into a blob of jelly.

'Look, I'm very sorry to keep you waiting but there was a fire in the apartment block I've moved into, and I wasn't allowed into the basement to get my ute. Fortunately, one of the cops gave me a lift or who knows when I'd have made it.'

'Guess we can't complain about that.' Leesa sighed. It wasn't as if he'd slept in or stopped at the supermarket to get lunch on the way. She was still aghast to learn he was the newest doctor at Flying Health Care. Of all people, he had to be the one she'd prefer not to bump into again. It had taken some time to put it behind her, and already hot images of Nick were reappearing at the front of her mind.

Not to mention the tightness in her gut. That was enough to put her off eating for the rest of the day.

She headed through the plane to confirm with the groundsman they were ready to have the stairway taken away so she could close the door. 'We'd better get a move along. Jacob gets stressed when he has to wait for us to pick him up.' And she needed to focus on work, ignoring Dr Sexy in every other respect.

'Our patient this morning?' Nick asked as he put his backpack away and buckled himself into the spare seat.

'Yes. Once a fortnight we transport him from Cook Town down here for treatment. He has acute lymphatic leukaemia and has just started his second month of chemotherapy. He stays overnight, sometimes two nights depending how he does, which lately has been tough on him. When he's cleared to go home, we give him a lift back. The road trip is too far for the little guy.'

'How old is he?'

'Eight. He's the cheekiest kid about and we all adore him. Even when he's stressed.' She hated when Jacob got upset. She might be a paramedic and see a lot of distress on the job, but it still hurt to witness anyone, particularly a child, in pain or ill or frightened about what they were going through. How parents coped was beyond her. These scenarios had to be their absolute worst nightmare.

Darren came through the headset. 'All tied in back there?'

'Ready and waiting.' Leesa sank into her seat and stared out at the tarmac beyond. In the distance a passenger plane was beginning take off. It was a superb day with the sun shining and no wind. That wouldn't last. The sea breeze would make itself known later in the day.

Dr Nicolas Springer. Nick, in other words. Dr Sexy. No,

she wasn't going there. That was behind them. Anyway, he was good looking and appeared to be a great guy— he probably wasn't on his own any more. Not that she one hundred percent knew if he'd had anyone special in his life back when they got together, but for some reason she'd trusted him. Which was plain dumb, considering how she'd trusted her ex not to be a bully and got that so wrong. Her trust was no longer given so easily under normal circumstances, and her affair with Nick had certainly been a moment out of time. One she hadn't regretted at all.

The propellers began spinning, rapidly gaining speed. Leesa watched as they rolled towards the tarmac, absorbing the thrill this always gave her. Sometimes she thought about getting her private pilot's licence for small planes, but then where would she fly to? Cairns was a long way from anywhere except the many small outlying communities. It was better to let the professionals give her a buzz.

'Is this the job you came to after leaving Brisbane?' Nick asked.

'Yes. It's the best one I've ever had. I especially get a kick out of helping kids and their families.'

'That's one reason I applied to work here. Helping people who want us there for them during difficult times. I've had enough of the abuse we get on the ambulances. Drunks thinking they should get special treatment, or fighting what you're trying to do to help them.' He shook his head. 'Sometimes it makes me wonder why we go to so much trouble to aid people, and then the next patient is wonderful and I have my answer.'

Blimey, he could be talkative. Not how she remembered him. The circumstances couldn't be more different though. They were at work, not having a drink or dancing. Or—yes, well, enough.

'I get what you're saying, and on these flights we mostly get gratitude.' There was the odd exception when someone thought they should be treated like royalty because they'd paid for their flight. Not all trips were provided by the health system. As far as she was concerned, everyone got the best help possible, irrelevant of who was paying and how old the patient was.

'Makes sense.' Nick settled back and studied the interior of the plane. 'I need to familiarise myself with everything. I like to be more than one hundred percent on board with it all. I don't want to waste time looking for equipment in an emergency.'

No one wanted that, and he was only doing what everyone did when they first started flying with this outfit. 'Go for it.'

Her pulse was still racing. All she'd known before he stepped on board minutes ago was that the new doctor was named Nicolas Springer and had been working on ambulances all over the country. Not once, even for a moment, had she thought Nicolas might be the Nick she'd spent those fiery nights with. 'What do you prefer to be called? Nick or Nicolas?'

'No one's ever asked me that before.' His focus was now on her. 'Nick. Nicolas is more formal.'

'What do your family call you?'

His mouth tightened. 'Either, or.' His focus returned to the emergency equipment.

Seemed she'd touched a raw nerve. Which was kind of sad if family was an issue for him. Everyone deserved a great family. In reality that wasn't always the case, but she'd been lucky with hers and still believed most people were, despite what she'd seen over the years, first as a nurse then a paramedic. 'I didn't recognise your name when Joy told us you were joining the gang. But we didn't exactly talk much about ourselves, did we?'

Jeez, Leesa, shut up, will you? Her head needed a slap. 'Sorry, forget I said that.'

'We can't avoid the fact we've spent time together, but it is in the past.'

Sometimes honesty could be a bit too blunt. He either wasn't wasting time remembering their time together or was letting her know how little it had meant, just as she should him.

'Yep, it definitely is,' she muttered and opened Jacob's case notes even though she pretty much knew them off by heart.

'I don't want to go to hospital.' Jacob stood near the steps up to the plane with his arms folded and tears pouring down his face. He stamped his foot and shouted, 'I'm not going.'

Leesa knelt down in front of her favourite little patient, resisting the urge to hug him tight. That wouldn't achieve anything until she knew what the problem was. 'Hey, Jacob, what's up, man? You love flying in the plane.'

'I don't want to.'

'Why not? What's happened to change your mind?'

'I don't like being sick. It's not fair.'

Leesa couldn't agree more. Glancing over to his mother, she noted the worry emanating from Kerry's tired eyes and gave her a smile that hopefully said, 'I've got this,' when she had no idea what was going on.

Even when he was stressed about what lay ahead in Cairns, Jacob was usually compliant when he had to board his ride. She sat down on the ground and reached out a hand. 'Sit with me.' She held her breath as the boy stared at her before slowly sinking down beside her. 'Isn't it cool being allowed on the airport tarmac?'

'It's my friend's birthday today and I want to go to his house and give him my present.'

Now she got it. Her heart broke for Jacob. Being so ill was hard for anyone, but for a child who didn't fully understand everything only made it twice as difficult. Though sometimes she suspected there wasn't much this boy didn't get about his condition. Today's reaction would be fairly normal even for adults.

'I bet you do, but you know what? He'll get lots of presents today so when you come home later in the week and give him yours it will be the only one that day, and that'll make it special.'

Jacob stared at her. 'I want to give it to him today. Everyone else is.' He wanted to be normal like his pals.

'I've got an idea. You could ring him later when you know he's home from school and sing *Happy Birthday*. That'd be special, wouldn't it?'

'Yeah.' A little bit of tension left Jacob's face. 'I s'pose.'

'You can practice singing the song all the way to Cairns.' Hopefully they had a quick flight.

'Will you sing with me?'

A gravelly laugh came from behind them. 'Go, kid.'

She grinned but didn't look over her shoulder at Nick, even though she wanted to see that sexy face with the neatly trimmed beard. What if she started calling him

Nicolas? Would that be less sexy? Except it wasn't his name that set her blood racing.

'You'll regret asking me. I sound like a dog under water when I sing.'

'Max's having a party on the weekend. I have to stop being sick by then.'

'Then the sooner we get you to hospital the sooner you will have your treatment and start getting over it.' Of course she was exaggerating, but if it worked then what the heck? This kid had to have his chemo. Along with as normal a life as possible.

Jacob stood up and held out his hand to her. 'Come on then.'

'Cool.' Relief filled her.

'Thank you so much, Leesa,' Kerry said. 'He's been upset all morning and I just didn't know what to do.'

'You were brilliant,' Nick said quietly, sounding a little awe struck.

She'd take that as a compliment, especially from this man. 'Jacob knows the drill and will be fine now.'

And he was, talking excitedly to the new doctor, telling him how the plane worked and where they were going to land and how the pilot had to look out for other planes flying in the sky.

Leesa relaxed, glad that Jacob had moved on from his distress. It was hard enough going through the treatment without being upset over missing out on fun with his friends.

When they disembarked at Cairns he was still yabbering to Nick, pulling him along by the hand and telling him not to be so slow because he had to get his treatment done so he could ring his friend.

'Quite the little charmer, isn't he?' Nick said when the ambulance had left with Jacob and Kerry.

'It breaks my heart to see what he's going through.'

'You're amazing. The way you took your time to persuade him to get on board made all the difference.'

'How else would I deal with it? He's got enough going on without needing a bossy paramedic telling him to do what he's told.'

Nick touched her arm. 'I agree with you wholeheartedly. But it was special, Leesa. I've never seen anyone deal with a distraught young patient quite like that.'

Someone else who was a charmer, huh? She knew all about them. Shrugging, she said, 'Let's grab a coffee while it's quiet.' There was a warmth where his hand had touched her that had nothing to do with the balmy warm winter temperature. It was a familiar sensation from the past. Except then there'd been nothing warm about what went on between them. No, it had been all hot. Searing hot. Something she wasn't meant to remember at all.

'Do we know what our next job is?' Obviously, Nick wasn't affected by her in any way.

'We're taking a teenage girl home to Mackay once she's been discharged from Paediatric Orthopaedics. She was in a serious quad bike accident two and a half weeks ago and has multiple fractures to both legs. Her mother is a solo mum and a GP. She's going to look after her daughter around her job as it's easier than coming back and forth to Cairns every night after work to be with her.'

'Who's going to be with the girl while her mother's at work?'

'I've been told she practises from rooms at home, and she employs a nurse as well who'll also keep an eye on

Matilda. It's going to be a difficult couple of months for them.'

'You certainly see a painful side of parenting in this job, don't you?'

'True, we do, but we also see wonderful parents coping with their worst nightmares while supporting and encouraging their children through hell.'

Another touch on her arm. 'You're very empathetic. I like that too.'

Too? What else about her was ticking his boxes? Did she even want that to be happening? As much as she'd liked him, she really wasn't ready to get to know him any better. Apparently, he moved around a lot and that wasn't her style. She preferred to be grounded in one place where she had family and friends.

She'd gone to Brisbane because her then husband had wanted to take up a great career opportunity, and in her book supporting him was part of being together. She should've read Connor's book first, then she'd never have married him, let alone left Cairns.

'You talk more than I remember.' Here she went again, raising the one subject that was taboo because she didn't need to go there. Make that she didn't want to, as it brought back wonderful memories that were unlikely to ever be repeated.

'We were usually too busy to talk.'

She had no idea how to respond to that statement. He definitely had no qualms about mentioning their time together. He'd have to learn that she did, except she wasn't actually doing any better thinking about it.

They reached the hangar where Darren was standing

in the kitchen doorway with a full coffee plunger. The tightness in her gut eased a tad.

'You drink coffee or tea?' Darren nodded at the man striding alongside her.

'Coffee's good.'

Joy appeared behind Darren and the conversation turned to work and all things acceptable in Leesa's thinking.

Not that she could drop the mental picture of that long, muscular body wrapped around hers after they'd made love. Nick had been extraordinary, and lifted the bar for her. Which could make things tricky going forward. She'd always be looking out for another Dr Sexy. Had been since she'd moved back here, though cautiously, in case she found another bad one.

'So, you two know each other?' Joy cut through her thoughts.

'Umm, briefly,' Leesa replied uneasily.

'Not really,' Nick said at the same time.

Joy gave them both a studied look. 'As long as nothing gets in the way of you working together then we'll leave the subject alone.'

It seemed Joy suspected there was more to the story than either of them were letting on. So what? It had nothing to do with work, hadn't even happened in Cairns, so there wouldn't be a problem. Apart from the rattled sensation she got when too close to Dr Sexy.

Leesa turned away to stir sugar into her coffee, ignoring the raised eyebrows of her colleagues. Nosey lot. She was hardly going to announce to everyone that she'd had a one-night stand with the new doctor—which had turned into a five-night stand. Dropping the teaspoon in the sink, she got her lunch out of the fridge and took a seat at the tiny table where everyone knocked elbows all the time.

Nick was leaning against the bench, coffee in hand.

Of course. 'You didn't have a chance to get any lunch, did you?'

'I'm good.'

In other words, no. 'There're yoghurts in the fridge and I've got a couple of bananas in my locker.'

'Girl food,' Darren retorted. 'Here, man, have one of my sandwiches. My wife always makes too many.'

'Cheers, Darren. If you're sure?' Nick reached for a sandwich, not looking her way once.

Awkward.

'Matilda, can you hear me?' Nick asked the teenager lying on the trolley bed.

Apart from the dark shadows beneath her eyes, her face was very pale. 'Yes, Doctor.'

'Good. We're going to get you inside the plane now. We'll be careful not to jar you in any way, but if you feel pain please tell us.'

Matilda did the defiant teen eye-roll thing. 'You think?'

'More pain than you're already feeling.' He knew from the notes she was on strong medication, but it wouldn't take much to inflict more hurt. 'Let's do this, Leesa.'

Leesa, the woman who'd toyed with his mind ever since their short fling in her apartment, which had then become his apartment. Until he'd packed up to come north, only to bump into Leesa so soon. It seemed as if something out there was toying with them, bringing them together at every opportunity. Were they meant to be together?

Try again. Nick shivered as he lifted his end of the trolley. They were stepping around each other, as if afraid to relax in each other's company, when not with a patient to deflect any thoughts they might have about their brief past. It could get tricky when they had to spend quite a bit of time together.

He usually dated women who loved having a bit of fun and then moved on. While getting involved with someone who wanted the whole shooting box was his dream, it was also scary beyond description. He had no idea if Leesa wanted the same. She appeared comfortable with her lifestyle, whatever that was, but that didn't make risking his heart again any easier.

His ex Ellie's revelation about the pregnancy, and that there'd been other men in her bed after they'd married, had taught him not to believe anyone when they said they loved him. Of course, he wanted nothing more than a woman to love for ever and who'd love him equally.

The only person he remembered ever loving him unconditionally was his grandfather, who'd passed away when he was twelve. He didn't remember anything about his parents, as they'd been killed in a car crash when he was barely a year old. Now here he was in Cairns working alongside Leesa, who'd got to him in lots of ways. Was that why he'd moved north? He wasn't sure, but suspected she'd had at least some part to play in it.

'How's that, Matilda?' Leesa asked their patient, more focused on the job than he apparently was. He'd say she was deliberately avoiding him as much as was professionally possible.

If Leesa was going to be such a distraction, then he'd have to ask Joy to roster him with other staff and never her. Might as well hand in his notice and move on now then, because that would be impossible with the small number of medics working the shifts. 'How's the pain level, Matilda?'

'You did a good job,' the teen retorted. 'No change.'

'Glad I'm good for something,' he grinned, comfortable with the patient if not his work partner. 'Let's get you tied down so we can get out of here.'

'You're making me sound like a wild pig you've just caught.' She giggled.

At last. Nick sighed, pleased to have lifted his patient's spirits, if only a little. He wasn't quite as good as Leesa with difficult patients, but he'd managed to make this one smile. 'One way of looking at it.'

Leesa was attaching monitors. 'Just keeping tabs on your blood pressure during the flight, Matilda.'

'Is that necessary?'

'I like to be cautious.' Leesa smiled. 'It's all part of the package.' Her gaze swept over him, wariness blinking out of those beautiful green eyes.

She hadn't been cautious the night they first met. Heat filled him. Just like that. Too easy.

Yep, he definitely should ask to work with someone else. Except Leesa had been so good with Jacob he wanted to work alongside her. He'd had to blink fast as she talked the boy into calming down and doing what was required. Leesa was special. But then he'd already suspected that. Which still wasn't a reason to spend more time than required on duty with her. Even then, he needed to keep her at arm's length. Like that was going to be possible inside a small plane.

Leesa shut the door and leaned into the cockpit. 'We're good to go, Darren.'

'We've got a five-minute wait. A flight from Sydney's on finals.'

'No prob.' Buckling herself in, she glanced his way. 'What do you think so far?'

About her? Amazing. *Yeah, right. Get a grip.* 'Flying in a plane certainly beats sitting in an ambulance, being held up in traffic mayhem at peak times.'

'Thankfully it doesn't get that busy in the sky.' She looked at the teenager and a frown appeared. 'Matilda, do you like flying?'

The girl was clenching and unclenching her hands. 'I've only been in a chopper and that wasn't nice.'

Nick asked, 'Was that the day of your accident?'

'Yeah.' Her hands tightened.

'You'll find riding in a plane a lot smoother than in a helicopter.' In an attempt to distract her, he asked, 'What happened? I heard you were in a quad bike accident.'

'I hit the accelerator instead of the brake and went over a bank. The bike landed on top of me.'

No wonder her memories of flying in a helicopter weren't wonderful. She'd have been in horrendous pain and shock, along with probably being frightened about what was going to happen to her. The case notes were on the end of the trolley. He picked them up. 'That must've been scary.'

'Try terrifying.'

Leesa stretched across to hold Matilda's nearest hand. 'Today will be a lot better. Darren's a great pilot, there's no wind to make it a bumpy ride, and you're in a lot better place than you were that day.'

'Were you with me?' Matilda asked her.

'I was. You gave that quad bike quite a fight.'

The signature eye roll appeared. 'I wish that were true.'

The notes Nick scanned made hideous reading. Three fractures in the left leg and two in the right. Five broken ribs added to the count. 'You're very lucky not to have sustained more serious injuries.' How Matilda avoided internal damage was beyond him.

'Thanks a lot, Doc. I don't see the luck in that, but if you say so I'll go along with it.'

Outside the windows the props began turning. Matilda's eyes widened and she gripped Leesa so hard it was a wonder bones weren't breaking in Leesa's hand. 'I remember this. It's like the chopper, how the noise gets louder and louder. I thought I was going to be in another accident.'

'Surely you were on strong painkillers?' Nick said.

'They didn't stop me thinking awful things.'

'They probably added to your mental confusion,' he told her. 'Today you can relax and take in what happens as we leave the ground and fly to your home town. You might even like the experience this time. How's that pulse?' he asked Leesa as she finished checking it with her free hand.

'As normal as any fifteen-year-old on an out-of-this-world experience can be.' She smiled at Matilda before turning and giving him one too. 'Up a little,' she mouthed.

Not surprised given Matilda's stress, he nodded. 'Wonder if we'll see any UFOs today.'

Another eye roll. 'You're nuts, Doc.'

'I've been called worse.' The silly talk was working though, as she didn't seem to realise they were already lined up at the end of the runway.

'Argh.' Matilda's cry of pain had him unclipping his belt and jumping out of his seat.

'What's up?'

'I moved my leg. Or I tried. It usually moves with a bit of effort.'

'Which leg?'

'The right one.'

The cast held it straight, so movement shouldn't have affected the fractures. 'Where exactly did you feel pain?'

Leesa was checking the BP monitor. 'All good.'

'Top of my thigh.'

The femur was fractured near the knee, not by the hip. 'Have you felt pain here before?' His fingers worked over the muscles.

Matilda winced. 'Sometimes when I've tried to roll over in my sleep.'

'I'd say it's happening in your muscles. Currently they're not being used, your movement went against what the casts are trying to prevent so they reacted.' He pressed lightly. 'How does it feel here?'

'All right. They told me the same in hospital but sometimes I forget.'

'You might need to have some massages,' Leesa said. 'Or get your mum to do it. I presume doctors have a basic idea?' she asked him.

'Very basic, but that's all Matilda needs.'

Matilda closed her eyes, like she had had enough of the conversation. She didn't appear to have noticed they were airborne and climbing rapidly, or wasn't concerned this time after all.

Nick returned to his seat. 'Where are we landing? I presume there's an airstrip near the town.'

'There's one right on the outskirts, about half a kilometre from Matilda's home. The local ambulance crew will transport her from there to the house.'

'Then we'll be on our way again.' Different to being in the ambulance, not knowing where or when the next call out will come. 'Do we know what's next?'

'Coffee?'

That cheeky glint in her eyes wound him up tight all over again. He knew what he'd like instead of coffee, and it didn't come in a mug. More of a rerun of some certain nights. 'Sounds like a plan.'

'Followed by taking a fifty-one-year-old woman to Townsville. She has early onset dementia, she's been in Cairns for respite care while her husband arranges permanent accommodation for her in the local rest home.'

Flying Health Care catered for all sorts of illnesses and emergencies. It was all about making the most of the staff and aircraft. They also covered emergencies with the Fire and Emergency Service with a helicopter when necessary. 'Every call is different, isn't it?'

'Makes the job exciting.'

At the moment Leesa was doing that. Not a good look for a doctor who needed to be fully focused on the case in hand. The doctor he'd always been until this morning. His phone pinged. Grateful for the interruption he looked at the message and glanced across to Leesa. 'The cop who drove me to the airport says the apartment building's been given the all-clear and everyone's allowed back in.'

'Did he say what caused the smoke? Or fire?'

'Someone on the floor below mine left a pot on the gas ring with oil in it and went out for a run.' *Idiot.* 'I'm glad the smoke detectors came on fast or who knows what the outcome might have been.'

'So you're renting another apartment.'

'Yes.' No ties that way. When he decided to move on,

he only had to pack his bags and call in the furniture moving company.

Leesa stared at him for a moment. 'Why not a house?'

His shrug was deliberate. 'Suits me best.'

'Right.' Disappointment blinked out of those thoughtful eyes before she turned away.

What did she expect? A full explanation about how, after his grandfather passed away, he'd grown up in foster homes, where no one cared about giving him a loving environment to enjoy and get used to? It was the driving force behind why he never stayed in one place for too long. The max was a couple of years, not always that long.

But that wasn't something he put out there. He didn't want anyone feeling sorry for him. He'd done enough of that all by himself in years gone by. Now he got on with making life work for him without getting too involved with anyone, though he stayed in regular contact with Logan.

'How're you doing, Matilda? That leg settling down?'

'Kind of.'

'I can't give you any more painkillers. You've had maximum dosage.'

'Whatever.' Typical teen response.

He leaned back and stared out the tiny window at the passing sky. The sense that the time had come to turn his life around had begun on the night he'd met Leesa at that barbecue, the ensuing nights only intensifying the idea.

She'd been the opposite of the women he usually knew, but there'd also been something about her quiet demeanour that had drawn him to her. She hadn't been quiet all the time, but for the first hour, as they'd sat having a drink and watching everyone else enjoying themselves, she had. He'd told himself to get up and leave, because there was a confident yet wary air about her. It had him wondering if he should try for a future that held the promise of the love he craved. But it had proved impossible to walk away. Look at the fun he'd had because of that—and the memories that haunted him.

Over the intervening months he hadn't stopped thinking about her, and what could be out there for him if only he could let go of the fierce need to protect himself. All because of a few nights spent with Leesa.

So was she the reason he'd come to Cairns? Along with the wake-up call after Patrick's cancer scare? Really? It couldn't be. That was too much to believe. Wasn't it?

He'd taken over her Brisbane apartment as a way of keeping her near in a vague kind of way. Though he'd quickly learned Leesa wasn't exactly unknown in the Brisbane emergency services, after all she'd done to help the women being abused by the previous boss of the ambulance station. Most people were in awe of her, but naturally there were a few who thought she should've minded her own business. Personally, he thought she had to have been very gutsy to do what she did, never mind the outcome for herself.

Had he truly moved north to get to know her better? Deeper? His mouth dried as he realised it was very likely why he'd gone online looking for a position up here, instead of reading all the situations vacant in the ambulance field over the whole country as per usual. Though not for one moment had he expected to be working out of the same base as her. He'd thought she'd be on the ambulances, not in the air. 'Idiot.'

'Pardon?' Leesa asked.

'Nothing. Ignore me.' For ever.

CHAPTER TWO

LEESA TOSSED HER car key in the air and caught it again.
Offering Nick a ride home since he didn't have his vehicle
would be the right thing to do. But then she'd have to cope
with him sitting in the car beside her, taking up all the air
and space, while setting a new rhythm to her heartbeat.

There were plenty of taxis over at the terminal building.
He'd be fine. And she'd be selfish to drive off without offering him a lift. It wasn't an invitation to get close again.

*Remember that the next time you get all hot around
him.*

'Nick,' she called, looking around for that tall, well-
honed body that had taken over the interior of the plane
like he owned it.

'What's up?' He came up behind her.

Her palms tingled. 'Do you want a lift to your apartment?'

'That'd be great, thanks.'

No hesitation about accepting her offer. More proof
she wasn't upsetting him the way he did her. 'Let's go
then.' She wanted this over and done, then she could pick
up Baxter, head back to the house Gran had lent her and
give the dog a walk before relaxing over a cold beer after
an unusual day.

The cases had been much the same as usual, except there'd been no emergencies or a patient going bad on them. It was Dr Sexy who'd really upset her equilibrium. Something she needed to get over fast because they would work together a lot. Not every shift was with the same person, but more than enough to worry her. He still had the power to turn her on fast. More than a year had gone by since they'd been so intimate, and yet the moment she'd heard his voice when he boarded the plane she'd been in trouble.

'I'll just grab my bag.'

'I'll be out in the carpark.' She wasn't hanging around inside waiting for him. That'd seem too eager, wouldn't it? Or normal for some people. Not for her. At the moment not a lot felt normal, all because Nick had turned up in her life again, and this time for more than a few nights.

Twenty minutes later Nick strolled out to join her. 'Sorry, Joy cornered me. She wanted to know how the day had gone and had I enjoyed the work.'

'Did you?' Did Joy mention again the fact Nick knew her?

'Absolutely. It's different to what I've done before in that we seem to get closer to the patients and learn more about them because there are repeat visits. If Jacob hadn't already spent time in your care, it might've been harder to calm him down and get him on board without a bigger fuss.' Then he shook his head. 'I take that back. You'd have managed no matter what. You have a way about you that has patients eating out of your hand.'

Nothing awkward about that. Opening her door, she looked at him over the car roof. He really thought that?

Yes, he would, because from the little she knew he wasn't a man to say something he didn't believe. *Wow.*

'Let's hope whatever it is, it keeps working,' Leesa replied. 'There're times when patients seriously need to calm down for their own safety, and if they didn't listen to us, we'd have a load of problems on our hands.'

She got into the car before she said too much. Just looking at Nick undid a lot of the determination to keep her distance. Pulling on her straight-face look, she turned on the ignition and music filled the car. One of the songs they'd danced to in the park by her old apartment, to be exact. Heat tore up her face. That was happening a lot today. She flicked the sound off.

'You don't have to turn it off for my sake.'

But she had to for hers. She'd downloaded the music and sung her heart out on the long drive home from Brisbane. She'd tried telling herself it was because she loved the tunes, that it had nothing to do with how she'd felt exhilarated and happy dancing and making out with Nick. 'I have it too loud sometimes.'

'It's the only way to listen to good music.' He grinned.

That damned grin was too sexy for her to be able to switch off the emotions it brought on. Putting the car in drive, she didn't waste any time heading out of the airport perimeter. The sooner her passenger was out of the car the better. She'd be able to breathe freely, for one.

'The apartment block's on George Street.'

'Right.' She hadn't thought to ask where they were headed. Another mistake, all because Nick was so distracting it was becoming embarrassing.

'Know where that is?'

'Yes.' She could do uncommunicative. Safer than saying something she'd instantly regret, which she seemed to do an awful lot around Nick.

He must've got the message because he said no more until she turned into his street and parked outside the apartment building. Looking around, he said, 'Not a sign of what went on this morning.'

'Why would there be?'

He shrugged. 'Don't know really. Want a beer?'

Love one.

'No, thanks. I've got to take my dog for a walk.'

'Okay.' He shoved the door open. 'Where do you go walking?'

'I'll take him along the promenade.' It wasn't far from here and Baxter would be chomping at the bit to get out and about. So much for going home first. Something else to put on Nick?

'Mind if I come with you?'

What? Nick wanted to join her for a walk? Outside of work? After she'd made an idiot of herself with that music.

He was watching her too closely. 'I think we need to clear the air if we're going to get along at work.'

'We got along fine today.' She'd liked working with him. He took his job very seriously. They all did. It was her dream job, and not once had she regretted returning home. But now Nick had landed on her workplace doorstep that might change everything.

Only if I let him.

True. She was in charge of her own destiny, something she'd repeatedly told herself over the years dealing with bullies. While Nick wasn't a bully—as far as she'd seen anyway, but she'd got that wrong in the past so would always be wary—he did seem to hold sway over her emotions. That needed dealing with sooner than later. He was already changing her, in that she did want to get to know him better and to have some fun. Like between the sheets again? It had been incredible before.

He was still watching her.

She sighed. 'You're right. Close the door and we'll go pick up Baxter.'

'I'm not trying to cause trouble, Leesa. I know I've landed on your patch and I don't want you to regret my arrival. We're adults. We can work together without that brief fling causing trouble between us.'

Blunt for sure. Also correct. 'Of course we can.' She went for honesty. 'I enjoyed today. You're a great doctor, and good with our patients. They liked you.'

I was relaxed when I wasn't recalling how your hands felt on my body, which was most of the time.

Feeling her face redden, she indicated to pull out and drove away from the apartment block.

Nick said nothing more until she pulled up outside a building with a high fenced yard, where a few dogs were waiting impatiently for their owners to turn up. 'You put your dog in day care?' He grinned. 'You are such a softie.'

'So what?'

'Just saying. I'm not surprised after seeing how you handled Jacob.'

Relax, Leesa. Give the guy a break.

'Baxter came from a rescue centre. His previous owners used to leave him tied up for days on end with little food or water, so I just can't tie him up and go out for very long. He gets distressed believing I'm going to leave him there for days, so when I've got something to go to other than work, I leave him with Mum and Dad.'

'How can people be so cruel?' Nick shook his head. 'Why have a dog if you're going to treat it like that?'

'The million-dollar question. Won't be a moment.' Out of the car, she strode inside to collect her beloved four-legged boy who was wagging his tail frantically as always. She knew he never expected her to come and pick him up, but at least here he was petted and loved by the staff running the centre while he waited for her to reappear.

'Hey, there, Leesa. Baxter's chomping at the bit to go home,' Karin said as she clipped the dog lead on. 'There you go, fella. Mum's here.'

Leesa dropped to her knees to hug her pet. 'Hello, Gorgeous. Had a good day?'

Baxter pushed into her, his lean body hard up against her.

'That's a yes then. We're off to walk the esplanade.' Standing up, she took the lead. 'See you tomorrow, Karin.'

Outside Baxter bounced up and down to the car, then stopped and stared at Nick through the window.

'It's all right, boy. Nick's a friend.' Sort of.

Nick opened his door and got out, holding his hands out for Baxter to sniff. 'Hey, Baxter.' He kept his voice light and calm.

Baxter sat back and looked up at him.

'Give him a moment,' she said. 'He's cautious around new people.'

'Wise dog.'

'There you go.' Her boy had stood up and was sniffing Nick's hand. 'You're in.' Easy as. But then she'd been much the same when she first met Nick. Would be again if she didn't keep a watch over herself. Sudden laughter bubbled up. She really was mad, and right now she didn't care at all.

'What's funny?' Nick looked as though he'd like something to laugh about too.

Good question. She wasn't really sure. 'Dogs. Men.'

He stared at her, then finally laughed too. 'Add women and we're on the same page.'

'Fair enough.' Opening the back door, she indicated for Baxter to get in so she could put on his safety harness. 'Let's go.'

Why had he suggested he join Leesa for the walk? Nick wondered as they strolled along the esplanade with Baxter bounding ahead. It was all very well saying they needed to iron out the hitches between them, but he had no idea where to start. Seemed Leesa didn't either, as she was staying very quiet except for an occasional word to the dog. She was probably waiting to see where he was going with this—it was his suggestion in the first place.

'Unreal.'

'What is?' she asked without looking his way.

He could say the stunning outlook across the harbour, but that'd be avoiding her. 'That I started work today at the same place you're employed. What were the odds?'

'Fairly high, I'd have thought. Cairns isn't a huge city and there aren't numerous air or road ambulance services.' Sarcasm dripped off her tongue. 'Did it never occur to you that you might end up at the same place?' It was coming across in spades that she wasn't pleased.

'I wondered if our paths might cross, but I didn't expect to end up at the same service centre.' He had thought about what it would be like to work for the same company, and hadn't really come up with a satisfactory answer. It was feeling more and more like he really had wanted to meet up again. Going by her reactions over the day, Leesa probably hadn't given much thought to their fling, other than maybe she didn't want anything more to do with him. She was blunt at times and friendly at others, but never fully relaxed.

'Face it, I know very little about you, and for all I know you might be like me and move around a lot.' He winced. He'd said too much about himself.

'I'm the dead opposite. I grew up here and the only other place I've lived is Brisbane.'

'I've no idea what it's like to live in one area for most of your life.' He could add that made him feel a little bit jealous, but best he didn't. She'd want an explanation he wasn't prepared to give.

Prepared? Or ready? As in he might eventually want to take the risk of exposing his inner demons? He'd already said too much. Coming on this walk with Leesa hadn't been his brightest idea. She had the ability to make him want to talk about things he never discussed with anyone.

'I'm sorry to hear that.' The tension had gone from her shoulders. There was a quizzical look in her eyes when she glanced across at him.

Don't ask why.

'Baxter's happy.'

'Nick, relax. I'm not going to pummel you with questions. Since we met in Brisbane, I have sometimes wondered what you were up to and if you were happy there. You're an okay guy and I'm happy to be working with you.' There was some heat creeping into her face and she'd begun walking faster. 'I don't see any reason for Joy to worry about us.'

'I agree.' He upped his pace to keep beside her. 'Thank you for making it easy. It can be tricky spending a lot of time with someone after what we enjoyed that week.' At least he hoped she'd enjoyed it. By the ecstatic sounds that came from her mouth at certain moments he was certain she had. He didn't believe she'd faked any of their love making. Sex, man. It was sex, pure and simple. Except never before had he spent so much time thinking about a woman he'd had sex with. Nothing pure and simple about that.

'My job is the most important thing I do and I won't let anything jeopardise it. Not even get offside with you,' she added with a tight smile.

'Good. Shall we start afresh by having a meal at one of the cafes on the other side of the road?'

'Meal? Flip. Sorry, I have to phone Mum. I'm meant to be having dinner with her and Dad.' She tugged her phone from her back pocket and tapped the screen. 'Mum? I'm going to be late. Sorry, but I was caught up in work stuff.' She glanced at him and grimaced. 'Now I'm walking Baxter and the doctor who started on the job today. He was at a loose end.'

'You're walking me?' He laughed.

She started to smile. 'Get in behind.' Then her smile vanished. 'Really? Maybe not.' Her sigh was dramatic. 'Okay, I'll ask him but we'll be late.' She held her phone away from her ear. 'Mum wants to know if you'd like to join us for dinner.'

Obviously, Leesa wasn't too happy with that idea. He

wouldn't mind spending more time with her, but not if she wasn't keen for him to join the family.

'Nick?'

He thought she didn't want him joining her. But it would mean he'd be getting to know Leesa better. No, not yet. If ever. 'Thank you but not tonight. I've some chores to do.'

'Did you hear that, Mum? Nick's got other things on.' He couldn't make out if she was happy or not. 'I'll head back to the car now and be on my way ASAP.' The phone slid back into her pocket. 'Come on, Baxter, we're going to Ma and Pa's for dinner.'

'Leesa.' He paused, uncertain what to say without making matters worse.

'It's fine, Nick. Probably for the best.'

Silence hung between them as they walked back to the car and set off for his apartment.

Finally unable to stand it any longer, he asked, 'Where do your parents live?'

'Twenty-five minutes north of the city. Dad grows sugarcane, has done for decades. He thought my brother might want to continue with the farm but Kevin took up commercial fishing. He works out of Port Douglas, about an hour from here.' It was as though she'd grabbed the chance to talk without going over what hung between them.

'Sounds like a busy family.'

'It was drilled into us as kids that you've got to work for what you want. Nothing comes in a Christmas cracker apparently, though I did keep pulling them in the hope Dad was wrong.'

Silence fell between them, making him wish he'd said yes to dinner with her family, but deep down he wasn't ready for that. Maybe when they were fully established as colleagues and not ex-lovers it would work. Or when he had the guts to follow up on the feelings of need and wonder for Leesa he was desperately trying to deny.

Leaning forward he turned the music up to fill the silence. The blasted song they'd danced to that night.

Leesa threw him a quick glance. 'You stirring, by any chance?'

'Not at all. I like that tune. Also, we agreed we needed to lay the past to rest, so turning music off because we heard it that first night isn't going to help.' Not saying he liked the memories it invoked—hot memories of Leesa dancing, kissing, sharing her body. Should never have turned the damned sound up.

'Of course.'

'Leesa, I'm not saying I want to forget the time we had together.' No way in hell could he. He'd tried and tried, and still the memories taunted him. 'Only now we work together things are different.' Get it? There wouldn't be any more time between the sheets for them.

'Right.'

He had no idea what she thought. Fortunately, his street appeared and Leesa turned the corner a little fast. Eager to get rid of him?

When she pulled up, she surprised him. 'Nick.' Her hand was warm on his bare arm. And electric. Like she'd flicked a switch so a powerful current raced through him. 'Your honesty is confronting but I'm grateful. I don't like ducking and diving around a problem, and yet I confess I've been doing exactly that all day.'

It was quite exciting realising he didn't, and wouldn't, always know what would come out of that sexy mouth. He gave her a smile. 'See you tomorrow.'

CHAPTER THREE

ON FRIDAY MORNING Leesa arrived at the hangar early, determined to find out who she was rostered with and sort her day out before Nick arrived. That way she'd feel in control of something at least.

'Morning, Leesa.'

So much for that idea. 'Hi there.'

Who are you working with?

Even on the days they hadn't worked together during the week she'd been aware of him whenever they were at the base at the same time, which had been often. The roster was lighter than usual.

'I'm on with you today.' So, he did mind reading too. Or just got on with the day. That was more likely as he was a practical man. Among other things.

'Have you checked the list for what's up first?'

Be tough, don't give in to the beating going on in your chest. Practise so that if you do apply for and get Joy's job, you'll know how to cope with left-field problems.

Like Nick, except she'd have to keep well away from anything more than a working relationship with him if she got the job. Since Joy had told her yesterday that she was leaving in eight weeks she'd been tossing the idea around about applying for the position.

A part of her wanted to advance her career, but a deeper part understood it was working with people needing medical help that really ticked her boxes, not sitting in an office doing paperwork for hours. There was nothing to lose thinking about what the job involved. She could always withdraw her application if she decided it wasn't for her. Plus, she'd have something other than Nick to think about.

'Should be a straightforward trip.'

'What?' She'd missed everything he said.

He stared at her and enunciated his words clearly. 'We're picking up a fourteen-year-old boy from Cook Town. He's got an infected club foot.'

'Not something they can deal with at the local hospital?' She really wasn't concentrating. The doctors up in Cook Town wouldn't send the boy their way unless there was a problem.

'Apparently it's serious, the lad didn't go to the doctor until he could barely stand on it.'

'Wonderful,' she muttered. Why did people wait until their condition was so far gone before getting help? It only caused more problems. 'You'd think he'd have learned what to do by his age.'

'Could be he gets teased about his foot and doesn't want to make a fuss.'

Air huffed over her bottom lip. 'I should've thought of that. I know all too well how kids love to tease or bully anyone who doesn't fit in.'

'I heard about what you did for those two women at the ambulance base in Brisbane. Pretty impressive. Not many people stand up to bullies the way you did.'

'I have experience of being bullied.'

His eyes widened. 'Why? You're beautiful and kind and not disdainful of anyone that I've seen.'

Her heart melted a little. 'Thanks. I was very tall as a teen, therefore I didn't conform with the others.'

'What a load of twaddle.'

Nick certainly knew how to make her feel good. But then so had her ex, until he'd got what he wanted, then he went into bully mode and never stopped. Not that she was saying Nick was bully material, only that she'd learned to be ultra cautious when it came to getting to know people. Might as well get it all out of the way. 'I was also married to a prize jerk who believed I was there to do as he wished all the time.'

'You left him?'

'Yes. There was only so much of his crap I could take. I deserved a lot better.' Always would. Be warned. Not that Nick seemed at all interested in her, other than as a colleague, something to be grateful about, but it was hard to raise that emotion. Especially when he was standing only a few feet away, his tall frame making her feel warm and happy. Like they were a match. It would be too easy to reach out and touch him.

She spun away and snatched up the medicine kit to put on board. Time to get to work. To focus on reality, not daydreams. She was not touching Nick.

He was standing beside her, looking impressed. 'You're tough. Go you.'

Tough enough to keep her hands to herself? Tugging her shoulders back, she said, 'I had to be.'

Have to be if I'm going to keep my heart safe.

Heart? That was going too far. Being attracted to Nick did not mean she was falling for him. No way.

But her head would not shut up. Its next question was, *Surely not every man you're attracted to will turn out to be a bully?* Definitely not, but how was she to know who to trust? Men didn't come with referrals.

Joy stood in the doorway. 'You're both here already. That's good because we have a prem birth with complications needing retrieving and taking down to Brisbane ASAP. It was called in by Dr Jones five minutes ago.'

'Matilda's mum, right?' Hopefully someone was with Matilda while her mother was seeing to her patient.

'Yes. The woman's at her clinic, it's been arranged for the ambulance to take her to the airfield when I let her know you're on your way.'

'Let's do it.' Leesa headed out to the plane where Darren was already waiting, ready to go. It was good to have something to think about other than her partner. Work partner. *Gorgeous partner*, added a cheeky part of her mind.

It was true. Nick was awesome. And not for her. The idea of a full-on relationship gave her warm fuzzies—and chilly shivers. Being single had its advantages. She didn't get told what to do all the time, could make her own decisions and stick to them—or dump them, whichever suited.

It could also be lonely not having that special person who was hers, at her side. Family and friends were great. Having a man to share the big and little decisions, the fun and not-so-fun moments, would be even better.

Nick was right beside her, case notes in hand and wearing an expression that said he was mentally running through the equipment they'd need and what was in the drug kit.

She nudged him. 'Everything's on board.'

'I know, but old habits don't go away.'

'They're the best.' She trotted up the stairs. 'Hey, Darren.'

'Morning you two. No rest for the wicked, eh?'

'You think?' Leesa gave a snort. If only she could have a bit of wicked in her life. Her gaze flicked over her shoulder to Nick as he closed them in. It might be better if they got down and dirty and she could get this craving for him out of her system. Yeah, nah. Best not. Disappointment filled her. But she could only laugh at herself. This was out there crazy.

Get over the guy.

Like it had worked last time.

'Can I take a front seat ride?' Nick asked Darren. 'I won't hold you up or get in the way.'

'Help yourself. I've already started take off procedures. Just get buckled in pronto.'

'Thanks, mate.'

Darren spoke to the control tower and the props began turning on one side of the plane, and then the other. 'Here we go. You'll get a clearer idea of the layout of the land from up above,' he told Nick, who was strapping himself in.

Leesa stretched her legs out in front of her. Great. Now she'd have all the air back here to herself.

'Do you want to read the notes?' Nick leaned back to her. 'There's not a lot to see.'

'Sure.' She took the paper he held out and shivered when their fingers collided. The man was a permanent fire sparkler with how he always set her alight. His hands were firm but gentle, hot while sensuous. Another shiver tripped down her back as she recalled them touching her. What she wouldn't do to share her bed with him again.

Biting her lip, she stared at the page in front of her. The words blurred as heat filled her. *Blink, blink. Swallow.* Her lungs filled, emptied.

The page slowly became clearer. Lucy Crosby, thirty-two, thirty-one weeks' gestation, had gone into labour at five that morning. Baby was born at six ten hours, was put into a ventilator and all functions were being monitored continuously. Mother had lost a significant amount of blood, and needed a transfusion on arrival at the designated hospital in Brisbane.

A glance at her watch told her the baby was barely an hour old. 'Come on, get cracking, there's a baby needing to be in the NICU.'

'We're airborne,' Darren replied through the headset.

'Oops, sorry, didn't mean to speak out loud.'

Both men laughed. 'Typical,' added Nick. 'But I know what you mean. These flying machines don't go fast enough sometimes.'

'This one will,' Darren sounded as though he'd been challenged.

Leesa watched the airport grow smaller as they rose quickly and listened to Nick's deep husky voice through her headphones. He could talk about paint drying on walls and she'd still be riveted. How pathetic was that? Definitely time to get out amongst it and find a guy to have some fun with. Not the one sitting in the right-hand seat up front. He'd be a lot of fun, but she feared he might snag her heart when she wasn't looking and that was not up for grabs. Not until she knew him very well anyway, because that was the only way to be safe. Besides, if she got Joy's job, she'd have to keep him at a distance.

'Leesa, can you set up the monitors while I get a needle into Alphie for fluids?' Nick leaned over the incubator. The little guy weighed fourteen hundred and twenty grams. It seemed an impossible number to survive, but he knew Alphie had every chance of putting on weight over the coming days as long as they got him to the intensive care unit ASAP.

'Onto it. His breathing's shallow and a little faster,' she said calmly.

'That's changed since we loaded him. I'll put a mask on him before anything else.'

'What's happening?' demanded the distraught father from the cockpit. He wasn't happy being there. He wanted to be with his son and wife.

Leesa looked up. 'Nick's going to help Alphie's breathing by putting an oxygen mask over his face. It won't hurt him at all.'

'What's wrong with his breathing? It was all right back at Dr Jones's.'

Nick carefully tightened the band around the baby's head just enough to keep it in place and turned to James. 'His breaths are coming a bit quick. I can't see anything else wrong with him.' He glanced at Leesa who nodded.

'BP's normal, heart rate good.'

Even though he expected that, Nick still felt relieved. These cases could go wrong very fast. This was when he was more than glad to have Leesa alongside him. Her competence was awesome.

'Can you check on Lucy?' Nick asked Leesa. The woman had haemorrhaged after giving birth, and while the bleeding had slowed, it hadn't stopped. Dr Jones had sutured the external tears but there was a serious internal wound that would see Lucy on her way to Theatre the moment she got to hospital.

'Onto it.' Leesa's smile warmed him through and through. At the moment they were a team, nothing else mattered other than getting their patients to hospital and giving them both all the care possible on the way. Would it be possible to get along just as well outside the job? It would be wonderful if they did, if he could give in to his feelings with no fear for his heart.

'Lucy, how are you doing?' Leesa asked. 'I'm going to check the bleeding.'

'Don't worry about me. Look after Alphie,' the woman whispered.

'Alphie's in good hands. Nick's watching over him like a hawk.'

His heart expanded at Leesa's words. She knew how to make him feel good. 'Alphie's doing great. He's a tough wee man. You need to be looked after, too.'

'Alphie needs you, Lucy,' James called from the front.

'It doesn't feel right to take your attention away from my baby,' Lucy said.

Leesa nodded. 'I understand, but your boy doesn't need two of us right now, whereas you need some help.' She snapped on fresh gloves. 'Let's get you sorted. You want to be cleaned up before we arrive at the hospital.'

Again, Leesa was being patient. Nick sighed. She was hard to ignore. Impossible, in fact. But he'd keep trying— until he couldn't any more. Which wasn't far off.

* * *

Darren raised his beer to everyone round the table, those not on duty who were at the pub down the road from the airport. 'Here's to the end of another week.'

'All right for some.' Leesa tapped her bottle against his and then everyone else's. 'I'm on all weekend.'

'Yes, and we know you love it.' Nick gave her a return tap.

It was true. She loved her job. Had even enjoyed working with the new doctor on the days they'd been rostered together. More than enjoyed. He was great company and just as sexy when he was being serious as he was when he was away from work. 'Most of the time I do.'

Nick looked surprised. 'Most? I'd have said all the time.'

'No job is that perfect.' She'd put her hand up to cover call this weekend because she wanted to be busy. It was the first anniversary of when her best friend was involved in a car versus bus accident that she didn't survive. It had been hard for everyone, especially her husband. John wasn't coping at all, to the point he'd been temporarily stood down from working as an aircraft engineer.

She looked around for him, having seen him with a couple of engineers when she'd arrived. He was leaning on the far end of the bar looking lost. She'd keep an eye on him and probably join him shortly. In the meantime, she'd focus on her workmates. This unwinding time was important for everyone after a week dealing with some heart-wrenching cases. Turning to Nick, she asked. 'What are you up to this weekend?'

Nick shrugged. 'Haven't planned anything really.'

'Sounds dull.'

'Not really.'

Strange how at work he talked more easily, but when they were away from work he seemed to go quiet. Just with her? No, he hadn't been very chatty with anyone. 'Have you ever come up this far north before?'

'No, never. It is a long way from anywhere,' he replied.

Hadn't she heard that before? 'Come on. We've got an airport. An international one to boot.'

'I've mostly spent my time in the large cities. This is a new experience for me.' Finally, a smile came her way. Plus a few more words. 'I do need to get out and see more of Oz, don't I?'

'I reckon.'

I'd make a good tour guide.

So much for keeping her distance. Thankfully she hadn't put that out there. Nick didn't need to know what she'd thought. Not that he'd be likely to take her up on the offer, he seemed as intent on keeping his distance as she was.

'I hear the Daintree's a great place to visit.'

'Watch out for the crocs,' she laughed. 'There are plenty of warning signs around the area, but still.'

'So, you want me back at work next week?' He grinned, making her head feel light.

Damn him. He did that too easily. 'Maybe.'

His grin remained fixed in place.

And she continued to feel light headed. Time to move away and get her mental feet back on the ground. She'd check on John and come back to the gang shortly.

'I'll be back,' Leesa said before heading over to the bar and hugging a man staring into the depths of his glass.

Nick sipped his beer and listened to the conversation going on around him at the table. They were a great bunch to work with. This past week had highlighted the reason he'd moved yet again. New faces, new challenges as far as the job went. Nothing exciting about the new apartment, but that was normal. Time to buy his own place? Thanks to Patrick he was very lucky not to have a student loan hanging over his head. Buying a house suggested permanence, something he longed for. Here? In Cairns, where Leesa lived? The million-dollar question.

'You hear Joy's handed her notice in?' said Carl, another doctor working for the same outfit as him.

'When did she do that?' Darren asked.

Nick was intrigued. Only a couple of hours ago Joy was telling him how pleased she was with the way he was fitting in. Not a word about her leaving had passed her lips, but he was the new boy on the block.

'A few days ago, apparently. She's not leaving for a couple of months, and then she and her husband are going to tour Europe for an indefinite period.'

'Does that mean her job's up for grabs? Or have management already got someone lined up?' asked Jess, a nurse he'd worked with yesterday.

Carl shrugged. 'Joy only said she was going to talk to the staff about it next week. No idea what that means, but could be they're looking for a replacement amongst you medics.'

Interest flared in Nick. He could apply. If he was going to settle down it would be perfect. It might help him stay grounded as it wouldn't be as easy to walk away.

Leesa.

It would mean no getting away from her. But did he

really want to? His gaze strayed across the room to that tall, beautiful woman who had somehow managed to start him thinking of a future he'd believed impossible. Hard to imagine not seeing her every day. But did that fit in with her being the one person who'd find him lovable enough to stay around for ever?

Leesa was holding the man's hand. Her head was close to his. She appeared to be talking quietly.

Nick's stomach dropped. It was one thing to hug a guy, but to hold his hand? No, there was more to this. Those two were acting like they had something going on. Yet she hadn't raced over to him when she arrived.

Just then the man ran his other hand down the side of his face, and Nick's mouth soured. He wore a wedding band. Married, and Leesa was holding his hand. He could not abide by that.

Leesa wasn't his girlfriend, but to see her with a married man like that had the warning bells clanging. Here he'd been thinking she might be the woman who could help him turn his world around. Wrong. His ex hadn't been honest with him, which was why he had to be able to trust whoever he fell in love with, when it happened. *If* it happened, and that had started to look possible—until now. Or was he over reacting? There could be a perfectly sane explanation. This was Leesa, after all.

'Want another beer?' Carl asked.

'No, thanks. I'm heading away.' Sitting here seeing Leesa getting all close and tender with that man was doing his head in. He'd been mistaken about her. All those sensations that heated his body, that had him looking at her, were a joke. She wasn't his type at all. He had to stick to dating women who were honest about their wish to have fun with no expectations about the future. Far safer that way. Except it was hard to believe Leesa would be dishonest about a relationship. But how well did he know her?

'Hey, I'll see you all at work.' Leesa stood at the table.

How had he missed her approaching? She sure didn't look guilty about anything.

She was still talking. 'I'm giving John a lift home. He's had a few too many to drive.'

'He's not looking great,' Darren noted.

'He's not in good shape,' Leesa agreed. 'It's the one-year anniversary.'

'Sure he's going to be all right home alone?' Carl asked.

'His father's staying the night. He was meant to be here but got held up at work and has gone straight to the house.' Leesa glanced Nick's way. 'John's wife passed a year ago tomorrow. She was my best friend.'

Guilt tore through him. How could he have immediately suspected the worst? Why hadn't he waited to find out what was going on before jumping to the wrong conclusion? Went to show how screwed up he was. How much Ellie's betrayal had affected him. Still did, apparently.

He wanted to move on, to create a happy, loving life while denying anyone near his heart. There was a lot to put behind him for that to work. 'Leesa, I'm really sorry to hear that.' In more ways than she could imagine. 'It's not going to be an easy day for you either.' Hence, she'd opted to work. She must be hurting big time. 'Who else is on tomorrow?'

Carl put his hand up. 'Going to miss my wife's first golf competition.' He laughed. 'Might be a blessing in disguise.'

'How about I cover for you?' Nick suggested. He could

be with Leesa if she wanted to talk about her friend, or support her silently if that suited.

'You serious? I owe you, Nick. Cheers.'

'No problem.' Unless Leesa wasn't happy with him, but he'd deal with that if it arose.

Darren stood up. 'Leesa, I'll come with you out to the car.'

'Thanks.' Leesa's face was grim. 'I'm hoping John's all right for the ride home.' She headed back to her friend.

'Poor bugger,' Carl said as he drained his bottle. 'Sure you don't want another?'

'No, thanks.' He stood up. Leesa was worried about her passenger. He'd offer to go with them. It was the least he could do for jumping to the wrong conclusion. His medical skills might be useful. Leesa wouldn't be worried without reason.

Leesa and Darren walked past with John between them. Leesa held the man's arm as he staggered.

Following them out to her car, he got a surprised look from Leesa. 'Thought I'd take a ride with you in case your friend needs help.'

'You don't have to do that.' She sounded snappy, but the relief in her eyes suggested she'd be glad of some help. He wasn't in the habit of jumping to conclusions, except when it came to trusting people not to let him down, so it only showed how much Leesa was getting under his skin. She was special, and he couldn't get past that. 'Not really. I'll sit in the back as the front might be best for John in his condition.'

John appeared to be past hearing what was going on. Not a good look.

'It'll be a slow trip but we don't have far to go,' Leesa

said as Darren helped John into the car. 'Hopefully his dad will be there by the time we arrive.'

'We can wait with him if not.'

Leesa glanced at him in the rear-view mirror. 'Thank you.'

'Where do you want me to drop you off? At work to pick up your ute or the apartment?' Leesa asked Nick, who was looking very comfortable in the front seat of her car. Despite all the warnings in her head, she couldn't deny how much she enjoyed his company at work and at play. Though there hadn't been any play so far, and might never be if she managed to keep her wits about her, which was proving difficult.

John's father had been waiting for them and, after they'd got John inside and sprawled over the couch, Nick had given him a quick check over. 'Sleep and a bucket at the ready is all I can recommend. Too much to drink and probably little or no food all day,' was his conclusion.

'Happening too often,' his father had muttered. 'He refuses to get help. Apart from tying him to the back of my truck there's nothing I can do.'

She'd hugged John, her own sadness at losing Danielle feeling heavier than usual. She missed her so much, it was almost unreal. No wonder John wasn't coping. Danielle had been the love of his life. Still was.

'The apartment's fine.' Nick brought her back to the here and now. 'Why don't you come up for a bite to eat? I'll order something in. You look done in, Leesa.'

She'd love nothing more than to sit down with him and not talk a lot, just relax in each other's company. 'I can't. I've got to pick up Baxter and take him for his walk. He'll be thinking his throat's cut since dinner hasn't arrived in his bowl.'

'Can I join you? Fresh air would be good for me too. We could stop for some food afterwards and take it back to my apartment. Baxter's welcome to join us.' Nick said.

It was impossible to fight the need to spend time with him right now. It was too hard when she was aching for her best friend. Good company would help ease the pain and, despite her misgivings about getting too involved, Nick was more than good company.

'You're welcome to,' she said.

At the dog care centre Baxter bounced around both of them as though he'd been imprisoned for a week.

'Freedom, eh, mate?' Nick rubbed his ears, making Leesa think she should bounce around too and get a few pats.

Baxter nuzzled in against Nick's leg, his tail wagging so fast Leesa figured it'd was about to fall off.

'He likes you. Let's go to the esplanade again. It's his favourite walk.' Hers too.

Once there, Nick threw a ball for Baxter to race after and bring back.

'I like you doing that. I don't cover half the distance when I throw it and Baxter doesn't get so worn out.'

Baxter dropped the ball in front of Nick and sat back, waiting impatiently for him to throw it again.

'As long as it doesn't go into the water,' Nick hurled the ball. 'A wet dog in the car would make me unpopular.'

'There're plenty of towels in the boot. Anyway, what's the point of having a dog if I can't deal with the odd mess to clean up?'

'I agree.'

'Have you ever had a dog? Or a pet of any sort?' He was so good with her boy, he seemed to understand what Baxter wanted.

'Never.'

The usual shutdown when she asked about his personal life. 'Ever consider it?'

'Sometimes, but I'm not home enough.'

No family, no pets. Friends? Best avoid that one. 'I mightn't have taken in Baxter if I hadn't known Karin. She's amazing, looking after him out of hours when I'm caught up with work. Mum and Dad take him if I'm really stuck, that's his favourite place to go to.'

'Gets spoiled rotten?'

'Totally. We always had a dog when I was growing up, but now Mum's got Parkinson's she's unwilling to get another as the day will come when she can't look after it. Dad disagrees but she won't budge on her decision, says having Baxter some days is enough. I think it's part of her way of coping with the Parkinson's.'

'I bet that's hard for both your parents.'

'A complete game changer. Mum mostly tries to carry on as she always has, but she did a lot of work on the farm driving tractors, fixing fences, you name it, and now she's had to give all that up. She was also a crack amateur golfer. I know there are days she can't deal with things, but she never lets Kevin, my brother, or I see it. Sometimes Dad talks to us about how he feels, but mostly he keeps it to himself.'

Not always the way to go, as things got bottled up, but Dad had taken up golf himself in the last year. While nowhere near as good as Mum, he said hitting the ball for as far as possible was a great way to let the frustrations go.

'How long has she had the disease?'

'About eighteen months. It was the main reason I came home. Not to hang around being a pest, but to support Ma and Pa as and when they need it. Besides, I can't imagine not being here. They're my family and that means everything to me.'

Nick took her hand and swung it between them as they walked along. 'I'm glad for you.'

Glancing sideways she saw a wistful look in his eyes. She wanted to tell him he could have that too if he really wanted it, but she suspected he already knew. From the little she'd learned she wondered what held him back from putting himself out there to find the special person to go through life with. 'Your family life wasn't so wonderful?' Her fingers tightened around his.

'No.' He dropped her hand, looking shocked he'd taken it in the first place.

'I'm sorry to hear that.' She took his hand back, and held him lightly.

The relaxed feeling when he'd first taken her hand had gone, replaced by a stiffness that told her to leave the subject alone. And him. If only he would talk, then he might get some of the angst off his chest and feel a little freer. Of course, she'd possibly misinterpreted his reaction to her question, but she didn't think so.

They were a right mixed-up pair: she wanting to settle down with a great guy while still nervous about him turning out to be all wrong for her, and Nick shutting down every time family was mentioned. How would he react if she asked him to join her for dinner tomorrow? He'd probably laugh at her and remind her he'd already turned her down once this week. Best not ask. She called

Baxter and turned around to head back to the car, Nick quiet beside her.

Baxter seemed to sense something wasn't quite right, trotting beside Nick all the way, totally ignoring her. It'd be funny if it didn't make her a little peeved. He was her boy, but truly she was happy he was looking out for her friend. If only she knew which buttons to press that'd make Nick relax as much with her. 'What do you feel like for dinner?' she asked. Then laughed. 'Not you, Baxter. You'll have the dried food that's in the car.'

'I don't get to share that?' Nick asked with a wry smile.

Leesa relaxed. They were back to normal, for now at least. 'Maybe.'

'I'm covering for Carl tomorrow,' Nick said quietly.

Forget normal. Her stomach knotted at the thought of more time together. It *would* be a diversion from thinking too much about Danielle. Sure thing. Funny how she could hear her friend laughing at her.

Go, girlfriend.

CHAPTER FOUR

FAMILY. IT WAS a big deal with Leesa. It was a big deal for him too, but from a completely different perspective, Nick acknowledged as he set the Thai takeout containers on the outdoor table. She had what he'd only dreamed of since his grandfather had passed. What he'd been looking for, yet afraid to give it all he had after Ellie did her number on him. Ellie had been the final straw.

He might've jumped into their marriage too fast, all because he wanted love and family so much that he hadn't stopped and really listened to Ellie and what she wanted. But he had learned a lesson. Listen to his head and heart. They had to be in agreement and, looking back, he saw that might not have been the case with Ellie.

Seemed the time had come to let go of the past and move on. If only he knew how do it safely. The idea of being hurt again made him shiver, while thinking it might all be worth the risk if it meant he could be happy. As Patrick said, 'Life's too short to waste it.'

'Want a glass for your beer?' the woman making him rethink a lot of things asked.

Shaking his head, he reached for the bottle she held out. 'It's fine as it is.' Then, before he could change his mind, he said, 'I was married once. It was a complete failure.'

Leesa studied him briefly. 'I know what that's like.'

'Yes, you do. My wife was unfaithful.' Among a few other things. But he'd said more than enough for now. 'Baxter doesn't seem fazed being five storeys off the ground.' The dog was peering between the balustrades at the street below, his tail wagging hard as he spied two dogs.

Leesa stared at him, then nodded. 'He's usually okay with any situation as long as I'm around.' Leesa rubbed her pet's ears. 'Aren't you, boy?'

'Can you give me the details of where you got him from? I think I'd like to get a dog, after all.' It was a sudden decision and yet it felt right. Another step towards settling down.

Another? Try the first. So far everything had been ideas, nothing fixed in reality. Warmth spread through him at the thought of having a pet. He'd never had one before. What the hell was going on? Swigging a mouthful of beer, he glanced at Leesa, and knew she was changing him, whether he liked it or not. Truly, he did like it. Even when he was coming up with reasons not to.

'I'll text you the website address.' She had her phone out and was tapping away. 'I'll recommend you to Karin as she's very protective of the rescue dogs, she usually wants so much background that it can take for ever, unless she knows the person giving a reference.'

'Cheers. It'll have to be a dog that can handle living without a backyard to play in. In the beginning anyway.'

'Lots of walks make up for that. There's also the dog care centre Karin runs for when you're at work.'

He'd seen the big yard there and the dogs running around pretty much nonstop. 'I'd be happy to use that service. I do not want to leave any dog of mine locked in-side the apartment alone all day while I'm out.' This was getting serious. None of the usual back-off feelings were in sight. Exciting really.

Leesa opened the containers and sniffed the air like she hadn't eaten for a week. 'Everything smells delicious.'

'Dive in.'

She didn't need a second invitation. Rice and stir-fried vegetables were piling up on her plate, followed by chicken red curry. 'Thanks for this.'

'Anytime.' He meant it. Despite his resistance she was becoming a part of his outside work life. He couldn't imagine not sharing a meal or going for a walk with her and Baxter—and the dog he would get. Quite an ordi-nary lifestyle by all accounts, and one he had little expe-rience of. One he would like almost more than anything else. Love would be the deal breaker to being beyond wonderful.

'It's nice just sitting and relaxing. I worry about John a lot. He needs help with his grief but won't listen to any-one about doing something about it.'

'He's not alone with that. People don't like admitting they're not coping. How long were they married?'

'Two and a half years. They were so happy it was unbe-lievable. I admit to occasionally having been a bit jealous. Then Danielle died and it seemed they'd been cramming in as much as possible before tragedy struck.' She looked at him with a wonky smile. 'Sounds crazy I know but…'

'Hardly crazy. No one knows what's around the cor-ner. They say we should grab everything we can while it's possible.'

Listen to yourself. You haven't exactly been following that advice.

'Danielle was always a bit that way, getting involved with sports, theatre and her career as a pilot. Sometimes I wondered how she fitted in her marriage, but they always seemed happy and there wasn't a moment they weren't doing something they enjoyed.' Leesa was staring out over the railing, sadness filling her face. 'I miss her so much.'

Nick couldn't help himself. He got up and crossed to her, lifting her up and wrapping her in his arms to hug her tight. His chin rested on her head as she snuggled closer. The scent of antiseptic and roses tickled his nostrils. He smiled. Reality was never quite as romantic as it was made out to be, but he liked that about being with Leesa. Reality was key to what he wanted in the future and, if it came packaged in this amazing woman, he could be ready to leap forward with her.

If she'd have him. But he was getting ahead of himself. This moment was about Leesa and her grief, not his heart. Though that was definitely getting more involved every day. 'One day at a time, eh?' He wasn't sure what he was referring to—Leesa's grief or his optimism.

'Only way to go.' She leaned back in his arms and looked at him. 'Thank you for being here for me. I don't usually let anyone see how I'm feeling.'

Everything inside him softened. Leesa was sharing herself with *him*. It meant a lot. 'I'm glad I was able to help.'

Her eyes brightened, tugging at his heart in an unfamiliar way, which was becoming too familiar. 'Funny how we seem to understand each other so easily.'

'Like that night we met in the park when we seemed to

click.' Did she understand he wanted to kiss her? Leaning in, his lips touched hers.

Her answer was to open her mouth under his and push her tongue inside, tasting him, winding him up so tight, so fast he felt as if his body would explode. 'Leesa,' he groaned into her.

She pressed her full length hard up against him. Those amazing breasts he still remembered flattened against his chest, her hips rocked against his, as she continued to kiss him with a passion that was mind-blowing.

He'd missed this, missed Leesa as he'd known her those few nights. Her buttocks were under his palms and turned him on even more. Hot, soft, sexy as. He was so hard he ached. 'Leesa?'

'Yes, Nick.' Her fingers were working at his trouser zip, making a job of what should be easy.

'Let me.' He wouldn't last if she didn't hurry.

'Uh, uh.' A couple of fingers slid under his trousers, hot on his abdomen.

Too hot. He pulled back. 'Slow down or I won't be there for you.'

'Can't have that.' She removed her hand so damned slowly those hot fingertips worked magic on his skin, sending his blood racing downward.

He had to bite down hard to hold himself together. 'Stop.'

'Can't do that either.' Her tongue ran over her lips.

'Come on. Inside.' He wouldn't make it to his bed, but there was a large sofa in the lounge.

She must've had the same thought because she headed directly for it, pulling him with her.

Not that he needed any encouragement.

Then she dropped his hand to pull her shirt over her head.

His mouth dried. His memory had failed him. She was so beautiful it hurt to breathe. Her breasts filled their lace cups perfectly. Her skin was creamy and soft, just as his dreams kept reminding him. He had to have her. Now.

No. That's not how this played out. Leesa came first.

'Nick.'

His name whispered against his mouth felt so sexy he nearly exploded.

'Condom,' she whispered.

'What?'

'Condom.'

Yikes. Showed how far gone he was. 'Be right back.' So much for the bedroom being too far away. They had to be careful, no matter how they were feeling.

He pulled the drawer so hard it hit the floor. At least the packet he needed was at the top.

Back to Leesa, who was sprawled over the sofa watching him as he raced towards her, his erection leading the way.

'Give me that.' She tugged the packet from his lifeless fingers and tore it open with her teeth. Then she reached for him, slid her hand down his length, squeezed softly, slid up again.

A breath stalled in the back of his throat. Lowering onto the sofa beside her exquisite body he found her wet heat. Ran a finger over her, and when she bucked under his touch, he did it again. And again. And again. He kept stroking her, drowning in her cries of ecstasy until she cried out and fell back, her eyes wide and her chest rising and falling fast. 'Nick,' she croaked.

Then she was up on an elbow, reaching for him, sliding the condom over his shaft so slowly he couldn't breathe for the heat and tension gripping him. 'Leesa, stop or I'll come.'

Her smile undid him. He tensed and then she was under him, guiding him inside, and he was joining her as she arched up into him. They were together. Completely.

Leesa stretched her whole body. She felt tender all over, and so relaxed and happy. Making out with Dr Sexy had been just what she needed. Hearing a rumbling sound coming from the man himself, she laughed. 'Hungry by any chance?'

'That was quite a work out,' he grinned and kissed her forehead. 'Seriously, thank you. I enjoyed every mo-ment.' He'd said thank you in a note after the first time. Pretty amazing that a man could openly thank her for being so intimate.

'I did too.' She hadn't had sex since their fling in Cairns, hadn't wanted to. Every time she thought that she should put some effort into finding a special man to start the life she longed for, memories of Nick and their lovemaking would stop her in her tracks. He had been wonderful and would be a hard, if not impossible, act to follow. Those few nights had meant so much. There'd been a depth to being with Nick—she knew she'd never settle for less again.

He was getting up. 'I'll get us some food.'

'It'll need heating up. Can I grab a quick shower while

you're doing that?' She hadn't had one before leaving work and was more than ready for one now.

'Go for it. Towels are in the large drawer beneath the basin.'

She hadn't even stepped under the water when Nick came through the bathroom door, roaring with laughter. 'Forget the Thai. Seems Baxter's into rice and stir fry. There's curry but it's on the deck, so guess he wasn't keen on that. He's got a very round stomach at the moment.'

'The little brat. I was looking forward to more. It's been ages since I had Thai.' She laughed. 'That'll teach me for being so easily side-tracked.'

'Can't blame him. We kind of neglected him.' Nick had his phone out. 'I'll order some more. Handy that they're only a few doors along the road.'

'I'll have my shower.'

'I'll join you in a moment.'

No food, but having Nick wash her back was going to be just as good. And the food wouldn't be too long. Quite the night.

And it only got better.

Just after midnight Leesa crawled out of Nick's bed and dragged on her clothes. 'I'm on duty at seven, and I need to take Baxter home so Mum can pick him up later in the morning.'

'We both probably need some shut eye. I'll see you down to your car.'

It was cool that he wanted to make certain she was safe. Not that she had any concerns, but still, Nick was a gentleman through and through. What's more, she really liked that about him. It was a first. Not even in the first months of their relationship had Connor been so kind.

Nick was nothing like him, hadn't shown any tendency towards bullying, and by now she did have experience to fall back on. She could start to trust her instincts.

After getting Baxter settled on the back seat, she turned to Nick and gave him a quick kiss. 'I've had a great time.'

'Me too.'

She was free tomorrow night to do it again. And the next one.

Don't rush things.

Good idea. Let the excitement and thrill of earlier settle a bit before making rash decisions.

On a sorry indrawn breath, she said, 'See you at work. Unless you want me to come by and pick you up, since your ute's still at the airport?'

'I'll grab a taxi.' Withdrawing already? Or saving her the hassle of having to go across town?

She'd run with that. It felt better. She had to stop looking for trouble and get on with having fun with a decent man. Nick was more than decent. He was sexy as all be it. He was so good looking she wanted to keep prodding him to make sure he was for real. His love making was beyond reality. She lost herself completely when he touched her. Maybe she did need to back off fast until her head was clear, so she could think carefully about where to go from here. 'No problem.' Clambering into the car, she headed for home, and time to dream about the hours she'd spent with Nick.

Leesa spent most of the rest of the night reflecting on Nick and their relationship. Whenever she closed her eyes, he was there behind her eyelids, smiling, laughing, being kind, gentle. And not giving much away.

Winding her up tight all over again, only this time it was all about her feelings and what to do about them. He was growing on her fast. Too fast, when she wanted to take one slow step at a time. She'd fallen for Connor quickly and look where that led. Part of her, a big part, wanted to let all that go so she could trust Nick. He really was nothing like her ex. Not in any way.

She was getting ahead of herself. There'd been nothing in their hours together to say that he might be interested in her, other than for a good time in the sack.

Now she was heading into work just as she had been a year ago when she got the call to say Danielle was gone. Her fingers whitened on the steering wheel. 'Miss you something terrible, girlfriend.' Would she ever get over losing Danielle? In some ways she probably would, but in others never. 'Damn it, Danielle, I need to talk to you, to hear you give me a speech about how, because I was a moron over Connor, it doesn't mean it'll happen again.'

Had Nick taken Carl's shift to be with her on the day she was mourning her friend? She suspected so. It would be second nature for him. Turning into the airport, she drove slowly towards the Flying Health Care hangar. She should be buzzing after last night, but now she suddenly felt nothing but trepidation. What if she was making a fool of herself with Nick? Everyone here seemed to think he was a great guy, but that wasn't a reason to fall in love with him. For her that had to be all about trust. The thing was, she did trust him. So why the hesitation?

'Morning, Leesa,' Nick called when she walked into the hangar. He was at the cupboard checking the drug kit they took on board. He didn't stop what he was doing to give her a smile or acknowledge the night before. Having similar doubts as her? Quite likely, considering he had some family issues.

'Hi, there,' she replied. 'How's things?'

'All good.'

Not super chatty. But when was he? When they were sitting on his deck eating Thai and getting hot and bothered. That's when. She shook her head and headed to the locker room, walking away from the temptation of wrapping her arms around him, along with a quick kiss. It wouldn't be professional to do that here. She probably shouldn't follow up on last night either, not when he seemed to have gone quiet on her.

Instead, she went to see if they had any flights arranged. Saturdays were usually quieter but she hoped today would be an exception.

'We're giving Jacob a lift home at eleven.'

She nearly leapt out of her skin at the sound of Nick's voice right behind her. So much for thinking he was keeping to himself. 'I didn't know he was still down here. He'll be fretting about his friend's birthday present.'

'Apparently, he had a rough time after his chemo and was kept in PICU for two days. He's doing all right now, but it's likely to happen again as the chemo takes its toll.'

'It will.' The build-up of the treatment always had a long-term effect, which she hated seeing with her patients. Especially the little ones. Being a parent was on her wish list, and it seemed nothing but exciting from where she stood, but she knew all too well that wasn't always the case. She did know, if she was lucky enough to become a mother, she'd love her kid to bits and be super strong for him or her no matter what.

'At the moment there's nothing else on our schedule,'

Nick informed her. 'I'm putting the jug on. Feel like a tea or coffee?'

'Tea, thanks. Is Darren here?'

'Doing his aircraft checks. He'll be in shortly.' Nick turned towards the kitchen.

Definitely not overly friendly. But she hadn't put herself out to be chirpy either. It was still hard not to rush over and hug him, to feel his long strong body against her.

The main phone rang sharply. Racing to answer it, she silently begged for a job so she didn't have to sit around in the kitchen for hours. 'Flying Health Care. Leesa speaking.'

'Hey, Leesa, it's Michael. We've got a call from Weipa to pick up a man who's been in a truck versus car accident. Internal injuries, fractures to both legs and pelvis.' Michael worked the phones for emergency services. 'I'll adjust the flight time for Jacob to early afternoon.'

Poor Jacob. Things weren't panning out for him this week. 'Right. On our way.' She hung up, feeling guilty. A seriously injured patient wasn't quite what she meant as a distraction. 'Forget the tea and coffee, Nick. We're on.'

'What've we got?'

Moving quickly to the plane, she filled him in on the scant facts. Once they were on the way more would come through on the laptop they took with them. 'Jacob's flight will be delayed until we're back.'

'He won't be happy about that. He so wanted to see his friend and give him his present. I imagine every hour is going to seem like another day to him.' Nick gave her a brief smile.

A smile that touched her, and loosened some of her

worries about them, despite it disappearing almost as soon as he'd produced it. 'You're not wrong there.'

'Why doesn't he go by car? It's only about three hours, isn't it?'

'Jacob gets car sick, and add in the chemo effects and it wouldn't be pleasant for anyone,' Leesa told him as she waved bye to the ground crew pulling the stairs away from the plane.

'Yet he's fine in the plane.' Nick buckled into his seat. 'But that's how it is for some.'

'Ready back here,' she told Darren through the headset she'd pulled on.

'It's going to be a bit bumpy over the hills,' the pilot warned them.

'No problem.' She didn't mind minor turbulence. It was a different story when they had a patient on board, as it added to the stress and pain for that person, and made helping them difficult as they had to remain strapped in their seats.

Nick had the laptop open and was reading the information about the patient they were flying to Weipa to pick up. 'Not looking good.'

'Fill me in.'

'Fractured ribs, both femurs, and right upper arm. Suspected perforated lung. Swelling in the abdomen so there must be more injuries in that area. We're going to be pushing it to get him to Cairns without a major problem occurring.'

'Going as fast as allowed,' Darren came through the headset.

'I figured you might be,' Nick responded. Then he looked her way. 'You good to go with whatever happens?'

'Always.' As if he had to ask. It was the nature of the job to be prepared for worst-case scenarios. They happened often enough for her to know wishful thinking didn't prevent them.

'You won't get a better paramedic than Leesa,' Darren said a little sharply.

'Thanks, Darren.' Turning to Nick, she removed the mouthpiece so Darren didn't hear. 'Do not question my ability. I am well versed in the medical requirements of our work.'

'I'm sorry. It was a reflex question. I don't doubt your medical skills.'

'Thank you.' They had moved on from their intimate night to being tense with each other. Not a good look for the future. Better to know now than later.

She turned to face out the window for the rest of the flight.

Nick knew he'd stuffed up big time. The anger in Leesa's expression told him she wasn't going to forgive him any time soon for questioning her ability to deal with the death of a patient. It had been a mistake. He hadn't deliberately set out to check she was comfortable with what might lie ahead, he'd been speaking aloud in an attempt to discuss what they might face. Except it came out as a question, and she was not happy with him.

Talk about going from a high to a low. Last night had been beyond fantastic. Making love with Leesa couldn't be better. She was so giving. And accepting. Almost loving. Almost. They were not falling in love. They couldn't. He wasn't ready, despite his feelings for her growing stronger by the day. After last night, it was going to be even harder to stay away from her.

Other than at work, and then they were professionals, looking after patients, keeping each other at arm's length. He was also about to apply for Joy's position, which meant he might have to take a step back to remain professional.

But right now, he wanted to reach out and touch Leesa, to tell her how much he believed in her medical skills. Other skills too. When it came to sticking up for herself, she was strong. She'd proved that by helping those women at the Brisbane base. There'd be no walking all over her, and he'd never want to. Leesa was his dream woman. His mind went back to last night when he was inside her and she was crying out as she came. More than a dream. She was real and near perfect, and he was still hesitant.

A while later she turned to look at him. 'Weipa's to our left. Darren must've had his foot to the pedal all the way.'

'No such thing as a pedal up here,' Darren retorted.

'Thank goodness for that or who knows how fast this plane might've gone.' Nick stretched his legs to loosen the kinks in his muscles. 'I've never been this far north and all I'm going to see is the airport.'

'Somewhere to come when you have leave to use up. Lots of people go through using four-wheel drive vehicles. I haven't done it, but know there's certain times of the year when it's safer. The rainy season's not one as the mud builds up and vehicles get bogged down. Not easy to get out when you're in the middle of nowhere.'

'Surely people go in groups?'

'Mostly, but there're always the exceptions. I remember one chopper flight we had to pick up a woman who'd had her leg broken when her husband revved the truck, it ran over her because it wasn't as stuck as he'd believed.'

Idiot. How could a man do that when his wife was in line with the vehicle? 'Lack of experience in the outback then.'

'Definitely.'

'Have you heard that Joy's leaving?' he asked. 'I'm thinking of applying for the position.'

'Me too.'

'That I didn't expect.'

'Why ever not? I'm as capable as anyone to do it justice,' she snapped, taken aback by the shock in his face.

'I know you are. It just never occurred to me you might want to run the outfit. You're so happy doing what you do.'

'I am, but there's nothing wrong with wanting to advance my career. Same as you want.'

'True.'

'It could prove interesting,' Leesa retorted as the wheels touched down on the tarmac and the plane slowed.

Unsure how she felt about his revelation, he moved on. 'There's an ambulance waiting by the shed. No, the driver's started backing towards where I presume Darren's going to park. A woman's already pushing the stairs this way.'

'They're obviously in a hurry. Not a good sign.' Unbuckling her belt, Leesa waited impatiently at the door for the plane to come to a halt, as near to the ambulance as possible without jeopardising anyone's safety.

'I agree.' Internal bleeding could lead to cardiac arrest. Or the man might've gone into a deep coma from a head wound. Worse, his lung might be compromised by a broken rib gouging a hole in it.

*Stop. Wait for the facts before starting to work out how
to get this man to Cairns safely.* 'I'd say we'll be back in
the air in minutes, Darren.'

'Gotcha.'

'Here we go.' Leesa slid the door open as the plane
stopped. The stairs were getting close.

They both grabbed a handle as the woman reached
them and applied the brakes.

Nick leapt down the steps two at a time and strode to
the ambulance as its back doors opened. 'Hi, I'm Nick,
a doctor.'

'Hey, Nick. Heard we had someone new.' A woman
began moving the trolley with their patient onto the tarmac. 'This is Maxwell O'Neill, forty-seven. Severe trauma
to head, lungs, abdomen and legs. He suffered cardiac arrest fifteen minutes ago. We resuscitated him, but his heart
rate's slow. Given the injuries blood loss is probably high.'

'Right, no hanging around then.'

Within minutes the stretcher was on the mini lift with
Leesa at the man's side, pressing the button that made
them rise up to the plane door. Nick shot up the stairs
to help unload the stretcher onto the bed. He was barely
aware of the plane lifting off as he read the monitors displaying Maxwell's heart reading, blood pressure and his
breathing. 'This is going to be one long trip.' Every minute would feel like an hour as they worked to keep Maxwell alive.

Leesa looked up from where she was preparing the
defibrillator in case Maxwell's heart stopped again. The
chances were high. 'We can do it.' Her smile was small
but warm, easing some of his tension.

It felt good to have her with him for this. She fed his

confidence so that he did believe in himself. Not that he didn't usually, but there were some cases when he knew the odds were stacked against saving a patient—this was one of them. Having Leesa here took away some of that pressure. 'Thanks.'

Her reply was another smile.

So he was back in the good books—for now at least.

Thirty minutes later the line on the heart monitor flatlined.

Leesa immediately placed the defib pads on Maxwell's bare chest and stepped back.

Nick pushed the button and waited, heart in his throat, for the electric current to get up to peek.

Maxwell's body lifted from the stretcher as the shock struck. Dropped back.

The air filled with a steady beeping sound.

Nick exhaled heavily. 'Phew. Thank goodness.'

Leesa wiped her brow. 'I can't believe his heart restarted at the first attempt.' There was a wobble in her voice.

'Hey, we were ready for it and wasted no time giving him a shock.'

'I know, but still.'

'Yeah, I get it.'

Twenty minutes out of Cairns it happened again. This time it took two shocks to get Maxwell's heart beating and the rhythm was all over the place.

Darren came through the headset. 'There's a helicopter on standby to take your patient to the hospital. There's been a crash on the main road and traffic's built up for kilometres either side.'

The last thing this man needed was a hold up. He probably wouldn't survive much longer without all the high-tech equipment only available in hospital. 'We'll go with him.'

'That's the plan,' Darren came back.

A thought came out of nowhere. 'Jacob's not going to be happy.'

Leesa glanced at him. 'I know. But we can pick him up in the chopper for the short hop back to the airport and the plane.'

Of course she'd think of that. 'Get onto whoever deals with these things and arrange it when you've got a free moment.'

'Tomorrow?' she laughed.

'Not if you want Jacob to still talk to you.'

'Good point.' Leesa grabbed a moment to call Michael and get Jacob and his mother's flight sorted.

Again, transferring their patient was fast and they were back in the air in no time, this time the thumping sound of rotors filling the cabin, and Maxwell was still oblivious to what was going on.

Nick knew he wouldn't relax until the man was off the chopper and being rolled into ED. Only then would he feel safe to breathe properly. They'd done all they could to keep Maxwell alive. It wasn't always enough, but there were limitations even for doctors. The down side to the job.

'Hey.' A light tap on his shoulder. 'Cheer up. We've done well so far.'

Dang, she read him so easily. And made him feel good when she did, not so alone. 'You're right. We have.'

Had the drama diverted her from thinking about her friend and what today meant? She'd been distracted in bed last night, but had thoughts of her friend's demise returned the moment she was back in her own place? Chances were, they had. Leesa didn't hide from pain, instead she seemed to confront it and work through it. He should take a leaf out of her book and do much the same.

CHAPTER FIVE

'SEE YOU NEXT TIME, Jacob,' Leesa waved at her favourite patient before heading out to the plane.

'Promise you will be here?' Jacob gave her a cheeky grin. He was happier than he'd been when he boarded the plane. Then he'd been sad and tearful, afraid his friend wouldn't talk to him because he was going to be so late home. His mother had managed to get a message through and the friend sent Jacob a text on *his* mother's phone saying he'd saved some cake to share with Jacob as soon as he got there. The lad hadn't stopped smiling since.

'You know I meant next time I'm rostered on to be your paramedic, you ratbag.' Which should be the next visit he had to make for treatment. Joy knew how much she liked being with Jacob and always tried to put them on the same flight. If she did get Joy's job, she wouldn't get to do those special flights with her favourite patients as often. Something else to consider.

Her application was in and still she wondered if it was the right thing to do. Did she really want to sit behind a desk for hours on end when she could be in the air caring for someone in pain or who was very unwell? Joy did her share of flights when she wasn't tied up with paperwork, as well as discussions with hospital management and other health units, but nothing like the number the rest of the medical crew members did.

There was a bigger question. Did she want to be Nick's boss? It would get in the way of being close friends, something they were rapidly becoming when they weren't being cautious around one another. Worse, it would mean they couldn't be intimate any more. Not when she had to treat all the staff equally. That was essential for good relations, and even if she and Nick continued their fling, she'd follow through on maintaining a level field with everyone. But it would only take one mistake or a perceived error where it appeared Nick was being favoured and she'd be out on her backside.

The other side of this was that Nick had applied too and could end up being her boss. Same issues arose. Plus, she might feel uncomfortable if he was in charge. So far, he came across as eager to work with people, not wanting to be in charge all the time. But she knew how that could be a farce. Hard to imagine that of Nick though. Talk about complicated.

As Darren took off, she leaned her head back and closed her eyes. So many things to consider since Nick had turned up in Cairns. Since returning home she'd been cruising through life, loving her work, enjoying time on the farm with the family and visiting Gran, spending hours with her friends when they were all free at the same time. Giving Baxter all he needed, not necessarily all he wanted. Life had been pretty good.

It still was. Except she'd been living in a vacuum. Taking each day as it came, not looking for more. Not thinking too seriously about her future and the dreams she'd always had about falling in love and raising kids and owning a piece of land with a lovely family home on it.

All very well to think she had years ahead to achieve those dreams, but look what had happened to Danielle. The babies she'd wanted, the trip to Norway to meet her nieces, the career she was building—gone in an instant. Thankfully Danielle hadn't waited to get started on fulfilling her dreams, or she'd not have achieved anything.

'Get a wiggle on, girlfriend. Make the most of today, not tomorrow.'

Leesa's eyes shot open and she looked around. She'd swear Danielle was right here, sitting opposite, locking her formidable gaze on her.

Instead, Nick asked, 'What's up?'

'Nothing. I was daydreaming.'

'What about?'

'Nothing important.' Not half.

'Really?' He sounded disappointed she wasn't sharing.

Something she understood. 'Really.' Some things weren't for imparting to a man she was still getting to know. She closed her eyes again. Hopefully she'd sleep till they reached Cairns. She was tired. Last night had been awesome. Making love with Nick was beyond amazing. She'd also been upset about Danielle. John had added to that with his despair. Yeah, sleep would be good. She sank deeper into the uncomfortable seat and tried to stop thinking about anything.

'Hey, wake up sleepy head. We've landed.' Nick was already out of his seat, looking eager to get going.

After knuckling her eyes, she straightened up and checked the time. Eighteen hundred had been and gone. 'With a bit of luck, we're done for the day.'

Darren poked his head around the cabin doorway. 'I haven't had any notification of another flight.'

'Nothing on the laptop either,' Nick confirmed.

Relief filled her. It had been stressful dealing with Maxwell's cardiac arrests and those horrendous injuries. She'd head out to the farm and have a shower there. Mum was cooking her favourite pasta for dinner as a cheer-her-up treat. Just the thought of diving into the bowl of sea-food and spaghetti made her feel a load better. The sleep might've helped too. 'What are you up to tonight?' she asked Nick as he slung the drug kit over his shoulder.

He shrugged. 'A quiet night in.' No smile was forth-coming. He looked tired. It had been as stressful for him working with Maxwell. Probably more so as the doctor on the job. Nick would've taken it hard if their patient hadn't made it as far as the hospital and into emergency care.

'It's been a long day.'

'It has.' He stood back for her to go down the stairs first, barely looking at her. Now that they'd finished work, he appeared to be taking a step back from her. Like her, he might want to think about where they were headed before he got in too deep. She didn't believe he regretted spending time with her. Nick was too genuine for that. He wouldn't have made love and then turned up at work as though they were merely colleagues if something wasn't bugging him. Like her.

Walking into the hangar, she thought about the warmth of being with her family. Something Nick clearly longed for. She sighed. To hell with all this toing and froing about how she felt. They both deserved to relax over a meal with a beer or wine and easy company.

Turning around, she crossed to the supply room. 'Nick,

how about joining me and the family for dinner?' If he turned her down it would be the last time she asked.

Slowly he looked across to her. 'Thanks, but think I'll give it a miss. I'm shattered.'

Fair enough. But studying him, her heart tightened at the despondency she saw. He wasn't being entirely truthful. But he also didn't do the feel sorry for me thing. 'Seafood spaghetti marinara is on the menu.'

'How did you know that's one of my favourite meals?' His smile was strained, but it was a smile.

'Something else we have in common. Mum makes it when she thinks I need cheering up.'

'Today you do because of Danielle.'

'Yes.'

'Have I got time to have a shower and throw on some decent clothes that don't smell of antiseptic?'

That was a yes then. Progress. She'd grab the moment and to heck with everything else. 'Go for it. Don't rush. I'll pop down to the supermarket to grab a couple of things Mum needs.'

'Can you add a bottle of wine to the list and I'll fix you up later?'

She shook her head. 'No. Tonight I've invited you out. Your role is to relax and enjoy yourself.'

Along with my company.

No holding back tonight. Danielle was right. Why wait for life to start? It was already here.

'Hey, Mum. I'm at the supermarket. Have you thought of anything else you need?'

'No, Leesa, just the Pinot Noir and tomato paste.' She laughed. 'Not to go together.'

'I'm bringing Nick, the new doctor, with me. Hope that's all right?' Her parents never made a fuss about her turning up with someone extra for a meal but, since it was Nick, she felt she had to say something so that her mum didn't get all gushy when they arrived. Since her Parkinson's diagnosis she'd been keen for Leesa to settle down with someone special.

Her mother laughed again. 'Not even answering.'

There was a bounce in Leesa's step as she made her way along the supermarket aisles. She added a second bottle of wine to the basket before grabbing a couple of items she needed at home, including biscuits for Baxter.

Nick smelt of pine soap when he slipped into the car beside her. His shorts moulded his tight butt, and the blue and white shirt, with two buttons open at the top, made her mouth salivate. Her fingers tightened on the steering wheel to prevent her from leaning over and rubbing his tanned skin. How did she possibly think she could remain aloof around him? He was stunning.

'I'm glad you persisted about me coming. I feel better already.' Nick glanced her way. 'Your family know I'm on the way?'

'Yep. I think Kevin's bringing a couple of mates too. Dad's got some chores to be done in the morning.'

'Count me in. Beats doing the housework.'

'From what I saw your apartment is immaculate.' Almost OTT in her book. 'You might get to drive a tractor tomorrow. There's early cane to be harvested.'

'Could prove interesting. Probably best I stick to the mundane chores.'

'It's no different to driving any other vehicle as long as you keep an eye out where you're going.'

'Could be a new skill to add to my CV.' He laughed for the first time all day, making her pleased she'd suggested he come with her.

She'd asked him as though it was a date, even if he didn't get that. Last night had been wonderful, today a lot less so, and she wanted to find a balance so they could get along—without watching every single thing they said or did for fear of tripping up. 'Being able to do things on a farm beats living in the middle of a large city.'

'I'm starting to see the benefits.'

'What did you used to do in your spare time?'

'In Brisbane I'd go to the Gold Coast to surf and kayak. I'd done some of that in Adelaide but prefer the Coast. In Sydney it wasn't so easy. It takes so long to get to anywhere when you live close to the Central Business District it's a drag.'

'Why the CBD?'

'I was working at the central ambulance station and the rules were that you had to live within sixty minutes of the station, so you could be called in for emergencies. It's a bit extreme really, as everyone on call stayed over at the station anyway, but the advantage for me was not having to take long, tedious train rides to get to work or home at the end of an arduous shift.'

When he relaxed, he could talk a lot. Showed how often he wasn't at ease with people. 'Central Sydney is fabulous,' Leesa said, 'but I could never live there. I prefer the outdoors being handy so I can get out and about any time I like.'

'You've got the farm for that, and all the beaches up the coastline.' He nodded. 'This is a great place. I could see myself staying here longer than my usual stints.'

'You what?' Had he really admitted that? To her?

'Surprised you, have I?' he asked with a serious look. 'Surprised myself, actually. It would be good to stop moving around.'

'Why do you?'

'Habit?' He hesitated. 'I'm looking for somewhere I feel comfortable.'

'Cairns is doing that?'

'Might be.' His uncertainty spoke volumes.

'Give yourself some time before making a major decision. You haven't been here very long.' He mightn't be either, but hope flared.

'True, but I already prefer the work. Flying all over the place to help people with ongoing issues, not having to sit in peak hour traffic when I'm coping with a touch-and-go case. There're a lot of pluses.'

'True.' What about his private life? Any pluses there?

'It's great being invited to dinner with you and your parents.'

She went with his change of subject. Pushing further might lead to him shutting down completely. 'Baxter will be happy to see you.'

He smacked his forehead lightly. 'How could I forget him? He's a big plus to living here.'

'Still thinking you might get a dog?'

'Yes, but if I do, I seriously have to consider moving into a place with a bit of a yard.'

She couldn't imagine Baxter being in an apartment. He loved bounding around the lawn too much. Indicating to turn left, she said, 'Here we go.'

Nick gave her a quizzical glance. 'You sound like you're uncertain about something.'

What about how her mother was going to act around Nick? 'Think the day's catching up.' Her energy level had fallen again, but not as low as when they'd finished work.

'I'm sure a wine and a bowl of spaghetti will have you bouncing around in no time.'

'Fingers crossed you're right.'

And that Mum keeps quiet about certain topics.

Nick would certainly head for another city if he heard a hint of what her mother hoped for.

'That was superb,' Nick told Jodi, Leesa's mother, as he pushed his plate aside. 'Seriously good.'

'Compliments will get you a third helping any day,' Kevin laughed.

He grinned. 'Except someone beat me to the last spoonful.'

'Only the fast win around here,' Kevin said.

'Relax, boys,' Jodi said. 'There's apple crumble and custard to follow.'

Nick shook his head. 'I can't believe this. Amazing.'

Family dinners had never been a part of his life. Not even when growing up with Grandad, who thought meals were to feed the body and not the mind with dreams of delectable offerings. As for what was doled out in foster care, forget it.

One dollop of something that could've been anything the pigs didn't want, and smelt even worse, did nothing for meal times except make them something that had to be got through as fast as possible. One home had been better, he conceded. Mrs Cole had cooked up decent solid meals that everyone had ate in a hurry, before leaving the table to get back to whatever they'd been doing before the plates were put down.

'Tomorrow it's a barbecue after we've finished in the paddocks,' Kevin told him.

'If you're trying to convince me to stay and help out, I'm in.' It was the least he could do for these kind people. Better than out and out admitting he wanted to spend more time with them.

'Might as well stay the night then,' Jodi said with a little smile. 'We've got extra rooms out the back.'

'I haven't come prepared for work. I'll need to pop home and get some rough clothes and boots.'

'Plenty here,' Leesa told him. 'All sizes.'

'Bathroom supplies available too,' Jodi told him.

With everything he needed on hand, he really couldn't insist on returning to town for the night. 'It's a done deal then.' Sipping his beer, he decided it wasn't such a bad thing either. He could get used to this easy way the Bennetts had about them, though no doubt there'd be nothing relaxed about harvest tomorrow. Standing up, he began clearing the dishes from the table.

Yes, he was comfortable beyond description, and for once he couldn't dredge up any enthusiasm over keeping his distance—especially from Leesa. She'd brought him into her circle without any concerns. Inviting him here tonight had come naturally, despite the tension lying between them throughout the day.

Leesa trusted him. Kapow. Just like that, she trusted him.

Talk about a first. Make that the first time he'd trusted in return so readily. Because, yes, he trusted her not to make a fool of him.

He could be making a fool of himself and she'd prove him wrong, but he couldn't find it within himself to believe so. Didn't mean he was going to leap into a relationship with her. They worked together and he didn't want to leave the job he was enjoying so much, especially if he did get the promotion. Also, he'd once fallen in love only to have it thrown back in his face. It had been the final blow to an already fearful heart. He'd lost enough people who mattered. Losing another would be impossible to cope with.

'Take that crumble through to the dining room,' Jodi told him.

'Yes, ma'am.' Leesa often sounded just like her mother, he realised. No arguing with either of them.

'Don't you "yes, ma'am" me.' She playfully flicked a tea towel at him. 'Pour my daughter another drink so she'll have to stay the night and not rush back to that empty house she lives in.'

'Trying to get me into trouble?' he grinned. He liked this woman. She pulled no punches, again like Leesa. And the rest of the family. 'Tell me, was it tough growing up here when Leesa and Kevin were young?'

'You'd have to ask Leesa. I will say we had no spare money, the kids didn't have fancy clothes or toys, but they both learned to work hard and be proud of what they achieved.'

Though in very different circumstances, he'd had much the same lessons. 'Sounds ideal.' For them, not him. He headed away with the pudding before he got hit with a load of questions he wasn't ready to answer, kind as Jodi was.

Kevin had moved away to talk on his phone and Leesa's father, Brent, was nowhere in sight.

'Would you like another wine?' He knew he was supposed to pour one without giving her the chance to say no, but he preferred to be more onside with Leesa than her mother if it came down to it.

Leesa looked from her empty glass to him, and nodded. 'Why not?' Her eyes shone with laughter. 'You seem comfortable.'

'You know what? I am. I'm even looking forward to going out in the sugar cane fields and getting down and dirty.'

'You might regret that tomorrow night when you've had too much sun, and muscles you aren't aware of ache like stink.'

'You suggesting I'm a townie?'

'Would you expect any different?' she asked and picked up the glass he'd filled. 'Joining me? Or saving yourself for tractor driving?'

A challenge was not to be ignored. He flipped the cap off another beer. Despite being momentarily alone with Leesa he leaned close to say quietly, 'Depends what you mean by joining you.' He could hand out challenges too.

Her smile was so sexy he nearly spilt his beer. 'You're sleeping in the staff quarters.'

'Who else will be there?' Kevin would have his own room in the house, surely? His mates weren't arriving till first thing in the morning as something had come up to keep them in town.

'I might,' Leesa teased.

'Better than me sneaking inside like a horny teen.' What with the noise Leesa made when she came, the whole house would know what was going on.

'I don't know. It could be fun.'

He shivered. He might be comfortable with this family, but there were limitations to how far he took it. 'I'd be too worried we'd be heard to actually let go.'

Leesa's laughter was loud and naughty, and brought everyone back to the table for dessert.

But later when she slipped in beside him on the narrow bed in the staff quarters, he had no handbrake on his feelings. Nor did Leesa.

The only downside was when she left him to go back to her room around three o'clock. 'I'm acting like that teenager you mentioned, but I can't bear to see a knowing look in my parents' eyes when my alarm goes off and I'm not there to stop it.'

After she'd gone, he slept the sleep of the dead. That was so abnormal he was stunned when Leesa's banging on the door woke him.

'What time is it?' The sun was streaming in the window he'd forgotten to cover with the blind.

'Six. I'm heading away. Mum's got breakfast going and the others are already downing mugs of tea.'

He'd been so deeply asleep he hadn't heard their vehicle arriving? 'Great. Now they'll all call me Townie.' He clambered out of bed.

'Take a fast shower before you head over to the house,' Leesa grinned. 'I'll see you tonight.'

He thought she was grinning because he smelt of their night together, but when the water remained cold he had to wonder if she'd been having him on. He wouldn't put it past her.

'Dang, forgot to turn the hot water cylinder on last

night,' Brent said when he joined the men around the table. 'We don't leave it on when no one's using the quarters.'

'I'll see to it before we get started in the fields,' Nick told him. 'I'll need a shower before heading back to town.' He didn't want to pong of sweat when Leesa drove him home, hopefully to his apartment for some more fun. Or she might decide to take him to the house she lived in, which he had yet to see. Apparently, it belonged to her grandmother who wasn't ready to sell it, despite living in a retirement village.

'Right. Let's get this happening.' Brent stood up. 'Nick, time for a driving lesson.'

'After I turn the water on,' he returned, feeling so good. Rinsing his plate, he stowed it in the dishwasher and followed the men outside with a spring in his step. To be doing something different and helping this family felt great. It showed how little he did beyond work.

After Patrick gave him his second chance, once he'd begun studying hard to get the grades that got him into university, he'd rarely looked sideways for other interests. His focus had been on proving he was as capable as Judge Crombie had suggested, and now it seemed he didn't know any other way to be.

Leesa was slowly changing him, and through her, her family seemed to be too. Another thing to be careful about? Could be, though a voice was nagging him to let it go and make the most of the opportunity to live a full life, not one that was devoted totally to medicine. He realised he really didn't know how to do that. Didn't have a clue.

'Climb up, Nick. We're heading to that field by the road.'

So began his experience of harvesting.

* * *

'How'd that go?' Leesa asked fourteen hours later when she sat down beside him on her parents' deck, where everyone was relaxing with a cold beer.

'He's not bad for a townie,' Kevin answered for him. 'His rows were straight and the cane wasn't mangled.'

'I really enjoyed myself.' Who knew he'd get so much pleasure out of driving a tractor up and down fields in the sweltering heat for hours on end? 'So much so I've put my hand up to help out again when I'm free.'

The smile Leesa gave him increased the happiness. 'Nothing like a new experience to give you a lift.'

She really did understand him. She mightn't know how messed up he was, but she certainly understood he wanted more out of life than what he already had.

'I wasn't down in the first place.'

'No, but you were looking for something to distract you from work.'

Thank goodness Baxter nudged his knee just then, or he might've grabbed Leesa into a hug that he wouldn't be able to pull back from. Instead, he rubbed the dog behind his ears. 'Hey, boy, is it your dinner time?'

'He's already had it. But no harm in trying to con you into a second round.' Leesa patted Baxter, but he wasn't moving away from Nick's hand.

'Fair enough.' Nick kept rubbing the dog. 'How was work? Busy?'

'Two short flights, one to take a man home after he was discharged from the cardiac ward, another to pick up a tourist who fell off a cliff up in the Daintree and sustained a fractured pelvis.'

'You go by chopper for that one?'

'Yes. It was only a short hop, but not near a road for

an ambulance to do the job.' She drained her beer and stood up. 'I'd better give Mum a hand. She seems more tired than usual.'

'She had a restless night,' Leesa's dad spoke up. 'There've been a few of those lately.' The man looked worried.

'The specialist did say that would happen, Dad. I think a lot of it's to do with her overthinking about what lies ahead.' Leesa frowned. 'Maybe she should have some counselling.'

'Good luck telling her that. She bit my head off the one time I mentioned it.'

'I'm not surprised.' Leesa sighed. 'Mum's always been strong and now she thinks she's letting the side down by being sick.'

'From what I've seen, she's still strong,' Nick said. 'She hasn't given up on getting out and doing her chores and having fun with the family.'

The shaking in her hands had been a bit stronger this morning, but that would happen as time went by. Sometimes it would be because Jodi had done too much, and would revert back to where it had been when she rested, and sometimes the intensity would remain, a sign of the Parkinson's strengthening.

Leesa squeezed his shoulder. 'Thanks for that. I think we're all watching too hard to find something.'

'You're not wrong,' Brent said.

'I imagine it's impossible not to,' Nick agreed. 'It's probably also what Jodi's doing.' He'd seen that with patients when he'd been training. Giving someone a prognosis that had no cure cranked up their anxiety level and had them on guard for more problems. 'It's only natural.'

Leesa was still standing beside him and her thigh was pressing against his arm. 'It's hard.'

He hugged her waist. 'Just remember, these days the outlook is good. Parkinson's can be controlled for years.'

'I know, but this is Mum.'

The only answer he had was to hug harder.

When Leesa stepped away to head to the kitchen she wiped her cheeks quickly, something he'd not seen before. Her mother was obviously her Achilles heel.

Nick's heart tightened for her and this family. There was nothing he could do but be there for her, and them. Something he really wanted. Which was a commitment in itself. One he fully intended sticking to. It was a huge step.

What's more, nothing was getting in the way of it. None of those warning bells were ringing in his head. Whether this meant he was committed to getting closer to Leesa he wasn't sure, but he'd go with this for now and let everything else unfold slowly.

And when they later reached his apartment block, he turned to Leesa. 'Want to come up for a while?' Strange how hard his heart was beating as he waited for her reply. 'Baxter can come too.' Not exactly following the 'slowly' part of his earlier thoughts, but it was impossible not to want to kiss her after what they'd shared last night.

'You didn't think you'd get away with leaving him in the car, did you?'

'I guess not.'

'I'm not staying the night, Nick. You're exhausted after working all day and need some sleep before turning up at the hangar tomorrow. But…' She gave him an impish grin that sent his blood racing. 'I do have an hour to spare.'

Better than nothing.

CHAPTER SIX

THE NEXT MORNING Leesa woke at five. It was a habit, no alarm necessary, though she always set it when on a shift. Today was a day off and she'd go spend some time with her mum.

Stretching as far as possible, she languished in the after sensations of amazing sex the night before. When she'd decided to leap in and see where she and Nick were headed she'd done it with all she had. He was everything she was looking for and more. But it had been physical, not getting close about their future or what each expected.

She couldn't share herself completely with a man who wasn't prepared to talk about himself. Obviously he had issues about family yet seemed completely at home with hers.

Being impatient wasn't going to get her anywhere, so she picked up her phone and texted him.

Morning. Haven't slept so well in ages.

Two hours later when Nick would've been at work, she still hadn't received a reply. Busy? Or playing cool again? Two could play that game, she decided. All very well getting together and having a hot night, and then going back to quiet mode, but she wasn't taking it any more. Either they cleared the air and at least remained friends—though how she'd walk away from their fling was beyond her—or the other option was to stick to being colleagues. Which might be best anyway if either of them got Joy's job.

Climbing out of bed, she hauled on shorts, t-shirt and running shoes. 'Come on, Baxter. I need to clear my head.'

At midday Nick still hadn't come back to her. The pleasure from the night before had well and truly faded. Now she was miffed and wondering if she was wrong about him, that he was another mistake. No, she couldn't accept that. He was special, through and through. Her head knew it, her heart felt it. And yet now she was feeling less inclined to carry on regardless.

Nick had the power to hurt her. A fling with him was no longer enough. It had to be all or nothing. Yet that was all that was on offer, and she knew she couldn't walk away.

She pressed his number to call him. 'Hey, busy morning?' she asked when he answered.

'Has been a bit.'

So that's how it was. 'Okay, I'll leave you to it then.'

'Feel up to going out for a meal tonight?' he asked.

Stunned, she decided she knew nothing when it came to reading men. This one in particular. 'I'd love to.'

'Great. I'll pick you up about seven, unless things turn upside down here.'

'Sounds good.'

'Got to go. There's an emergency come up.'

Wow. Where did that come from? Now she was totally confused. A date with Nick. The first one they'd been on. So far everything had been about sex. Other than Saturday night at the farm, she reminded herself, when she'd invited him to dinner.

Doing a little dance on the spot she hugged herself. If she wasn't in love with Nick, she was so damned close it was scary. Because there were no guarantees everything would go as she hoped. So, she'd go back to taking it slowly, one day at a time, enjoying what time they had together and see where it led.

Which is what she did over the next couple of weeks. Nick was no more forthcoming about his past when they talked over dinner, always bringing the conversation around to work or her family and the farm. Leesa bit down on the questions she needed answers for, hoping that giving him space would eventually lead him to relaxing completely with her.

At the end of one long and difficult day she told Nick she had to go and see her mother. 'I won't drop around to your place tonight. Mum needs me to pick up some meds for her. I want to spend some time with her too.'

'Fair enough.' He looked fine with that apart from a slight shrug.

'It's what I do, Nick, okay? This is my family.' Her life didn't revolve entirely around Nick. She was independent and didn't need him in her life twenty-four-seven. It might be an old hang up from her marriage, but if she didn't take heed she'd only get more wound up. Being around Nick had her freeing herself of the past, but there was a way to go.

'I get it. Truly,' he added sharply.

From the little he'd said, her family life wasn't what he'd known as normal. But he had to understand it if he wanted more than a fling. 'I need to catch up on a few jobs too,' she said. Grocery shopping and tidying the house before Gran came to visit in the weekend were top of the list.

'Me, too.' Finally, he relaxed a little. 'See you back here in the morning.'

'Will do.'

'Leesa.'

Spinning around, she found Nick right behind her. 'Have I forgotten something?'

He shook his head. 'No. I want to say sorry for the way I reacted. I don't expect you to spend every hour of your time with me. We both have more to our lives than work and our fling.'

She stared at him. Coming from Nick that was quite an admission. 'Yes, we do have other things needing our individual attention that can't be ignored for ever.'

I will never become yours or anyone else's total life. Connor tried to make me do that and it was as though he was taking over my mind, dictating who and what I was.

Nick would never be like that, but she still had to stand up and be counted, for her own confidence if nothing else.

Then something dawned on her. 'If you get Joy's job you won't be moving away.'

'No. Think it's time I got on with getting a dog, too.'

'You are looking at more permanence in your life, aren't you?'

That had to be good for him. Might be for her too, because there was no way she wanted to get involved with a man who couldn't put down roots somewhere. But, most importantly, she believed Nick really needed to create his own place and start to feel he was home.

'A pet's a good start,' she added. She wasn't so sure

she wanted to go up against him for Joy's job. The consequences might make for more problems.

'One step at a time?'

She dipped her head in agreement. 'Absolutely. Now I have to run or the pharmacy will be closed before I get there.' She touched his stubbly chin. 'Sleep tight.'

'Might do that with no distraction between my sheets.' He stepped away. 'See you in the morning.'

She couldn't wait. Nick had got to her in ways she'd never have believed. He accepted her as she was, didn't even hint at wanting to change her. When she'd said she had other plans for tonight he did tense up a bit, but then he apologised for his reaction. Yes, he was a great guy and she was falling deeper and deeper for him.

Her skin tightened. Was this truly good? Nothing dishonest or untrue was ever reflected in his character, whether they were working together or sharing a meal and bed. Going with her gut instincts felt right. If those needed back up it was there in the way her family accepted Nick. Not what they'd done with her ex. No, they'd tried to warn her Connor wasn't good enough but love could be blind. It had been with Connor. It wasn't going to be with Nick.

Next morning when she walked into the staff kitchen her heart melted at the sight of Dr Sexy perched on a stool, stirring sugar into his tea as he read what appeared to be case notes. 'Morning.'

His head flicked up. 'Back at you. Kettle's just boiled.'

'Who's flying us today?'

'Darren. He's giving the plane the once over.'

Mark, a helicopter pilot, strode into the room. 'I'm on the chopper if you need an exciting ride.'

'Not unless an emergency crops up,' Nick told him with

a laugh. 'Our list is all about going to places with landing strips, not pocket-sized squares.'

'What time did you get in?' Leesa asked.

'Just after five. I was out of milk and bread so figured I might as well grab some and come in here for breakfast.'

Sounded like he hadn't slept well. Missing the fun they'd been getting up to?

'Thought you were going shopping last night.' She wasn't going to tell him she'd slept like a log. He might think she didn't miss him much, and she had.

She'd also been glad of time to herself to think through everything going on between them. The past fortnight had sped past, all fun and not serious in any way. Which was fine, but nothing had changed. All fun and no depth.

'I went home to shower and change, then couldn't be bothered going out again.'

'Where are we headed for our first job?' she asked, ready to get to work and away from wondering if Nick ever relaxed enough to get out and have a life. He'd helped at the farm but that had been at her instigation. It was as though he didn't know what to do with himself when he wasn't being a doctor.

'Taking a woman down to Brisbane for a heart valve replacement. She's expected here at eight thirty.'

'I'll go check stock levels and everything else.' With a mug of tea in hand, Leesa headed out to the plane, all the time trying not to think about Nick. Impossible when they spent a lot of time together.

'How was Jodi?' Nick asked as they waited on board for their patient to arrive.

'Not as tired as I'd expected. I do wish she'd take things easier though.'

'You might be asking too much.'

She knew that, but she didn't want her mum's condition getting worse before it had to. 'Of course I am. It's to be expected.'

'I get that.'

Did he though? When he'd said he didn't have family to care about? She sucked air over her teeth. Now she was being bitchy for no reason. It was because he rattled her. They were opposites in so many ways but they still understood each other. Could they have a future? One that was for ever and not just for a few nights having amazing sex?

'You've gone quiet.'

'It happens occasionally,' she put out there.

'Can't say I've noticed.' Nick tapped her shoulder. 'We've got company.'

The ambulance was backing up to the plane. 'Good. Now we can get going.'

'Impatient, aren't we?' He flicked her a puzzled look.

'It's a long haul to Brisbane and back.'

'Part of the job.' The puzzlement remained.

Fair enough. She didn't know why she was being terse other than she needed more time away from Nick to do some serious thinking. She was in a relationship that she wasn't sure was quite what she wanted, or needed. A fling had its upsides, but they weren't really her thing. She was an all or nothing kind of girl. And that didn't seem to be what Nick wanted.

'Hello, Leesa, Nick. This is Maggie Oldsmith.' The ambulance medic was pressing the button to bring the stretcher up to their level. 'She's been given a mild sedative as she's not keen on flying.'

'Hi, Maggie. I'm Leesa, your paramedic for the duration of the trip.'

'And I'm Nick, the doctor keeping an eye on you.'

'Hello. I'm the old bat needing a new heart valve.' Maggie's smile was tired, as were her eyes. It all went with her heart condition.

'You'll be a new woman when we bring you home,' Leesa told her.

'I hope so.'

'Is there anyone coming with us to keep Maggie company in Brisbane?' Nick asked the medic as he looked outside.

'Maggie's son is already down in Brisbane. He'll be at the hospital when the ambulance arrives.'

'Right, let's get this show in the air.' Nick checked the trolley was secure. Leesa watched the medic lower the lift and move away so she could close the door.

'All set,' she told Darren.

Once they were airborne and levelled out, Nick gave Maggie a thorough check over, leaving Leesa redundant as the two of them chattered about any number of things.

She knew Nick was trying to divert Maggie from worrying about flying. It must've worked, or the sedative had had an effect, because she was soon snoring. The monitors were showing no changes in her readings from what they'd been at the start of the flight. 'Well done.'

'Not sure I like the background music,' he grinned, then pulled up the laptop and began going through Maggie's medical data, the grin gone.

So no chatting to fill in the time. Leesa sighed. They did do this at times, pulled back from one another without reason. It was quite likely Nick required space to think it all through too. That was a wet blanket on her emotions even when she was doing the same. Talk about mixed up, she smiled internally. But then the experts said love wasn't meant to be easy. She wouldn't know other than her experience definitely hadn't been a walk in the park.

Staring out the window she watched the coastline bend and curve all the way south. It was a beautiful landscape. The beaches, the blue water and the Great Barrier Reef further out attracted visitors from all over the country and around the world. She lived in one of the most amazing places.

Time to check on Maggie. She unclipped her seatbelt at the same moment Nick did.

'I've got this,' he said.

She could get picky and point out she usually did the obs, but what was the point? They were as capable as each other and Maggie was in good hands, be they hers or Nick's.

'No problem.' Pulling her phone from her pocket, she read her emails and answered two.

On the return flight Nick studied Leesa from under lowered brows. Damn she ripped him up and had his heart speeding without any encouragement. She was beyond wonderful. The nights they spent in bed were amazing. He couldn't get enough of her. So much so he was teetering on the edge of the love cliff. More than anything he wanted to let go and hand his heart over. Yet the buts remained, holding him firmly on the ground. He knew his love would be safe with Leesa if she reciprocated it.

That was the question. Did she? There was so much he hadn't told her, and the longer he left it the harder it

SUE MACKAY											129

became to put everything out there. As though the more
he gained from being with her, the more he had to lose
when she learned about his past and how he'd raced into
his marriage without so much as a backward glance.

He gave a tight grunt. Seemed these days the only way
he looked was backwards. Keeping safe. Staying lonely
and fed up. Desperate for something most people had.
Afraid of being hurt and of hurting someone else.

'Cleared to land,' Darren told them.

'Good, I'm starving.' Leesa slid her phone into her
pocket.

'When aren't you?' Nick asked. He wasn't only referring to food, but sex. Leesa had a huge appetite for that.

They'd barely started lunch when an emergency call
came in. It had them heading to Cook Town, to pick up a
fisherman who'd got his hand caught in the winch while
bringing in a laden net, and had severed two fingers.

'How awful was that?' Leesa commented after they'd
loaded the man into an ambulance back in Cairns. She
shuddered at the thought of losing some fingers.

'I bet it won't stop him fishing once the stubs have
healed,' Nick said. 'He sounded like a tough bugger. Apparently, he once had a large fish hook stuck in his abdomen for two days while the skipper got the boat back to
port in the midst of a storm.'

'How did the hook end up in his stomach?' she asked.
'Kevin's told me some crazy stories about what happens
on board fishing trawlers.'

'It's not the safest job about.'

Joy was waiting outside the hangar when they arrived
back at base. 'You two are needed on the chopper. A six-
seater fixed-wing with four people on board has gone

down in the forest behind Hartley's Falls. Fire and emergency have one chopper on its way and need another. You're the first crew I've got available.'

'Let's go.' Leesa was already striding towards the chopper where Mark was sitting in the cockpit.

Nick strode out to keep. 'No rest for the wicked, eh?'

'I'm wicked?' she teased.

'Very,' he grinned. The tension had eased.

'Takes one to know one,' she added as she leapt up into the helicopter.

Nick slammed the door closed behind them.

Mark instantly started the rotors spinning. 'Buckle up, guys. I'm going low and fast.'

Which meant they could get knocked about by wind off the hills. But it was totally reasonable to do that. They weren't going too far and Mark wouldn't want to waste time gaining height that he'd soon have to lose.

'What do we know about the passengers?' Nick asked when they were airborne.

'Four men returning from a safari up north,' Mark answered, 'One of them the pilot. The plane lost contact with the tower about an hour ago. A chopper from Port Douglas was in the vicinity and located the plane. There's no movement, no sign of anyone.'

'We're to expect the worst-case scenario and hope we're wrong.' Nick leaned back in his seat, his eyes closed. 'I hate these jobs.'

'Don't we all?' Leesa agreed.

Nick sat up straight. 'Let's run through what we need to take down when we arrive.'

Leesa tapped one finger. 'The medical packs.' Tapped a second finger. 'The drug kit.'

He nodded. 'Stretchers, oxygen.'

They continued with the list, both working on the assumption they'd be retrieving men who were alive. It was the only way to approach the scene, unless they heard differently.

The closer they got to Hartley's Falls the tighter the tension in Leesa's face got. They hadn't heard from the other chopper yet.

Nick touched her thigh. 'Breathe.'

'I'm trying,' she gasped.

'I get that.' He kept rubbing her thigh.

Mark came through the headset. 'All four men are alive. Three with serious injuries. Fire and Rescue are lifting two out soon, the medics have stabilised them and got them onto stretchers.'

'We're going to have to hover further away?' Nick asked.

'If I can't find a safe place to put down nearby, then yes.'

'What if you got the other chopper to move away so we can be lowered to the site to help out?'

'We'll do it only if the guys on the ground give us the all-clear, but chances are they'll be too busy retrieving their two patients.'

'We don't want to delay their operation.'

A low groan came through the headset.

'Mark, what's up?' Leesa asked.

Silence.

'Mark? Talk to us,' Nick demanded.

'Buckle up tight,' Mark shouted. 'I'm going down.' Even before Mark finished speaking the chopper was dropping. Fast. Frighteningly fast.

His heart in his throat, Nick glanced at Leesa as she pulled her seatbelt tighter. 'What's going on?' His stomach was a tight ball. Something was very wrong. 'Hey, Mark, what's up?'

'Don't feel good.'

'How? Where?'

'Head.'

'Not good.' Leesa stared ahead.

Nick reached for her shaking hand, held it between both his. 'We'll be fine.' They had to be. Leesa had to be. Nothing bad could happen to her.

Leesa would've given Nick an eye roll if fear wasn't gripping her so hard no part of her moved—except her mind, and it was in panic mode.

'Yeah, sure.' Her fingers tightened around his, probably about to break them. What was wrong with Mark? Something to do with his head. Pain? Blurriness? She glanced out the window, and immediately looked away.

The forest was barely metres below, rushing at them. Then trees were all around and the chopper was tipping sideways. A horrendous racket filled her head of tearing metal, rotors ripping into the trees. *Bang! Ka-thump!* Metal screeched, buckled inwards. She was flung sideways, then backwards.

The movement stopped.

Nick's hand had gone.

She blinked once, twice. Stared around, breathed in deep. 'Nick?' she cried. 'Nick. Answer me.'

'I'm here.' His voice came from beyond where he'd been sitting. 'You okay?'

No idea. She tried to stretch her legs but didn't get far

because the cockpit had been shoved back. The stretcher in front of her was at an odd angle. Her upper right arm was throbbing. Her neck was stiff and painful. Otherwise, 'Think so. What about you?'

His reply was a deep groan as he tried to shift.

Her heart jerked. 'Nick? What's happened?' *Please be all right.* Unclipping the safety harness, she stood up only to bang her head on metal. The top of the chopper was caved in. Down on her knees, she forced her way over obstacles to reach Nick.

His face was contorted with pain.

Her heart slowed. 'Where are you hurting?' Nothing could be wrong with Nick. Anything but that.

'My chest. Probably my ribs. Check Mark. I'll follow you.'

'No.' She wanted to stay with Nick, check him over thoroughly. Laying her hand on his chest she touched his ribs as gently as possible.

He winced. 'Something slammed into my chest, possibly cracked a rib or two. I don't feel bad otherwise. Mark was having a medical event. He needs your attention.'

Nick was right. Dammit.

'You stay here.' She was already backing out of the small space beside him. It was the hardest thing she'd ever done. Her arms ached with the need to hold him, to confirm what she knew. They were alive.

Leesa grabbed a seat as the chopper lurched and dropped further to thud onto something solid, hopefully the ground. The thought of falling further gave her the heebies.

'Agh…' Nick groaned loudly.

'Nick?' she called, her heart in her throat as she prepared to go back to him.

'Carry on to Mark. He didn't respond to your call.' Then Nick groaned again, followed by a curse.

'Mark, can you hear me?' She pushed and shoved through the crumpled wreck of the helicopter. 'Mark? Where are you?'

Silence. But only from him. Trees were cracking and metal was groaning as the chopper rocked. She closed her eyes and waited for it to fall further.

Nothing happened.

Slowly she exhaled. Phew. A pounding started behind her eyes. She couldn't feel a wound on her skull, didn't remember hitting anything with her head.

Get over it.

Squeezing through the unrecognisable flying machine, nothing appeared to be where it should. A pair of legs stopped her progress.

'Mark.' Leesa knelt and began to run her hands up Mark's legs to his arms and hopefully a pulse. A branch had bust through the windscreen making it impossible to see his head. Her hand touched a hand, and she felt for a pulse. Very weak but there *was* one. Relief filled her. Not that it meant he was going to be all right, but he was alive. Holding the back of her other hand in front of his mouth and nose she felt erratic, short breaths. 'What happened?' she asked no one in particular.

He'd said 'head' when Nick asked where the problem was. Could be an aneurism or a stroke. Impossible to tell.

Unwilling to try moving Mark on her own when she didn't know what other injuries he might have, she began to carefully and methodically check over the parts of his body she could reach.

'What have we got?' Nick asked from behind her.

She nearly leapt out of her skin. 'Jeez, you scared the living daylights out of me. You were supposed to stay where you were.' She wasn't going to admit she was glad he was with her. This whole disaster was freaking her out. Her hands shook and the throbbing behind her eyes was increasing in intensity.

A steady hand touched her shoulder. 'It was getting a bit lonely back there.'

Looking at him, she bit her lip. He was whiter than white. 'It's a tight squeeze in here but I'm glad you're with me.' So much for not telling him. 'You're bleeding from your chin.' She ran a finger over his jaw.

'Took a bit of a whack. Is Mark alive?' Forthright for sure. But sensible—there was no point in trying to move the man if he was gone.

'He's breathing and his pulse is shallow and hard to find. I haven't managed to check him all over. That branch's in the way. Before you even think of trying to move it with those ribs giving you grief, you are staying away.'

Talking like a kid on steroids, Leesa.

'Sorry, I'm a bit shaken up.'

Nick ran a finger down her cheek. 'It's understandable. I'm feeling much the same.'

She leaned closer, drew a slow breath to ease the tension gripping her. It was so good having him here, if only he hadn't been injured. 'Take it easy. You're hurting.'

'I hear you, but let me take a look at Mark. There might be some way we can shift him without causing any more problems. We need to make certain his spine's not damaged first.' Nick was already removing one of Mark's shoes. A hard pinch on the sole got a small twitch. 'Don't think we need worry about the spine at least.'

'Something on his side.' Seemed all she could do was hope for more good news to come.

Worry belied Leesa's words and Nick wanted to haul her into his arms and never let go. The crash had been close to being dreadful for all of them. Holding Leesa would calm his shattered nerves, but Mark needed his attention more than anyone. Scrambling closer, he bit down hard as pain flared in his chest. The odds of fractured ribs were high. He was thankful his breathing was fine or he'd be scared witless that a rib had penetrated a lung.

'I wonder how long before someone realises we're missing.' Leesa had a hand on Mark's wrist, her finger searching for his pulse. She must've found it because relief filtered through her worry.

'They must've heard from Mark that we were closing in.' Quite the day for aircraft crashes. 'Someone will be asking why he hasn't reported in shortly.' The pilot's left arm was at an odd angle. 'Possible shoulder dislocation here.' Nothing he could do about it. Mark needed to be in an open space for the joint to be manipulated into place, and until help arrived that wasn't happening. Not a lot was.

'Can you reach his head to check it over?' Leesa sounded stronger.

Relieved, Nick held his breath as he lay down prone next to Mark, reaching his right arm up to Mark's head. Pain engulfed him. He waited for it to pass, trying not to breathe too deeply, then took his time feeling for contusions. 'Nothing.' But… 'Hang on. Yep, swelling on the left side.' A bleed? Quite possible, though prior to the crash or as a result of that branch whacking was impossible to know yet.

'Should we try to put him into the recovery position?' There was a hitch in Leesa's voice. 'Just in case.'

In case things went pear-shaped. 'Let's give it a go.' It was going to hurt like stink but they had to do everything they could for Mark. 'You'll have to do most of the work, I'm sorry.' His left side was pretty useless.

'I'll try pulling him my way if you want to work at keeping him free of the branch.'

It was an operation in hell, painful for all of them, though Mark knew nothing. Eventually they had him on his side with his head tipped back enough to keep his mouth open.

Nick took a couple of deep breaths and pushed up onto his backside. 'You cried out a couple of times. Are you sure you're not injured somewhere?'

His heart pounded at the thought. He didn't want Leesa hurting at all. The chances of that were nigh on impossible. The severe landing and then the chopper rolling and twisting meant there was no escaping some serious bruising for all of them. They were lucky both of them weren't far worse off. That's if she wasn't downplaying an injury—something that wouldn't surprise him. Leesa was one determined woman when it came to showing how strong she could be.

Her eyes met his. 'I honestly don't think I've got anything more than lots of bruises. We're going to look a funny colour for a few days.'

'A matching pair.' Crash survivors. What if he'd lost her

for ever? Strong shivers rocked him. No way. He couldn't face that. She was special, wonderful. She—

His heart stopped. Leesa meant so much to him it was terrifying thinking about what might've happened.

Leesa's delicious lips finally lifted into one of her beautiful, gut-twisting smiles. 'Does purple match the blue of our uniforms?'

He shuffled closer, needing to put his good arm around her. He had to feel her, to know they'd made it. Kissing the top of her head, he whispered, 'We're very lucky.'

'We are. For a moment…'

His arm tightened around her as she shivered. 'Don't go there.' He already had. It was dark and gut wrenching.

'I'll try not to.' Her lips brushed his. 'Hold me close.'

He twisted to bring her in closer, and gasped as pain shot through his chest.

Leesa pulled back carefully. 'Nick. I'm so sorry. I didn't think. Where's it hurting?' Her fingers were slipping under his shirt, going right to the very spot where he thought the ribs were broken.

'How did you know?'

'That that's where it's painful? There's a lot of swelling. Plus, some bleeding from a surface wound.' Her fingers were moving all over his ribcage, checking, feeling, touching. Then she moved lower to check his abdomen, up to his shoulders and around his neck. 'Otherwise, I think you're up to muster. Unless,' her eyes were fierce when she locked them on him. 'Unless there's something *you're* not mentioning?'

He started to laugh and immediately regretted it as his ribs told him they weren't in the mood. On a light inhale he croaked out, 'I'm fairly certain all's good inside.'

'Thank goodness.'

Another gentle kiss came his way, soft on his mouth, yet tormenting—he couldn't follow up by embracing her hard and kissing her like there was no tomorrow, because there nearly hadn't been.

But they did have a tomorrow. They'd survived the crash, were able to move and talk and be together. For now. He pressed his mouth over Leesa's, savouring the moment, her warmth and softness. Who knew when they'd get a chance to do this again? A crowd would soon arrive to help. Far more important, he knew, but he did need to hold Leesa, if only to confirm she had survived.

She pulled back and stared around. 'Where is everyone? Come on, guys. We need you.' Her gaze returned to him. 'I presume the locator beacon still works after a crash like this.'

'They're made to withstand huge impact. The rescue crews already had their hands full, and they're now one chopper down. Literally,' he added quietly.

'I wonder if Kevin's with a crew. He's a volunteer for Port Douglas's Fire and Rescue and wasn't out on the boat today.'

'Do they bring that station in on these events?'

'Yes. We're closer to Port Douglas than Cairns.' Leesa tipped her head to one side. 'Listen. Is that what I think?'

A low *thwup* sound reached him, getting louder by the second. 'Only a chopper makes that racket.' Hopefully those on board were looking for them. 'That hasn't taken too long.'

'They'll do a recce to see what's happened and then assess how badly injured we are.'

The helicopter seemed to be doing a circle above them,

creating a sharp wind and causing small objects to flip around the wreckage. Then it moved away a small distance and hovered briefly before retreating further. 'We might be getting some company.'

Leesa had leaned over Mark to shield him from the dust filling the air. 'Hope so.'

'Hey, Mark, you there?' a familiar voice called. 'Leesa, Nick?'

'We're here. Everyone's alive,' Nick called back as Kevin appeared through the trees. 'Leesa's bruised but otherwise seems in good nick.' The guy would've been worried sick once he heard his sister was on board the chopper. 'Mark needs evacuating ASAP.'

'Kevin, am I glad to see you.' The relief in Leesa's face nearly undid Nick.

He knew she'd been holding it together, but now that help had arrived in the form of her brother, she was obviously letting go a little. He wasn't someone she'd feel she had to keep her game face on for. Which she'd been doing with him, he realised. That hurt. Yet it was who she was, and that was the woman he was falling for more and more. He gripped her hand. 'You're doing well, Leesa.'

She blinked at him, then dredged up a smile. 'Sorry, just had a wee lapse of concentration.' Turning back to Kevin, she said, 'Have Mum and Dad heard about this?'

'What do you think, Leesa? It's not a large town when it comes to these scenarios.'

'True.'

Kevin hugged her carefully, obviously not taking his word about her condition for granted. 'Hell, girl, you know how to frighten us all.' Pulling back, he swallowed hard. 'Nick, how are you faring? Any injuries?'

'Think I've got a broken rib or three, otherwise all good. It's Mark who's the worry.'

'Fill me in on the help required.'

Leesa nodded to him. 'You're the doc.'

Kevin listened while sussing out how to get Mark out of the wreckage. 'Got it. I need Tony down here to give me a hand.' He talked into his handset, then told them, 'We'll take Mark to hospital now, but I'm afraid you two will have to wait a while. The two people at the original accident site you were going to need attention.'

'No problem,' Leesa and Nick said at the same time.

Nick managed a smile. They were in sync and it felt good.

'Though there is a seat for one of you on this trip, but I don't like the idea of leaving either of you on your own.'

'Take Leesa.'

'No way. I'm staying,' she snapped. 'We'll be fine. Get Mark sorted. He's in a bad way.'

'On to it. Leesa, I'll let Ma and Pa know you're okay.'

'Tell them Nick's all right too.'

An unfamiliar tenderness struck him in his chest. Leesa included him in what to tell her family like it was nothing unusual. Given how open and friendly they all were to him, he wasn't really surprised. They had no idea how foreign that was for him.

Spending time with Leesa's family didn't make them his. They had treated him how he imagined they treated most people—with open hearts and kindness. All the more reason to step back before he got too involved and hurt Leesa by messing it up somehow. Because he wasn't great at family relationships, if his history was anything to go by.

It was awfully quiet after the helicopter had left with Mark. Nick held Leesa against his good side and laid his chin on top of her head. 'You doing okay?'

'I've had better days.'

She wasn't opening up to him, but that could be her coping mechanism. She hadn't said much to Kevin either after that first comment.

'Haven't we all? I hope Mark's going to come out of this all right. It's amazing how he did his best to get us on the ground while he still could.'

'We owe him our lives.'

A shiver went through him. They certainly did.

Leesa held his hand tight against her thigh, her fingers shaking. 'I—' Tears streaked down her face.

His heart thumped against his ribs, creating even more pain. He needed to take her in his arms and never let go again. What if? It was a question he knew he'd be asking himself for a long time to come. Reaching for her, he held her carefully, knowing he *would* have to let her go eventually. He'd nearly lost her. As he had lost others he'd loved. It was too much.

He wasn't meant to love. He was meant to run solo. Yet how could he leave her?

CHAPTER SEVEN

IT WAS CRAMPED and beyond uncomfortable sitting in the wreckage. Leesa slowly turned in his embrace, being careful of Nick's ribs, and gazed at him before finding a weak smile. 'Still enjoying your job?'

'I'm getting new experiences every day.'

'Glad to hear it. I'd hate for you to think you'd prefer to be on the ambulances instead the planes.' Though that would be a lot safer. Unless some crazed driver drove into the ambulance.

Doing glum again, Leesa. You're alive and so is Nick.

'What made you choose ambulance work over other options when you qualified?' Time to see if she could learn more about this mysterious man. She was done with messing around, deciding what she wanted to do. Today had woken her up. She adored Nick.

'I like the intensity of picking up people from all sorts of places and traumas and working to save them. I have to be at my best all the time.'

'Doesn't any doctor worth their weight?'

'True, but there's often an urgency that doesn't come with sitting in an office talking about symptoms and past medical history. I like being out and about rather than tied into one place all the time.'

'I know what you mean. It's why I swapped from nursing to the ambulances.'

Was that really why he did this kind of emergency medicine? It sounded a bit like how he moved from city to city to town every year or two. He didn't seem to do getting close to people. They were already involved, though for how long she had no idea.

Last night she'd been thinking about slowing down and taking a long hard look at what she was doing. Today she'd come close to not having that choice—and she wanted him. Badly. To prove she had survived. That Nick had survived. To prove she did have a future. Hopefully with Nick. She wasn't going to waste any more time procrastinating. If the crash had shown her anything, it was to get on and make the most of what came her way.

Turning the conversation onto him, she said, 'Tell me more about why you keep moving around the country.'

He tensed.

She waited for him to change the subject. Or not speak at all.

Finally, 'I don't know what it's like to stop in one place. To live in the same town, or home even, permanently.'

Her heart plummeted. She couldn't imagine what that was like. 'Not even when you were growing up?'

'No.' His fingers were rubbing soft circles on her arm. 'My parents died about the time I turned one. My grandfather took me in but he passed when I was twelve.'

'Nick, that's terrible.' Taking his hand in both hers she held tight.

'It sucks all right.'

'No one deserves that. I don't know how you coped.' She'd always had her family beside her. A loving, caring family who looked out for each other no matter what. Even when she went ahead and had married Connor. They'd believed he was wrong for her, but they'd never left her to deal with the aftermath on her own.

'Who says I did?'

'I do. Look at you. A doctor helping others. A kind man who doesn't put himself before everyone else. You work hard, and—' She found a smile for him. 'You love dogs. Baxter anyway.'

Nick stared at her as if she'd gone mad.

'I didn't hit my head in the crash.' At least she didn't think she had. 'I mean every word.'

One corner of his mouth lifted. He flattened his lips but the smile returned, this time with his whole mouth involved. 'No wonder I moved up here. You say the most wonderful things.'

Her heart clapped. Damn he was wonderful. Even when she wasn't looking for a future with him, he was so tempting. Dr Sexy. 'Glad to make you happy.'

'Remind me to buy Baxter a bone next time I see him too. Seems I've made another friend.'

'You've made a few. Everyone at Flying Health Care thinks you're great. As for my family, Mum's always asking when you're next coming to dinner.' She winced. That info should've stayed in her head.

There'd been a few times where Mum had quizzed her about Nick to the point she looked for excuses not to phone. A girl had to look out for herself, sometimes even from interfering mothers.

'You need to buy a whole bag of bones,' she added. Might as well go for light-hearted and keep him onside.

It would be mighty lonely in here if he decided to clam up on her.

'I'll do that.'

'Where did you live with your grandfather?'

'Adelaide. Although he was tough, Grandad was good to me, gave me the basics in life. In some ways he was my father, my only parent, because I don't remember anything about my mum and dad.' Then he'd lost the man replacing his parents.

'Of course you don't remember. Have you got photos of your parents?'

'A box full. But the weird thing is they've never grown up. They were only twenty and twenty-one when they died. I know that probably doesn't make sense, but I can't help it.'

'It makes perfect sense to me. I can see you as a boy looking at those photos and hoping for something to change. You're now older than they were, and that must seem strange.'

'Leesa, you're so understanding it's scary.' He leaned in to kiss her, wincing as he moved. Guess the shock of the crash was causing havoc with the sensible side of his brain.

'Careful, Nick. You can't take that pain for too long. How about I get you a strong opioid? You've got to get through moving out of here and onto a chopper yet.'

'Might be a good idea, though I'm not supposed to prescribe them to myself.'

'I'm qualified to give drugs out, remember?'

'Glad one of us has their wits about them. My doctor head is getting in the way. I'll put that down to the unusual circumstances I find myself in.'

She wasn't so sure she had any wits, but she could pretend. 'I'll find the kit.'

On her hands and knees, she crawled through the wreckage to search for the drug kit. Equipment lay everywhere, bags and packs broken open. One monitor was smashed, the other looked as though nothing was wrong with it. Unbelievable.

Scrabbling around she finally found what she needed. Hopefully everything inside was in good shape, or Nick might miss out on dealing with that pain. He couldn't swallow a handful of powder if he didn't know what it was.

Swallow. Water. Looking around again she spied a pack of six bottles they carried for patients and staff. Two remained whole. Damn, it was almost pitch dark now. Torch. Where were they kept? Top shelf of the cupboard by the bed. She squinted through the dark to see where the cupboard was. There, twisted on the floor. The door was warped. She pulled to open it but it wouldn't budge. Swearing gave her some satisfaction, but did not help get the door to move.

'Damn. No torches.' She needed to get back to Nick while she could still see enough to read the labels on the bottles of tablets.

Back beside Nick, she went through the bottles of drugs. 'Which one do you want?'

'Codeine.'

Holding a bottle right before her eyes, she laughed, although a bit sharply. 'Good choice. Here it is. At least I think that's what it says.' She handed it to Nick. 'What do you see?'

'Codeine.' He handed it back.

Tipping one tablet into the palm of his hand, she opened a water bottle and pushed it into his other.

Nick's head reared. A tight groan ripped out of his mouth.

'Did I hurt you? I'm so sorry.' Her heart was thudding. She'd hurt him. How could she be so thoughtless? Guilt assailed her. 'Nick, I didn't mean to.'

He placed his palm on her cheek. 'It's all right. You didn't do anything wrong. I moved sharply and paid the price.'

Her heart skittered. It hurt her to see him in pain. 'We might have to ban kissing for a few days,' she said.

That would be bloody hard to stick to. Kissing Nick was her favourite pastime these days. As much as making love. Sometimes a kiss from Nick made her feel right, happy and content, and she didn't need the excitement of sex to do that.

'Not if I have a say in the matter.' He sagged back against the metal upright that had avoided being bent in the hard landing. 'But I will give things a rest for now. We might have a longish wait before help arrives. It's going to take a while to airlift the others to hospital.'

Time alone with Nick. She'd love it, except he was in pain. 'I reckon everyone's working their butts off to get here ASAP.'

They'd better be. She surreptitiously watched Nick's chest rise and fall with each breath he took. Consistent, not deep, but not too shallow, nor out of kilter. Good. If his lung had been punctured by one of those fractured ribs he'd be in a much more serious condition.

'Because we're part of the team?' He nodded. 'Makes sense I suppose. I've seen police go that extra mile for their own when something terrible has happened.'

'It's a natural response. Look after your own first.'

They sat squashed in the confined space as darkness took over completely. Now that she was sitting still with nothing to do, aches all over her body were starting to get ferocious.

'I got lucky as a teen when I stole a car.'

'You what?' She'd never have believed it if she'd heard it from anyone else, but Nick didn't do lying.

'I wanted to learn to drive and no one would teach me. The judge gave me a second chance and I grabbed it with both hands, never did anything so stupid again.'

Now she was learning what made him tick. 'Tell me more.'

'His son was in my class and cruised through every lesson like he didn't need to put in any effort. I made him my target, to beat him in all subjects.'

That she believed. 'And did you?'

'Not all, about fifty-fifty. It meant he had to knuckle down and work hard for the first time. Patrick—Judge Crombie—credits me for Darian's success, says he'd never have done so well if I hadn't caused him a headache.'

'Patrick. So you're still in touch?'

'He's been my mentor ever since, though we don't catch up often. I flew down to Adelaide to see him before I came up here. He had cancer but is in remission. Who knows for how long? He's been warned to get on with ticking things off his bucket list.'

Leesa grabbed his hand. 'That's hard for you too. But you did get lucky with him.'

'I did.' He removed his hand. 'Tell me about your husband.'

Blindsided by the sudden change, she took a moment

to collect her thoughts. This was part of moving forward into a stronger relationship, and yet she felt he was suddenly aware of how much he'd given away about himself and regretted it.

'Connor was amazing,' Leesa began. 'So kind and generous, helpful, keen to be a part of my life. I fell for him fast and we married, against my family's wishes I admit, and we moved to Brisbane for his career. End of the happy days. It was as though he was free to do what he liked being so far from my family. He was clever, changing slowly, not showing his true colours straight up. I wasn't good enough for him. Didn't matter what it was, cooking his favourite meal, parking the car in the garage, mowing the lawns, I couldn't do anything right, and I paid by being snubbed, then access to our bank accounts was closed off to me.'

Leesa shivered. He'd never hit her, but there were days when she half expected it.

'But you left him.'

'I did.' She could hear the pride in her voice. 'I had to or submit for ever, and I wouldn't do that. It wasn't easy, but I did it and stayed on in Brisbane to prove to myself I didn't need to run home.'

'Except you then faced another bully.'

'By then I'd wised up. He didn't stand a chance. Not with me, and he backed off. The other women didn't do so well until I supported them. After dealing with my husband, I knew how hard it can be for some people to leave these situations. I couldn't stand by and not help them.'

With one finger on her chin, Nick turned her face so he was looking directly at her with empathy. 'I imagine trust doesn't come easy for you.'

Like she thought, smart. 'You got it.' She was working on getting over her issues about her ex, but it wasn't as easy as packing up and leaving him had been, and that hadn't been a picnic either, with him refusing to accept that she was never going back. He kept telling her she'd never manage on her own, which only reminded her how she'd coped at school and could do it again, even if it was trickier.

'How's your trust radar after your marriage fell apart?' she asked.

His sigh was long and slow. 'Not great. Makes me wonder if I'm cut out for a relationship, or if I should remain single and get on with being a good doctor instead.'

'Don't think like that. One mistake doesn't make a lifetime's worth.' Said she who'd thought the same for so long.

Not any longer. Danielle had always said she had to move on, and after today that's exactly what she intended doing. With Nick. And if that didn't work out? She'd keep trying. Her chest ached. As a result of the impact, or because she wanted a man to love and kids to raise under that love, she couldn't be certain. Probably both. She shuffled her butt, trying to get comfortable, not doing well. Tipping her head back she closed her eyes, exhaustion filling her, closing down her mind.

'Chopper's coming,' Nick nudged her.

She hadn't heard it but now it was very obvious. 'Phew. I've had enough of this place.'

'No food or anything to drink,' Nick smiled. 'The TV screen was useless too.'

'Funny man. Now we can get you checked over and make sure those ribs haven't done any damage to your lung.'

'My breathing's normal.'

'Yeah, I have been keeping an eye on your chest movements,' she admitted. Not hard when his chest was so damned distracting. She still worried he was hiding another injury from her.

'No surprise there.'

Tenderness filled Nick as Leesa gave him a wobbly smile. As though now they were about to be lifted out of here, she was letting go of whatever had kept her calm till this moment.

He wanted to kiss her once more before they were surrounded by their rescuers. It hurt to lean closer but, hell, he could deal with that to taste Leesa under his lips.

'I'm glad I had you with me today,' he said. 'It made all the difference. But I'm sorry you were in the crash. I don't like that one bit.'

'We had no choice over what happened and who we were with. But having you by my side made it easier to cope. You took everything so calmly.'

'Much like you.' She'd have been tough no matter who'd been with her, but he'd take her words to heart and enjoy them. Because he believed her. He believed *in* her. She wasn't lying, or trying to earn points to cash in on something he could provide her with later.

Remorse struck. His old cautions were still in place and, unless he let them go, there wasn't going to be a later. He might have to be careful going ahead if he was to avoid more heartbreak, but he had to learn to trust. It wasn't fair on Leesa, or anyone, if he didn't. That was like expecting her to turn out to be another Ellie.

Yeah, he sighed. He was falling for this amazing woman. Falling harder than the chopper hitting the ground earlier. Hopefully Leesa didn't break anything inside him. Or he didn't do the same to her.

Bright lights shone through the carnage from the hovering chopper. The noise was deafening. Handy since he'd run out of things to say without putting his foot in it and telling Leesa the thoughts tripping through his mind. He wasn't ready to divulge where his feelings were at. Not yet. Slowly was the only way to go. If at all.

So, he went with practical, carefully leaning close to shout, 'We need to start moving out of this wreckage.'

Leesa was getting up on her knees when Kevin appeared, holding out his hands to pull her through the narrow space.

Then she was gone and it was his turn. Holding his breath, in an effort to keep the pain under some form of control, he shuffled through to where Kevin reached out for him.

He shook his head. 'No.' Being hauled upright would be agony. It wasn't so great doing it all by himself either. What he hadn't mentioned to Leesa was his ankle was in a bad way too. Hopefully only sprained and not fractured. Whichever, walking wasn't going to be fun.

Kevin led them through the scrub and up to where their rescue helicopter had landed, helping Leesa through the rough terrain, turning back regularly to make sure Nick was with them.

Nick hobbled along, biting his tongue to keep the groans to himself. When Kevin reached to help him into the chopper he didn't refuse. He knew when he was being stubborn for the sake of it. Within minutes Kevin had settled him in a seat and buckled him in, then the chopper was lifting off the ground.

'How're you doing?' Leesa asked.

Nick opened his eyes and stared straight into hers. 'Glad we're out of there.'

'What's wrong with your left foot?'

'Think I've sprained the ankle.'

'Not likely considering you were sitting down when we hit the ground. Most likely a fracture.' She was unclipping her seatbelt, in paramedic mode.

'Leave it, Leesa,' he snapped. 'I'm fine sitting here. The doctors will sort it out when we get to hospital.'

Her head shot up. 'I'm only trying to help,' she snapped back.

'I know. I don't like the situation, that's all.'

'What situation? I thought we were getting along fine.'

Too well, if the thumping in his chest was an indicator. 'We are. But it has been a bit of a wake-up call.'

As she kept staring at him, her face filled with worry. But finally, she said, 'That's understandable. We've had one hell of a shock. It's all catching up with us now we're on our way to hospital.'

He suddenly felt exhausted. 'Certainly is.'

'Yep.' Her smile was tentative.

He took her hand in his. It was becoming his go-to move when he wanted to be close to Leesa. Which it shouldn't if he was serious about backing off. Dropping her hand, he leaned his head back against the seat and closed his eyes to wait out the time till they landed.

'Wake up.' Leesa was shaking him gently.

He jerked upright, groaning as pain slammed under his ribs. 'Have we landed?' The door was opening and bright lights filled the cabin. Guess that was a yes.

Kevin appeared from forward. 'We have. Let's get you

two inside to ED. Ma and Pa are in the waiting room. Pacing the floor to oblivion, I imagine.'

'Did anyone pick up Baxter?' Leesa asked. 'I didn't think to ask you to tell Mum. What sort of doggy mum does that make me?'

'One who had a lot else going on in her head,' Kevin told her. 'Your boy's fine. He's in Dad's truck, chewing on a bone, I'm told.'

'That's good. He's used to me being late, but not to turn up at all will have freaked him out.'

'Hate to tell you this, but Dad says he's fine. Karin was about to take him home with her as she figured you were on a callout. Come on, let's get this over and done with.' Kevin helped Leesa out, then turned to give Nick a hand.

'There's a wheelchair coming for you,' Kevin told him.

'How...' Oh, Leesa. Of course she'd have got Kevin to call ahead. 'Thanks.'

Looking into those beautiful but tired eyes, his head and heart were all over the place. He did want more with her. That much he was not going to deny any longer. What was the point? He knew he was done for. But that didn't mean he was ready to rush in. After what had happened, the caution had grown even bigger and he wasn't totally sure why. So forget backing off, and try going slowly.

'I'm discharging you,' the ED doctor told Leesa. 'You were quite right. Lots of bruising that you'll know about for days to come, but nothing more serious.'

'Thanks, Laurie.' She wasn't going anywhere until she knew if Nick would be kept in overnight. She swung her legs off the bed and gasped when her thighs protested. 'Painful bruises.'

'The result of severe impact,' Laurie nodded. 'Take it easy for the next couple of days. Stay away from work.'

'I'll see that she does,' Joy answered before Leesa could argue. 'The same goes for you, Nick.'

Joy had turned up within minutes of the chopper delivering them to the hospital. She hadn't been allowed to see Mark, who had had a brain bleed and was now in ICU.

'I'm not arguing,' Nick growled as he lay sprawled on the bed in the next cubicle, looking shattered.

'Is Nick staying overnight?' she asked Laurie.

'I see no reason for that once we've finished with him,' the doctor grinned.

'Just as well or we'd have argued,' Nick told Laurie.

His X-rays had shown four broken ribs and a fracture in his wrist, none in his swollen ankle. He'd been right on that score. Thankfully, as they'd thought, his lung hadn't been punctured. That was the best result. It would've been horrifying if that had happened. There was nothing she'd have been able to do to help him other than keep him on oxygen, and with a hole in his lung that'd have been an exercise in futility.

Her chest tightened. She could've lost Nick. And she wasn't thinking of a work colleague. No, this was the man who had ignored her boundaries and walked right on into her head and heart. Throw in his injuries and she was going to insist he come back to her place.

'Nick, a nurse is going to put your wrist in a soft cast. You'll have it on for a week then, when the swelling's gone down, it will be replaced with a plaster version,' Laurie told him.

He was looking at Laurie as if it was hard to understand what she was saying. 'Then I'm free to go, too?'

'Yes. Nothing we can do about your ribs except pre-scribe strong analgesics, along with antibiotics for that cut on your chin I stitched. *And*—' she emphasised the word '—I insist you don't get too physical. For the sake of your ribs and that ankle.'

'The pain will keep me in line.'

Leesa blinked. He was admitting that? Showed how ev-erything had got to him, because normally he was averse to revealing his feelings.

A nurse slipped into the cubicle. 'Nick? I'm Enid and I'm here to sort out your left wrist.'

Then Kevin strode into her cubicle. It was getting like a circus in here, but rescue staff were given more leeway than general patients because of what they did for people.

'Hey, sis, how're you doing?'

'All good. I can go home any time I like.'

'That's what I was hoping. I'll take you home when you're ready. What about you, Nick?'

'I'll be on my way as soon as this cast's on.'

Leesa said, 'Come back to my place, Nick. You don't want to be on your own tonight.' She didn't want to be alone. The crash had been horrendous, and now that they were safe and sorted, she was beginning to feel more shaken than when they'd first hit the ground. Her par-ents would be happy for her to go to their house, but she wanted her own place with her own things around her. And Nick with her too, because he'd understand how she felt. He'd been through it too.

'Nick?'

He was looking at her as though he wasn't sure what to do. Finally, he nodded. 'Okay. Thank you.'

She couldn't decide if he was happy going home with

her or merely agreeing because being on his own wasn't a good option at the moment, but now wasn't the time to delve deeper. They were beyond making sense after all that had happened.

'Good idea, Leesa,' said Kevin. 'What about some clean clothes, Nick? You look like something the butcher chopped up.'

'Tactful. Could we swing by my apartment?' Nick asked.

'Only if I go in and get what you want. I don't think it's a good idea for you to move around any more than necessary,' Kevin told him.

Nick looked from him to her, and Leesa laughed. 'Don't even think about arguing.' She sensed he was on the verge of doing exactly that and it bugged her, though she didn't know why.

'With a Bennett? Not likely.' Then he turned serious. 'Thanks, but—'

She cut him off. 'But nothing. It makes sense for you to be with someone tonight.' Her heart dipped. Was something wrong? She'd have to wait to find out. She was shattered and could barely string a sentence together.

'I don't want to be a nuisance when you're a train wreck too, but you're right, Leesa. I'd feel more comfortable knowing you're there.'

That wasn't so hard, was it? 'Good. Let's get out of here.'

CHAPTER EIGHT

NICK LOOKED AROUND HIM. He'd thought as it was Leesa's grandmother's house it would be small, but it was huge. The lounge he sat in was the size of a football field. Okay, a small one toddlers played on, but it was still large. Light and airy with big bay windows that looked out over what appeared to be an expansive lawn and flower gardens. Someone had forgotten to turn the outside lights off.

'Who does the gardens?' he asked Leesa. 'They're stunning.'

'I do. Gran set them up over many years, and when I moved in I couldn't let them go to ruin.'

'You like gardening?' Of course she did. It was pretty darned obvious. 'You must if you keep them in such good order.' So this was one of her interests outside of work. Probably the most dominant one, given the size of the plots.

'I get a thrill out of planting a shrub or bulb and seeing the result when it blooms.' She was sitting on a leather rocker with her legs stretched out on the foot rest, a plate of the fried chicken and salad her mother had prepared for them on her knees.

'I wouldn't know a bulb from a shrub,' he muttered. Gardens came with homes.

'There's always time to learn.'

'You know what? You're right.' He was thinking about having a garden? Where? If he got a dog, he'd said he'd move, so how about a place with a lawn *and* a garden? 'I might give it a go sometime.'

'Sometime?'

'Okay, if I move from the apartment, I could be tempted to look into buying a house with a small yard.'

'If?'

'Will you stop questioning everything I say?' He'd just told her what he was thinking of doing and she kept at him, wanting to know more. Frustrating to say the least, because he was so unsure of his next step, of how to follow through on the love he held for her.

He snapped. 'It's new for me to be talking about this. I need to get my head around it.' It was huge to even be thinking about stopping his nomadic life to settle in one place, even more so to tell Leesa what he thought. Although he couldn't guarantee how long for. He had a feeling that if he started on this change of lifestyle he might adhere to it—because he might've found what he'd spent most of his life looking for. The only thing wrong there was he was worried about hurting Leesa if he failed. He needed to toughen up and make some decisions, not drag it out because his heart was involved.

'I'm trying to support you in a backward kind of way.' Leesa bit into a drumstick and chewed thoughtfully. 'I can't imagine what it's been like not to have a house to call home, where gardens, decorating, renovations are all part of everyday things to attend to. You've missed out on a hell of a lot.'

She never minced her words.

He should be thankful, but sometimes they came too close to be easily accepted. Tonight, he'd try. He and Leesa had been through a traumatic experience together and needed to put it behind them without arguing. Now he thought about it, his reaction to her questions might be because he'd felt so out of sorts since the crash.

No, there was more to it than that. He was out of sorts because he'd woken up to the fact that he loved Leesa. Which was downright scary. There was a lot at stake.

'You're right, I have, but I do not want you feeling sorry for me.'

'I don't. I admire how you've got on with your life, and seem to be starting to look for what it is you really want.'

She read him well. Too well, if he was honest. No one had ever done that like she did. Except Patrick, and that had turned out good for him. Did that mean Leesa could be good for him if he stayed around? Frightening. It could mean everything, or it could turn to dust because he wasn't sure he understood how to make it work well.

'It's taken years but you're right, I have started thinking of my future and not my past.' If that wasn't huge then what was? Falling in love most definitely was. As would giving his heart freely. Those would be the final winners. And the largest hurdles. He'd nearly lost her today, and that scared the pants off him. Others had left him in the past. For that to happen again—well, he had no idea how he'd get through that. Yet he wanted so much to try to make it work with Leesa.

'I'm pleased for you, Nick. Everyone deserves happiness.'

Says she who'd struggled to put her past behind her.

They really were two peas in the proverbial pod. 'Including you.'

'What's more, we shouldn't sit around waiting for happiness to arrive. We should get on and make it happen.' Leesa was watching him closely, no doubt looking for a reaction to that statement.

And he had one he'd love to share. She was his dream woman. He was making inroads into getting on with living life to the full. He opened his mouth to speak, closed it again. One thing to think how he felt, quite another to tell Leesa.

What if he'd misunderstood her and she didn't want anything more than a friendship with him? What if, when she said everyone was entitled to be happy, she only meant he was too, and wasn't saying it would be with her? The mistakes he'd made in the past reared their ugly heads and shut him down.

'I see.' She stood up slowly, wincing with pain all the way.

He got to his feet even more slowly, the throbbing in his ribs diabolical. But the pounding in his heart was more painful. He had to keep Leesa onside, and the only way to go was by being open with her as much as he dared, so they could at least talk more.

'No, Leesa, you don't. I haven't explained myself. I know that. It doesn't come easily for me, but that's not a good excuse. Spending time with you is a priority. I always feel the best I have in a long time, if not for ever, when I'm with you.'

'I can live with that for now.' Her crooked smile showed how exhausted she was. Holding out her hand to him, she added, 'Let's go to bed. I'm shattered, and you look no better.'

'Your mother made up a spare bed for me.'

Leesa blinked. 'You're serious? There's a surprise. I'd have thought she'd have locked the doors to the spare bedrooms so you had to join me.'

So Jodi liked him being with her daughter. His heart swelled. Another good thing to happen. Except if he let Leesa down, in any way, he'd be letting down her family as well. 'Could she be thinking I need to be very careful in bed right now?'

'Definitely.' Taking his hand, she tugged him gently. 'We can share a bed without getting active.' Another blink. 'I'd say that'll be difficult, but right now all I want is to be stretched out and comfortable so I can sleep. Not very sexy, I know.' She shrugged.

He laughed lightly, aware of not moving his chest too much. 'It's about all I'll be able to manage.' As he followed Leesa through the house, he noted three spare bedrooms with perfectly arranged furniture. 'Which bedroom would Jodi have chosen for me?'

'The one on your right. It's the second largest and the one I use for visitors if I have any.'

'Not many then?' He'd have thought with her caring, friendly manner she'd always have someone dropping by for a night or two.

'Most of my friends live around here.' She didn't sound sad.

'Where does Baxter usually sleep?'

'Where do you think?'

'Your bedroom.' Where else would she have him? This was Leesa, the soft-hearted dog mum. Baxter was with

Leesa's parents, as everyone thought it would give Leesa a chance to sleep and not be nudged in those painful places.

'I'm going to have a shower. If you want one, there's a bathroom further along the hall. Towels are in the drawer beneath the basin.'

'Sounds idyllic. Hot water to soak away the grime and loosen my muscles.'

Leesa spun around to face him and gritted her teeth. 'Ow.' Her chest rose as she drew in a deep breath. 'Silly girl. Do you want a hand getting your shirt off? I can't imagine it'll be a picnic.'

'Yes, please.' It'd be the first time she'd removed his clothes without him getting hard.

Her grin told him she'd read his mind. 'Who'd have thought?'

'Not me.'

'Now that you're in my room you can use the ensuite. You can fall out of the shower and into bed with only a few steps. I'll use the main bathroom.' She was already turning the sheets back.

He hated that she was taking so much care of him, but right now he didn't have the energy to argue. After being settled in that comfortable chair in the lounge, walking down the hallway had taken a lot of effort, with pain ricocheting around his body in all directions. 'You're a gem.'

'And you hate being in this situation. I get that.' Heading into the ensuite, she took a towel off a shelf and laid it on the counter. 'There you go. See you in bed shortly.'

Still no reaction from his body. He really was a mess. Hopefully he'd be able to cuddle into her long, warm frame and fall asleep holding her with the arm on his good side.

* * *

Leesa stood under the hot water and let the heat soak into her bruised and battered body. It was wonderful. Never mind she'd be too hot and probably sweat some when she got out. Right now, she needed this to relax her muscles, which were tight and damned sore. That crash landing had been horrific, jarring every part of her body. But she was grateful that's all she'd suffered.

Nick hadn't been so lucky.

As for Mark, he was gravely ill and would be for a while to come, by the sound of it. Brain bleeds were no picnic.

It all went to show you didn't have a clue what a day would bring when you got up in the morning.

She shampooed and conditioned her hair, then realised she'd have to waste time drying it before she could crawl in beside Nick. But she couldn't have left it as it was when she felt dirty from top to toe. Now she was deliciously clean. Finally flicking the water off, she grabbed her towel and dried off, feeling so much better.

She was spending the night in *her* bed with Nick. It was the first time he'd come to the house, and it was another step forward in their relationship. He'd seemed concerned he'd given too much away earlier, but for her it was progress. It meant he trusted her, and she felt special that he had talked about how he was changing, because she wasn't holding back any longer.

Nick was lying on his back when she returned to her room. 'How's that working?' she asked.

'Not bad.' There was a familiar twinkle in his eyes.

'Oh, no. We are behaving tonight.' No way would she have Nick in pain from anything they got up to.

'Hate to say it but you're right. I can lie on my right side though. You can back in so we can cuddle.'

'Sounds perfect. I think I'll be asleep in thirty seconds flat.' Which meant missing out on feeling his arm around her. 'I'll do my best to stay awake for a while.'

'Don't even try. We both need sleep more than anything.' He rolled carefully onto his good side.

Leesa slipped under the sheet and leaned over to kiss him. 'What a day. Good night.' Moving carefully, she turned onto her side, back towards him and smiled as their bodies came together. His skin was warm and his breath tickled the back of her neck. Sheer bliss.

'Leesa. Wake up.' A hand was shaking her. 'Wake up, Leesa.' It was Nick's voice.

Dragging her eyes open, she stared around the dark room, feeling cold and shaky. 'Where am I?'

'In your bed. I think you were having a nightmare.'

It came rushing back. 'The chopper crashing. The trees hitting us. You unable to move. Me hurting.' She gulped air. 'It was awful.'

Nick wound an arm around her, beneath her breasts, tucking her close. 'Going through it once was bad enough.'

'That's put me off wanting to sleep.' She couldn't keep reliving the nightmare. It was awful. 'At least we're no worse off than we were the first time.' Her mouth tasted of bile. 'Have you slept?'

'A little. I wake every time I move.'

'Time for some more analgesics.' Except she didn't want to leave the safety of Nick's arms. Shaking her head, she admonished herself. Not safety, comfort. She *was* safe.

It was her head causing problems now. 'I'll get them in a moment.'

'I can get them.'

She sat up immediately. 'No, Nick. That'd mean more pain for you. I'll get some for myself too.' They'd ease the aches and might drag her under to sleep, even if she fought it.

After they'd taken the tablets, Nick lay on his back and Leesa stretched out beside him, holding his hand. She felt her heart melting for Nick. He'd opened up some more during their wait in the chopper. Could the crash have been something good in disguise?

Staring upward, the tension that started from the moment Mark shouted they were in trouble slipped away at last, leaving her languid and comfortable. Nick was her dream man. She trusted him completely. He'd never deliberately hurt her. Was he falling for her? More than anything she hoped so. For now, she'd go with the flow. She was too tired for anything else.

It had been the strangest day of her life, yet she was happy. Yes, happy to have found this man. All she had to do now was make him understand they could have a future together. But not tonight. Tonight was for unwinding and being comfortable together without firing up the lust and getting hot. They needed to be able to share time that didn't involve sex, only love. And if Nick wasn't into loving her then she'd deal with that another day. Right now, she was happy to roll with her own feelings.

Shuffling closer to him, she laid a hand on his chest

and closed her eyes. This was near perfect. If she didn't move too much and set off the aches.

'Time I got back to work,' Joy said as she stood up the next day after dropping by to see how they were doing. 'Glad you're both feeling a bit better.'

'I'll be back on the job tomorrow,' Leesa told her. 'Thanks for the filled bread rolls. They were delicious.'

'You're welcome.' Joy paused, looked from her to Nick. 'Does the accident change either of your minds re my job? Last week's interviews went well I hear.'

'The job's the last thing on my mind at the moment,' Leesa told her.

'I'm in,' Nick told Joy.

'If one of you gets the job is the other going to throw their toys out of the cot?' Joy asked.

'Not at all.'

'No way.' Leesa glanced at Nick, then back to Joy. 'My concern is how the rest of the staff will see it. They might read too much into situations where say I give Nick a job to do that someone else wanted, and vice versa.'

Nick was watching her closely. Looking for what? She was only putting the truth out there.

'We're a small crew compared to ambulance stations you've worked in previously, Leesa. We're close. I've never had any problem with any member thinking they should've been given a job over someone else. I can't see it happening if either of you take my place.' Joy was focused completely on her. 'I know you well, and I can't see you giving Nick, or anyone else, more than their fair share of the good jobs. It's not like you.'

Her heart softened at the compliment. 'Thank you. I should've talked to you sooner, then I could've stopped worrying.'

'So your application remains in place?'

'Yes. I don't know if I'll be comfortable flying in choppers any more. Spending time in the office seems far safer.'

Nick watched Leesa as she made a plunger of coffee. She looked thoughtful, as though he'd done something wrong applying for Joy's position. 'You still okay with us competing for the same job? First time we've come up against each other.'

'Interesting area to be doing so.' Her finger was scratching at the hem of her shorts, where a huge bruise covered most of her thigh. It had to be painful but she never mentioned it, or any of the others he'd noticed during the night.

'Look, Leesa, if you're really worried about being my boss—' he paused and gave her a smile '—I promise to behave.'

His smile hadn't worked. She looked unsettled. 'I am nervous about flying now.'

He tried another smile. 'That's natural but you'll get over it.'

'You don't know that.'

'I know you. You're tough.'

'Is this you trying to talk me out of trying for the job?' The spoon she'd been holding slammed onto the bench.

Nick came straight back. 'Not at all. I don't need you to do that to make me feel more optimistic.' Why were they even talking about this? It hadn't been an issue before, as far as he knew.

Her head shot up. 'I know that. You'd be brilliant as chief of operations.'

Knock him down. Now he was confused. 'Thank you, but so would you.'

Her mouth twitched. 'We're doing well so far. Everything feels like a big deal at the moment, probably as a result of what happened yesterday.'

Just like that the angst left him. 'Good idea. Who gets the job's not up to us anyway.'

'We won't be the only applicants.'

'True.' If he got the position it would be a step forward in changing his life. He'd be stopping in one place. The place where Leesa lived. Could he do it?

'What are you thinking now?' she asked. 'I can't read you.'

Leesa never let him away with a thing. 'I'm wondering what it would be like to live in one place for more than a year or two. To settle down permanently.' If yesterday had taught him anything it was that he loved Leesa to bits. The ramifications were huge after he'd lost others he'd loved. What if he lost Leesa? He'd lost too many people who were important to him already.

'Nick, before you go any further, hear me out.'

His chest was tightening. What was coming next? He should leave before his heart was shattered. Or before she showed how much she expected of him. But it wasn't that easy. He cared too much. He wanted to believe they could make this happen, he just didn't trust life to give him a chance.

'Meeting you has been the best thing to happen to me in a long time.' Her gaze was steady.

His heart wrenched at her words. But there was something in her voice that said there was more to come. 'Carry on.'

'Like you, I have problems from my past.'

He gasped. 'You think I'd bully you? No damned way. How can you even begin to think that?'

'The same way you feel about settling down and trying to make a life for yourself. I want to follow my instincts but they've got me into trouble before.'

The anger disappeared. 'I get that. Believe me, I would never pressure you to do something for me that you didn't want to.'

'I know that. Truly. It's just that—' She stopped, hauled in a huge breath. 'I'm scared. I've fallen for you, Nick.'

This time it felt as though his heart had stopped. 'Leesa—'

Her hand went up in a stop sign. 'Wait. I've spent years not believing I could find a man who'd treat me well and accept me for who I am. A man to love for ever and have children with, to establish a loving environment for a family. I have finally found him—you. Despite what I've just said it is you.' Her breasts rose on a deep breath. There was more to come.

He waited, heart in his throat.

'I know you still struggle with trust, or admitting you might be there now. I'm taking a huge leap here, but this is my heart speaking, so if you're not interested then please tell me.'

His mouth dried. His head spun with what she'd told him. She loved him. He loved her, but how to tell her when he couldn't put the past completely behind him? Ellie had said she loved him and look what she'd done.

Leesa's not Ellie.

She'd never play around behind his back. She'd tell him outright if she'd stopped loving him. He'd had a lifetime of learning not to trust people, which led to him not trusting himself, hence wanting to step back from Leesa before he hurt her. 'I don't know what to say.'

After the crash he'd thought he could walk away to save them both from more hurt. Now it seemed he was wrong. He couldn't turn his back on her for any reason.

So talk to her—speak from your heart.

Therein lay the problem. He didn't know how to. The last time he'd done that it had come back to wreck his heart.

Silence fell between them.

Finally Leesa stood up and crossed to look out the window at the garden beyond. After a few minutes she turned, and the sadness in her face shocked him. 'You don't believe you're ready. I get that. If I'm putting pressure on you, it's because I think you are ready to make the changes you've been looking for.'

She paused, fidgeting with her hair. 'It's obvious you need some space, and I'm pushing you. I've told you my feelings. I don't want to hear anything you don't one hundred per cent believe.' She shoved a hand through her hair and sighed. 'Or I've just made a complete fool of myself.'

'Leesa, it's not that.' Her family had stood by him last night, and brought home the fact that if he was involved with Leesa he was also involved with them. They'd share their lives with him. They'd also have him for dog tucker if he hurt her. And he couldn't trust himself not to. He had no experience of true loving family. Messing up would not be hard.

She waited, her foot tapping the cork tiles.

What to say? What to say?

Finally Leesa shook her head at him and said, 'Go away, Nick, and think long and hard about what you're really looking for. You can't go to work at the moment, so use the time to sort yourself out. If I'm not going to be in the picture then let me know sooner rather than later.'

His heart was breaking as he watched her walk out of the room, her head high and back ramrod straight. His heart tightened for this amazing woman, who he was already hurting. She was strong, and not afraid to show him.

'Goodbye, Leesa.'

For now. She was right about one thing. He had to sort himself out, starting now. When he did tell her he loved her there couldn't be any hesitation. No looking back. It would be an all or nothing decision. He wanted all.

He pulled his phone from his pocket to call a taxi. Leesa was right about one thing—he had decisions to make, and the sooner the better for both of them.

She'd told him she loved him. Hope was flapping around inside his chest like a stranded fish. He'd followed her here on a whim, which he hadn't been able to admit to himself until recently. They'd happily reconnected and had been getting along well. Now he had to find the courage to follow his heart.

The taxi pulled up and he got in, taking a long look at Leesa's home with him.

CHAPTER NINE

'WELCOME BACK, LEESA,' Jess said and got up from the table to give her a careful hug. 'Love the colours on your face.'

'I'm going to scare my patients, for sure.' Leesa filled a mug from the coffee plunger. Everyone was here, as if they'd been waiting for her.

'How are you feeling?' Darren asked. 'Apart from sore all over.'

Heartbroken. I haven't heard from Nick for nearly two days.

'Wary of helicopters, but otherwise ready to get back in the seat.' Planes seemed a whole lot safer at the moment.

'Here's the thing,' Darren said. 'The helicopter didn't fail. Mark did, and I'm not being nasty about that. The poor blighter had a serious medical issue.'

'He did an amazing job getting us so close to the ground before he lost consciousness. That's what Nick and I think happened anyway. We owe him, for sure. But I still think I might find my first ride in a chopper a little scary.'

'I don't doubt that for a moment,' Darren agreed.

'How's Nick doing?' Jess asked. 'Joy says he's not coming back to work for ten days or so. Lifting trolleys or boards with patients on will be a no-no for quite a while.'

Ten days? Her heart sank. That was longer than Laurie had said was necessary. So he wasn't in a rush to see her and become a part of her life. He could've done other less physical jobs. 'Broken ribs are nasty by all accounts.'

'They hurt like hell with every little move you make,' one of the paramedics said. 'Speaking from experience after a particularly rough rugby game years back.'

'He could do the paperwork and let Joy have some air time,' Darren noted, unaware he was on the same track as Leesa.

'Hey, good to see you.' Joy walked in carrying a plate with a large chocolate cake. 'Here's to you, Leesa, and having you back on board.'

She stared at Joy. 'A cake? Chocolate too.' She wiped a hand over her eyes. 'You're spoiling me.'

Placing the plate on the table, Joy gave her a gentle hug. 'You gave us a huge fright, you three.'

Leesa swallowed down the lump in her throat. She hadn't given much thought to how everyone else would've felt when they heard the chopper had gone down. Just knew they'd have been in a hurry to help them. 'Thanks, guys.' She reached for a tissue and blew her nose. So unlike her to get emotional in front of people. 'We'd better put some aside for Nick and Mark.'

Joy handed her a knife and some plates. 'Nope. They get their own cakes when they return.'

Nick might miss out altogether, she thought as she cut into the layered cake, if he chose to move on yet again. He had said goodbye to her, not see you at work. Should she call him and ask how he was doing?

No. She'd said she'd give him space and she had to stick to that. The last thing she needed to do was upset him all over again. But she missed him more than she could believe. Every minute of the day and night. Listening out for him, looking for his ute in the driveway, holding the pillow he'd used, burying her face into it and breathing in his scent. Pure male with a hint of spice. The best smell in the universe. Her universe anyway.

'Here, get your teeth into this.' Joy had taken over cutting slices of cake and plating up. 'When we've finished here, I'd like a moment of your time, unless a call out comes in.'

Her stomach sank. Time to face reality. 'No problem.' *Liar.*

The cake sat heavily in her stomach when she went into Joy's office. Had Joy heard from Nick? Had he handed in his notice and was in the throes of leaving town?

'Wipe that grim expression off your face, Leesa. I'm not here to make things difficult for you.' Joy took a seat opposite her. 'I want to reiterate that I believe you and Nick can work together if one of you has my role.'

If Nick comes back to me. Or comes back at all.

'You haven't heard from him?'

'Only to say he wanted a few more days off than originally agreed on when we discussed his injuries.' Joy was watching her closely. 'Is there something more to this?'

'Not really. Nick has some sorting out to do.' She'd spent a lot of time since he'd gone considering her future with or without him in it, and had realised changing roles at work wasn't what would make her happy. Even if Nick didn't want to be a part of her life, she now knew she wanted to make more of her life outside work. Clenching her hands in her lap, she returned Joy's steady gaze. 'I'm withdrawing my application as of now.'

'Can I ask why?'

'I've been too focused on work and it's time I had some other interests. Apart from Gran's gardens,' she added with a small smile.

'What if I told you the board members are going to offer you the job?'

Her eyes widened. 'Seriously?' Pride filled her. She was thrilled, but it didn't change a thing. 'That's amazing, but sorry, I won't be changing my mind again.' She wasn't tempted at all. 'Sorry to muck you all around.'

'You haven't. We've a firm second contender.' Joy stood up. Conversation over. 'But I admit I'd have loved seeing you in my role. You'd have been great at it. Maybe at a later date.'

Somehow, she doubted that. Her pride grew though. It was good to hear she was appreciated. 'I'd better get to work. And Joy, thanks for being so patient.'

Walking out to the plane she couldn't help thinking about what lay ahead. The fact was she didn't have a clue, and for once that didn't worry her. Except when it came to Nick, and that was out of her hands. He'd come back to her or he wouldn't. It was beyond hard waiting to find out, and for every hour she did her heart cracked open a little wider. It was going to be decimating if he didn't, but better now than further on. Damn it, it was already bad enough that she struggled with getting on with all her jobs.

But she would. She was strong. She'd made a decision to show Nick her love for him. If it backfired, she could still feel relieved she'd done all she could.

But was it enough? That was the burning question.

* * *

Nick's finger hovered over the 'pay now' icon. The air ticket to Adelaide was a mere tap away. Did he really need to visit Patrick and talk about his feelings for Leesa, to explain why he was in such a quandary? He already knew what the judge would say. *'Get on with following your dream and stop wasting your life.'* Patrick wouldn't come up with any new answers to the questions filling his head.

Leaning back in his chair, Nick looked around the apartment and sighed. The same old same old. No different to every apartment he'd lived in over the years since graduating. The views altered, as did the room sizes, wall colours, floor levels. In other words, unexciting, uninteresting. A place to sleep at the end of a shift, no more, no less. He was over it, and ready to move somewhere permanent. In Cairns. With Leesa. She meant everything to him.

'See, I don't need to talk to Patrick. I know what to do.'

There would be no avoiding the truth any longer.

He was ready to settle down and try to make a go of having a home life. A full life, not one focused entirely on being a doctor.

There. The truth. And he wanted to do it all with Leesa. He wanted to love her freely, with no fear of letting her down or hurting her. He understood life didn't run that smoothly all the time though. People had to take chances. Including him.

His phone played the tune to the dance he and Leesa had got up close and personal to in Brisbane. The caller ID was unknown.

'Hello?'

'Nick, mate, it's Kevin. How're you doing?'

Why was Leesa's brother calling him? 'I'm good.'

'Those ribs still giving you grief?'

'Unfortunately, yes. What've you been up to?' What was this about? Who gave Kevin his number? Leesa? He doubted it. She'd been adamant about no contact until he'd made up his mind about their future. She wouldn't involve her brother in this.

'I'm heading out on the boat for a few days to catch a load of prawn tomorrow and thought I'd check in on you before I go. Is there anything I can do for you?'

Knock him down. This wasn't a seek and tell call. Kevin was being as decent as the rest of his family. Not really surprising. 'No, all good here. But thanks for the offer. We should catch up for a beer when you get back.' See? Small steps.

'There's a plan. Once those ribs are up to scratch I'm taking you out on the boat for a couple of days, show you how we catch your favourite food.'

Staying here was sounding better and better. 'I'd enjoy that. How's Leesa doing?' he asked without thought. Because she was constantly on his mind. Because she just never went away.

'You should ask her yourself,' Kevin told him. Then relented. 'She's back at work and seems to be recovering from the battering she took.'

That was a relief. 'I'm glad to hear that.'

'Talk to her, man. She's missing you.'

So Kevin knew they weren't in touch, which probably meant so did Jodi and Brent. 'I have to get a few things in order first. I don't want to hurt her by rushing it.'

'Don't take too long. I'll give you a buzz about that drink when I get back at the beginning of next week. See ya.' The guy was gone.

On the laptop the 'pay now' icon had disappeared, replaced with 'time's up'.

Time's up. How appropriate. The decision was made. He was staying. He loved Leesa beyond measure. It was what he was going to do about it that needed fixing. And he knew the answer to that too.

For the first time since the crash a cold beer beckoned. Getting a bottle from the fridge he headed out onto his balcony. He leaned on the balustrade and stared out at central Cairns and the airport beyond. His new home town. The feeling of achievement over reaching his decision filled him with contentment.

Kevin calling to see how he was doing made him feel good. Like he belonged somehow. And while that had worried him, now he grabbed it, accepted it. All because of one amazing woman he'd sat down beside at a party in Brisbane over a year ago, he'd found what he'd wanted for so long. Leesa and love, things he could not walk away from. Ever.

Kevin had raised the subject of Leesa. It sounded as though he knew more than he was letting on. He couldn't imagine Leesa talking about him to the family, but then they knew her well and would have figured out something was up.

The dance tune rang again. He never got this many calls.

This time it was Joy. 'What's up, boss?'

'You have a new job. Congratulations.'

His heart stopped. Did he want this? 'What about Leesa?'

'She pulled out.'

'When?' *Why?*

'Yesterday. I'll leave it to Leesa to explain why.'

Had he said 'why' out loud? She'd better not have done it for his sake. He didn't want that and it would make him very uncomfortable.

'I'm—' What was he? Only a couple of days ago he was going to retract his application. But now that he had made up his mind to stay in Cairns, climbing the career ladder was a start to settling in and making that life with Leesa he so desperately wanted. 'Do you want me to come in and go through everything?'

'You're on sick leave. We'll talk when you're back on duty. And Nick?'

'Yes?'

'I won't tell the rest of the crew until you've had a couple of days to think about it.'

Joy got that he had concerns. But he didn't. He was ready. 'I don't need to think about it, but I'd appreciate you keeping quiet for now. I'd like to talk to Leesa first.'

'Fair enough.'

'Thanks again. Have you got someone covering for me?'

'We're managing. Everyone's pulling their weight and making sure Leesa doesn't overdo it. She might say she's fine, but she struggles with lifting bags, let alone patients.'

Of course Leesa would be downplaying her pain. There was no arguing with her—ever. 'Right, I'll see you on Monday. I don't need those extra days I asked for any more.' He didn't need Patrick to tell him what he already knew.

After finishing the call he stared at the laptop as ideas of what to do next bounced into his mind. He got another beer and sat down to study the real estate options for the area.

Rural or beach? Definitely not in the city. That wouldn't suit Leesa, nor him, now he was coming to understand how much he wanted this. As different to boring apartments as possible for starters. Space for Baxter and the dog he intended getting.

He was getting ahead of himself. Leesa liked living in her grandmother's house and might not want to shift. Only one way to find out, and in the meantime he'd do all he could to get this happening. She'd said she had fallen for him. He could not let her down—ever. He trusted her with his heart. He really did. So he was going to do everything imaginable to make her happy. And more.

There was a buzz in his veins. This was the most exciting thing he'd ever done. He was finally coming home.

Leesa dragged herself through the front door, glad to be home and that the week was over. First stop—the fridge, and a glass of pinot blanc to unwind. The days at work since the accident had been tiring and her heart hadn't been in it.

It had been tied up with Nick, as she wondered if he was still in town or if he'd already packed his bags, headed away to the next city on his radar.

Baxter raced through the house, headed for the kitchen and his food bowl.

Okay, the wine came second to dog roll and biscuits. 'Give me a minute, boy.'

Wag, wag. His tail swished back and forth on the floor.

Her heart expanded at the sight of his face full of hope and love. Dogs were so easy to please. She adored him.

The door chime sounded.

Baxter was off in a blur, tail still wagging, no hackles up.

Who would be calling in now? Not any of her family. They walked in like it was home to them, which in a way it was.

'Hey, boy, how are you?'

Her heart leapt. Nick. Baxter had known. Was this good or bad?

'Leesa? Are you there?'

'Coming.' Slowly.

Suddenly she was afraid. She'd been kidding herself if she thought she'd cope with Nick saying he wanted nothing more to do with her. Her skin tightened and bumps lifted on her arms. Rubbing them hard she made her way back to the door. And Nick.

'Hey, Leesa.' Nick stood tall and confident, a bunch of tulips in his hand. Not a clue to what he was going to tell her. The flowers could be a closing gift. His confidence might be because he'd made some decisions he was happy with that didn't include her. 'I've missed you.' His eyes were full of love, or so she wanted to believe.

Her heart was pounding like a drummer, like it knew that was love streaming her way. Locking her eyes with Nick's, she whispered. 'I've missed you too.'

He didn't move. 'Leesa, I love you with all my heart.' His voice was firm. But his hand shook as he held out the tulips. 'For you, my darling.'

Nick loved her? Nick loved her. Yes. As she took them, she said, 'My favourite blooms.' Had he known that?

'Jodi told me.'

'You've been talking to Mum?' That had to be good, didn't it? As were the flowers. She couldn't quite take in everything, was still waiting for a catch. 'Come in.' Nick was right behind her as she headed to the kitchen. 'I'm about to pour a wine. Want one?'

'I'd love one. But first there is something else I want to tell you.'

Her heart slowed. Damn it. She was done with guessing. 'What?'

'I'm not moving away. I'm going to be a permanent fixture in Cairns, or around the area anyway. And I want to share that with you.'

'You're staying?' She had to check.

'Yes, I am. I meant it, Leesa. I love you.'

'Oh, wow.'

The tulips got a little crushed in the ensuing hug and kiss.

'Easy,' Nick gasped.

Hell. His ribs. Placing her palm on his cheek, she leaned in to brush a light kiss on his lips. 'I'm sorry. In the heat of the moment, I forgot.'

'So did I.' His laughter sent a thrill of desire pulsing through her.

But they had to restrain themselves. Broken ribs didn't make for active lovemaking. 'Damn.'

'We'll find a way round the problem, I'm sure. But let's start with that wine you mentioned. I built up a thirst coming here, stressing over whether you'd be happy to see me or not.'

'Why wouldn't I? I told you I love you.' Oh, not in quite those words. Placing the flowers on the bench she faced him. 'Nick Springer, I love you with everything I've got. I love you,' she repeated, because she loved saying it.

He reached for her again, held her with a small gap

between them and leaned in to kiss her senseless. 'Love you too, Leesa.'

It was Baxter head-knocking her knee that drew her back. 'Okay, boy, I guess you've been patient enough. Nick, you pour the wine while I feed hungry guts here.'

'Sure.' He found the glasses and got the bottle from the fridge, while watching her feed Baxter then find a vase for the tulips.

'Simply beautiful,' she said as she placed them on the sideboard. 'Let's sit out on the deck.'

'I've been offered Joy's job and I'm taking it,' Nick told her as he sat down beside her on the cane couch. 'I know you withdrew your application.'

'If Mark hadn't been so ill, I'd thank him for the crash and waking me up to a few things.' She sipped the wine and continued. 'I don't want to be in charge of operations. I just want to do an honest day's work helping people and then come home to do other things I enjoy.'

'Like gardening and walking Baxter.'

She nodded. 'And establishing a home that's mine, not keeping Gran's going as hers. She's not coming back here, and I'm ready to be creative with the house and grounds.'

'You want to stay in this house?'

'I haven't got that far with future plans. I was waiting till I heard what you were going to say about us being to-gether.' Loving each other meant living together. It had to or any relationship was off the agenda.

Damn but she loved it when he brushed his lips over her cheek.

'Here's what I've been doing these past few days.' He sat back with a smug look on his face. 'I've been look-ing at properties for sale north of the city, mostly on the coast and one inland with five acres and the potential to buy the neighbour's.'

'You have?' Her head spun with amazement. 'When you make up your mind you certainly get on with things.'

'About time, don't you think?'

She answered with a kiss. 'So is there a property you prefer above all the others?'

'I'm tossing up between the inland one and a stunning house near Trinity Beach. But I'd like you to see them first. You mightn't like either of them.'

'You're asking for my opinion? Does that mean what I think it does?'

'Of course.' His smile was devastating. 'But here's the big question. Will you go on dates with me? Give us time to get to know each other really well? As in looking forward and seeing what we both want individually and together?'

Her knees weakened as she looked into those beautiful blue eyes. 'Yes, Nick Springer, I will date you. But be warned, I already know what I want and you're a part of it all.'

'Afraid I'll get away?' he grinned before kissing her again.

'Too right,' she managed between kisses. 'Let me warn you, you won't get a chance. I love you too much.'

'Good, because I love you back. And, just so you know, one of the two houses I preferred had five bedrooms, while the other had three.'

'Let's go for five.'

'That means we'll be living by Trinity Beach.'

'Bring it on. Dogs love the seaside.'

Their next kiss sealed the deal.

EPILOGUE

LEESA SPRINGER'S HEART was singing as she gazed into her daughter's eyes. 'You are so beautiful, Courtney.' Tears welled up, and she brushed them away impatiently. She'd become a right old softie the night Courtney arrived in the world.

'Just like her mother,' Nick sprawled out in the lounger beside them. He never stopped telling her how much he loved her and that he thought she was beautiful. They'd been married eighteen months and everything was wonderful. More than she'd ever hoped for.

Handing her the tissue box, he said to Courtney, 'I'd never have believed my wife had so many tears stored up until you came along, poppet.' He ran a finger lightly over his daughter's arm.

Leesa grinned and gazed around at the front lawn she'd spent the last year working to turn into a spectacular sight, even if she said so herself. The last two months of her pregnancy had seen a halt in progress as she struggled to get down on her knees or to wield a spade. But it was a work in progress, and being a garden, one that would never stop. 'I need to plant those tulip bulbs or I won't have any flowers in the spring.'

'There's a carton of bulbs waiting in the shed.'

'You bought some?'

'They're your favourites. Besides, we've filled the first spare bedroom, so I figured you'd want to get back to the garden before we start on the next room.'

She laughed. 'You hear that, Courtney? You're going to get a brother or sister but not for a while yet.' Courtney was barely three months old and they wanted to enjoy her before adding to the family again.

'We probably do need to slow down a bit. It's been a whirlwind since the night I proposed, hasn't it?'

'I like whirlwinds when you're in them.'

They'd bought the house by the beach within weeks of Nick coming to Gran's house to tell her he loved her. Then they had a beautiful wedding at her family's farm a few months later.

And out of the blue, Leesa found herself pregnant with Courtney days after they returned from their honeymoon in Fiji.

Life didn't get any better.

'Kevin phoned. He's bringing prawns and his girlfriend for dinner. In that order,' Nick laughed. 'He mentioned Jodi and Brent might join us too.'

Okay, life could get better. Her heart swelled with love for all the people she cared about, and especially for these two, who she loved more than anything or anyone. Along the way she made the right choices and this was the reward. 'Love you two.'

Nick took his little girl and cradled her in one arm. Then he wrapped his other arm around the love of his life. 'Love you both back.'

He couldn't believe how happy he was. Every morning

he got out of bed with a spring in his step. Every night he returned to their super king-sized bed with excitement in his veins to hold his wife against him.

Life was perfect. It wasn't glamorous or OTT, just idyllic and happy.

He'd come a long way from Adelaide, and he wasn't measuring that in kilometres. No, he'd found a life that involved family and a real home right here. All because of Leesa. She was the best thing to ever happen to him.

To think he'd only gone to that barbecue in Brisbane to give his mate and his mate's girlfriend some time to themselves. He might never have found love if not for that night.

He gazed around their property and love tugged at him. Leesa had done a magnificent job of turning what had been a bald, dry area into stunning, colourful gardens and lots of green lawn for Baxter and Levi, another rescue dog, to play on. One day Courtney and any siblings that came along would play there too.

Yes, his heart was light and full of love. Life couldn't get any better.

* * * * *

COMING SOON!

We really hope you enjoyed reading this book.
If you're looking for more romance
be sure to head to the shops when
new books are available on

Thursday 15th August

MILLS & BOON®

Coming next month

REUNION WITH THE ER DOCTOR
Tina Beckett

Her whole being ignited.

It was as if Georgia had been waiting for this moment ever since she'd come back to Anchorage. Eli's mouth was just as firm and warm as she remembered. Just as sexy. And it sent a bolt of electricity through her body that morphed into some equally dangerous reactions. All of which were addictive.

And she wanted more.

Her hands went behind his neck and tangled in his hair as if afraid he might try to pull away before she'd gotten her fill of him. Not that she'd ever been able to do that. No matter how many times they'd kissed, no matter how many times they'd made love, she still craved him.

Despite the three years she'd spent away on Kodiak, that was one thing that evidently hadn't changed.

She pulled him closer, relishing the feel of his tongue pressing for entrance—an entrance she granted far too quickly. And yet it wasn't quick enough, judging from the way her senses were lighting torches. Torches that paved the way for an ecstasy she could only remember.

How utterly heady it was to be wanted by a man like this.

Continue reading
REUNION WITH THE ER DOCTOR
Tina Beckett

Available next month
millsandboon.co.uk

FOUR BRAND NEW STORIES FROM
MILLS & BOON MODERN

The same great stories you love,
a stylish new look!

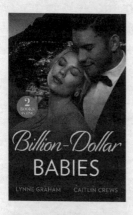

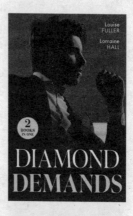

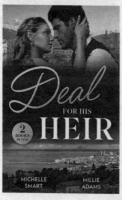

OUT NOW

MILLS & BOON

Afterglow Books is a trend-led, trope-filled list of books with diverse, authentic and relatable characters, a wide array of voices and representations, plus real world trials and tribulations. Featuring all the tropes you could possibly want (think small-town settings, fake relationships, grumpy vs sunshine, enemies to lovers) and all with a generous dose of spice in every story.

♪ @millsandboonuk
◎ @millsandboonuk
afterglowbooks.co.uk

#AfterglowBooks

For all the latest book news, exclusive content and giveaways scan the QR code below to sign up to the Afterglow newsletter:

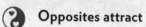

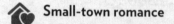
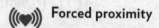
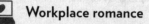

LET'S TALK

Romance

For exclusive extracts, competitions and special offers, find us online:

f MillsandBoon

X @MillsandBoon

◎ @MillsandBoonUK

♪ @MillsandBoonUK

Get in touch on 01413 063 232

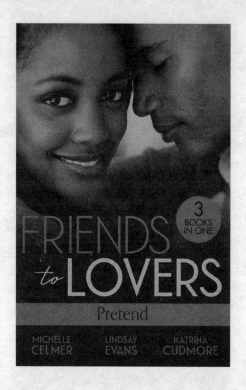

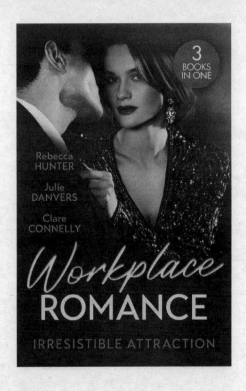